MILLION-DOLLAR MAVERICK

BY
CHRISTINE RIMMER

MILLS & BOON

Published in Great Britain 2014
by Mills & Boon, an imprint of Harlequin (UK) Limited,
Eton House, 18-24 Paradise Road, Richmond, Surrey, TW9 1SR

© 2014 Harlequin Books S.A.

Special thanks and acknowledgement are given to Christine Rimmer for her contribution to the MONTANA MAVERICKS: 20 YEARS IN THE SADDLE! continuity.

ISBN: 978-0-263-91299-9

23-0714

Harlequin (UK) Limited's policy is to use papers that are natural, renewable and recyclable products and made from wood grown in sustainable forests. The logging and manufacturing processes conform to the legal environmental regulations of the country of origin.

Printed and bound in Spain
by Blackprint CPI, Barcelona

Christine Rimmer came to her profession the long way around. Before settling down to write about the magic of romance, she'd been everything from an actress to a salesclerk to a waitress. Now that she's finally found work that suits her perfectly, she insists she never had a problem keeping a job—she was merely gaining "life experience" for her future as a novelist. Christine is grateful not only for the joy she finds in writing, but for what waits when the day's work is through: a man she loves who loves her right back, and the privilege of watching their children grow and change day to day. She lives with her family in Oregon. Visit Christine at www.christinerimmer.com.

For my mom.
I love you, Mom,
and I'm so grateful
for every moment we had together.

"I shouldn't have been kissing you," he muttered darkly, as a warning.

"I'm not a good bet. There's something…broken in me, you know? I haven't been such a good man in the years since I moved back home. I've been a Crawford through and through, you might say—too proud and too sure I knew every damn thing. You are a quality woman. You deserve a better man than me."

She only looked at him, eyes wide, bright with the sheen of unshed tears. He wanted to grab her and start kissing her all over again.

And that couldn't happen. He made himself clearer. "The last eight years, since I've been back in town, I've gone out with several women. But it never ends well."

Callie kept her gaze level. He couldn't tell what she might be thinking. "I understand," she said.

He leaned a little closer. "Do you really?"

"I do, Nate. Although I happen to think you're a much better man than you're giving yourself credit for."

"You're just softhearted."

She gave a tiny shrug. "Maybe I am."

3 8014 05235 8360

Prologue

January 15

On the ten-year anniversary of the day he lost everything, Nate Crawford got out of bed at 3:15 a.m. He grabbed a quick shower and filled a big thermos with fresh-brewed coffee.

Outside in the yard, his boots crunched on the frozen ground and the predawn air was so cold it seared his lungs when he sucked it in. He had to scrape the rime of ice off his pickup's windshield, but the stars were bright in the wide Montana sky and the cloudless night cheered him a little. Clear weather meant he should make good time this year. He climbed in behind the wheel and cranked the heater up high.

He left the ranch at a quarter of four. With any luck at all, he would reach his destination before night fell again.

But then, five miles north of Kalispell, he spotted a woman on the far side of the road. She wore a moss-green, quilted coat and skinny jeans tucked into lace-up boots. And she stood by a mud-spattered silver-gray SUV hooked up to a U-Haul trailer. With one hand, she held a red gas can. With the other, she was flagging him down.

Nate grumbled a few discouraging words under his breath. He had a long way to go, and the last thing he needed was to lose time playing Good Samaritan to some woman who couldn't be bothered to check her fuel gauge.

Not that he was even tempted to drive by and leave her there. A man like Nate had no choice when it came to whether or not to help a stranded woman. For him, doing what needed doing was bred in the bone.

He slowed the pickup. There was no one coming either way, so he swung the wheel, crossed the center line and pulled in behind the U-Haul on the far shoulder.

The woman came running. Her bright-striped wool beanie had three pom-poms, one at the crown and one at the end of each tie. They bounced merrily as she ran. He leaned across the seats and shoved open the door for her. A gust of icy air swirled in.

Framed in the open door, she held up the red gas can. Breathlessly, she asked, "Give a girl a lift to the nearest gas station?" It came out slightly muffled by the thick wool scarf she had wrapped around the bottom half of her face.

Nate was known for his smooth-talking ways, but the cold and his reluctance to stop made him curt. "Get in before all the heat gets out."

Just like a woman, she chose that moment to hesitate. "You're not an ax murderer, are you?"

He let out a humorless chuckle. "If I was, would I tell you so?"

She widened her big dark eyes at him. "Now you've got me worried." She said it jokingly.

He had no time for jokes. "Trust your instincts and do it fast. My teeth are starting to chatter."

She tipped her head to the side, studying him, and then, at last, she shrugged. "All right, cowboy. I'm taking a chance on you." Grabbing the armrest, she hoisted herself up onto the seat. Once there, she set the gas can on the floor of the cab, shut the door and stuck out her hand. "Callie Kennedy. On my way to a fresh start in the beautiful small town of Rust Creek Falls."

"Nate Crawford." He gave her mittened hand a shake. "Shooting Star Ranch. It's a couple of miles outside of Rust Creek—and didn't you just drive through Kalispell five miles back?"

Pom-poms danced as she nodded. "I did, yes."

"I heard they have gas stations in Kalispell. Lots of 'em."

She gave a low laugh. "I should have stopped for gas, I know." She started unwinding the heavy scarf from around her face. He watched with more interest than he wanted to feel, perversely hoping he wouldn't like what he saw. But no. She was as pretty as she was perky. Long wisps of lustrous seal-brown hair escaped the beanie to trail down her flushed cheeks. "I thought I could make it without stopping." Head bent to the task, she snapped the seat belt closed.

"You were wrong."

She turned to look at him again and something sparked in those fine eyes. "Do I hear a lecture coming on, Nate?"

"Ma'am," he said with more of a drawl than was strictly natural to him. "I would not presume."

She gave him a slow once-over. "Oh, I think you would. You look like a man who presumes on a regular basis."

He decided she was annoying. "Have I just been insulted?"

She laughed, a full-out laugh that time. It was such a great laugh he forgot how aggravating he found her. "You came to my rescue." Her eyes were twinkling again. "I would never be so rude as to insult you."

"Well, all right, then," he said, feeling suddenly out of balance somehow. He put the pickup in gear, checked for traffic and then eased back onto the road again. For a minute or two, neither of them spoke. Beyond his headlight beams, there was only the dark, twisting ribbon of road. No other headlights cut the night. Above, the sky was endless, swirling with stars, the rugged, black shadows of the mountains poking up into it. When the silence got too thick, he asked, "So, did you hear about the great flood that took out half of Rust Creek Falls last summer?"

"Oh, yeah." She was nodding. "So scary. So much of Montana was flooded, I heard. It was all over the national news."

The Rust Creek levee had broken on July Fourth, destroying homes and businesses all over the south half of town. Since then, Rust Creek Falls had seen an influx of men and women eager to pitch in with reconstruction. Some in town claimed that a lot of the women had come with more than helping out in mind, that they were hoping to catch themselves a cowboy. Nate couldn't help thinking that if Callie Kennedy wanted a man, she'd have no trouble finding one—even if she was more annoying than most.

Was she hungry? He wouldn't mind a plate of steak and eggs. Maybe he ought to ask her if she wanted to stop for breakfast before they got the gas....

But no. He couldn't do that. It was the fifteenth of January. His job was to get his butt to North Dakota—and to remember all he'd lost. No good-looking, mouthy little brunette with twinkly eyes could be allowed to distract him from his purpose.

He said, "Let me guess. You're here to help with the rebuilding effort. I gotta tell you, it's a bad time of year for it. All the work's pretty much shut down until the weather warms a little." He sent her a quick glance. She just happened to be looking his way.

For a moment, their gazes held—and then they both turned to stare out at the dark road again. "Actually, I have a job waiting for me. I'm a nurse practitioner. I'll be partnering up with Emmet DePaulo. You know Emmet?"

Tall and lean, sixty-plus and bighearted to a fault, Emmet ran the Rust Creek Falls Clinic. "I do. Emmet's a good man."

She made a soft sound of agreement and then asked, "And what about you, Nate? Where are you going before dawn on a cold Wednesday morning?"

He didn't want to say, didn't want to get into it. "I'm on my way to Bismarck," he replied, hoping she'd leave it at that.

No such luck. "I went through there yesterday. It's a long way from here. What's in Bismarck?"

He answered her question with one of his own. "Where you from?"

There was a silence from her side of the cab. He prepared to rebuff her if she asked about Bismarck again.

But then she only said, "I'm from Chicago."

He grunted. "Talk about a long way from here."

"That is no lie. I've been on the road since two in the morning Monday. Sixteen hundred endless miles, stopping only to eat and when I just had to get some sleep…."

"Can't wait to get started on your new life, huh?"

She flashed him another glowing smile. "I went through Rust Creek Falls with my parents on our way to Glacier National Park when I was eight. Fell in love with the place and always wanted to live there. Now, at last, it's really happening. And yeah. You're right. I can't wait."

It was none of his business, but he went ahead and asked anyway, "You honestly have *no* doubts about making this move?"

"Not a one." The woman had a greenhorn's blind enthusiasm.

"You'll be surprised, Callie. Montana winters are long and cold." He slid her another quick glance.

She was smiling wider than ever. "You ever been to Chicago, Nate? Gets pretty cold there, too."

"It's not the same," he insisted.

"Well, I guess I'll see for myself about that."

He really was annoyed with her now, annoyed enough that he said scornfully, "You won't last the winter. You'll be hightailing it back to the Windy City before the snow melts."

"Is that a challenge, Nate?" The woman did not back down. "I never could resist a challenge."

Damn, but he was riled now. Out of proportion and for no reason he could understand. Maybe it was because she was slowing him down from getting where he needed to be. Or maybe because he found her way too easy on the eyes—and then there was her perfume. A little sweet, a little tart. Even mixed with the faint smell of gasoline from the red can between her feet, he liked her perfume.

And it wasn't appropriate for him to like it. It wasn't appropriate for him to be drawn to some strange woman. Not today.

She was watching him, waiting for him to answer her question, to tell him if his mean-spirited prediction had been a challenge or not.

He decided to keep his mouth shut.

Apparently, she thought that was a good idea because

she didn't say anything more, either. They rode in tense silence the rest of the way to the gas station. She filled up her can, paid cash for it and got in the pickup again.

He drove her straight back to her waiting SUV.

When he pulled in behind the U-Haul, he suggested grudgingly, "Maybe I'd better just follow you back to town, see that you get there safely."

"No, thanks. I'll be okay."

He felt like a complete jerk—probably because he'd been acting like one. "Come on." He reached for the gas can. "Let me—"

She grabbed the handle before he could take it and put on a stiff smile. "I can do it. Thank you for your help." And then she leaned on the door, jumped down and hoisted the gas can down, too. "You take care now." In the glow of light from the cab, he watched her breath turn to fog in the icy air.

It was still pitch-dark out. At the edge of the cleared spot behind her, a big, dirty For Sale sign had been nailed on a fence post. Beyond the fence, new-growth ponderosa pines stood black and thick. Farther out in the darkness, perched on a high ridge and silhouetted against the sky, loomed the black outline of a house so enormous it looked like a castle. Built by a very rich man named Nathaniel Bledsoe two decades ago, the house had always been considered a monstrosity by folks in the Rust Creek Falls Valley. From the first, they called the place Bledsoe's Folly. When Bledsoe died, it went up for sale.

But nobody ever bought it. It stood vacant to this day.

Who was to say vagrants hadn't taken up residence? And anyone could be lurking in the close-growing pines.

He didn't like the idea of leaving her there alone. "I mean it, Callie. I'll wait until you're on your way."

Unsmiling now, she gazed at him steadily, her soft chin

hitched high. "I *will* last the winter." The words had steel underpinnings. "I'm making myself a new life here. You watch me."

He should say something easy and agreeable. He knew it. But somehow, she'd gotten under his skin. So he just made it worse. "Two hundred dollars says you'll be gone before June first."

She tipped her head to the side then, studying him. "Money doesn't thrill me, Nate."

"If not money, then what?"

One sleek eyebrow lifted and vanished into that bright wool hat. "Let me think it over."

"Think fast," he muttered, perversely driven to continue being a complete ass. "I haven't got all day."

She laughed then, a low, amused sound that seemed to race along his nerve endings. "Nate Crawford, you've got an attitude—and Rust Creek Falls is a small town. I have a feeling I won't have any trouble tracking you down. I'll be in touch." She grabbed the outer handle of the door. "Drive safe now." And then she pushed it shut and turned for her SUV.

He waited as he'd said he would, watching over her until she was back in her vehicle and on her way. In the glare of his headlights, she poured the gas in her tank. It only took a minute and, every second of that time, the good boy his mama had raised ached to get out and do it for her. But he knew she'd refuse him if he tried.

In no time, she had the cap back on the tank, the gas can stowed in the rear of the SUV, and she was getting in behind the wheel. Her headlights flared to life, and the engine started right up.

When she rolled out onto the road again, she tapped the horn once in salute. He waited for the red taillights of the U-Haul to vanish around the next curve before turning his truck around and heading for Bismarck again. As he drove back through Kalispell, he was shaking his head, dead certain that pretty Callie Kennedy would be long gone from Rust Creek come June.

Ten and a half hours later he rolled into a truck stop just west of Dickinson, North Dakota, to gas up. In the diner there, he had a burger with fries and a large Dr Pepper. And then he wandered through the attached convenience store, stretching his legs a little before getting back on the road for the final hour and a half of driving that would take him into Bismarck and his first stop there, a certain florist on Eighth Street.

Turned out he'd made good time after all, even with the delay caused by giving mouthy Nurse Callie a helping hand. This year, he would make it to the florist before they closed. And that meant he wouldn't have to settle for supermarket flowers. The thought pleased him in a grim sort of way.

Before heading out the door, he stopped at the register to buy a PayDay candy bar.

The clerk offered, "Powerball ticket? Jackpot's four hundred and eighty million now."

Nate never played the lottery. He was not a reckless man, not even when it came to something as inexpensive as a lottery ticket. Long shots weren't his style. But then he thought of pretty Callie Kennedy with her pom-pom hat, her gas can and her twinkly eyes.

Money doesn't thrill me, Nate.

Would four hundred and eighty million thrill her?

He chuckled under his breath and nodded. "Sure. Give me ten dollars' worth."

The clerk punched out a ticket with five rows of numbers on it. Nate gave it no more than a cursory glance as she put it in his hand.

He had no idea what he'd just done, felt not so much
as a shiver of intuition that one of those rows of numbers
was about to change his life forever.

Chapter One

At seven in the morning on the first day of June, Callie Kennedy knocked on the front door of Nate Crawford's big house on South Pine Street.

Nate hadn't shared two words with her since that cold day last January. But he'd seen her around town. He'd also kept tabs on her, though he would never have admitted that. Word around town was that she was not only a pure pleasure to look at, she was also a fine nurse with a whole lot of heart. Folks had only good things to say about Nurse Callie.

He pulled the door wide. "Well, well. Nurse Callie Kennedy," he drawled. Then he hooked his fingers in the belt loops of his Wranglers. "You're up good and early."

She gave him one of those thousand-watt smiles of hers. "Hello, Nate. Beautiful day, isn't it?"

He knew very well why she'd come. It wasn't to talk about the weather. Still, he leaned on the door frame and played along. "Mighty nice. Not a cloud in the sky."

"Happy June first." She beamed even wider, reminding him of a sunbeam in a yellow cotton dress with a soft yellow sweater thrown across her shoulders and yellow canvas shoes on her slim little feet.

"Let me guess…." He wrinkled his brow as though deep in thought. "Wait. I know. You're here to collect on that bet I made you."

"Nate." Her long lashes swept down. "You remembered." And then she looked up again. "I love your new house."

"Thank you."

"That's some front door."

"Thanks. I had it specially made. Indonesian mahogany." It had leaded glass in the top and sidelights you could open to let in a summer breeze.

"Very nice." She looked at him from under impossibly thick, dark lashes. "And the porch wraps all the way around to the back?"

"That's right, opens out onto a redwood deck." And they might as well get on with it. "Come on in."

"I thought you'd never ask."

He stepped out of the doorway and bowed her in ahead of him. "Coffee?"

"Yes, please." She waited for him to take the lead and then followed him through the central foyer, past the curving staircase, to the kitchen at the back. He gestured at the breakfast area. She took a seat, bracing an elbow on the table and watching him fiddle with his new pod-style coffeemaker.

"I've got about a hundred different flavors for this thing…."

The morning light spilled in the window, making her skin glow and bringing out auburn gleams in her long dark hair. "Got one with hazelnut?"

"Right here." He popped the pod in the top and turned the thing on. Thirty seconds later, he was serving her the steaming cup. "Cream and sugar?"

"I want it all. How many bedrooms?"

He got her the milk and the sugar bowl. "Three to five, depending."

"On what?"

"I have an office down here in the front that could be a bedroom. The master also has a good-sized sitting room with double doors to make a separate space. That sitting room could be a bedroom, too." He got a cup for himself and sat opposite her. "Not a lot of bedrooms, really, but all the rooms are nice and big."

"More than enough for a man living alone, I'd say."

He wasn't sure he liked the way she'd said that. Was she goading him? "What? A single man is only allowed so many rooms?"

She laughed. "Oh, come on, Nate. I'm not here to pick a fight."

He regarded her warily. "Promise?"

"Mmm-hmm." She stirred milk and sugar into her cup. "I heard a rumor you're planning on leaving town."

"Who told you that?"

"You know, I don't recall offhand." She sipped. "This is very good."

"You're welcome," he said gruffly.

She sipped again. "It's odd, really. Three months ago, you moved from the ranch into town, and now people say that you're leaving altogether."

"What people?" He kept his expression neutral, though his gut twisted. How much did she know?

No more than anyone else, he decided. To account for his new, improved lifestyle, he'd started telling folks that he'd had some luck with his investments. But as for the real source of his sudden wealth, even his family didn't know. Only the Kalispell lawyer he'd hired had the real story—which was exactly how Nate wanted it.

"You know how it is here in town," she said as though she'd been living in Rust Creek Falls all her life. "Everybody's interested in what everyone else is doing."

"No kidding," he muttered wryly.

"Several folks have mentioned to me that you're leaving."

Why not just admit it? "I'm looking for a change, that's all. My brothers can handle things at the ranch, so my bowing out hasn't caused any problems there. At first, I thought moving to town would be change enough."

"But it's not?"

He glanced out the sunny window, where a blue jay flew down and landed on the deck rail and then instantly took flight again. "Maybe I need an even bigger change." He swung his gaze to her again, found her bright eyes waiting. "Who knows? Maybe I'll be heading back the way you came, making myself a whole new start in Chicago. I'm just not sure yet. I don't know what the next step for me should be."

She studied his face with what seemed to be honest interest. "You, living in Chicago? I don't know, Nate. I'm just not seeing that."

He thought, *You don't know me well enough to tell me where I might want to live.* But he didn't say it. She'd seemed sincere just now. And she was entitled to her opinion.

She wasn't through, either. "I heard you ran for mayor last year—and lost to Collin Traub. They say you're bitter about that because of the generations-long feud between the Traubs and your family, that it really hurt your pride when the town chose bad-boy Collin over an upstanding citizen like you. They say it's personal between you and Collin, that there's always been bad blood between the two of you, that the two of you once got into a knock-down-drag-out over a woman named Cindy Sellers."

"Wow, Callie. You said a mouthful." He actually chuckled.

And she laughed, too. "It's only what I've heard."

"Just because people love to gossip doesn't mean they know what they're talking about."

"So none of it's true, then?"

He admitted, "It's true, for the most part." Strangely, today, he was finding her candor charming—then again, today he wasn't on his way to North Dakota to keep his annual appointment with all that he had lost.

She asked, "What parts did I get wrong?"

He should tell her to mind her own business. But she was so damn pretty and she really did seem interested. "Well, the mayor's race?"

"Yeah?"

"I'm over that. And it's a long story about me and Collin and Cindy, one I don't have the energy to get into right now—and your cup's already empty."

"It was really good." She smiled at him coaxingly.

He took the hint. "More?"

"Yes, please."

Each pod made six cups. All he had to do was put her mug under the spigot and push the brew button. "You've collected a lot of information about me. Should I be flattered you're so interested?" He gave her back her full cup.

She doctored it up with more sugar and milk. "I think about that day last winter now and then...."

He slid into his seat again. "I'll just bet you do." *Especially today, when it's time to collect.*

Her big eyes were kind of dreamy now. "I wonder about

you, Nate. I wonder why you had to get to Bismarck, and I keep thinking there's a lot going on under the surface with you. I love this town more every day that I live here, but sometimes people in a small town can get locked in to their ideas about each other. What I think about you is that you want…more out of life. You just don't know how to get it."

He grunted. "Got me all figured out, don't you?"

"It's just an opinion."

"Yeah, and that and five bucks will get you half a dozen cinnamon buns over at the doughnut shop."

She shrugged, her gaze a little too steady for his peace of mind. Then she asked, "So, what about Bismarck?"

He was never telling her about Bismarck. And, as much as he enjoyed looking at her with all that shiny hair and that beautiful smile, it was time to get down to business. "Excuse me." He rose and turned for the door to the foyer, leaving her sitting there, no doubt staring after him.

In his study at the front of the house, he opened the safe built into his fine wide mahogany desk and took out what she'd come for. Then he locked up the safe again and rejoined her in the kitchen.

"Here you go." He set the two crisp one-hundred-dollar bills on the table in front of her. "I get it. You like it here. You've made some friends. They all say you're an excellent nurse, kind and caring to your patients. You're staying. I was wrong about you."

"Yes, you were." She sat very straight, those soft lips just hinting at a smile now. "I like a man who can admit when he's wrong." She glanced down at the bills and then back up at him. "And I thought I told you way back in January that money doesn't do much for me."

Okay. Now he could start to get annoyed with her again. "Then what *do* you want?"

She turned her coffee mug, slim fingers light and coaxing on the rim. "I've been staying in one of the trailers they brought in for newcomers, over on Sawmill Street."

"I know," he admitted, though he hadn't planned to. Her pupils widened slightly in surprise. It pleased him that he'd succeeded in surprising her. "Maybe I think about you now and then, too."

She gazed at him steadily for a moment. And then there it was, that hint of a smile again. "I'm tired of that trailer."

"I can understand that."

"But as I'm sure you know, housing is still kind of scarce around here." So many homes had been damaged in the flood the year before, and they weren't all rebuilt yet. "I really like the look of the empty house next door to you. And I heard a rumor you might own that one, too."

The woman had nerve, no doubt about it. "You want me to give you a house just for sticking out a Montana winter?"

Her smile got wider. "Not *give* it to me, Nate. Sell it to me."

Sell it to her....

The former owners of both houses had chosen not to rebuild after the flood, so Nate got them cheap. He'd been a long way from rich at the time. His plan then had been to fix the houses up slowly, starting with the smaller one next door. He'd figured he would put money in them when he had it to spare, getting his brothers to lend a hand with the work.

But after his big win, he found he could afford to renovate them both without having to drag it out. With everyone believing his cover story of a windfall on the stock market, he'd told himself it was safe to go for it. He could fix them up and do it right.

He should have been more cautious, probably. Not spent so much on the finishes, not redone both houses. Or at least, if he had to go all out, he should have had his lawyer advise him, maybe put them under the control of the trust he'd established to make sure he would remain an anonymous winner.

Callie kept after him. "Oh, come on, Nate. You can't live in two houses at once, can you? I'm guessing you fixed that other one up with the intention of selling it, anyway."

He thought again that she was one aggravating woman. But she did have a point: he'd bought both houses with the idea that he would eventually turn them around. And really, she didn't seem the least bit suspicious about where his money might have come from. She just wanted to get out of the trailer park. He needed to stop being paranoid when there was absolutely nothing to be worried about. "Finish your coffee."

"And then what?"

"I'll give you a tour of the other house."

Those fine dark eyes gleamed brighter than ever. She pushed back her chair. "I can take my coffee with me. Let's go."

An hour later, after he'd shown her the property and then gone ahead and fed her breakfast, Callie made him an offer. It was a fair offer and he didn't need to quibble over pennies anymore. She stuck out her soft hand and they shook on it. He ignored the thrill that shivered along his skin at the touch of her palm to his.

On the first of July, Callie moved into her new house next door to Nate Crawford. The day before, she'd had a bunch of new furniture delivered, stuff she'd picked out in a couple of Kalispell furniture stores. But she still had to haul all her other things from the trailer park on Sawmill Street.

Emmet DePaulo insisted she take the day off from the

clinic and loaned her his pickup. Then, being Emmet, he decided to close the clinic for the morning and give her a hand.

He got a couple of friends of his, Vietnam veterans in their sixties, old guys still in surprisingly good shape, to help load up the pickup for her. Then he drove it to her new house, and he and his pals carried everything inside, after which they returned to the trailer and got the rest of her stuff. With the four of them working, they had the trailer emptied out and everything over at the new house before noon.

In her new kitchen, Callie served them all takeout from the chicken-wing place on North Broomtail Road. Once they'd eaten, Emmet's friends took off. Emmet told her not to work too hard and left to go open the clinic for the afternoon.

She stood out on the porch and waved as he drove away, her gaze wandering to Nate's big house. She hadn't seen him all day. There were no lights shining from inside and no sign of his truck. But then, it was a sunny day, and his house had lots of windows. He could be inside, and his truck could very well be sitting in that roomy three-car garage.

Not that it mattered. She'd bought her house because she liked it, not because of the man next door.

After living in a trailer for six months, her new place felt absolutely palatial. There were two bedrooms and a bath upstairs, for guests or whatever. Downstairs were the kitchen, great room, front hall and master suite. The master suite had two entrances, one across from the great room in the entry hall and the other in the kitchen, through the master bath in back. The master bath was the only bathroom on the first floor. It worked great that you could get to it without going through the bedroom.

Callie got busy putting her new house together, starting with her bedroom. That way, when she got too tired to unpack another box, she'd have a bed to fall into. She put her toiletries in the large downstairs bath and hung up the towels. And then she went out to the kitchen to get going in there.

At a little after three, the doorbell rang.

Nate? Her silly heart beat faster and her cheeks suddenly felt too warm.

Which was flat-out ridiculous.

True, she found Nate intriguing. He was such a big, handsome package of contradictions. He could be a jerk. Paige Traub, her friend and also a patient at the clinic, had once called Nate an "unmitigated douche." There were more than a few people in Rust Creek Falls who agreed with Paige.

But Callie had this feeling about him, a feeling that he wasn't as bad as he could seem sometimes. That deep inside, he was a wounded, lonely soul.

Plus, well, there was the hotness factor. Tall, with muscles. Shoulders for days. Beautiful green eyes and thick brown hair that made a girl want to run her fingers through it.

Callie blinked and shook her head. She reminded herself that after her most recent love disaster, she was swearing off men for at least the next decade. Especially arrogant, know-it-all types like Nate.

The doorbell rang again and her heart beat even faster. Nothing like a visit from a hunky next-door neighbor. Her hands were covered in newsprint from the papers she'd used to wrap the dishes and glassware. She quickly rinsed them in the sink and ran to get the door.

It wasn't Nate.

"Faith!" Like Paige Traub, Faith Harper, Callie's new

neighbor on her other side, was a patient at the clinic. Also like Paige, Faith was pregnant. Both women were in their third trimester, but Faith was fast approaching her due date. Faith had big blue eyes and baby-fine blond hair. She and Callie had hit it off from the first.

Faith held out a red casserole dish. "My mom's chicken divan. It's really good. I had to make sure my favorite nurse had something for dinner."

Callie took the dish. "Oh, you are a lifesaver. I was just facing the sad prospect of doing Wings to Go twice in one day."

Beaming, Faith rested both hands on her enormous belly. "Can't have that."

"Come on in...." Callie led the way back to the kitchen, where she put the casserole in the fridge and took out a pitcher of iced herbal tea. "Ta-da! Raspberry leaf." High in calcium and magnesium, raspberry-leaf tea was safe for pregnant women from the second trimester on. It helped to prepare the uterus for labor and to prevent postpartum bleeding. Callie had recommended it to Faith.

Faith laughed. "Did you know I'd be over?"

"Well, I was certainly hoping you would." Callie poured the tea, and they went out on the small back deck to get away from the mess of half-unpacked boxes in the kitchen. The sky had grown cloudy in the past hour or so. Still, it was so nice, sitting in her own backyard with her first visitor. And it was definitely a big step up from the dinky square of back stoop she'd had at the trailer park.

They talked about the home birth Faith planned. Callie would be attending as nurse/midwife. Faith had everything ready for the big day. Her husband, a long-haul trucker, had left five days before on a cross-country trip and was due to return the day after tomorrow.

Faith tenderly stroked her enormous belly. "When Owen

gets back from this trip, he's promised he's going nowhere until after this baby is born."

"I love a man who knows when it's time to stay home," Callie agreed.

"Oh, me, too. I— Whoa!" Faith laughed as lightning lit up the underbelly of the thick clouds overhead. Thunder rumbled—and it started to rain.

Callie groaned. Already, in the space of a few seconds, the fat drops were coming down hard and fast. She jumped up. "Come on. Let's go in before we drown."

They cleared a space at the table in the breakfast nook and watched the rain pour down. Faith shivered.

Callie asked, "Are you cold? I can get you a blanket."

"No, I'm fine, really. It's only… Well, it's a little too much like last year." Her soft mouth twisted. "It started coming down just like this, in buckets. That went on for more than twenty-four hours straight. Then the levee broke…."

Callie reached across the table and gave Faith's hand a reassuring squeeze. "There's nothing to worry about." The broken levees had been rebuilt higher and stronger than before. "Emmet told me the new levee will withstand any- and everything Mother Nature can throw at it."

Faith let out a long, slow breath. "You're right. I'm over-reacting. Let the rain fall. There'll be no flooding this year."

It rained hard all night.

And on the morning of July second, it was still pouring down. The clinic was just around the block from Callie's new house, and she'd been looking forward to walking to work. But not today. Callie drove her SUV to the clinic.

Overall, it was a typical workday. She performed routine exams, stitched up more than one injury, prescribed painkillers for rheumatoid arthritis and decongestants for summer colds. Emmet was his usual calm, unruffled self. He'd done two tours of duty in Vietnam and Cambodia back in the day. It took a lot more than a little rain to get him worked up.

But everyone else—the patients, Brandy the clinic receptionist and the two pharmaceutical reps who dropped by to fill orders and pass out samples—seemed apprehensive. Probably because the rain just kept coming down so hard, without a break, the same way it had last year before the levee broke. They tried to make jokes about it, agreeing that every time it rained now, people in town got worried. They talked about how the apprehension would fade over time, how eventually a long, hard rainstorm wouldn't scare anyone.

Too bad they weren't there yet.

Then, a half an hour before they closed the doors for the day, something wonderful happened: the rain stopped. Brandy started smiling again. Emmet said, "Great. Now everyone can take a break from predicting disaster."

At five, Callie drove home. She still had plenty of Faith's excellent casserole left for dinner. But she needed milk and bread and eggs for breakfast tomorrow. That meant a quick trip to Crawford's, the general store on North Main run by Nate's parents and sisters, with a little help from Nate and his brothers when needed.

Callie decided she could use a walk after being cooped up in the clinic all day, so she changed her scrubs for jeans and a T-shirt and left her car at home.

It started sprinkling again as she was crossing the Main Street Bridge. She walked faster. Luck was with her. It didn't really start pouring until right after she reached the store and ducked inside.

Callie loved the Crawfords' store. It was just so totally

Rust Creek Falls. Your classic country store, Crawford's carried everything from hardware to soft goods to basic foodstuffs. It was all homey pine floors and open rafters. The rafters had baskets and lanterns and buckets hanging from them. There were barrels everywhere, filled with all kinds of things—yard tools, vegetables, bottles of wine. In the corner stood an old-timey woodstove with stools grouped around it. During the winter, the old guys in town would gather there and tell each other stories of the way things used to be.

Even though she knew she was in for a soggy walk home, Callie almost didn't care. Crawford's always made her feel as if everything was right with the world.

"Nurse Callie, what are you doing out in this?" Nate's mother, Laura, called to her from behind the cash register.

"It wasn't raining when I left the house. I thought the walk would do me good."

"How's that new house of yours?" Laura beamed.

"I love it."

"My Nathan has good taste, huh?" Laura's voice was full of pride. Nate was the oldest of her six children. Some claimed he'd always been the favorite.

"He did a wonderful job on it, yes." Callie grabbed a basket. Hoping maybe the rain would stop again before she had to head back home, she collected the items she needed.

Didn't happen. It was coming down harder than ever, drumming the roof of the store good and loud as Laura started ringing up her purchases.

"You stick around," Laura ordered as she handed Callie her receipt. "Have a seat over by the stove. Someone will give you a ride."

Callie didn't argue. "I think I will hang around for a few minutes. Maybe the rain will slow down and…" The sentence wandered off unfinished as Nate emerged through the door that led into the storage areas behind the counter.

He spotted her and nodded. "Callie."

Her heart kind of stuttered in her chest, which was thoroughly silly. For crying out loud, you'd think she had a real thing for Nate Crawford, the way her pulse picked up and her heart skipped a beat just at the sight of him. "Nate. Hey."

For a moment, neither of them said anything else. They just stood there, looking at each other.

And then Laura cleared her throat.

Callie blinked and slid a glance at Nate's mother.

Laura gave her a slow, way-too-knowing smile. Callie hoped her face wasn't as red as it felt.

Nate lurched to life about then. He grabbed a handsome-looking tan cowboy hat from the wall rack behind the counter. "I moved the packaged goods out of the way so they won't get wet and put a bigger bucket under that leak." He put the hat on. It looked great on him. So did his jeans, which hugged his long, hard legs, and that soft chambray shirt that showed off his broad shoulders. "I'll see to getting the roof fixed tomorrow—or as soon as the rain gives us a break."

"Thanks, Nathan." Laura gave him a fond smile. And then she suggested way too offhandedly, "And Callie here needs a ride home…."

Callie automatically opened her mouth to protest—and then shut it without saying a word. It was raining pitchforks and hammer handles out there, and she *did* need a ride home.

Nate said, "Just so happens I'm headed that way. Here, let me help you." He grabbed both of her grocery bags off the counter. "Let's go."

Callie resisted the urge to tell him she could carry her

own groceries. What was the point? He already had them.
And he wasn't waiting around for instructions from her,
anyway. He was headed out the door.

"Um, thanks," she told Laura as she took off after him.

"You are so welcome," beamed Laura with way more
enthusiasm than the situation warranted.

Chapter Two

"My mother likes you," Nate said as he drove slowly down Main Street, the wipers on high and the rain coming down so hard it was a miracle he could see anything beyond the streaming windshield.

Callie didn't know how to answer—not so much because of what Nate had said but because of his grim tone. "I like her, too?" she replied so cautiously it came out sounding like a question.

He muttered darkly, "She considers you quality."

Callie didn't get his attitude at all—or understand what he meant. "Quality?"

"Yeah, quality. A quality woman. You're a nurse. A professional. You're not a snob, but you carry yourself with pride. It's a small town and sometimes it takes a while for folks to warm to a newcomer. But not with you. People are drawn to you, and you made friends right away. Plus, it's no hardship to look at you. My mother approves."

She slid him a cautious glance. "But you don't?"

He kept his gaze straight ahead. "Of course I approve of you. What's not to approve of? You've got it all."

She wanted to ask him what on earth he was talking about. Instead, she blew out a breath and said, "Gee, thanks," and let it go at that.

He turned onto Commercial Street a moment later, then onto South Pine and then into her driveway. He switched off the engine and turned to her, frowning. "You okay?"

She gave him a cool look. "I could ask you the same question. Are you mad at your mother or something?"

"What makes you think that?"

She pressed her lips together and drew in a slow breath through her nose. "If you keep answering every question with a question, what's the point of even attempting a conversation?"

He readjusted his cowboy hat and narrowed those gorgeous green eyes at her. "That was another question you just asked me, in case you didn't notice. And *I* asked the first question, which *you* failed to answer."

They glared at each other. She thought how wrong it was for such a hot guy to be such a jerk.

And then he said ruefully, "I'm being an ass, huh?"

And suddenly, she felt a smile trying to pull at the corners of her mouth. "Now, that is a question I can definitely answer. Yes, Nate. You are being an ass."

And then he said, "Sorry."

And she said, "Forgiven."

And they just sat there in the cab of his pickup with the rain beating hard on the roof overhead, staring at each other the way they had back at the store.

Finally he said, "My parents are good people. Basically. But my mom, well, she kind of thinks of herself as the queen of Rust Creek Falls, if that makes any sense. She married a Crawford, and to her, my dad is king. She gets ideas about people, about who's okay and who's not. If she likes you, that's fine. If she doesn't like you, you know it. Believe me."

"You think she's too hard on people?"

There was a darkness, a deep sadness in his eyes. "Sometimes, yeah."

"Well, Nate, if your mother's the queen, that would make you the crown prince."

He took off his hat and set it on the dashboard—then changed his mind and put it back on again. "You're right. I was raised to think I should run this town, and for a while in the past seven or eight years, I put most of my energy into doing exactly what I was raised to do."

"You sound like you're not so sure about all that now."

"Lately, there's a whole lot I'm not sure of—which is one of the reasons I'm planning on leaving town."

She shook her head. "I don't believe that. I think you love this town."

"That doesn't mean I won't go." And then he smiled, a smile that stole the breath right out of her body. "Come on." He leaned on his door and got out into the pouring rain. He was soaked through in an instant as he opened the backseat door and gathered her groceries into his arms. "Let's go." He made a run for the house.

She was hot on his tail and also soaked to the skin as she followed him up her front steps.

Laughing, she opened the door for him and he went right in, racing to the kitchen to get the soggy shopping bags safely onto the counter before they gave way. He made it, barely. And then he took off his dripping hat and set it on the counter next to the split-open bags. "A man could drown out there if he's not careful."

It was still daylight out, but the rain and the heavy cloud

cover made it gloomy inside. She turned on some lights. "Stay right there," she instructed. "I'll get us some towels."

In the central hall, a box of linens waited for her to carry them upstairs to the extra bath. She dug out two big towels and returned to the kitchen. "Catch." She tossed him one.

He snatched it from the air. They dried off as much as possible, then she took his towel from him and went to toss them in the hamper. When she got back to him, he was standing in the breakfast nook, studying a group of framed photographs she'd left on the table last night.

She quickly worked her long wet hair into a soggy braid. "I'm going to hang those pictures together on that wall behind you." And then she gestured at the boxes stacked against that same wall. "As soon as I get all that put away, I mean."

He picked up one of the pictures. "You were a cute little kid."

She had no elastic bands handy, so she left the end of the wet braid untied. "You go for braces and knobby knees?"

"Like I said. Cute. Especially the pigtails." He glanced at her, a warm, speculative glance. "An only child?"

"That's right." She went to the counter and started putting the groceries away. "They divorced when I was ten. My mother died a couple of years ago. My father remarried. He and his second wife live in Vermont."

He set the picture down with the others. "I'm sorry about your mom."

She put the eggs in the fridge. "Thanks. She was great. I miss her a lot."

"Half siblings?"

"Nope. They travel a lot, my dad and my stepmom. They like visiting museums and staying in fine hotels in Europe, going on cruises to exotic locales. He really wasn't into kids, you know? My mom loved camping, packing up the outdoor gear and sleeping under the stars in the national parks. So did I. But my dad? He always acted like he was doing us a favor, that having to deal with sleeping outside and using public restrooms was beneath him. And having a kid cramped his style. I never felt all that close to him, to tell you the truth. And after he and my mom split up, I hardly saw him— Sheesh. Does that sound whiny or what?"

He watched her for a moment. And then he shrugged. "Not whiny. Honest. I like that about you."

She felt ridiculously gratified. "I… Thank you."

He nodded, slowly. They stared at each other too long, the way they had back at the store.

And then she realized that one of them should probably say something. So she piped up with, "On a brighter note, I have a couple of girlfriends in Chicago who are like sisters to me. They'll be coming to visit me here one of these days— Beer?"

He left the pictures and came to stand at the end of the granite counter. "Sure."

She got a longneck from the fridge. "Glass?"

"Just the bottle." He took it, screwed off the top and downed a nice, big gulp. She watched his Adam's apple working, admired the way his wet shirt clung to his deep, hard chest. He set the bottle on the counter and ran those lean, strong fingers through his wet hair. "You leave anyone special behind in Chicago?"

She stopped with the carton of milk held between her two hands. "I told you. My girlfriends."

He picked up the beer, tipped it to his mouth, then changed his mind and didn't drink from it. "I wasn't talking about girlfriends."

She didn't really want to go there. But then, well, why

not just get it over with? "There was a doctor, at the hospital where I worked. A surgeon."

"It didn't work out?"

"No, it did not." She glanced toward the bay window that framed the breakfast nook. The rain kept coming down. The wind was up, too. "Listen to that wind."

He nodded. "It's wild out there, all right." Lightning flashed then, and thunder rumbled in the distance. Callie put the milk in the fridge and threw the ruined paper bags away. He held up his beer bottle. "I'll finish this up and get out of your hair."

She had plenty of boxes left to unpack, and the sooner he went home, the sooner she could get going on that. Still, she heard herself offering, "Stick around. Faith Harper brought me a jumbo baking dish full of chicken divan last night. I have plenty left if you want to join me."

He took his hat off the counter and then dropped it back down. "You sure?"

She realized she was. Absolutely. "Yes."

Half an hour later, he'd cleared all the stuff off the table and set it for them with dishes she'd unpacked the night before. She'd cut up a salad and baked a quick batch of packaged drop biscuits. He said yes to a second beer and she poured herself a glass of wine. They sat down to eat.

After a couple bites, he said, "I remember this casserole. Faith's mom always brought it to all the church potlucks. It was a big hit. The water chestnuts make a nice touch."

Callie chuckled and shook her head.

"What?" he demanded.

"I don't know. It's just… Well, that's a small town for you. I love it. I give you chicken divan and you can tell me its history."

He ate another bite. "It's the best." He took a biscuit,

buttered it, set down his knife. "So how do you like working with Emmet?"

"What's not to like? He really is the sweetest man, and he's good, you know, with the patients. Everyone loves him, me included." She sipped her wine. "The equipment we're working with, however, is another story altogether."

His brows drew together. "I thought Emmet got some grants after the flood, that everything was back in shape again."

"That's right. He had the building restored. It *is* in good shape now, and he saved most of the equipment by moving it to the upper floor before the levee broke. But was all that stuff even worth saving? It's a long way from state of the art, you know? The diagnostic equipment is practically as old as I am. And the exam table cushions are so worn, they're starting to split."

"You're saying you need funding?" He was looking at her strangely, kind of taking her measure.…

"What?" she said sharply. Did she have broccoli between her teeth or something?

"Hey, I'm just asking." That strange expression had vanished—if it had ever been there at all.

She spoke more gently. "Yeah, we could use a serious infusion of cash. So if you know anybody looking to give away their money, send them our way."

"I'll do that," he said. And then he picked up his fork and dug into his food again.

A few minutes later, he helped her clear the table. It was a little after seven. If he left soon, she could still get a couple more hours of unpacking done before calling it a night.

But the longer he stayed, the more she didn't want him to go.

In the back of her mind, a warning voice whispered that she was giving him the wrong signals, that she was supposed to be swearing off men for a while, that she might be really attracted to him, but her friend Paige Traub had called him a douche—and he'd acted like one the first time they met. Plus, well, he kept saying he was moving away, and she never wanted to live anywhere else but Rust Creek Falls.

It couldn't go anywhere. And the last thing she needed was to get herself all tied in knots over a guy who wouldn't be sticking around.

But then, instead of waiting for him to say how he should get going, she opened her big mouth and offered, "Coffee? And if you're lucky, I may even have a bag of Oreos around here somewhere...."

He rinsed his plate in the sink and handed it to her. "Oreos, did you say?"

"Oh, yes, I did."

"And I know you've got milk. I saw you put it away."

She bent to slide the plate into the lower dishwasher rack. "Have I found your weakness?"

He moved in a step closer. "There are just some things a man can't resist...."

She shut the dishwasher door and rose to face him, aware of the warmth of him, so close, of the gold striations in those moss-green eyes, of how she loved the shape of his mouth, with that clear indentation at the bow and the sexy fullness of his lower lip.

He lifted a hand and brushed his fingers along the bare skin of her arm, bringing a lovely little shiver racing across her skin. Outside, the sky lit up and thunder rolled away into the distance. The rain just kept pouring down, making a steady drumming sound on the roof.

She whispered, "Nate..."

And his fingers moved over her shoulder, down her back. He gave a light, teasing tug on her unbound braid.

"I keep thinking of those pictures of you, with your braces and your pigtails. I'll bet you had a mouth on you even then."

This close, she could smell his aftershave, and beneath that, the healthy scent of his skin. "What do you mean, a mouth?"

"You know. Sassy. Opinionated."

Her lips felt kind of dry, suddenly. She started to stick out her tongue to moisten them but caught herself just in time and ended up nervously pressing her lips together. "I am not sassy." She meant it to sound firm, strong. But somehow, it came out all breathless and soft.

He chuckled, rough and kind of low. She felt that chuckle down to her toes. It seemed to rub along her nerve endings, setting off sparks. "Yeah," he said. "You are. Sassy as they come."

"Uh-uh."

"Uh-huh."

"No, Nate."

"Yes, Callie." Now his voice was tender.

And she felt warm all over. Warm and tingly and somehow weightless. She'd gone up on her tiptoes and was swaying toward him, like a daisy yearning toward the sun.

His hand was on her shoulder now, rubbing, caressing. And then he said her name again, the word barely a whisper. And then he did what she longed for him to do. He pulled her closer, so she could feel the heat of him all along the front of her body, feel the softness of her own breasts pressed to that broad, hard chest of his.

He made a low questioning sound. And in spite of all her doubts, she didn't even hesitate. She answered with a slow, sure nod, her eyes locked to his as his mouth came down.

And then, in the space of a breath, those lips of his were

touching hers, gently. Carefully, too. To the soft, incessant roar of the rain, the constant harsh whistling of the wind, she lifted her arms and wrapped them around his neck, parting her lips for him, letting him in.

The kiss started to change. From something so sweet it made her soul ache to something hotter, deeper. Dangerous.

A low growling sound escaped him. It seemed to echo all through her, that sound. And then his tongue slid between her lips, grazing her teeth. She shivered in excitement and wrapped her arms tighter around him.

He held her tighter, too, gathering her into him, his big hands now splayed across her back, rubbing, stroking, while she lifted up and into him, fitting her body to his, feeling that weakness and hunger down in the core of her and the growing hardness of him pressed so close against her.

Her mind was spinning and her body was burning and her heart beat in time to the throb of desire within her.

Bad idea, to have kissed him. She knew that, she did— and yet, somehow, at that moment, she didn't even care. She was on fire. Worse, she was right on the verge of dragging the man down the hall to her bedroom, where they could do something even more foolish than kissing.

But before she could take his hand, the whole kitchen lit up in a wash of glaring light so bright she saw it even with her eyes closed. She gasped.

Lightning. It was lightning.

And then thunder exploded, so close and loud it felt as if it was right there in the kitchen with them.

Callie cried out, and her eyes popped wide open. Nate opened his eyes, too. They stared at each other.

He muttered, "What the hell?"

She whispered, "That was way too close," not really

sure if she meant the lightning strike—or what had almost happened between the two of them.

He only kept on watching her, his eyes hot and wild.

And right then, the lights went out.

"Terrific," Callie muttered. "What now?"

It wasn't dark out yet—but the rain and the cloud cover made it seem so. He was a tall shadow, filling the space in front of her, as her eyes adjusted to the gloom.

That had been some kiss. Callie needed a moment to collect her shattered senses. Judging by the way Nate braced his hand on the counter and hung his head, she guessed he was having a similar problem.

Finally, he said, "I'll check the breaker box. Got a flashlight?"

She had two, somewhere in the boxes still stacked against the wall. But she knew where another one was. "In my SUV."

So he followed her out to her garage, where she got him the flashlight and then trailed after him over to the breaker box on the side wall. The breakers were perfectly aligned in two even rows.

He turned to her, shining the flashlight onto the concrete floor, so it gave some light but didn't blind her. The rain sounded even louder out here, a steady, unremitting roar on the garage roof. He said what she already knew. "None of the breakers have flipped. I had all the wiring in the house replaced. This box is the best there is. I'm thinking it's not a faulty breaker. A tree must have fallen on a line, or a transformer's blown." The eerie light bouncing off the floor exaggerated the strong planes and angles of his face.

She stared up at him, feeling the pull, resisting the really dumb urge to throw herself into his arms again. Suddenly, she was very close to glad that the power had gone out. If it hadn't, they would probably be in her bedroom by now.

Her throat clutched. She had to cough to clear it. "We can call the power company at least." They trooped back inside. She picked up the phone—and got dead air. "Phone's out, too."

He took a cell from his back pocket and she got hers from her crossbody bag. Neither of them could raise a signal. He tipped his head up toward the ceiling and the incessant drumming of the rain. "I'm not liking this," he muttered, grabbing his hat and sticking it back on his head. "I'll be right back."

"Where are you going?" she demanded. But she was talking to an empty kitchen.

He was already halfway down the central hallway to the front door.

"Nate…" She took off after him, slipping out behind him onto the porch.

No light shone from any of the windows up and down the block. It looked like the power was out all around them. And the rain was still coming down in sheets, the wind carrying it at an angle, so it spattered the porch floor, dampened their jeans and ran in rivulets around their feet. Scarier still, Pine Street was now a minicreek, the water three or four inches deep and churning.

He sent her a flat look. "Go inside. I'm having a look around."

"A look around where?"

But of course, he didn't answer. He took off down the front steps and across her soggy lawn, making for his pickup.

Go inside? No way. She needed to know what was going on as much as he did.

She took off after him at a run and managed to get to

the passenger door and yank it open before he could shift into gear and back into the rushing, shallow creek that used to be their street.

"You don't need to be out in this." He glared at her, water dripping from his hat, as she swung herself up to the seat, yanked the door shut and grabbed the seat belt.

She snapped the belt shut and armed water off her forehead. "I'm going. Drive."

He muttered something low, something disparaging to her gender, she was certain, but at least he did what she'd told him to do, shifting the quad cab into gear and backing it into the street. He had a high clearance with those big wheels cowboys liked so much, so at that point the water running in the street posed no threat to the engine. He shifted into Drive, headed toward Commercial Street, which was also under water. He turned left and then right onto Main.

They approached Rust Creek and the Main Street Bridge. In the year since the big flood, the levee had been raised and the bridge rebuilt to cross the racing creek at a higher level.

He drove up the slope that accommodated the raised levee and onto the bridge. The water level was still a long way below them.

"Looks good to me," she said.

With a grudging grunt of agreement, he kept going, down the slope on the other side and past the library and the town hall and the new community center with its Fourth of July Grand Opening banner drooping, rain pouring down it in sheets.

"Um, pardon me," she said gingerly. "But where are we going now?"

He swung the wheel and they went left on Cedar Street. "I'm checking the Commercial Street Bridge, too," he said grimly, narrowed eyes on the streaming road in front of them. "It's the one I'm really worried about. Last year, it was completely washed out."

They went past Strickland's Boarding House and the house where Emmet lived and kept going, turning finally onto a county road just outside town. It was only a couple of minutes from there to Commercial Street. He turned and headed for the bridge.

It wasn't far. And there were county trucks there, parked on either side of the street. A worker in a yellow slicker flagged them to a stop and then slogged over to Nate's side window, which he rolled down, letting in a gust of rain-drenched wind.

Nate knew the man by name. "Angus, what's going on?"

Angus was maybe forty, with a sun-creased face and thick, sandy eyebrows. Water dripped off his prominent nose. "Just keepin' an eye on things, Nate."

"The levee?"

"Holding fine and well above the waterline. It'll have to rain straight through for more than a week before anybody needs to start worryin'."

"Power's out."

"I know, and landlines. And a couple of cell towers took lightning strikes. But crews are already at work on all of that. We're hoping to have services restored in the next few hours." Angus aimed a smile in Callie's direction. "Ma'am." She nodded in response. He said, "With all this water in the streets, it's safer not to go driving around in it. You should go on home and dry out."

"Will do." Nate thanked him, sent the window back up and drove across the bridge and back to South Pine, where he pulled into her driveway again and followed her inside.

As she ran across the lawn, her shoes sinking into the waterlogged ground, she knew she should tell him to go, that she would be fine on her own. But for someone he'd called mouthy, she was suddenly feeling more than a little tongue-tied, not to mention downright reluctant to send him on his way.

Which was beyond foolish. If he stayed, it was going to be far too easy to get cozy together, to take up where they'd left off when the lights went out.

She decided not to even think about that.

Inside, she kicked off her shoes and left them by the door. "I'll bring more towels. And it's pretty chilly. If you'll turn on the fire, we can dry off in front of it." Her new energy-efficient gas fireplace required only the flip of a switch to get it going.

With a low noise of agreement, he turned for the great room off the front hall.

When she came back to him he stood in front of the fire. He'd taken off his boots and set them close by to dry. She gave him a towel and then sat down cross-legged in front of the warm blaze. He dropped down beside her. They got busy with the towels. Once she'd rubbed herself damp-dry, she set her towel on the rectangle of decorative stone that served as a hearth. He tossed his towel on top of hers, bending close to her as he reached across her, bringing the smell of rain on his skin and that nice, clean aftershave he wore.

"Feels good," he said.

And she was oh, so achingly aware of him. "Yep," she agreed. "We'll be dry in no time."

Her makeshift braid was dripping down her back, so she grabbed her towel again and blotted at it some more, letting her gaze wander to the bare walls he'd painted a warm, inviting butterscotch color and on to her tan sofa, and from there to the box of knickknacks by the coffee table, which she'd yet to unpack....

She looked everywhere but at him.

And then he caught the end of the towel and tugged on it.

Her breath got all tangled up in her chest as she made herself meet his eyes.

And he asked, soft and rough and low, "Do you want me to go?"

She should have said yes or even just nodded. There were so many reasons why she needed *not* to do anything foolish with him tonight.

Or any night, for that matter.

But the problem was, right at the moment, none of those reasons seemed the least bit important to her. None of them could hold a candle to the soft and yearning look in his eyes, the surprisingly tender curve of his sexy mouth, the way he took the towel from her hands and tossed it back over her shoulder in the general direction of the other one.

"Yes or no?" He pressed the question.

And, well, at that moment, by the fire, with him smelling so wonderful and looking at her in that focused, thrilling way, what else could she say but, "No, Nate. I want you to stay."

He smiled then. Such a beautiful, open, true sort of smile. And he laid a hand on the side of her face, making a caress of the touch, fingers sliding back and then down over her hair, curving around her wet braid, bringing it forward over her shoulder.

And then reaching out his other hand, using his fingers so deftly, unbraiding and combing through the damp strands. "There," he said at last. "Loose. Wet. Curling a little."

She felt a smile tremble on her mouth. And all she could say was, "Oh, Nate…"

And he said, "That first day, back in January?"

"Yeah?" The single word escaped her lips as barely a whisper, a mere breath of sound.

"You had that heavy scarf covering the bottom of your face. And then you took it off. What's that old Dwight Yoakum song? 'Try Not to Look So Pretty.' That was it—how I felt. I hoped you wouldn't be so pretty. But you were. And you had that hat on, bright pink and green, with those three pom-poms that bounced every time you shook your head. And your hair, just little bits of it slipping out from under that hat, so soft and shiny, curling a little, making me think about getting my hands in it...."

She said, feeling hesitant, "You seemed so angry at me that day."

He ran his index finger along the line of her jaw, setting off sparks, in a trail of sensation. "I had somewhere I needed to be."

"I, um, kind of figured that."

"I wasn't prepared for you." Gruffly, intently.

And then his eyes changed, moss to emerald, and he was leaning into her, cradling the back of her head in his big, warm hand.

And she was leaning his way, too.

And he was pulling her closer, taking her down with him onto the hearth, reaching out and pulling the towels in closer to make a pillow for her head.

She asked his name, "Nate?" And she was asking it against his warm, firm lips.

Because he was kissing her again and she was sighing, reaching her hungry hands up to thread her fingers into his damp hair. She was parting her lips for him, inviting his tongue to come inside.

And he was lifting a little, bracing on his forearms to keep from crushing her against the hard floor, his hands on either side of her face, cradling her, kissing her.

Outside, lightning flashed and thunder rumbled and the rain kept coming down.

She didn't care. There was only the warmth of the fire and the man in her arms, the man who could be so very aggravating, but also so tender and true and unbelievably sweet.

He lifted his head and he gazed down at her and she thought that his eyes were greener, deeper than ever right then. He opened that wonderful mouth to say something.

But he never got a word out.

Because right about then, they both realized that someone was knocking on the front door.

Chapter Three

Nate stared down at Callie. He wanted to kiss her again, to go on kissing her. Maybe whoever was at the door would just go away.

But the knocking started in again. And then a woman's voice called, "Callie? Callie, are you in there?"

Callie blinked up at him, her mouth swollen from his kisses. "I think that's Faith…."

Bad words scrolled through his mind as he pushed back to his knees and rose, bending to offer a hand. She took it and he helped her up.

Once they were both on their feet, they just stood there, gaping at each other like a couple of sleepwalkers wakened suddenly in some public place. He took a slow breath and willed the bulge at his fly to subside. Just what he needed. Their neighbor knowing exactly what she'd interrupted, spreading the word that he and Callie had a thing going on. And, okay, yeah. He did have a thing for Callie. But it was a thing he'd never intended to act on….

The knock came again. "Callie?" cried a woman's voice.

Callie called, "I'll be right there!"

Both of them got to work smoothing their hair and straightening their still-damp clothes. Tucking in her snug T-shirt as she went, Callie headed for the door. Since he didn't know what else to do, he trailed in her wake. She disengaged the lock and pulled the door back.

Faith, barefoot in a pale blue cotton maternity dress, stood dripping on the doorstep, holding a battery-powered lantern, a relieved-looking smile on her face. "You're here. I'm so glad…."

Callie stepped back. "Come in, come in…."

Faith spotted Nate. "Hey there, Nathan."

"Ahem. Hi, Faith." He felt like a fool.

But Faith didn't seem especially concerned with what he might be doing in the dark at Callie's house. She said to Callie, "Actually, I came over to get you."

Callie frowned. "Get me?"

Faith's head bobbed up and down. "It's happening. The baby's coming. I've been timing contractions, getting everything ready. They're four minutes apart, about fifty seconds each."

"Active labor," Callie said in a hushed, almost reverent tone.

And Faith chuckled, as if having a baby in the middle of a rainstorm with the phones out and no electricity was something kind of humorous. "I've been waiting for the phones to come on so I could call my mom and call you over. But the phones aren't cooperating. And it feels to me like this baby is going to be born real soon now. I… Uh-oh." She doubled over with a groan, her free hand moving to cradle her giant belly. "Here…comes another one…."

Callie took the lantern from her and shoved it at him.

"Here." Blinking, stunned, he took it. This couldn't be happening.

But it was.

Nate stood there, holding the lantern high, gaping at the two of them in complete disbelief.

"Come on," Callie urged. "Just come inside by the fire for a minute…."

Faith made a low, animal sort of sound. "But I…have everything ready, just like we planned…."

"Good. Wonderful. As soon as this one passes, I'll get my equipment and we'll go to your house. Now come on, lean on me." Callie coaxed and coddled, guiding a staggering, moaning Faith into the great room and over to the sofa, not far from the fire.

Still holding the lantern high, Nate watched them go. He stood rooted to the spot, his heart pounding out a swift, ragged rhythm, his worst nightmare unfolding all over again.

They needed to do something. *He* needed to do something. But right at the moment, he found he couldn't move.

Callie had Faith at the sofa by then, near the light and heat of the fire. "Right here, sit down. Easy now, easy…."

Faith panted, groaning some more as she went down to the cushions and Callie went with her.

Right about then, Nate finally made his frozen body move. The blood rushing so fast in his veins it sounded like a hurricane inside his head, he set down the lantern, dug his cell from his pocket, punched up 9-1-1 and put the phone to his ear.

Nothing.

With a muttered oath, he pulled the phone away from his face and stared at the screen. No bars. So he shoved the useless thing back into his pocket and took off like a shot toward the kitchen, grabbing up the house phone from the counter when he got there and trying it.

It was dead, too.

Dead.

Not a word he wanted in his mind at the moment.

He dropped the phone and raced back to the front of the house. When he got to the foyer, he stopped in the doorway to the great room. By then, Faith seemed to be breathing more normally, and Callie glanced over and saw him standing there.

She gasped at the sight of him. "Nate, what's wrong? You're white as a sheet. Are you all right?"

He made his mouth form words. "I tried my cell and your house phone. Both are still out. We need to get her to my truck, take her to the hospital in Kalispell. We need to do that now."

Faith let out a cry of protest. "No. No, I'm not going to do that." She grabbed Callie's hand again. "Callie, tell him. This is going normally, beautifully. I don't need a hospital. I want the home birth I planned for."

"Home birth." Nate swung his gaze back on Callie and accused, "Are you crazy? Have you both lost your minds?"

Faith said, "You should sit down, Nate. Before you fall down."

He braced a hand on the door frame and wondered why his knees felt weak. "I'm fine. There's nothing wrong with me."

Faith shook her head. "Seriously, now. You don't look so good."

Nate clutched the door frame harder. "Like I said. Fine. I'm just fine." And then he noticed that Callie was on her feet and coming toward him. He demanded, "What is the matter with you two? It's not safe, not right." He glared at Callie. "She needs a hospital…."

Callie reached for his hand. "Come on. Over here."

"What? I don't…"

"Come on." She had his hand and she put her other arm around him. And he found he had let go of the door frame and was letting her guide him over to the easy chair close to the fire. "Here," she said gently, the way you talk to a sick child. "Sit right here." She pushed him slowly down onto it. "There you go. That's it.…"

He felt light-headed, and he wildly stared up at her as a low, angry sound escaped him.

She kept talking slowly and calmly. "Lower your head, Nate." She put her hand to his upper back and pushed. At first he resisted, but then he gave in and let her guide him down so his head was between his knees. "Good," she soothed. "Excellent. Now just stay there for a little while, please. I want you to concentrate on your breathing, make it even, deep and slow.…"

"This is crazy," he insisted to the space on the floor between his stocking feet. "It's not safe. We have to get Faith to the hospital, where they can take care of her, where she and the baby will be safe."

Callie kept on in that slow, soothing voice. "It will be okay, Nate. I promise you. Just stay there with your head down. Just breathe slowly and deeply."

He wanted to yell at her, to yell at *both* of them, to get it through to them that they were insane, out of their minds to take a chance like this. He knew what would happen if they did. He knew it from the worst kind of personal experience.

However, he was afraid if he sat up right then and tried to explain to them what idiots they were being, he would throw up. That wouldn't help anyone.

Eventually, Callie asked, "Better?"

He stared at his socks and muttered, "Yeah. Better. I think so."

"Good. Because I need you. I need your help. I need you to pull it together, please. Will you do that for me?"

"Please, Nate," said Faith from over there on the sofa. "Callie's not only a nurse. She's certified as a midwife. We have this handled. It's going to be okay."

He sat up. By some miracle, he didn't throw up and he didn't pass out. He looked from one woman to the other and realized that Callie was right about one thing. He really did need to pull it together. "You're determined to do this?"

"Yes, we are," the women said in unison.

It wasn't the answer he'd hoped for, but it was the answer he got and now he needed to deal with it. "What do you want me to do?"

"Wonderful." Callie let out a long sigh. "Put on your boots and help Faith back to her house. I need to dig my midwife bag out of a packing box upstairs. I'll get it and I'll be right over, I promise."

Out on the porch, it was still raining as if it was the end of the world. Nate handed Faith the lantern. "I'm just going to carry you."

She bit her lip and nodded. "Okay."

So he scooped her up in his arms and ran with her, down the steps and across the yard, with the rain pelting down on them and his boots sinking into the saturated ground with every step he took.

But at least it wasn't far. He was mounting the steps to the shelter of her porch in seconds. He shoved open the front door as another one of those contractions started.

Faith moaned and almost dropped the lantern. He managed to catch it, keeping one hand on her for support as she slid her feet to the floor, all the while fervently praying that Callie would get over there quick.

The house was warm. Faith had a fire going in the living room heat stove. And she had fat candles lit and more of those electric lanterns set around.

She pointed down the central hallway. "My room," she moaned. "That way...." He waited for the worst of that contraction to pass and then scooped her up again and carried her down there, detouring into the room she indicated.

He set her on the bed, which had been stripped except for a sheet and some kind of plastic cover beneath the sheet, which made faint crinkling sounds as it took her weight. There were candles on the dresser and a lantern by the bed. In the soft glow of light, he saw a basin, stacks of clean towels and diapers and those small cotton blankets that you used on newborns.

Perched on the end of the bed, Faith had started rocking gently back and forth, kind of humming to herself. He stood over her, feeling like a lump of useless nothing. She actually did seem kind of peaceful and relaxed about the whole thing.

Nothing like Zoe, nothing like that awful day in January so long ago...

He cleared his throat. "Is there anything I can get you?"

Faith looked up at him, big blue eyes so calm. "I didn't know, about you and Callie...." He had no idea what to say to that, so he said nothing. He'd known Faith forever, been five years ahead of her in school. He used to hang out with her older brother Stan. She pinched up her mouth at him and added sternly, "You treat her right, Nate Crawford. She deserves the best."

He gave her a slow nod, figuring that was the easiest way to get off the subject of Callie and him and what might be going on between them.

Faith softened toward him then and granted him a gentle little smile. "What you can do is go to the kitchen and get me some ice chips."

"Ice chips," he repeated.

"That's right. Metal bowl in the high cupboard on the right of the sink, ice pick in the drawer to the left of the stove. Break up some ice into small chips for me. It helps, to suck on the chips, keeps me hydrated."

Relieved to have something constructive to do, he left her.

Callie came in as he was breaking up the ice. She stopped for a moment in the open doorway to the hall. "Ice chips. Good." She gave him a smile. She had a purple rolling canvas bag, like the largest size of carry-on suitcase, with a stylized logo of a mother and child on the front. "Just bring them in when they're nice and small."

"Will do." He kept poking with the ice pick.

She turned and wheeled her midwife suitcase off down the hall.

When he took them the ice chips, Callie met him at the door. "Thanks," she said softly. "We've got it from here."

Did she want him to go back to his house? Well, he wasn't. If something went wrong, at least he would be there to take them wherever they needed to go. "I'll just… wait in the other room, keep the fire going. Anything you need, you give me a holler."

She nodded. "Maybe more ice chips later."

"Whatever you need, you just let me know."

He went back to the kitchen and stood at the sink, gulping down a tall glass of water, and then wandered into the living room to check on the fire in the heat stove. After that, he had no idea what to do with himself.

So he paced for a while. Eventually, Callie came out

and asked for a pitcher of water, two cups and more ice chips. He got those things for her.

The time crawled by. He checked his phone frequently and also the landline phone on the side table by the sofa. But the power stayed out and the phones, as well. And the rain just kept on, curtains of water falling out of the sky.

About two hours after Callie joined Faith in the bedroom, he heard a really loud moaning sound coming from in there. He went to the door and put his ear to it.

He heard Callie's soft, soothing voice. And he heard Faith. She was the one moaning, making hard, guttural sounds—loud, harsh grunting noises that reminded him of the way female championship tennis players sounded when they hit the ball.

He wanted to tap on the door and ask if everything was all right, but he figured they wouldn't appreciate him interrupting.

He returned to the living room, stoked the fire, checked the phones. And waited.

And waited some more.

He heard occasional noises from the bedroom but nothing that alarmed him. And he knew that Callie would shout for him if things got out of hand or if she needed him to get her something.

And then, at ten minutes before midnight according to the crystal clock on the spindly little desk in the corner, the lights came on. Nate was pacing the living room floor at that moment, and he stopped in midstride to look up at the ceiling fixture, which had just burst into brightness. He took another step. And then he stopped again, tipping his head to the side, listening.

Silence. He rushed to the front door and pulled it open.

The rain had stopped. Porch lights glowed up and down South Pine. The minicreek of rushing water in the street had drained away. There was only the wet blacktop gleaming in the reflected glow of the street lamps.

"Let there be light," Callie said softly from behind him.

He shut the door and turned to her, his heart suddenly surging into overdrive, a weird coppery taste in his mouth. "Faith? The baby? Are they…" He couldn't quite seem to finish the question.

She put her finger to her lips and whispered, "Come with me."

Terror was messing with him, his heart bouncing around in his chest, his stomach spurting acid. But then her expression got through to him, brought him a degree of calm. If things had gone bad, no way would she be looking up at him with that smug little half smile.

"This way." She turned and started back down the hall. He fell in behind her. When they got to Faith's room, Callie put a finger to her lips again and then gently pushed the door open.

Faith lay propped on a pile of pillows in the now properly made-up bed. She wore a green robe and held a pink bundle in her arms—and she looked up and gave him a tired, happy smile. "Hey, Nathan. Look who's here."

He hardly knew he was moving, but then he found himself standing by the side of the bed.

Faith's hair hung lank around her face and there were dark smudges under her eyes. But still, she looked good, had a kind of glow about her. She seemed so happy, so proud. "We're calling her Tansy," she said.

Nate nodded. He knew her husband's family. "After Owen's grandmother."

"That's right. You want to hold her?"

He wasn't sure about that, but then Callie eased around him and took the pink bundle from Faith—and what could he do?

Callie laid the little girl in his arms. He looked down at her, at Tansy, at her tiny, pink mouth and her button of a nose. She yawned, a giant yawn, and then she gave a big sigh and settled into sleep again without ever opening her eyes.

He dared to hold her for a minute longer, a deep and familiar sadness flowing through him, mingling with his joy for Faith and Owen, with the awe he felt just being in the presence of a person so tiny and perfect and fine.

"She's beautiful," he said and held her out for Callie to take her.

Callie passed her back to Faith, and then she asked him, "How about a cup of coffee?"

He realized he'd been holding his breath and let it out slowly. "Sounds good to me."

In Faith's kitchen, Callie gestured for him to sit at the breakfast bar. He slid onto one of the three high stools, and she got to work, finding coffee and filters in the cupboard, loading up the coffeemaker. He checked the phones again, but they were still out.

Once she had it brewing, she took the stool beside him and braced her cheek on her hand. "You okay?"

He looked into those big brandy-brown eyes and thought about how much he'd liked kissing that sweet, soft mouth of hers, about how he would love to kiss her again.

But he wouldn't. After tonight, he was going to make a concentrated effort to steer clear of pretty Callie Kennedy. Because Faith was right. Callie deserved the best. She deserved a good man to love her and marry her and give her babies, like that angel back in the bedroom in Faith's arms.

He wasn't that man. All that was over for him.

His gaze fell on that purple bag of hers, all packed up

and waiting in the corner. "A midwife, a nurse. You kind of do it all, huh?"

She chuckled. "I always wanted a practice like the one at the clinic, but somehow, I ended up in a big Chicago hospital on the administration end. It was better money and I…" She pressed her lips together and he knew there was something she'd decided not to say. "Anyway, I took the midwife training a few years back and got certified. I kept telling myself that maybe someday I would give up the rat race and become a real, hands-on nurse and midwife in some homey small town where everybody knew everybody."

"And just look at you now." He didn't try to hide his admiration.

She beamed. "Living my dream, and that is no lie."

For a moment or two, neither of them spoke. The coffeemaker sputtered away.

Callie spoke again, her voice low now and kind of careful. "You were white around the mouth, back at my house. Faith and I… We both thought you were going to pass out."

He breathed in the reassuring scent of brewing coffee and thought how he was going tell her it was nothing, just a guy thing, that some men were terrified at births.

But instead, he opened his mouth and said, "I was married once."

Softly, she answered, "I didn't know."

He meant to stop there. But then he went and opened his mouth and told her more. "I met my wife in Missoula, when I was in college. At Johnny's Downtown Cafe, where she waited tables. She had red hair and freckles and big hazel eyes. Her name was Zoe Baker and she was the love of my life." He fell silent. He waited for the woman next to him to break the spell, to say something so he could change the subject.

She didn't say a word, only looked at him, her expression tender and gentle and completely accepting.

So he just kept talking. "Me and Zoe, we had two great years together in Missoula while I finished school. When I graduated, I wanted to bring her home to Rust Creek Falls with me. But she'd met my parents, and my mom wasn't warm to her. Zoe didn't feel welcome here. She knew they wanted more than 'just a waitress' for their wonderful firstborn son." He muttered those words. They tasted so bitter in his mouth.

Callie lifted a hand and put it gently on his arm. He felt that touch right down to the center of himself. He knew he ought to shut up.

But he didn't. The old story just kept pushing, demanding to be told.

So he went on with the rest of it, how he and Zoe moved to Bismarck, where Zoe's mom, Anna, lived. How he got a job running a fast-food place, and they were doing all right.

"I loved her," he said. "I loved Zoe so much that I was happy even living away from Rust Creek, away from home. Then Zoe became pregnant." God in heaven. He shut his eyes, breathed in slow through his nose. "The sweetness of that time, I can't begin to tell you about it. I was the happiest man alive. But I did want to move home, and my parents promised to be more welcoming to Zoe. They wanted their grandchild born in Rust Creek Falls. So Zoe agreed to spend Christmas with my family, to see how it went."

Callie didn't say anything. She just kept her hand there, on his forearm, steady and soothing. And she listened, those big brown eyes never shifting, never looking away.

He kept going. "I was so sure of everything, sure it would work out just how I wanted it. Figuring I was coming home for good soon, I quit my job, and we stayed at the Shooting Star, the ranch Grandfather Crawford left to me and my brothers when he passed. At the time, there was only a foreman and a couple of hands living there. I opened up my grandfather's house and Zoe and I stayed there. I hoped she would like that, be impressed with how big and comfortable the house was…."

Callie patted his arm and then left his side to get down the coffee cups. "And was she impressed?"

He shrugged. "Zoe never cared about stuff like that, about money and fancy things." *She was a lot like you that way,* he thought but didn't say.

"How did the visit go?"

"Pretty well. My parents still didn't really warm to Zoe, but they wanted me back home, so they were on good behavior." He watched as she filled two cups and pushed one across the counter at him. He sipped and she put milk and sugar in hers.

She took the stool next to him again.

And he continued, "On Christmas Eve, Zoe had some bleeding. There was cramping, too. I rushed her to the hospital in Kalispell, and the doctor there put her on bed rest. We agreed she would take it easy at the ranch until the baby was born and then we would talk about what to do next. I was glad that we would have to stay in Rust Creek Falls for a while. I was just so sure that the longer Zoe stayed, the more she'd come to love it here. Zoe's mom volunteered to come and help out, but Anna really couldn't afford to take the time off from her job. We told her we were fine, and she stayed in Bismarck…." He stared at Callie, wondering why he was telling her this, wishing he'd never gotten started, knowing he should stop.

And then, not stopping, just going on, telling her the rest of it. "The fourteenth of January, the snow started. By the morning of the fifteenth, it was a blizzard, one for the record books, whiteout conditions. And Zoe was in labor.

The phones were out and the roads were closed, with six feet of snow and more coming down. It was just the two of us, and our baby trying to be born, alone in my grandfather's house. There were... How do they always say it?" He sipped his coffee, slowly, set the cup down. "There were complications. They both died, Zoe and our little boy."

Callie didn't say anything. He was grateful for that. And she didn't need to say anything. She understood. He could see that in those big eyes. She touched his arm again, a brief brush of a touch. And then she folded both hands around her coffee cup and waited for him to finish it up.

So he did. "After we buried them I took off. I lived in Wyoming for a while, and Colorado, and Utah, traveling around, picking up odd jobs. I didn't stay in one place for long. I kept moving, kept trying to outrun the pain of what had happened, kept trying to forget. And then, eventually, when I realized there was never going to be any way to forget, I gave up and just came home. I didn't know where else to go."

"I had no idea," Callie said in a whisper.

He shrugged. "Nobody in town remembered Zoe, really. She and I had our life together away from here. And my parents, they prefer to forget her, not to think about the grandson they never saw. Mostly, everyone's forgotten I was ever married. And I'm good with that. I don't want to talk about it. It hurts too much—and don't even ask me why I'm talking about it now."

Callie shook her head and answered in a gentle voice, "Okay. I won't ask."

He muttered darkly, as a warning, "I shouldn't have been kissing you. I'm not a good bet. There's something... broken in me, you know? I haven't been such a good man in the years since I moved back home. I've been a Crawford through and through, you might say—too proud and too sure I knew every damn thing. You are a quality woman. You deserve a better man than me."

She only looked at him, eyes wide, bright with the sheen of unshed tears. Her mouth was so soft. He wanted to grab her and start kissing her all over again.

And that couldn't happen. He made himself clearer. "The last eight years, since I've been back in town, I've gone out with several women. But it never ends well. They get fed up with waiting for me to get serious. But I never get serious. I've never felt anything like what I had with Zoe. I've pretty much accepted that there's no one else for me."

Callie kept her gaze level. He couldn't tell what she might be thinking. "I understand," she said.

He leaned a little closer. "Do you really?"

"I do, Nate. Although I happen to think you're a much better man than you're giving yourself credit for."

"You're just softhearted."

She gave a tiny shrug. "Maybe I am." Her eyes seemed so sad. "Just tell me the rest, will you please? Tell me about Bismarck."

Why not? He'd come this far. And he knew she would keep it to herself. She was that kind of woman, the kind a man could depend on to respect his secrets and guard his privacy.

And it seemed only right somehow, to finish the story. "Every year, on January fifteenth, I drive to Bismarck to put flowers on their graves."

Callie made a soft, mournful little sound, but she didn't say a word.

He went on with it. "I used to go and pick up Anna, Zoe's mom, and we would take the flowers together. But then, two years ago, Anna remarried and moved to Florida. I'm glad for her. She's happier than she thought she would ever be, after losing her only child and her grandbaby, too. But she can't make it back to North Dakota every year. So now I make the trip on my own. And then, once I've delivered the flowers, I go straight to a certain roadhouse I know of with a motel out back. I get good and plastered and I remember—all of it, everything that's lost. And I do it a long way from Rust Creek Falls, where no one will see me drunk and disorderly and crying like a fool. Then, when I've finally had enough of the memories and the whiskey, I sleep it off in that motel I mentioned, the one out back behind the bar."

She looked at him for a long time, a patient sort of look. He thought he could stare into her eyes for a century and never want to stop.

He also knew that if he stayed in that kitchen with her much longer, there would be no telling what he might do or say. He could end up telling her everything, including about the lottery ticket he bought the day he met her, about his big win, that not even his family knew about, about how it kind of felt to him that she had brought him good luck, a new start on what, for a decade, had always been the darkest, hardest day of the year.

No. He wasn't going to go there.

"I should leave." He pushed his cup away.

She didn't argue, just went on looking at him as though she could see right down to the core of him.

He got up and headed for the door.

"Good night, Nate," she said softly.

He just kept walking. He knew if he stopped, if he turned back to look at her, he wouldn't be able to go.

Callie heard the front door open and the soft click as he closed it behind him. A minute later, she heard his pickup

start up next door—he would be moving it from her driveway to his garage.

Her heart ached for him. And she was way too attracted
to him.

And he'd made it more than clear that whatever this
thing was between them, it wasn't the kind of thing that
could last. Plus, hello, hadn't she promised herself she
would steer clear of men in general for a while?

It was all just completely unworkable, and she needed
to get over it, get over *him*—which was a ridiculous way
to think of it. She didn't know him well enough to need
to get over him. Tonight was the first night she'd spent
any real time with him, the first night they'd even shared
a kiss. She didn't need to get over him. She just needed to
forget about him.

The phone on the counter started ringing, the sound
startling her, so she let out a sharp, "Oh!"

It was Faith's mom, Brenda. Callie reassured her that
there'd been no flooding on South Pine and Faith was fine.
Then, before Brenda could ask more questions, Callie told
her to hold on and carried the phone down the hall to see
if Faith was awake. She was sitting up among the pillows,
Tansy in her arms.

Callie held up the phone and mouthed, "Your mom."

"Did you tell her?" Faith whispered back.

Callie shook her head.

Faith gave her a wobbly smile and picked up the extension by the bed. "Mom." A sob escaped her. Fat tears
overflowed and trailed down her cheeks. But she was
smiling at the same time. "Mom, you won't believe what's
happened…."

Callie backed out of the bedroom and shut the door.
And then she returned to the kitchen, where she poured a

second cup of coffee she really didn't need and tried not to think of Nate, alone in his big, beautiful house with only sad memories to keep him company.

Chapter Four

Nate didn't get a whole lot of sleep that night. He kept thinking of Callie, of how focused and still she'd been when he told her about Zoe, the way she just listened, not needing to fill the air with words or fall all over him with a flood of sympathetic noises.

He kept thinking of the way she'd handled him—and really, there was no other word for it. She had handled him good and proper when he almost lost it over Faith having the baby. Gently and firmly, she had calmed him down and gotten him reluctantly on board with their plan.

And then there were those kisses they'd shared. The woman could get a dead man going.

He wouldn't mind kissing Callie Kennedy again, and frequently.

She was something, all right. Something really special.

And that was why he would keep his distance from here on out. The woman just *did* something to him, made him feel as though she could see inside his head—and his heart, too. He wasn't up for that. After losing Zoe and the baby, he never wanted to care that much again. He had a feeling that with Callie he could get in deep, and it would happen fast. Giving her a wide berth was the best option.

Yeah, that could be a little tricky, given that she lived right next door. But he could be damned determined when he set his mind to it.

The next morning, the third of July, there wasn't a cloud in the sky. Nate had business in Kalispell at nine, so he was up good and early, showered, shaved and dressed and frying himself some eggs when the house phone rang.

It was his mother. "Nathan. Good morning. Everything all right on the south side of town?"

"It's fine here at my house."

"Did you lose power and phone service, too?"

"Yeah." He turned the heat down under the pan and poked at the eggs and had a very strong feeling his mother was leading up to something.

"But everything's back on now?"

"That's right. I woke up this morning, and even my cell was finally showing bars."

"Terrific." A pause and then, way too sweetly, "You and Callie get home all right?"

"Just fine, Mom."

"She's a wonderful person, don't you think?"

He gritted his teeth and kept his voice neutral. "Yep. She's great." He tucked the phone into the crook of his shoulder and slid the eggs onto his plate, then turned to pop the toast from the toaster.

His mother kept on. "She just loves it here in town. Never wants to leave. Did you know that, Nathan?"

"She mentioned that once or twice, yeah." And a change

of subject was in order. "Faith Harper had her baby last night." He slathered butter on the toast.

"Now, where did you hear that?" his mother demanded. Laura Crawford never liked it when she wasn't the first to know about a new baby coming or who got engaged or was getting divorced.

"I was there."

"What?"

"Faith had the baby at her house. It was during the storm. She came over to get Callie to help her."

"Over to *your* house?"

"No, Mom. To Callie's house."

"Oh. You were at Callie's house?"

"I drove her home, remember?"

"Do not treat me like I'm senile. Of course I remember."

"Callie's a midwife. Did you know that?"

"Of course I knew. I told you I *like* Callie. She's more than a very pretty face. She has a good head on her shoulders. She's helpful to everyone and a good listener, too. Most times, when she comes in the store, we have a nice chat, Callie and me. Emmet's lucky to have her. More people are going to the clinic when they need a doctor now, because Callie is a top-notch medical professional."

He knocked back a slug of coffee. "So, anyway, Callie delivered Faith's baby."

"I'm so glad she was there when Faith needed her."

"Faith had a little girl and named her Tansy, after Owen's grandma."

"Well, I guess I remember Tansy Harper better than you do."

He stifled a chuckle at how his mom could get all huffy if you dared to think you knew more than her—and then he thought of Zoe, of how his mother had said more nice things about Callie in the space of two minutes than she'd ever said about the woman he'd loved more than life. "Mom, I have to go. My breakfast is getting cold."

"What's the matter? What'd I say now?"

"Not a thing," he lied. There was just no point in plowing that old ground again. "I'll call Delbert Hawser to come fix the roof for you, see if he can get over there today."

"Can't you or one of the other boys do it? I hate to spend good money on a handyman when I've got four strong, capable sons." His mother had plenty of money to pay for the roof repair. But she'd always prided herself on her frugality. She knew how to make a penny beg for mercy.

"I'll tell Delbert to send me the bill. Don't you worry about it."

"I hate for you to waste your money, even though I know you've done well for yourself, investing your inheritance so wisely and all." That was the story he'd given them when he'd fixed up the two houses and then moved off the ranch, that he'd made a killing investing the money that came down to him from Grandpa Crawford.

"It's not a problem," he assured her. "I'm happy to take care of it for you."

"I am proud of you, son." Her voice was soft now, loving. "You know that, don't you?"

"Thanks, Mom."

"I just hope you're rethinking that crazy plan of yours to move away. And you know, if you started seeing someone you really liked here in town, well, you just might come to your senses and realize that you don't even *want* to leave."

"Gotta go. Really. 'Bye, Mom."

She was still talking as he hung up.

He ate his breakfast and called Delbert, who agreed to fix the roof leak at the store that afternoon and send Nate the bill. As he pulled out of the garage for the drive to Kalispell, he couldn't help but glance over at the house next door.

No sign of Callie. No lights on inside that he could see. Would she be at the clinic now or still at Faith's helping out? He really would like to know how Faith and little Tansy were doing....

But he fought the urge to stop the pickup in the driveway and jog across the lawn to see if she might be there. Instead, he backed to the street, shifted into forward gear and hit the gas so hard he laid rubber getting out of there.

Twenty-five minutes later, he was pulling into a parking space behind an office building in downtown Kalispell. He went in the back entrance and took the elevator to the third floor, which housed the offices of Saul Mercury, Attorney-at-Law. The elevator doors opened on a black marble foyer and a middle-aged receptionist behind a wide front desk.

"Hello, Mr. Crawford. Mr. Mercury is expecting you. Go right on back."

He took the hallway on the right, down to the large corner office where Saul was waiting.

"Nate. Always great to see you." The lawyer, tall and broad-shouldered with a thick head of hair so blond Nate was certain it had to be a dye job, met him at the door. They shook hands. "Sit down, sit down," Saul encouraged with a smile that proudly displayed an orthodontist's fantasy of big, straight white teeth. Nate settled into the visitor's chair opposite Saul's giant desk of chrome and glass.

They got down to business.

Saul handed him a folder, and they went over the lawyer's report on what Nate's money was doing under the umbrella of the trust Saul had created for him.

As he did every month during their meeting, Saul suggested that besides all the "good works" Nate kept putting money into, he ought to find—or let Saul find him—some real investment opportunities for his fortune.

Nate said what he always said. "I'll get to that. But for now, I just want to take care of some things that need doing before I leave Rust Creek Falls."

Saul asked what he'd asked every month since Nate had started talking about moving away. "Decided where you're going?"

"I've been thinking Chicago…."

"When will you leave?"

"I haven't firmed anything up yet."

"Ah." Saul's expression said it all. The lawyer found it humorous that Nate kept saying he was leaving and yet he never managed actually to go.

Nate brought them back around to the business at hand. "I have a new project I want you to handle."

Saul's look turned hopeful. "Real estate? The markets? An internet start-up?"

"A donation. Let's say two—no, three—hundred thousand."

"A donation." Saul seemed to stifle a groan—after which he flashed those big white teeth again. "Why am I not surprised?"

"I have plenty of money now," Nate reminded him. "More than I'll ever need."

Saul put up a hand. "Not arguing, Nate. Just advising."

"The point is I've never been what you would call a generous man. It's good for me to give a little."

"And that's admirable. It's only that I think you should let your money *make* money, too."

"I get it, Saul. And I'll start looking for investment opportunities that interest me."

"You could let me help you look." Now the lawyer put up both big hands and patted the air. "Not a big deal, no pressure. But whenever I see an interesting possibility, I'll email you the information. You see one that intrigues you, get back to me. We'll talk."

"I don't want to be rushed into anything."

"Nate. C'mon. I won't send more than a couple of possibilities a week. You're not interested, do nothing."

"Fine. Send them my way. Now, ready for the details on that three hundred K?"

Saul tapped a key on his laptop. "Fire away."

After the meeting with Saul, Nate stopped in at Target to pick up a few things.

And then, on the way home, he turned off the highway at the winding road that led to the Traub family ranch, the Triple T. His sister Nina lived there now. She ran the family store most days, but lately she'd been taking Wednesdays and Thursdays off. Last Christmas, she'd had a daughter, Noelle, and married Dallas Traub, one of Collin's five brothers. Now she and Dallas had a nice ready-made family, with little Noelle and Dallas's three boys.

When Nate pulled into the big yard, there were no Traubs in sight. Not that it would have mattered if there were. The Traubs were civil to him now, as a rule. Yeah, most of them remained leery of him and he didn't blame them. He'd spent way too many years buying into the old family feud between his people and theirs, talking trash about Traubs whenever he got a chance. And then there'd been the long-time, personal animosity between him and Collin and the way he'd played dirty in the mayoral race.

But then he'd lost that race and had to eat an extra-large slice of humble pie. And Nina went and married one of Collin's brothers. And then Nate went to Bismarck in January and ended up a multimillionaire.

Things had changed, as far as he was concerned. True,

it was a convoluted relationship between the Crawfords and the Traubs. For generations, they'd hated each other, competed with each other for love and for land, done each other dirty in any number of business deals. But that was then. Nate just couldn't see a reason anymore to keep on with the old feud. Even his parents, who'd clung all their lives to the longtime animosity, couldn't really say specifically what the feud was about in the here and now, let alone why it should continue. There had been rotten behavior on both sides for generations. It needed to stop.

So now he made it a point to speak politely to every Traub he happened to meet on the street. The Traubs weren't exactly wild over him, but they were getting so they kind of put up with him, which meant that when he stopped in to see Nina on the Traub family ranch, no one came out to greet him with a loaded shotgun.

That day, Dallas's boys, Ryder, Jake and Robbie, were off at summer school in town, and Dallas was out in one of the far pastures, tending cattle. It was just Nina and the baby at home. Nate got to hold Noelle, and Nina fussed over him and made him lunch. At Target, he'd bought toys for each of the boys and a few things for Noelle, too.

Nina chided, "You don't always have to bring presents, you know."

"But, Nina, that's what uncles do." In his lap, Noelle giggled and reached for the ring of bright plastic keys he'd brought her. Each one made a different sound when you shook it. He handed them over and she crowed with delight when the blue one made a chiming sound. "See? She loves it."

Nina finished the last of the clothes she was folding and set the hamper aside. She pulled out a chair and sat down across from him. "That was some storm yesterday."

"But it's over now and the levee held."

"Life is good." Nina wore a pleased smile. "Mom called earlier. She said Faith Harper had a little girl during the storm and you were there for the birth."

"Well, I was in the house, but essentially useless. I brought her ice chips when she needed them and did a lot of pacing in front of the fire."

"Mom also says you're sweet on Nurse Callie Kennedy. She's real happy about that."

"Mom doesn't know what she's talking about."

"Well, now, Nathan," Nina teased. "You did move her in next door to you."

"Move her in? I was selling the house, and she's the one who bought it. That's hardly moving her in."

"Pardon me for saying so, but it seems to me your tone is just a tad defensive."

Noelle leaned back against him and shook the key, which made a rattling sound. He said, "Nope. Not defensive in the least."

"Everyone likes Callie. She's a lovely person. I'm thinking you're a lucky man."

"Callie's great. I like her a lot. But there's nothing going on between her and me." It was the truth, as of now, anyway, he told himself—and tried not to remember the feel of her in his arms or the scent of her hair or the way those big eyes seemed to see down into his soul.

Nina observed, "You seem a little too determined to convince me."

"Not determined. Just telling you how it is, that's all."

She studied him for a count of five. He braced to keep insisting that there was nothing happening with him and Callie.

But then she said, "It's the Fourth tomorrow. Grand opening of the new Grace Traub Community Center."

Nate had donated to the center—anonymously, through

the trust. But most of the money had come from a weird old guy named Arthur Swinton, who'd once been mayor down in Thunder Canyon, a town three hundred miles southeast of Rust Creek Falls, where a lot of Traub relatives lived. Swinton had ended up in prison for embezzlement at one point and then managed to get his sentence commuted by the efforts of the Roarke family, led by Shane Roarke, who it turned out was Arthur Swinton and Grace Traub's illegitimate son. Swinton then vowed ever after to do good works. Like…building a community center in Rust Creek Falls and naming it after the woman he'd loved before she'd even been a Traub. It didn't make a whole lot of sense to Nate, but, so what? The community center would be a real plus for Rust Creek Falls.

Nina went on, "And then there'll be the usual street fair on Main and the street dance and fireworks at night."

He gave her a patient look. "I know what goes on for the Fourth of July."

"You're going, right?"

"I haven't decided yet."

"Come on, Nathan. You should be there. Everybody's going. It's a big deal this year, the anniversary of the Great Flood." Nina looked a little misty-eyed. The year before, all the usual events had been canceled due to the incessant rain. And then, in the afternoon, the levee gave way. It had been a dark day for Rust Creek Falls. "We've come back stronger than ever. Mom says she'll run the store so Dallas and I can take the kids to the fair. And then Ellie says she'll help out if we want to try and stay for the dance and the fireworks." Ellie was Dallas's mom, the Traub family matriarch.

Amazing. Laura Crawford, the mother-in-law of a Traub, and Ellie Traub, with a Crawford for a daughter-in-law. He'd never thought to see such a thing in his life.

In his arms, Noelle started fussing. He surrendered her reluctantly when Nina rose and reached for her.

Nate got up, too. "Thanks for the lunch."

Dark eyes flashing with mischief, Nina rocked from side to side and kissed the fussing baby on her fat, pink cheek. "See you tomorrow. Bring your sweetheart."

"I don't have a sweetheart," he grumbled.

"That's not what Mom says…."

"Knock it off." He headed for the door.

"There is nothing quite as beautiful as young love in bloom," she called after him.

He kept his mouth shut and got out of there, closing the door a little harder than he needed to behind him.

When he got home, Nate saw Owen Harper's red pickup parked in the driveway of the house on the other side of Callie's. So he took over the baby gift he'd bought. Owen invited him in, and Faith's mom came out of the kitchen with a beer for each of them. They toasted the new baby, and he learned that Tansy and Faith were both doing fine.

Faith's mom brought out chips and dip and he hung around some more—longer than he should have, he realized, when Callie showed up at the door.

She wore Hello Kitty nurse's scrubs and hot-pink clogs, and something in his chest ached just at the sight of her, with those unforgettable dark eyes and all that seal-brown hair pinned up haphazardly, making his hands itch to take it down. Faith's mom grabbed her in a hug, and Owen insisted she should have a beer.

But she shook her head. "I would love one, but I have to get back to the clinic. Thought I'd just drop in and have a quick look at Faith and the baby, see how they're doing…." She slid him a glance then. "Hello, Nate." Careful. Contained.

"Hey, Callie." He raised his almost-empty beer to her because he didn't know what else to do, and he felt awkward and empty and kind of forlorn.

Ridiculous, to feel this way. Just because he'd held her in his arms and she'd felt way too right there. Because she was tenderhearted and tough, too. Because she was the kind of woman who made a man want to blather on, pouring out the secrets of his soul that, until her, he'd always had sense enough to keep to himself.

And then, Faith's mom was wrapping an arm around her, turning her toward the back of the house. "They're just resting. Come on...."

He watched her go and wished she would come back, come back and sit with them, have some chips and dip and a cold drink and tell him all about her day.

Really, he could almost start to think that his mom was right. He was gone on Callie Kennedy, mooning around after her like some lovesick teenager.

He finished his beer, shook Owen's hand again and said he really had to go.

Independence Day dawned as bright and sunny as the day before.

Nate got up, thinking he would hang around home for a while and then maybe drive out to the Shooting Star, see how his brothers were doing, ask if they needed a hand with anything on the ranch.

But then his brother Brad called and said that he and their other brothers, Justin and Jesse, were going to the opening of the community center. "We'll meet you on the town-hall steps." The town hall was directly across from the new center. "We'll make a day of it, the four of us, check out the booths at the street fair, head over to the Ace in the Hole for a beer or two later. And go to the dance tonight."

"I don't know, Brad."

"What do you mean, you don't know? You sound like some crabby old man. Do you know this town is now full of good-lookin' women who have come to help us continue our recovery from the flood of the century?"

"I do know that, yeah."

"And you know they'll all turn out for the Fourth of July, don't you? Nothin' a pretty do-gooder enjoys so much as a quaint small-town celebration and the chance to dance with a cowboy. We need to get friendly with some pretty women, Nate. We need to forget all our troubles." Brad's wife, Janie, had divorced him three years ago. He'd been kind of cynical ever since.

"I think I'll skip it."

"Nathan. I want you to listen and listen good. We're goin'. *You're* goin'. You've been in a funk for months now and you need to snap out of it."

"*I'm* in a funk?"

"You know what I mean, ever since you lost the election to that no-good Collin Traub."

"I'm over the election, Brad." How many times did he have to say it?

"You should look on the bright side. Your investments paid off and now, all of a sudden, you've got money to burn."

"Well, I wouldn't say that." Even if it was true.

"You live in a fancy house and you don't have to spend your days knee-deep in cow crap anymore. You can afford to show a pretty do-gooder a really fine time."

"Damn it, Brad. I mean it. I'm *over* the election, and I don't like the way you're—"

"Be there. In front of the town hall. Ten o'clock."

Before Nate had a chance to say no again, Brad hung up on him.

Nate put the phone down with a sigh of resignation and hit the shower.

On the Fourth of July, Main Street drew the crowds and parking was scarce. So Nate left his pickup at home and walked across the Main Street Bridge to North Main, where most of the festivities would take place.

From the bridge clear to Sawmill Street, people were everywhere. Volunteers had looped patriotic bunting from every available railing and storefront. Old Glory waved wherever you looked—from the flagpole in front of the library to the ones at the town hall and at the new community center, to every possible pillar and post where a flag might be mounted.

The biggest crowd had gathered around the new center, which was all dressed up for the holiday with red, white and blue draped in swags across the facade. A newer, bigger Grand Opening banner replaced the one that had been sagging to the ground during the storm two days before. And a giant blue ribbon with an enormous bow on it had been tied across the big double doors, no doubt to be cut by some beaming official when it was time for everyone to go inside.

They had a band set up on the grass. It was made up of old guys who played for the dances at the Masonic Hall, and several youngsters from the high school. When Nate got there, they were playing a marching song, not very well but really loud and with a lot of enthusiasm.

Brad, Justin and Jesse waited on the town-hall steps, as promised. Brad and Justin were acting like a couple of ya-hoos, whistling at every pretty girl who walked by. Jesse, the youngest and most sensitive of the four of them, stood a little to the side, looking as if he wished he'd just stayed at the ranch with the horses he loved so much.

Nate was a little embarrassed, too, at the way Brad and Justin were carrying on. But he was also kind of happy to be out in the sunshine on a nice summer day, hanging with his brothers. Even if two of them *were* behaving like fools.

And Brad had been right about the women. There were a lot of new women in town, and most of them were good-looking.

Brad nudged him in the ribs. "See that gorgeous blonde over there? The newcomer? Ponytail?"

The blonde in question turned her head at that moment, and Nate could see her face. She really was a stunner. "I see her."

"Name's Julie Smith. That's all I know, even though I've asked around. Kind of a mystery woman, really. Which is fine. When a girl looks like that, her name's all I *need* to know."

Jesse shook his head. "Brad, you're an embarrassment, you know that?"

"Lighten up, little brother. I'm just having fun."

Nate admired the scenery as the band played on.

Jesse left them temporarily. He wandered down the steps and out to the street and started chatting up Maggie Roarke, an attorney from Los Angeles. Maggie was tall and sleek and blonde. Nate had seen her around town in her classy business suits, looking as if she'd just stepped out of a Calvin Klein ad. She seemed about as wrong for Jesse as a woman could get.

And that got him wondering if maybe sleek, sophisticated Maggie Roarke might be Jesse's problem lately. He'd seemed quieter and more withdrawn than usual. When he came back to join them on the town-hall steps, Nate almost asked him if he had something going on with the lawyer from L.A.

But then the speeches started. Collin got up first. He was a damn fine speaker, Nate had to admit. Collin had a way of connecting with folks when he got up in front of them. He was funny and he gave it to them straight, and people picked up on his sincerity. He spoke of the flood last year and the toad-strangler of a storm two days before, about how the levee had been tested more than once now and come through with flying colors, proving that Rust Creek Falls really was being rebuilt better and stronger than ever. Their town, Collin said, had taken a tragedy and remade it into a triumph of the human spirit.

Though Justin and Brad grumbled under their breaths the whole time about the damn upstart Mayor Traub, Nate only found himself more convinced that Collin was doing a fine job. The thunderous applause rising up from the crowd when Collin finished seemed a seal of approval, not only for his words, but for the man himself and his dedication to the safety, prosperity and betterment of Rust Creek Falls.

Arthur Swinton stepped up next. The old man looked frail, with thinning silver hair and a deeply lined, drawn face. His speech was a rambling one that finally seemed to be wrapping up with: "I dedicate this community center to the beautiful Grace Traub, may she rest in peace. I know I have led a far from exemplary life. But it is my fervent, my true, my lasting hope that, in the end, a man is defined not so much by his past transgressions as by his dedication, now and in the future, to do what's right, to love others more than himself and to…erm, offer all he has in the pursuit and fulfillment of the, uh, greater good." He paused. People began to clap—but then he started in again. "Love each other more, everyone! Give each other all you have! Don't let bitterness or sadness or the failure

of your dreams steal away your will to…to…" He seemed
to lose his train of thought completely then.

But someone yelled, "Yay! You said it, Arthur! God
bless you, old man!" and that got the applause going again.
Everyone joined in clapping, and Arthur Swinton blinked
and looked around and finally, smiling in a bemused sort
of way, sat down—only to pop back up again when the
sheriff, Gage Christensen, signaled him over to the center's double doors.

Swinton took the giant pair of scissors from the sheriff's offered hand and cut the ribbon.

And the band started up with a patriotic song, and everyone clapped, hooted and hollered as the doors of the
Grace Traub Community Center swung wide.

"Come on," said Justin. "I didn't get breakfast. I heard
they got doughnuts and coffee inside."

Nate followed his brothers across the street and joined
the crowd pouring through the open doors.

In the auditorium, folding tables had been set up along
one wall. There was coffee, juice and sweet rolls for all.
Nate got in line for a paper cup full of coffee and a Danish.

He almost spilled the coffee all over himself when he
spotted Callie a few feet away, sipping coffee and chatting with a very pregnant Paige Dalton Traub. The Daltons
were all fast friends with the Traubs. Last Thanksgiving,
Paige had reunited with her high-school boyfriend Sutter
Traub, the oldest of Collin's brothers—and also the man
who'd run Collin's mayoral campaign and done an excellent job of it.

Nate was not proud of the rotten stunt he'd pulled at the
campaign's last debate. He'd known he was losing, that
Collin was beating him both on the stump and head-to-
head in debate. It had galled him no end at the time that
not only was he losing, but the man who would beat him

was his lifelong nemesis, the biggest troublemaker of all the Traubs.

So he'd fought dirty, going after Collin's campaign manager, Sutter, exploiting a sensitive subject from the past.

All it had taken was a call to an old friend, a decorated veteran. Master Sergeant Dean Riddell stood up at the end of the final debate and called Sutter on the carpet for having once spoken up against the Iraq war.

In actuality, Sutter had never said a word against the war. He'd simply tried to keep his brother Forrest from re-upping; Sutter had felt that Forrest had given enough for his country already. But folks in town had accused Sutter of speaking out against the war itself.

In Rust Creek Falls, you supported your country. You didn't express doubts about the war. Sutter had left town at the time of the uproar, the anger against him had been so strong. He'd only returned after the flood, to help out with recovery and then to try and get his brother elected mayor. By then, folks were willing to forgive and forget.

Until Nate had his friend the war hero rub the past in all their faces.

But Nate's triumph had lasted only a matter of minutes.

Paige, still a Dalton then, had stood up right there in the town meeting and backed Sutter. She'd called Sutter an honest and ethical man whose sin was to express the doubts he felt in his heart. It had been a strong, impassioned argument, and with it, she'd completely pulled the rug out from under Nate and his candidacy.

Nate had been ready to spit nails at the time. Looking back, though, he just felt ashamed of himself. He knew he'd gotten exactly what he deserved.

His gaze strayed to Callie. God, she looked good. In a snug pair of jeans and a fitted red-and-white-checked shirt, she lit up the room. She hadn't spotted him yet.

But Paige had. And though he'd been making headway at better relations with most of the Traubs, Paige had yet to forgive him for trying to drag Sutter through the mud during that last debate. She gave him a look of icy scorn.

And Callie caught the direction of her gaze and saw him.

They had one of those moments, like the other day at the store. They just stared at each other. He knew he shouldn't do that, shouldn't gape at her like a love-struck fool. But for a long, magic string of seconds, he just couldn't look away.

Apparently, neither could Callie.

Until Paige broke the spell by putting a hand on Callie's shoulder. Callie blinked and turned to Paige and Paige leaned in close to her and started talking fast, shaking her head.

Nate couldn't hear a word of it and he doubted anyone else but Callie could, either. Paige kept her voice down. But he had a pretty good idea she was talking about him and what she was saying was not the least flattering.

Paige and Callie turned together and walked the other way, leaving him standing there by the refreshment tables with his coffee and Danish, feeling about two inches tall, trying to remind himself that it was a good thing if Callie thought less of him. He needed to look on the bright side. If she decided he was a rat bastard, fair enough.

If she wanted nothing to do with him, terrific.

If she hated him, wonderful.

If she couldn't stand the sight of him, then she wouldn't let him near her.

And that would make it a lot easier for him to stay the hell away from her.

Chapter Five

Outside, Callie and Page found an empty bench by the library, in the dappled shade of a cottonwood tree. The spot was tucked back from the street, along the side of the building, far enough from the crowd that they could talk undisturbed.

Paige said, "I know I told you before that I didn't think much of Nate."

Callie blew out a breath. "'An unmitigated douche,' that's what you called him. I guess I kind of understand why you said that now."

Paige winced. "Look. I can see there's… Well, it's obvious you've got a thing for him. And the way he was looking at you… Whoa. That look could burn down a barn. But I just thought you should know what happened last fall, because I don't think he's any kind of bet for a boyfriend."

Callie was still reeling from what Paige had whispered to her back in the auditorium. "I can't believe he pulled a dirty trick like that on poor Sutter, to discredit Collin. Not only because Sutter's a good guy who only wanted to look out for his brother, but also because nothing Sutter ever did has any bearing on whether or not Collin should be mayor. It's so low, so completely unlike the Nate I know."

Paige rested both hands on the ripe bulge of her pregnant belly. "Well, maybe you don't know him all that well."

"Maybe I don't," Callie said regretfully as her heart cried that she *did* know him, that he was a good man, that if he'd once been something less than good, he'd changed and he'd grown.

Paige said, "And he's been out with lots of women over the years, but he seems to have some kind of problem with the concept of getting serious with a girl. Because he never does. From what I've heard, the women get tired of waiting for there to be more with him. Sometimes he breaks it off, sometimes the woman does. But the result is the same. It doesn't last."

Callie longed to ask Paige if she even remembered the wife Nate had loved and lost, if she knew about his baby, who had died being born, if she had any clue how Nate had suffered, how he still hadn't really gotten over losing the family he'd loved so very much.

But she didn't feel right mentioning Zoe and the baby. She didn't think Nate would appreciate that, even if she brought it up in the service of defending him. He'd said that Zoe and the baby weren't common knowledge in town. And he'd told her straight-out that he preferred to keep it that way, that he didn't want his private pain made public.

Plus, even losing a wife and child didn't give a man a right to play dirty, the way he had during the mayor's race. Strangely, she had a feeling Nate would agree with her on that; he wouldn't even want her defending him to Paige. So she kept her peace.

Paige said, "Look. I've still got issues with him, so

yeah. Maybe I'm being a little unfair to him. People say he's been…kinder and gentler in the past several months. It seems like losing the mayor's race really took him down a peg, and that was good for him. It's clear he's trying to be a better man. Even I see that. But still, every time I set eyes on him, I want to give him a very large piece of my mind."

"Hey. It's understandable. Really, Paige. I get it."

"Just think about it before you get in too deep with him."

Callie couldn't hold back a rueful chuckle at that. "Get in too deep? Don't worry. Yeah, the attraction is…" She sought the word.

Paige provided it. "Smokin'?"

"Exactly. But we do understand each other, Nate and me. He's leaving town and doesn't want a relationship. And I've sworn off men for the foreseeable future."

"Hold that thought," Paige advised wryly. "At least when it comes to Nate Crawford."

"Hey, Paige! Callie!" Mallory Franklin and her eight-year-old niece, Lily, strode across the grass toward them. Last winter, Mallory had moved with Lily to Rust Creek, seeking the slower pace of small-town life.

Lily, in pink jeans and a yellow shirt, with her shining, stick-straight black hair tied into two ponytails, seemed to be adapting to the move just fine. She dropped to the grass. "Aunt Mallory, can we *please* go to the street fair now?"

"In a minute." Mallory took the free space on the bench next to Callie. "Gorgeous day…" Callie and Paige nodded agreement. "Want to check out the street fair with us?"

"Say yes and we can go." Lily looked up hopefully at them.

Callie was grateful for the interruption. Enough had been said about Nate for now. "Absolutely. Paige?"

"Love to," Paige agreed. Callie got up and offered her a hand. Paige laughed. "I may look like a beached whale, but I can still get off a bench on my own." She braced a hand on the bench back, rose and then took a minute to rub the muscles at the base of her spine. "Nine weeks to go. I cannot wait."

"Let's go!" Lily bounced to her feet.

So they all strolled up the street and browsed the booths run by local farmers, cooks and craftspeople. Callie bought a dozen cookies from the Community Boosters' bake sale and a bib apron fringed with rickrack and printed with cherries from a booth run by the Daughters of the Pioneers.

It was fun, being with her friends and with chatty, gregarious Lily, enjoying the festivities on this sunny holiday. There were other kids running around. Some of them had firecrackers. Lily laughed every time a string of them went off.

Callie tried really hard not to look for Nate. But every time she saw a tall, broad-shouldered cowboy, her heart gave a hopeful little lurch in her chest. Since Rust Creek was wall-to-wall with tall cowboys, her heart got quite a workout that morning.

Twice when her pulse beat faster, it actually was Nate. She saw him by the Daughters of the Pioneers' booth with his brothers and again near the Forest Service booth. Both times, she looked away before he could catch her watching him. And both times, she couldn't help wishing he might march right up to her and ask her if maybe she'd like to spend the day with him.

In spite of everything—swearing off men, Paige's warnings, the way he'd told her right out that she should stay away from him—in spite of all that, if he'd asked her, she would have boldly laced her fingers with his and strolled from booth to booth with him.

But he didn't ask her. And she just kept telling herself she was glad about that.

She didn't believe it, though. Not for a minute.

Around noon, she decided to take her purchases back to her house and try to get a few more moving boxes unpacked.

Paige said she was done with the fair, too. "I'm heading home to put my feet up."

"You two coming back for the dance and the fireworks tonight?" Mallory wanted to know.

"I'll see how I'm feeling." Paige patted her belly. "Sutter said he'd take me if I'm up for it. So maybe I'll see you."

Yet again, Callie thought of Nate. She couldn't help wishing that he might be there that evening, might ask her to dance. And the fact that she couldn't stop thinking of him deeply annoyed her.

Really, she needed to give all things Nate a rest. "I'll probably be there," she answered at last.

Mallory touched her shoulder. "If I don't see you, remember. First Newcomers' Club meeting. Monday night, seven o'clock, in our new community center."

"Oh, come on," Callie teased. "We've both been in town for more than six months. We're hardly newcomers."

Paige laughed at that. "Six months is nothing in Rust Creek Falls. If you weren't born here, you're a newcomer."

Callie heaved a big pretend sigh. "Well, I guess I better make that meeting, then." She agreed she would be at the center Monday night.

At home, she grabbed a sandwich, then unpacked four more moving boxes and put them away in the hall cabinets.

She still had several boxes to go, but she was getting there. And she felt pretty proud of herself to have the unpacking almost finished in only four short days since she left the Sawmill Street trailer. Her new house was not only beautiful, it was beginning to feel like home.

Inspired by how great everything looked, she unpacked more boxes. By seven that night, she'd done them all. To celebrate, she had a glass of the white wine she'd been saving and finished off the casserole Faith had brought over on moving day.

Then she indulged in a long, lazy bath and took her time with her hair and her makeup. She put on her tightest pair of jeans, a sparkly red top, her fun red straw cowboy hat and her fabulous red Old Gringo cowboy boots. It was a little after nine and she was on her way out the door when the house phone rang. She almost just let it go to voice mail.

But then, what if it was something important? She shut the door and hurried to grab the extension in the great room.

All day long, Nate had been telling himself he was about to go home.

But right after the opening of the community center, Brad had insisted they visit the street fair. Just what a guy needed. Endless booths selling pot holders and afghans and all manner of handcrafts. Women could be damn clever with the stuff they made. But what use did a single man have for a toaster cover or pink towels embroidered along the hems with rows of yellow daisies? Uh-uh.

He saw Callie twice. Both times, she was way too careful not to look his way. He tried to tell himself it was a good thing, that it was what he wanted, for her to avoid him.

But really, it wasn't so good. In fact, it made him feel like crap.

Next, Brad and Justin wanted to head for the Ace in the Hole Saloon, where the beer flowed freely and you could play pool or pick up a card game in the back.

"Just for lunch," he agreed. "Then I've gotta get home."

They had burgers at the Ace—or at least Nate and Jesse did. Justin and Brad were more interested in liquid refreshment. By three or so, Jesse got tired of hanging around the bar and left. Nate would have followed, but his other two brothers were getting pretty plastered. He hung around to provide a little damage control.

He took Brad aside and actually got him to promise to slow down on the alcohol intake. Then Justin started playing pool with a cute little blonde. She was a good player and Justin had his pride. He started concentrating more on the game and the girl than on bending his elbow.

Nate and Brad joined in a game of Texas Hold'em with a couple of carpenters from down in Thunder Canyon, and Delbert Hawser, the handyman. Brad drank Mountain Dew and won steadily, which kept him happy, even without more beer.

It was getting around dinnertime when Nate stood up from the table. Brad was still winning and focused on his cards, so he didn't put up much of a fight when Nate said he was leaving.

By then, the booths on Main Street were starting to close up. Nate got a hot dog and a root beer from one of them. After that, he remembered that the family store was still open and his mom had been working all day. On the Fourth of July, they usually did a landslide business and didn't close until nine. He went to the store instead of home.

His mom stood at the register ringing up a sale when he walked in. She looked tired, he thought. So he hung his hat on the peg by the door to the back rooms and told her he would stay and close up for her.

She gave him one of her warmest smiles. "You're a good boy, Nathan." She said it so fondly, he didn't even take offense or feel the need to remind her that he hadn't been a boy for a very long time. But then she added, "And the street party won't really get going until after nine. You'll have plenty of time for dancing with Callie— Where is she, anyway?"

Nate just shook his head. "I don't even know how to begin to answer that one, Mom."

"She's a prize and I don't want you to let her slip away, that's all."

He reminded himself that she was tired and she meant well. But still, he didn't need her butting in. "Let it go, Mom."

She hitched up her chin. "I hate when you're snippy with me."

"Let it go."

She pursed her lips at him then, but she did keep them shut.

He spotted his father over behind the candy counter. Todd Crawford looked as weary as his wife.

"Take Dad with you. You've both been working long enough today."

Ten minutes later, they left him and his gorgeous blond-haired, blue-eyed baby sister, Natalie, to handle the last two and a half hours. The time flew by. It wasn't too crowded, but customers kept coming in and they had plenty to do.

At eight-thirty, Natalie came up behind him and wrapped her arms around him. She gave a squeeze and wheedled, "Mind if I take off now? I want to go home and put on something sexy for the street dance."

He grumbled, "The last thing a man wants to hear is that his baby sister plans to put on something sexy."

She leaned her head against his back. "Okay, okay. Scratch that. Something pretty."

"Too late. Now I'll have to come to the dance just to beat up any cowboy who makes a wrong move with you."

"Don't you dare. I can handle myself."

The thing was, she could. In a dangerous kind of way. When she was three, she'd figured out how to unlock the front door. Then she climbed into his dad's favorite pickup and actually managed to start it up and roll it several feet into the creek.

He clasped one of her hands and pulled her around in front of him so he could look at her. "Get lost. And have fun."

With a giggle of delight, she bounced on tiptoe to kiss his cheek. "Later, big brother." And she took off.

At nine, he turned the sign around and got busy closing up. There was a list of closing chores, including doing the final count for the day and putting all but a few hundred in change into the safe under the floor in the office.

He had the money in order and put away and was just emerging from the back, pushing through the swinging door into the space behind the main counter, when someone tapped on the double entry doors out front.

Through the etched glass at the top of the door, he saw a red cowboy hat, long, wavy brown hair, a pair of very pretty bare shoulders and arms and a red sequined top. The hat obscured her face.

But he knew it was Callie.

He shouldn't have been so glad. He ought to just turn around and go out through the parking lot in back.

Right. His boots couldn't carry him to her fast enough. He unlocked the door and pulled it open. Out in the street, someone lit up a chain of firecrackers and a cool evening breeze brought him a hint of her tempting scent.

She tipped up her chin and he saw those shining eyes beneath the brim of her red hat, noted the rather determined set of that plush mouth. "Whatever it is, I'm listening," she said.

He had no idea what she might be talking about. Not that he could bring himself to care. She was right there in front of him, close enough to touch, and the night was falling, the band setting up on the sidewalk in front of the store. He felt like a bottle rocket, about to go off, straight up in the air, shooting off sparks.

"Come on in." He stepped back. She stepped forward. He closed the door behind her.

"Okay," she said, kind of breathless and so damn sweet. "What?" There was a row of pegs by the door. He reached up, lifted the red hat off her head and hung it up. "Hey!" she protested, but those soft lips were smiling and a teasing laugh escaped her. She gazed up at him expectantly.

He leaned an arm on the door frame and stared at that mouth of hers and remembered how fine it had felt to kiss her. "What can I do for you, Callie?" It came out low and a little rough, as though he was trying to seduce her.

And hey. Maybe he was.

She blinked and the tip of her pink tongue came out and touched the beautiful bow of her upper lip. "I..." A frown creased her brow. "I thought you wanted to talk to me."

If he said no straight-out, this moment would be over. He didn't want it to be over, even though he knew he should have never let it get started in the first place. He had so many good intentions when it came to her. But right now, he didn't give two red cents for good intentions.

He wanted only to go on standing here in front of the door in the family store after closing time, standing here with Callie, her perfume on the air and her shining eyes locked with his.

As he tried to decide whether to kiss her or put a little effort into pretending he knew what she was talking about, she spoke again. "Your mother just called me?" she asked hopefully. "She said you were here at the store and you really needed a private word with me...."

"Mom." He shook his head. "Why am I not surprised?"

"So you...didn't ask her to call me?" Her cheeks had turned the most gorgeous shade of pink. And then she groaned and let her head drop back against the door. "Oh, right. Of course you didn't. If you had something to say to me, you would pick up the phone and call me yourself."

"She's shameless, my mother. She doesn't want me to miss my chance with you."

A smile bloomed—and then she seemed to catch herself. The smile dimmed a little. "But what about you, Nate? What do *you* want, really?"

He couldn't resist. He lifted a hand and ran his thumb along the velvet plumpness of her lower lip. Amazing. Touching her. It got to him, got to him real good. She was something special, something real and true. Someone honest to the core, all wrapped up in the prettiest package. Someone he'd tried so hard to be cynical about. Someone the likes of which he'd never thought to find again.

"Nate. Will you please answer me?"

"So beautiful..." He hadn't really meant to say that out loud.

She cleared her throat. "So, um, I should go?"

He touched her chin, traced the soft, firm shape of her jaw with his index finger. "Yeah. You should go. Stay."

Her tender mouth quivered. "You have to pick one or the other."

He guided a swatch of glossy hair behind her ear and then, with his index finger, followed the perfect shape of that ear. Up and around and down—and after that, he just kept on going, trailing his finger along the side of her astonishingly silky throat. She shivered a little, and her eyes lowered to half-mast.

"I'm having trouble," he confessed gruffly. "I can't seem to get you out of my mind." He caught her chin and lifted it higher, positioning that unforgettable mouth of hers for a kiss he knew he shouldn't claim. She let out a slow, shaky breath. He breathed her in, gratefully. "So maybe my mother was right, after all. I did want to talk to you in private. I just couldn't admit it to myself until you got here. And I have to tell you, I hate it when my mother's right."

Those eyes, deepest brown with golden lights, searched his face. "Then...what—"

He could only repeat, "What?"

"—did you want to say to me?"

He went with the first thing that popped into his desire-addled brain. "I saw you talking to Paige today...." Not the best choice of topics, he decided. But it couldn't be helped. All his conversational filters just stopped working around her.

She drew herself up a little straighter, closed her softly parted lips. And swallowed. "She told me about the war hero you invited to the final debate of the race for mayor."

He still had his hand under her chin. He let it fall. But he didn't step away. He just couldn't bear to put distance between them. Every time he saw her it was like this. And the need to be close to her just kept getting stronger. "It's true," he said in a flat voice. "I went after Sutter to discredit Collin. But I got what I deserved. It backfired on me big-time because Paige stood up and exposed what I'd done for the dirty dealing it was."

She looked at him kind of wonderingly. "You're not going to even try to make excuses for yourself?"

He did step back then. Because if he couldn't stay away

from her, she at least had a right to understand—who he was, what he'd done, what kind of man she was dealing with.

"There is no excuse," he said. "I started out on the town council wanting to serve the people of Rust Creek Falls. I really did. But I ended up...losing my perspective, I guess you could say. The day after the flood, for example...."

She stared up at him, waiting. "Yeah?"

Why was he telling her this? Why had he told her half the things he'd already revealed?

"Nate. Please. Go on."

He shook his head. But he did go on. "The mayor had been killed during the storm. I was on the council, and the other members deferred to me. We had nine trained guys on search and rescue. I decided that was enough. That we should get all the volunteers together and put them to work on cleanup. I was more worried about flood damage than the people who might be stranded or injured...or worse. Collin stood up and said we needed everyone on search and rescue first. I tried to back him down. But he knew he was right—and he was. And the whole town got behind him. We did the right thing first, search and rescue.

"Later, when Collin decided to run for mayor, he did it because he wanted to serve, wanted the best for Rust Creek Falls. By then, I only wanted to *win,* to beat him. Serving was an afterthought. I see that now."

"You've changed since then."

"God, I hope so."

"What changed you?"

He shrugged. "I lost. Sometimes a little humbling is good for a man. And then my sister married a Traub. And Collin's turning out to be a better mayor than I ever would have been. And then I...came into a little money. They say money's the root of all evil. I wouldn't say it's been that way for me. I can do what I want now. I've had to do some thinking about that, about what I really want. That's turned out to be good for me. And…" He knew he shouldn't go on.

But she wasn't letting him off the hook. "And what?"

He gave it to her. There was no point in lying about it anymore. "And now there's you. You're…in my mind, Callie Kennedy."

"Oh. Well…" She looked at him as though he'd hung the moon. She shouldn't do that.

He didn't deserve that. "I said I was broken."

"Yeah?"

"Sometimes you make me think I just might be fixable."

She watched him so steadily. And then she reached out her slim hand and wrapped it around the back of his neck. Her fingers were cool. Still, they made him burn. She pulled him into her.

He went without protest—eagerly even—moving back into place with her, up close and personal, bracing his arm against the door frame again.

She said, "Paige doesn't trust you."

"I don't blame her. You probably shouldn't trust me, either."

"She sees the old you. She doesn't know how much you've changed."

"People don't change. Not really."

She tipped her head to the side, considering. "Maybe not. But sometimes they do lose their way. And then some of them manage to find it again. I, um…"

He bent a little closer. He couldn't seem to stop himself. He pressed his rough cheek to her soft one and he whispered in her ear, "You what?"

"I believe you, Nate," she whispered back. "I believe that, wherever you went wrong once, you've found your way again."

He kissed her cheek, heard her soft, sweet sigh. "I don't feel all that confident about where I'm headed. I don't even know where that might be."

"But you're on the right track. I...believe in you. And that's pretty wild, because I'm a girl who wasn't going to believe anything a guy told me ever again, a girl who was supposed to be swearing off men."

He kissed her lips then. They tasted softer, sweeter, better than ever. "You better go ahead and tell me about him."

"Him?"

"Don't play coy. You know what I mean. Tell me about that other guy, the guy in Chicago."

She wrinkled up her nose at him. "It's nothing new, nothing that hasn't happened before. And I feel like such an idiot whenever I think about it."

He stroked a hand down her hair, caught a stray curl and wrapped it around his finger. It made a loose corkscrew when he let it free. "Tell me. I need to know these things about you."

"All the dumb things I've done, you mean?"

"I'm guessing you weren't dumb in the least. You were just your true self, and whoever he was, he let you down."

She shut her eyes and leaned her head back against the door. "All right. Here goes. His name was David. Dr. David Worth."

He nuzzled her neck, pressed a row of kisses along the tender ridge of her collarbone. "A surgeon, you said the other night...."

"Yeah."

"I hate him." He kissed the words onto her skin.

She gave a low chuckle. He drank in that sound. "A plastic surgeon, as a matter of fact."

"I hate him more."

"I guess I was dazzled at first. He had a penthouse

apartment downtown, in the Loop, which is arguably the best of the best when it comes to living in Chicago. And... well, you know. Everything money can buy."

"I thought money didn't thrill you."

"And I'm trying to explain to you why it doesn't, how I learned my lesson not to be impressed with some jerk just because he's got money to burn."

"So there's no hope, then?"

"Hope of what?"

"Of changing your mind and thrilling you with the size of my bank account," he teased.

She chuckled. "None."

"I had a feeling you would say that." And then he bent a little closer, close enough to rub noses with her. "Go on."

"I was with him for five years. I kept my own place, but I considered him my guy. I was serious about what I had with him. He took me to the best restaurants. We vacationed all over the world."

"All over the world, huh? The way your dad does with your stepmom?"

She gave him a wry smile. "Yeah. Pretty much."

"The guy was like your dad?"

"Oh, yeah. It was classic, I guess. My father deserts our family—and I grow up and start dating a guy just like him. And David pushed me to stay in administration, where I wasn't happy. He wanted me to be more of a businesswoman than a real nurse. With him, I was someone I didn't want to be."

"So you dumped him." He stroked her cheek with the backs of his fingers and she trembled a little. "Good for you."

"Dumped him?" She sifted her cool hand up into his hair. He wished she would just keep on doing that and never, ever stop. "Not exactly. He wanted me to move in with him. I stalled. I had this feeling that it just wasn't right with him and me. He said he understood, that he would give me time to think it over. And then I decided I was being an idiot, that I loved him and he loved me. I couldn't wait to tell him. I went to his fabulous penthouse apartment to surprise him. And did I ever surprise him. He was there with another woman."

Nate dipped his head to her and breathed a bad word against her neck.

She said, "I decided not to move in with him, after all."

"Good choice."

"I wrote to Emmet instead, and when he said he could make a place for me, I packed up my things in a U-Haul and… Well, you know the rest."

Out on the street, the band had started up. They were playing a great old song by the Man in Black.

Nate framed her face between his hands. "You really loved him?"

She held his eyes. And shook her head. "I look back and, well, I thought I did at the time. But now I just wonder how I got it so wrong. I never really even *wanted* him. It was more that I thought he was what I *should* want, you know? I didn't even see that I was choosing a man way too much like the father who left me until that moment of truth when I found David with that other woman."

"So it was a good thing, that you caught him cheating."

"Well, Nate, it certainly didn't feel that way at the time."

"I'll bet. The bastard."

"But you're right. It was. A good thing in so many ways. I can't begin to tell you. I might never have come here to Rust Creek, never have found the life I always wanted if Dr. David Worth hadn't been such a complete tool."

"And so you swore off men."

"Well, yeah. I did. But then *you* came along. I liked you

that first day, when you picked me up by the side of the road. I liked you even though you really pissed me off."

He laughed low at that. "I was a real SOB to you. I wanted you to hate me. I liked you too much."

"And you didn't *want* to like me," she put in softly. "Because that day was Zoe's day, Zoe's and the baby's."

His throat felt tight. "Yeah."

She reached up, laid her slim, smooth hand on the side of his face. He caught her wrist and turned his mouth into the heart of her palm as she whispered, "This thing with us…"

"Yeah?"

She hitched in a ragged breath as he nipped the soft pad at the base of her thumb. "It feels strong to me, Nate. It feels real."

He was through lying about it. He brought her hand against his chest and held it there. "For me, too."

Her fingers moved against his shirt, caressing him, and her gaze didn't waver. "I want to go with it, see where it takes us."

"Me, too."

"Are you still…thinking about leaving?"

"Not when I'm lookin' at you."

"But you are. I can see it in those green, green eyes of yours. You're still thinking about it."

"Yeah."

"I'm not. This is my home now. Rust Creek Falls is the place for me."

With the hand that wasn't holding hers, he guided a soft curl of hair away from her eye. "I know."

"I'm never again making my life over to fit what a man wants."

"And I will never ask you to." Right then, outside, the band did something downright amazing. They launched into Dwight Yoakum's "Try Not to Look So Pretty." He laughed. "Will you listen to that?"

She looked adorably bewildered. "What?"

He brought her hand to his lips again and kissed her knuckles one by one. "They're playing our song."

She cocked her head, listening. "*That's* our song? I don't think I'd choose *that* one...."

"You're not lookin' at what I'm lookin' at. And come on." He tugged her away from the door and into his waiting arms. "Dance with me."

Her smile lit up the shadowed store. "Nathan Crawford..."

"What?"

"Oh, I don't know. All right. Let's dance."

She tucked her fine, curvy body against him, and they danced across the old pine floor, skirting the pickle barrel, turning in circles around the wine display, stepping up onto the platform that defined the dry-goods section and then dancing right back down to the main floor again.

When the song ended, they stood near the checkout, swaying together. She had both arms twined around his neck, and he had his hands resting nice and snug on the sweet outward curves of her hips.

It was a simple thing, the *only* thing, to pull her closer, to settle his mouth on hers.

She sighed and opened for him. He tasted the slick, hot places beyond her parted lips and wanted the kiss to go on forever. She affected him so strongly.

Too strongly, probably. But he was so gone on her, he didn't even care.

When he lifted his head, she looked up dreamily at him through those gold-flecked dark eyes and asked, "What now?"

They probably ought to get out of here. If they stayed and he kept kissing her, he wouldn't want to stop with just kisses. And no way their first time was going to happen in the family store.

Their first time...

Until tonight, he'd never really believed there would be a first time for them.

But he did now. And he realized he found that pretty terrific.

She clasped his shoulders. "Nate. Yoo-hoo. You in there?"

"Right here." He dropped a quick kiss on the end of her beautiful nose. "You want to check out the street dance?"

"Sure."

"Get your hat and I'll grab mine."

He locked up and they went out the front door and down to the street, where at least a hundred couples were dancing under the moon, in the added glow of party lights strung from tree to tree and between the street lamps. He was feeling pretty good about everything.

Until he saw Paige Traub dancing with Sutter a few feet away at exactly the same moment that Paige caught sight of him with Callie in his arms.

Chapter Six

Paige gave him a look. It wasn't a good look. It was an unhappy combination of surprise and dismay at the sight of her friend dancing with him.

Nate wanted to sink right through the asphalt beneath his boots and keep going clear to China.

And, apparently, Callie didn't feel so good about the situation, either. She stiffened in his hold, sucked in a sharp breath—and then seemed to collect herself. "Hey, Paige." She waved.

Paige gave a tiny flick of her hand in response. But she didn't manage an actual smile.

A minute later, the song ended. With a hand at the small of her back, Sutter guided his very pregnant, still-unsmiling wife away.

Callie said, "I'll talk to her." He heard the regret in her voice. "I probably should have talked to her before…" She let the sentence trail off.

He finished for her. "Before being seen in public with me?"

She tried to deny it. "No, I…" The band launched into the next song, a faster number in a two-step rhythm. She leaned in close. "Walk me home?"

Might as well. The good-time feeling had gone from the evening. He took her hand and led her off the street, onto the sidewalk across from the band. People waved and said hi. He and Callie both nodded and smiled, spreading greetings as they went.

But he didn't slow in his brisk stride and she kept up with him.

The crowd thinned out once they passed the library. By the time they crossed the bridge, the music was much fainter behind them. There were no party lights past the bridge. The half-moon glowed brighter above them, suspended in the darkness, surrounded by the thick scatter of the stars.

It wasn't far. In no time, they were turning onto their block. At her place, he led her up the walk and into the shadow of her front porch.

She opened the door and then waited for him to go in ahead of her.

"Beer?" she asked, once they'd hung their hats on the pegs just inside the door.

He shook his head.

She turned on the lights and gestured him into the great room, where he sat in the easy chair and she perched on the sofa. For a minute or two, neither of them knew where to start. He stared at the dark fireplace, trying not to think of the two of them lying there the other night, of kissing her and kissing her and never wanting to stop.

Might as well get down to it. "Look, Callie. I get the

picture. You told Paige not to worry about you and me, that you would have nothing to do with me."

The sequins on her top caught and cast back the light, sparkling brightly as she wrapped her arms around herself and launched into denials. "No. I didn't. I mean…" She chewed on her lower lip a little before adding, "Not exactly."

"Then, what exactly *did* you say?"

"That I'd sworn off men and you were leaving town and nothing was going to happen between us." She leaned toward him. "Oh, Nate. At the time I said it, I meant it."

"When was that?"

She winced. "Um. This morning. But then, tonight, your mother tricked me into coming to find you. And then we started talking and…well, I just had to admit to myself that I'm wild for you and I don't care about all the reasons it might not work out. I want us to have a chance together."

"You're wild for me?" The depressing moment took on a hopeful tinge.

She looked exasperated. "Didn't I already tell you that?"

"I think I would have remembered if you had."

"Well, all right." She tipped that cute chin higher. "I'm wild for you—and I should never have said never about you to Paige. I get that now."

He didn't blame her for what she'd said to Paige. It all made sense to him. If anyone had asked him about him and Callie earlier in the day, he would have done what she had—in fact, he *had* done what she had, essentially, when his mother started in on him about not missing out with her.

"Oh, I don't like that look on your face." Callie jumped to her feet, all urgency now. "Really. It's not like that. Not like I know you must be thinking…."

He couldn't bear to see her so torn up, so sure he would

lay blame on her. So he rose, too, and he went to her. "You don't know what I'm thinking." He said it gently.

And she let out a cry and slid around the coffee table and into his arms.

He guided her dark head against his shoulder and stroked her shining hair. "Listen. Are you listening?"

"Yeah." Small. Soft. Unhappy.

"I'm not blaming you." He cradled her sweet face between his hands. "If I seem harsh, it's only because I hate that you might lose a friend over me."

"No. That's not going to happen."

"Callie. It's the way things go here."

"Here?"

"Yeah. In Rust Creek Falls, you're with the Crawfords or you side with the Traubs. Most of us are trying to put the old feud behind us, but sometimes it still gets rocky. I don't like you in the middle of it."

Her eyes narrowed mutinously. "Please don't say you're going to stay away from me. Tonight, I've felt that we're finally getting somewhere. And if you turn your back on me now... I mean it, Nate Crawford. Do not do that to me again."

"I won't, I promise you. We're past that now."

"Good."

"It's just that there's something I need to do, something I should have done months ago."

"What?" she demanded.

He bent to press a soft kiss on those upturned lips. "Don't worry. It's nothing that awful."

"But what *is* it?"

"I'll explain, I promise. After I figure out how to go about it, after I...get it done."

"Nathan. Honestly. You are the most aggravating man."

He laughed.

She glared. "This is not funny."

"Yes, it is. Think about it. For so many years, I was the good boy, the fine, upstanding Rust Creek Falls citizen, the one people admired and counted on to take a leadership position. And Collin Traub was the bad one, the trouble-maker, the one you couldn't trust with your daughters. And now look what's happened. Our positions have reversed. Collin's happily married to the prim and pretty kinder-garten teacher Willa Christensen. Have you met Willa?"

"Yeah. She and Paige are good friends. I really like her."

"Everybody does. She's a great person, and she and Col-lin are pillars of the community. And I'm the lowlife who used dirty tactics to try and win the mayor's race. I'm the guy Paige is certain is going to do you wrong."

"I *will* talk to her. I'll make her see that you're a much better man than she realizes."

He smoothed a long, thick lock of silky dark hair back over her shoulder. "Thank you. But it's not your mess to straighten out."

She huffed a little. "I don't like where this is going. I don't even *know* where this is going."

He could understand her confusion. He felt it, too. He wanted to soothe her, to promise it would all work out all right. But that would be a promise he might not be able to keep.

She started to say something.

With a muttered oath, he bent his head and kissed her. She made a low, tender noise in her throat, slid her arms up around his neck and kissed him back.

For a few dreamy minutes, he forgot everything but the feel of her mouth under his, the warmth of her sweet body pressed close against him and the hungry thudding of his own yearning heart.

Finally, with aching reluctance, he lifted his head. "I should go…."

She scowled at him. "I don't get it. Here we are, finally working things out…and you want to go."

"I didn't say I *wanted* to go. I just think it's best if I go."

"Well, you're wrong."

"Before we get in any deeper together, I have to do what I can to fix what I've broken." He peeled her arms from around his neck and held her away from him, her hands between his. "Give me a few days to make things right— or at least, as right as I *can* make them."

"What are you planning? Why can't you just tell me?"

"Stop nagging, woman," he commanded, grinning to take the edge off the words. He kissed her again—a hard, quick one—and then he let go of her hands and stepped back from her. "A few days. Please?"

"You always make things so difficult."

"Trust me?"

She braced her fists on her hips. "Actually, I do trust you. Don't make me live to regret it."

"I will be back." He headed for the door.

"And don't just assume I'll be waiting with open arms when you do," she called after him.

He snagged his hat from the peg and pulled open the door. "With you, Callie, I don't assume anything." And he left before he could give himself an excuse to stay.

Callie called Paige the next morning. She got right to the point. "Okay, I'm sure you're probably wondering about what you saw at the street dance last night. I realize I said there was no chance of anything going on between me and Nate. I was wrong. Last night, before the dance, we talked, Nate and me. And, well, yes, now something is definitely going on between us." *Even if he did walk out on me when I told him I wanted him to stay.*

Paige answered carefully, "I just don't want you to get hurt, you know?"

"I know. And *he* knows he did wrong by Sutter. He says he's going to try to make it right."

"How?"

"Well, he didn't exactly explain himself."

"Somehow, I don't feel very reassured by that news." At least there was humor in Paige's tone. "And if he hurts you, he'll be answering to me."

Callie felt equal parts warm-fuzzy and apprehensive. "You're a good friend, Paige. But Nate is a lot better man than you think."

"Just tell him he'd better treat you right or else."

"He's a good man. I believe that."

Paige wasn't buying. "Just…be careful. Please."

What could Callie say to that? Clearly, she *wasn't* being careful. And after all her brave talk about swearing off men, too.

She thought of David. Her brain had kept insisting that David was the right guy when her heart had known all along that he was all wrong.

With Nate, it was the opposite. Her brain warned her that Nate had too many issues, that he might be a good guy deep down, but that didn't mean he was a good bet for love.

Her heart, on the other hand? It kept pushing her toward Nate. With every beat, her heart seemed to whisper his name.

Was she doing it again, falling for the wrong kind of guy and heading for a big, fat heartbreak? Paige certainly seemed to think so.

And Callie understood Paige's doubts. She just didn't

share them. Not in her heart, anyway. And with Nate, her heart ruled.

They talked for a few minutes longer. When she hung up, Callie felt better, knowing Paige was still her friend. She also felt thoroughly annoyed at Nate for deciding to "make things right" and then walking out on her without giving her a clue as to how he planned to do that.

Nate spent Saturday checking on what his money had been doing. It soothed him somehow, to witness the results of his financial contributions. It made him feel that he was finally doing something right, that a guy *could* turn his life around—even if he wasn't sure where he was going now he was facing in a whole new direction.

Yeah, all right. Money didn't buy everything. But it sure made life better for folks if they had it when they needed it. He visited three small ranches in the Rust Creek Falls Valley where his lottery winnings had been at work. The money had rebuilt a damaged barn and paid for a new well. It had replaced a house too flood-damaged to salvage and provided college educations for a couple of promising ranchers' daughters who wouldn't have been able to afford to go otherwise.

The ranchers he called on were all good people, people he'd known all his life. They invited him in and offered him coffee and assumed he was just stopping by to be neighborly. They had no idea he was the one behind the mysterious foundation that had helped them to pay for the things they really needed but hadn't known how they would afford.

When he got back to town, he went to the library. Before he checked out a few books, he toured the addition recently built on in back. The new nonfiction wing had increased the library's square footage by 50 percent.

The trust had done that, too. Just as it had paid for the computer room in the new community center, where people who didn't have access to a PC or tablet or smartphone of their own could surf the internet or check their email, where schoolkids could do their homework using state-of-the-art equipment.

By the end of the day, after seeing that he actually had done some good in his town, he felt calmer inside himself. He felt almost able to let go of a little more of his false pride and do what he should have done long before now.

At home alone that night, he sat out on his back deck with a tall, cold one and watched the darkness fall and the stars fill the wide, clear sky. Over the back fence, he could see the top of the window in the side wall of Callie's kitchen. The light was on in there.

He wanted to jump the fence and pound on her back door until she answered. He wanted to grab her close and cover her mouth with his and kiss her until he forgot everything but the wonder of holding her in his arms.

But he did no such thing.

He'd promised himself he wouldn't. Not yet.

Sunday he went out to the Shooting Star and worked alongside Jesse taking care of the horses. In the afternoon, they rode out to check on the other stock, and that night, he went to his parents' house for Sunday dinner. All evening, his mom kept giving him significant looks, waiting for him to say something about the way she'd manipulated Callie into coming to find him at the store.

He praised her pot roast and kissed her cheek as he was leaving. But never once did he give her even a hint of how her matchmaking tricks might have worked out.

Monday morning, he was up well before dawn. It was pitch-dark outside as he backed his pickup from the garage and headed out of town.

* * *

Sutter Traub bred and trained horses for a living. He owned a successful stable in Seattle and he'd bought a ranch in Rust Creek Falls Valley when he moved back home. Talk around town was that Sutter and Paige would eventually be renovating the run-down house at the ranch and moving out there to live. But for now, the couple lived in Paige's house at North Pine and Cedar Streets, and Sutter got up good and early most mornings to drive out to the ranch and spend his day with his horses.

Nate was waiting on the steps of the old ranch house when the lights of Sutter's pickup cut through the dark and shone on him sitting there. He rose and stood waiting as Sutter stopped the truck and turned off the engine, dousing the lights. Nate heard the pickup door open and shut as Sutter got out.

"Nate Crawford," Sutter said from the darkness. "I can't say you're welcome here."

"I can't say I blame you," Nate answered slow and clear. "But I would very much appreciate a few minutes of your time."

"Do I need to get my shotgun from the rack?"

Nate didn't know whether to chuckle—or duck. "I'm hoping you won't feel the need to shoot me."

Boots crunched gravel as Sutter approached. He was built broad and brawny and stood an inch or two under Nate's six-three. He kept coming until his dark form was close enough that Nate could have reached out and brushed his sleeve.

For about ten never-ending seconds, the two stood facing each other.

Finally, Sutter broke the thick silence. "Sit." Nate dropped back to the bottom step and Sutter sat down, too. "Okay. What brings you out here before the crack of dawn?"

"I think it's time I made amends to you, Sutter."

There was a silence filled with cricket sounds and the whinny of one of the horses in a nearby paddock. "Amends for what?" Sutter asked as if he didn't know.

"For coming after you at that last mayoral debate in an attempt to get at Collin. It was a low-down, rotten thing I did that day."

Sutter held his peace for several seconds. Nate braced for a fist in the face. But in the end, Sutter only said mildly, "Yes, it was."

Nate continued with his apology. "I knew the truth, but I twisted it for my own ends. I was willing to do just about anything to win the race for mayor. Even drag you through the mud again to make Collin look bad."

"And how'd that work out for you, Nate?"

Nate's pride jabbed at him. He had to fight the urge to say something hostile. The whole point was to take his licks and convince the man beside him in the dark that he knew he'd done wrong and wanted to make up for it. "It backfired on me, big-time. I got what I deserved."

There was another silence. Nate's nerves stretched taut. Finally, Sutter said, "Well, it all worked out just fine for me. My candidate won. I moved back home where I always wanted to be. And I married the love of my life. I'll be a father soon. I want to teach my son or daughter not to grow up holding grudges. But before I shake your hand, Nathan Crawford, I think you got someone else you need to say sorry to besides me."

Had Nate known that was coming? "Collin," he said so low in his throat it came out like a curse.

Out on the horizon, he saw a sliver of light: dawn on the way.

Sutter got up. Nate rose to stand beside him.

Sutter said, "Tonight. Seven o'clock. The Ace. You can buy me and Collin a beer."

Chapter Seven

Collin Traub had thick black hair and eyes to match. Growing up, there wasn't a dare he wouldn't take. He rode the rodeo, broke a lot of hearts and never went to college. Everyone said he would come to no good.

He'd fooled them all. Collin was a talented saddle maker by trade and, as it turned out, a politician by avocation. He'd married Willa Christensen a year ago. They were happy together, Collin and Willa. Everyone remarked on it, even Nate's mother, who'd never in her life until then had a kind thing to say about Collin Traub.

Nate dreaded the meeting with Collin. It was tough enough to try and make amends to Sutter, who had never called him dirty names or punched him in the face hard enough to black both his eyes.

Making amends to Collin Traub? Uh-uh. Never in his life had he planned to do any such thing.

For the rest of the afternoon, Nate considered ways he might back out of apologizing to his lifelong nemesis. But every time he just about convinced himself there was no way he was meeting Collin at the Ace in the Hole, he would think of Callie. He would see her shining eyes looking up at him, see the faith she'd put in him, the trust she had in his supposed deep-down goodness.

And he would know that he had to do it. He had to be... better than he'd ever thought he was capable of being.

He walked into the Ace at six-thirty, figuring he'd do well to get there first, to try and take a little control of a situation in which he found himself at a total disadvantage. He knew of a certain booth in back, in the corner, where he and the Traub brothers could take care of business without the whole town watching.

Unfortunately, the Traub brothers were way ahead of him.

Sutter and Collin were already there, sitting at the bar with Dallas and one of their other brothers, Braden. Collin spotted Nate instantly in the mirror on the back wall.

Their eyes met and locked.

And Nate felt dread and something like fury, all in a lead-weighted ball in the pit of his stomach. He thought of all the names Collin had called him when they were growing up: "Goody-boy" and "Mama's little sweetheart," "butt-wipe" and "Little College Man," among so many others too down and dirty to ever repeat.

And then there were the fights they'd had, the way they'd go at each other, no holds barred, punching and kicking, each of them determined to finish the other off for good every time.

Never in a hundred million years had he imagined he would come to this moment: to be standing in the Ace, staring eye to eye in the mirror with Collin Traub, planning to humble himself, to tell his enemy that he had gone too far and wanted to apologize.

Collin turned around and faced him. "Nate."

Nate gave him a nod. "Collin."

"You're early," the other man said mildly.

Nate took off his hat. "Not as early as you."

A whisper went through the Ace. And after the whisper, the place went dead silent. You could have heard a tooth-pick drop to the peanut-shell-strewn floor.

Then Dallas stepped forward. His sister's husband of-fered his hand. "Hey, Nate."

Nate took it and shook it. "Hey." Gratitude washed through him. He was thankful to his brother-in-law for stepping up like that, for reminding every staring eye in the place that Crawfords and Traubs *could* get along, gen-erations of bitter feuding to the contrary.

And then Sutter said, "How 'bout that corner booth in back?"

Nate knew the one—it was the same one he'd been thinking of. "Sounds good."

Sutter led the way back there, with Collin behind him and Nate taking up the rear. Braden and Dallas remained at the bar. The booth was empty. Collin and Sutter sat on one side, Nate on the other.

One of the waitresses stepped up. They all ordered long-necks.

There was no small talk while they waited for the beer. Nate put his hat on the seat beside him and reminded him-self that he could and would do this, that he would be a better man for it.

Finally, the girl came back with the beers. She put them down quick and hustled away.

Nate lifted his longneck. "To…our town," he said, be-cause it seemed like he ought to say something.

They clinked bottles and drank.

And then, there it was. The moment that was never supposed to happen.

His turn to grovel to a couple of Traubs and be a better man.

He set down his beer, straightened his shoulders and made himself look straight into his lifelong enemy's black eyes. "Okay, it's like this. Collin Traub, I apologize for bringing Sergeant Dean Riddell to that last debate, for coming after Sutter to try and bring you down. It was wrong and it was low and I never should have stooped so far. You have turned out to be a damn fine mayor, so it all worked out as it should, the way I see it now. But I have owed it to you to step up and tell you I know what I did and I know it was wrong and, if it's possible, I would like to find a way to…ahem…" His throat kind of locked up about then. He kept his gaze steady on the man across from him and pushed at the point of lockdown until the words broke through again. "I want to make things right, make it square between us. Or if not square, well, at least I want you to know I regret being such an SOB and I won't be pulling any crap like that again." What else? There was more he should say, wasn't there?

But it was all too unreal. Sitting in a booth across from Collin, trying to make things right.

Could anyone ever make things right after years and years of hatred and bitter battles and continued bad behaviors on both sides?

Collin took another long pull off his beer. He set the bottle down. "Sounds good to me." He turned to his brother. "What do you say, Sutter?"

Sutter gave a slow nod. "Yeah. I'm good with it. Things are changing in this town. And it's about time we all got past hating each other just because hating is what we've always done."

Nate stared from one man to the other, not really be-lieving what they were telling him. "So…that's it, then? You accept my apology?"

Both men answered, "Yeah," at the same time.

"Well, all right. That's great. I…" He realized he wanted out of there, right away. Before one of them changed his mind. He reached for his hat. "Guess I'll be on my way."

"Wait a minute," said Sutter.

Dread coiling in his gut again, Nate set his hat back down.

Collin said, "I heard you came into a little extra money…."

Money? He had a moment's absolute certainty that they knew he'd won the lottery. But then he remembered the cover story, about his supposed investments paying off. Everyone knew about that. "Right. I did the apologizing. Now comes the part where I actually have to make the amends. And that includes money somehow?"

Collin laughed. There didn't seem to be any malice in the sound. Just humor. And plenty of that. "Well, yeah. But we're not shaking you down or anything. Right, Sutter?"

Sutter grunted. "Not too much, anyway. And it's for a good cause."

Nate eyed them warily. "What cause?"

"People left town after the flood." Collin was suddenly stating the obvious. "But then a whole lot more people came to help us recover. As of now, we've got something of a population boom in Rust Creek Falls."

"Yeah?" Nate encouraged, hoping the other man was getting to the point.

"This town needs jobs," Collin said. "When the re-building is over, the new people are going to need work or they're gone. We don't want them to leave. We don't want Rust Creek Falls to turn into one of those towns with a bunch of boarded-up houses and more people getting out every year. We want this town to grow and prosper."

"And we want your help with that," added Sutter.

Nate put in gingerly, "You may have heard that *I'm* planning on leaving town...."

Both men gave him the deadeye. Sutter asked, "Well, *are* you?"

"I haven't decided yet, but it's more than a possibility."

Collin and Sutter shared a speaking glance. Then Sutter said, "Whatever. Your money's good either way, right?"

And Collin went on, "We're thinking a resort, like the one down in Thunder Canyon. The Thunder Canyon Resort has been a real economy booster down there. A successful resort brings in the tourists, which means money for the merchants and jobs for the citizens."

Nate put up both hands. "Look, boys. I know nothing about running a resort—plus, as I said, I'm considering a move."

"We don't want you to run it," said Collin. "We don't expect your participation in the planning or the building, either. We just want you to invest in it, put your money in it."

Nate wondered why he hadn't heard about this resort project before. After all, news traveled fast in Rust Creek Falls. "You have a group of investors together?"

The brothers shared another look, this one kind of rueful. Then Collin said, "We got nothing. It's an idea at this point."

Sutter threw in, "But everything starts with an idea, right?"

Collin added, "*And* with the money."

Nate asked, "You got anything on paper?"

The brothers shook their heads in unison.

And Nate almost laughed. But then he thought about how, if money was needed, he did have that. He thought about what it really meant to make amends. The Traub brothers had been better than civil to him. They'd been downright generous. They'd accepted his apology without making him sweat as much as he probably deserved to.

He wasn't about to laugh in their faces because they brought up some half-baked idea to bring jobs to town. "So it's in the beginning stages, this project," he suggested.

Collin said, "We just want to know, is a resort something you would invest in, given we had a real plan for one, given that we could get a group together?"

Nate thought about all the money he'd given away already. What was a little more in the interest of peace between the Crawfords and the Traubs?

"Yeah," he said finally. "You bring me a plan, and I'm in."

"Welcome to the Rust Creek Falls Newcomers' Club," said Lissa Roarke Christensen. She stood at the portable podium next to the refreshment table in the large meeting room of the Grace Traub Community Center.

Lissa had come to Thunder Canyon early last fall to write about the flood, about the spirit of the little town that could not be broken, even by a disaster of epic proportions. Lissa's blog and articles had raised nationwide awareness and brought a lot of help to Rust Creek Falls. And while she was doing all she could to see that the town recovered, Lissa had found love—and marriage—with the Rust Creek Falls sheriff, Gage Christensen.

"It seems only right," Lissa said, "that we newcomers band together, for the sake of the town we now call home—and for the sake of the friendships we share and hope to build. Tonight, it's a social night only. We'll visit, get to know each other better and maybe start talking about the direction we want to take as a group, the things we want to see accomplished in our new town. There's coffee and soft drinks, cookies and brownies." She gestured at the refreshment table. It was covered with goodies provided by just about everyone present. "All completely calorie free, of course." Everyone chuckled. "So help yourselves," Lissa said, "and thanks for coming. It's great to be neighbors in our new hometown."

Enthusiastic applause filled the room.

Mallory leaned close to Callie. "Come on. Let's get some coffee."

So Callie helped herself to a cup of decaf and a large, delicious brownie as laughter and conversation filled the air. She and Mallory chatted and she thought how she was glad to be there. It kind of took the edge off waiting around for Nate to show up at her door and tell her he'd done whatever mysterious thing he needed to do before the two of them could continue their relationship.

If they even *had* a relationship. Since he'd left her in her great room Friday night, she'd wondered more than once if the thing between them could even be called a relationship.

She doubted it sometimes.

And sometimes she just wanted to march over to his house and tell him to get over himself. They needed to take this thing between them to...wherever the heck it wanted to go.

Mallory said, "Callie? Did you hear a single word I said?"

Callie shook herself and apologized and said, "I guess you'd better tell me again."

Mallory reshared the latest gossip. Apparently, there was some mysterious benefactor giving out cash around town under cover of a trust called Brighter Horizons.

Lissa Christensen, who was standing with them, nodded. "True. I've been looking into it. I'm sure there's a story there. Brighter Horizons contributed about a third of the money that built this center. And not only that, the trust has put a couple hundred thousand into repairs at the high school and into more upgrades of the elementary school." The elementary school had been badly damaged in the flood and then mostly rebuilt. It had reopened at New Year's. "Not to mention there have been Brighter Horizons' checks going out to several of the local ranchers who are now able to replace equipment, farm buildings and homes destroyed by the flood."

"Wow," said Callie. "We need funds at the clinic. How do I get in touch with Brighter Horizons?"

"I wish I knew," said Lissa. "Nobody seems to know. But whoever's behind all this generosity is deeply familiar with this town and the valley. Whoever it is knows which people and institutions are in need—and has whipped out a very large checkbook to fix a lot of problems. I would love to find out who's behind Brighter Horizons. It would make a great story, an uplifting story. And that's my favorite kind. But so far, Rust Creek Falls's benefactor seems determined to remain anonymous."

The meeting broke up at a little after nine.

It was a beautiful evening and Callie had left her SUV in her garage. She walked home through the gathering darkness thinking about Rust Creek Falls's mysterious benefactor, imagining ways she might let Brighter Horizons know that a needy institution, the clinic, seemed to have slipped under its donation radar.

She stopped on the Main Street Bridge and gazed down at the clear, rushing creek waters and considered maybe putting up notices around town:

Attention Brighter Horizons: The Rust Creek Falls Clinic Needs Your Money, Too!

Chuckling to herself at the idea, she started walking again.

And the thought of Nate kind of drifted into her mind the way such thoughts often did. Her smile faded as she turned onto Commercial Street.

What was he doing tonight? A girl could get discouraged waiting around for him to do whatever it was he just *had* to do and come back around again. A girl could start thinking she'd made another big romantic mistake to get her hopes up over a guy like him.

As she approached her own house she couldn't help but notice that the lights were out at his place.

So, where was he tonight? She told herself to give it up, let it go, don't even wonder.

But then she turned onto her front walk and the man in question materialized from the shadows of her front porch, holding his hat.

Chapter Eight

She really did consider playing it cool.

For like maybe a second and a half.

But then she looked in his eyes and she saw so much. Gladness. Hope. Yearning.

All the things she guessed were reflected in her eyes, too.

With a soft cry, she ran to him.

He opened his arms and gathered her in, laughing. And she was laughing with him as he picked her up and swung her around in a circle right there in front of her bottom step.

Her feet touched the ground and she beamed up at him. "Is it done...whatever it is?"

"Yeah," he said. "Tonight. It's done. At last."

And she punched him in the shoulder—not too hard but hard enough. "Are you ever going to tell me *what* you're talking about?"

He tipped up her chin and brushed the sweetest kiss

so lightly across her waiting lips. "Are you ever going to invite me in?"

Fair enough. She took his hand and led him up the steps and into her house. He hooked his hat on the peg by the door as she pulled him into the great room and switched on the lights. "Okay. You're in. And I'm listening."

He took her in his arms again. "You look so good." He ran a hand down her hair. "Really good. But then, that's no surprise. You always do. From the first moment I saw you, standing by the side of the road with your pom-pom hat and your red gas can."

She gazed up at him, thinking that he looked good, too. And not only handsome but...happier inside himself somehow. "Thank you—and I'm waiting."

He cleared his throat. "All right. I'll tell you. Tonight I had a beer with Sutter and Collin at the Ace in the Hole. I apologized for my behavior during the mayor's race. I... took responsibility for being a low-down jackass."

She was more gaping than gazing now. "Seriously?"

"Yeah."

"And?"

"They accepted my apology."

She thought of Paige. Maybe, just maybe, Paige would stop worrying now. "Just like that? You're friends with Collin and Sutter Traub?"

"Well, I wouldn't say we're friends, exactly, but we parted on good terms—after they asked me to contribute to a little project of theirs to get investors together and open a resort."

"I think my head is spinning. Sutter and Collin are opening a resort?"

"It's just in the early stages, something they're trying to get off the ground."

"And you said you'd help them?"

"I said I would invest. And I will, if it goes anywhere."

She pulled him over to the sofa, pushed him down and sat beside him. "Amazing."

He threaded his big fingers between her smaller ones. She rested her head on his shoulder. It felt really good there. "I've been missing you," he said, his voice just a little rough.

"I've been right next door the whole time," she scolded.

"I know. It's been driving me crazy."

"Good. I'm glad."

"You make me think I don't want to move away, after all. You make me think that all I could ever want is right here in my hometown."

"Good," she said again and felt a sharp prick of sadness. "But you still haven't decided, have you, whether to stay or go?"

"No." He said it quietly. But firmly, too.

And she whispered, "Tell you what. Let's not talk about your leaving."

His fingers tightened on hers. "Maybe you'll want to come with me."

"Maybe you don't want to go, not really."

He said her name gently, a little regretfully, "Callie..."

And she put her other hand over their joined ones. "Shh. Let it be."

He made a sound that might have been agreement. And then he turned his head and pressed a kiss into her hair. A shiver moved over her skin. Delicious. Exciting. "I walked back here from the Ace at a little after eight. I didn't even go to my house. Just came here and sat on your porch and waited for you."

She snuggled in closer. He eased his hand from hers, but only so that he could wrap his arm around her and draw her even closer to him.

"I went to the first meeting of the Newcomers' Club," she said. "It's mostly the women who've come to town since the flood." He tugged on a loose lock of her pinned-up hair, then traced a figure eight on her arm with a playful finger. She smiled at the tenderness in his touch. "Lissa Christensen gave a welcome speech and we all ate too many brownies and shared the latest gossip—ever heard of Brighter Horizons?"

His teasing finger stopped in midtrace. "Uh. No, I don't think so...."

Something in his voice—in the stilling of his touch—alerted her. She lifted her head to look at him.

He frowned, asked, "What?" a little too innocently.

She stared at him a moment longer and then shook her head. "I don't know...." And then she settled against him again. "Nothing. Where was I?"

He pressed another kiss into her hair. "Something called Brighter Horizons?"

"Right. Lissa says it's some foundation or something—a trust, I think she said. Nobody knows who's behind it, but the trust has donated a lot of money all over town. Lissa wants to get the inside scoop and write about it."

"I'll bet." He growled the words against her hair.

"Lissa says it has to be someone who knows Rust Creek Falls, because Brighter Horizons seems to be putting money where it's really needed." She chuckled to herself. "While I walked home, I tried to think up ways to get in touch with them, whoever they are, to let them know they forgot about the clinic and we will be glad to make excellent use of any random funds they toss our way."

"How do you know they forgot about you? Maybe they're on it, and you just haven't gotten your big check yet."

"I wish."

"Aw, come on. Have a little faith, will you?"

She lifted away from him and then reached out and clasped the back of his warm, strong neck. "Faith. All right. If you say so...."

He was looking at her as though he never wanted to look away. "I've missed you," he said again. Tonight, his eyes were moss-green, a ring of gold and amber around the dark irises. He smelled so good, of that fresh, outdoorsy aftershave he always wore and something else that was all Nate, all man.

"I'm just glad you're here." She pulled him toward her, wanting his kiss.

He didn't disappoint her. His lips touched hers. She sighed and opened, inviting him in. He kissed her for a long time, sitting there on her sofa with her as night fell outside.

And when he finally pulled back from her, they both opened their eyes at the same time. She thought that he looked at her trustingly, and longingly, too.

She understood that look. She felt the same way. For months she had tried to deny this thing between them, not even letting herself speak to him until the first of June when she came to collect on that bet she'd won. She'd seen him a lot around town in the months between January and June, and every time she saw him, she yearned to walk right up to him and get him talking, maybe even to ask him if he'd go to dinner with her sometime.

But she hadn't done it. She'd told herself to stay away, that her friend Paige said he was trouble and she was taking a break from the male of the species, anyway.

In the end, though, the attraction she felt for him would not be denied. And now, at last, she'd come to the place within herself where she didn't want to deny it.

He wasn't like David. She knew it to her bones. He'd

done wrong things, but he had owned that wrongness, wrestled with it, come to grips with the need to make things right and then taken steps to do just that.

No, not like David, though she knew that, like David, he would probably hurt her. But when he did, it wouldn't be out of cruelty and thoughtlessness and a lying heart. He wouldn't betray her the way that David had, the way her father had when she was only a child. He would hurt her because of that need in him to go, to leave the home she'd come to love. Because of that broken place in him that maybe wasn't quite so broken anymore.

But wasn't completely healed, either.

He wouldn't be happy if he went. She knew that, down in the deepest, truest part of her. But she couldn't make him see that. He had to figure it out for himself.

He touched her face the way he liked to do, his fingers light and cherishing on her cheek. "What now, Callie Kennedy?"

She caught his hand again and stood.

He held on to her fingers, but didn't rise. Instead, he looked up at her from under his brows, a lazy look, more than a little bit hungry, a look that excited her, a look that made that lovely weakness down in the womanly core of her.

"Come on," she whispered and gave a tug.

Still, he didn't rise. "Are you sure?"

"I am, yes." That time, when she pulled on his hand, he rose and stood with her, guiding their joined hands around her and pulling her sharply into him. She gasped at the feel of him, pressed against her, hard and wanting. Their twined hands held her tight at the base of her spine. "Nate..."

"Shh." He lowered his mouth and kissed her again, a

hard, hot kiss that time, a kiss that plundered the secrets beyond her parted lips, a kiss that made his intentions clear.

She kissed him back, eagerly. And that time, when he lifted his head, she didn't say anything. She just unwound her body from the circle of his arm and led him out of the great room, across the front hall, past the stairs to the upper floor and into her bedroom.

At the side of the bed, she switched on the lamp and turned back the covers, smoothing open the sheets. And then she went into his arms. He drew her close again.

There were more kisses, lingering and sweet.

Until she pulled away a second time to open the drawer in the nightstand. She took out a box of condoms and removed one, setting it within easy reach of the bed.

He chuckled.

She slid him a look. "Yeah, well, I bought them Saturday in Kalispell, when I went for groceries. Because a girl never knows when the right cowboy will come calling."

He reached into his back pocket and pulled out three more. "Makes perfect sense to me." He set them with hers on the nightstand.

She put the box back in the drawer and pushed it shut. "Call us prepared."

He snaked out a hand and hauled her into him again, cradling her chin with his other hand, his eyes dark green now and intense in their focus, his body hard and ready, calling to hers. "I never thought…" He said it low and a little bit ragged.

"Never thought what?"

He searched her face with those green, green eyes. "This. You. Me. How it is with us. It's really good."

She only nodded. It was the best she could do. Her throat had clutched. And the words wouldn't come.

He didn't seem to mind. "I want to see you. All of you."

Again she nodded.

And he reached up with one hand and pulled out the pins that held up her hair, setting them next to the condoms on the nightstand. He took his time about it, spreading her hair on her shoulders, smoothing it down her back, combing it with his fingers, pausing to wrap it around his hand, only to unwind it carefully once again.

"Silky, warm," he whispered, taking another thick lock of it, bringing the strands to his mouth, rubbing them there. "Smells like flowers and cinnamon."

He began to undress her, his tanned fingers nimble on the buttons of her shirt, easing them out of the buttonholes one by one, carefully spreading the shirt open once he had them all undone. "So pretty..." He bent his head and pressed a kiss on the slope of her right breast, just above the lace of her shell-pink bra. "Callie..." He breathed her name against her flesh, and she relished the hot shiver that skated along the surface of her skin. "Callie." He kissed the top of her other breast.

And then he got back to the business at hand.

He unwrapped her like a much-anticipated present, taking her by the waist and sitting her down on the bed so he could kneel at her feet and pull off her boots and her socks. And after that, rising, taking her hand, urging her to stand again. He took down her snug jeans. When she had just her panties and bra left to cover her, he gathered her close, bent his head and captured her lips for more of those long, slow kisses.

She tried to reciprocate, to get him out of his shirt, at least. Or maybe his big-buckled belt. But every time she got to work on some article of his clothing, he gently took her hands away and kissed her again, and she forgot everything but the hot, wet perfection of his mouth on hers, the hardness of his body pressing along hers, the touch of his hands on her willing flesh, the need to clutch him closer, hold him tighter, never, ever let him go.

He took off her bra, eased away her little panties. She was naked and it was glorious. "Soft." He whispered the word against her throat. "So smooth…" He nipped her collarbone, making her moan.

And then he bent his head to her breast. She speared her fingers into his hair, pulling him closer, urging him to kiss her, to draw her nipple into his mouth, to flick his tongue around it, swirling.

She made noises, shameless sounds—hungry, yearning, encouraging sounds. His hands caressed her, cradling her breasts, his touch both thrillingly rough and heartbreakingly tender, those clever, knowing fingers moving lower, gliding between her thighs, where she was waiting and wet and longing for him.

He touched her there, where she wanted him most, and she gasped and cried his name and whispered, "Yes, oh, yes. Please, just…there." And he gave her what she begged for, his fingers moving right to the spot that brought her a swift, shining bolt of pure pleasure.

He stroked and he teased. And then he touched her more deeply, opening her. And she was gone, lost, over the moon with the feel of him, the way he knew just where to touch her, how to make her burn and lift her hips to him and beg him not to stop, to give her more.

When he guided her down to the bed again, she went happily, stretching out across the white sheets, her knees at the edge and her feet dangling to the floor.

He knelt. Moaning, she opened her heavy eyes and lifted her head to look down at him. He smiled at her.

"Nate, I…"

"What?"

But already she had forgotten whatever it was she had

meant to say. So she only moaned again and let her head drop back to the mattress.

She felt his warm, rough-tender hands on her thighs, rubbing. Slowly. Clasping, too, spreading her legs wider, revealing every last secret her body might have kept from him. She had no secrets, not now.

And it didn't matter in the least. Except that it was good and right and she didn't care to keep secrets from him, anyway. She rolled her head from side to side against her soft, white sheets and felt those hands of his moving.

Down and inward, finding the burning womanly core of her again. Stroking, teasing. She moaned some more. And then he moved in closer. There was the sweet friction of his shirt against her inner thighs, the warmth of him beneath the crisp fabric…

And then he kissed her.

There.

Just there.

He kissed her and he went on kissing her, using his lips and his tongue and his knowing fingers in the most lovely and exciting ways. She rocked her hips up to him and called his name and clutched at the sheets.

And then it happened. The heat and the wonder spiraled down to that one most sensitive spot—and then opened up wide, coursing in sparks and a swift flow of heat all through her, opening her up and tossing her over the edge, sending her spiraling, spinning, setting her free as she whispered his name.

He stayed with her, easing her down from the peak with gentle kisses at first and then, after, rising up enough to rest his head on her belly. She stroked her fingers through his thick gold-streaked brown hair and thought how right and good it felt to be there with him.

Eventually, he turned his head and placed a long, soft kiss on her belly. Then he levered back on his heels.

"Oh, don't go...." She reached for him. But he was already rising to stand above her. "Come back here," she commanded lazily, her arms still outstretched to him.

"I will," he said, and his eyes said he meant that. "Count on it." He looked at her and she was fine with that, with lying there completely naked under his admiring gaze, her hair all wild and tangled, spread across the sheets.

With a hard sigh, she let her arms drop back to the mattress. "Hurry up." She pouted.

So he got to work undressing. He did it quickly, with a sort of ruthless efficiency that she found almost as exciting as his kiss, as the brush of his strong hands on her skin.

He was a beautiful man, broad and strong, with big shoulders and a deep chest tapering down to a tight waist and narrow hips. A beautiful man who wanted her. The proof of his desire rose up from the dark nest of hair between his heavily muscled thighs. She looked at it and then up into his waiting eyes.

And then she reached out her arms once more.

That time, he didn't hesitate. He came down to the sheets with her, gathering her up into his big arms and rearranging her, until she lay with her head on the pillows and her feet toward the headboard.

"At last." She sighed, pulling him close to her, taking the weight of him and glorying in it, widening her thighs so he could slip between them.

"Callie." He said her name as though it was an answer to some question. A good answer. The right answer. He lifted up on his big arms and gazed down at her and she stared back up at him....

A great moment. One of the best. A moment with nothing of regret in it. Only anticipation and the promise of more pleasure. Only this man who had seemed so impossible, so difficult.

This man who was turning out to be more than she'd understood at first. Tough and tenderhearted, he really got to her. Whatever happened in the end, she would not regret her time with him.

He whispered her name again. "Callie..." Her hair was everywhere, spread out in coils and snarls around them. He buried his fingers in it, bent to rub his cheek against it where it fell along his arm.

And then he was kissing his way over her shoulder, up the side of her throat, scraping his teeth there, sucking a little, hard enough that she knew it would probably leave a mark, a mark that would fade quickly, unlike the one he was making on her heart.

Nipping, nuzzling, he kissed his way into the cove just below her chin, and higher, until his wonderful, warm mouth closed over hers.

They shared another kiss, better than the last one, his tongue sweeping the inner surfaces beyond her parted lips, beckoning hers to follow. And she did follow, tasting him deeply, sharing breath with him, sighing her desire into his mouth. As they kissed, he touched her, his hand straying down to find her wet and open and eager for him.

When he lifted his lips from hers, she moaned and blinked up at him, drowning in the feel of him, lost in his touch.

"Now?" he asked in a rumble so low it came out like a growl.

And she nodded. "Now."

And somehow he already had the condom in his hand. He fumbled with it.

She giggled, a silly, happy sound, and got her hands up between them to take it from him. The top tore off easily.

He pushed back, away from her. She missed the hard, hot weight of him. But, oh, he did look fine, looming above her on his knees, looking down at her with an expression that stole the breath right out of her body.

She took the condom from the wrapper and tossed the wrapper away, reaching for him. He moaned when she touched him and she couldn't resist a few slow, testing strokes. He was silk over steel and she wanted to taste him.

But he shook his head. "I want you, *you,* Callie. Now."

"But I—"

"Now."

She looked into his eyes again, saw heat and hunger and couldn't bear to deny him. So she rolled the protection down over his hard length, carefully so as not to tear it, easing it in nice and close at the base.

And then he was reaching for her, lifting her up and over.

With a cry of surprise, she found herself straddling him, staring down into those beautiful eyes. "What…?"

"Ride me," he commanded in a rough growl.

That sounded like a wonderful idea to her. So she went up on her knees and he positioned himself beneath her and then, with slow, thrilling care, she lowered herself onto him. They both groaned at the feel of that. Her body gave to him, welcoming him, taking him in.

And then he was clasping her hips in his big, strong hands, pulling her down, seating himself in deeper, all the way.

She gasped again and braced her hands on his broad, hard chest.

"Move for me, Callie."

She obeyed. It was only exactly what she wanted to do. She rocked her hips and he lifted his to meet her, keeping rhythm with her, the two of them in matching time. She tipped her head back as she rocked on him and he brought his hands up, caressing, over the outward swells of her hips, inward at her waist and around to her back, which she arched for him. His fingers caught in her tangled hair and he played with it, wrapping it around his hands, tugging on it hard enough to hurt just a little, spiking her pleasure even higher.

And then he was taking her by the waist, rolling her back under him, claiming the dominant position once more, moving on her and in her, filling her so completely. Her mind spun and her body caught fire. She lifted her legs and wrapped them tight around his narrow hips as her climax expanded up from the feminine core of her, rocking through her, rolling over her in waves. When she cried out, he only lowered his mouth and took that cry into himself as he kept on moving within her, filling her so completely, burning her up with pleasure, turning the world inside out.

And then he went still, pressing into her so close and deep that she felt him pulsing, felt his completion as it took form from hers. He broke the endless kiss they shared, his head straining back, the tendons of his powerful neck drawing hard and tight. A low, wordless sound escaped him.

And she reached up, wrapped her fingers around the back of his neck and pulled him close to her again, guiding his head to rest in the curve of her throat.

"Callie..." He groaned her name, his breath hot against her skin.

She held on, sighing, cradling him close to her heart as they eased down from the peak together and slowly settled into afterglow.

In time, he lifted up onto his forearms again. He looked down at her, frowning. "I'm crushing you...."

"Yes, you are." She brushed at his hair where it fell across his forehead. "But I don't mind at all."

"Don't want to crush you," he grumbled. And then he rolled them again. That time they ended up on their sides, still joined. He wrapped his leg across her hip, smoothed her hair back from her face so it flowed out behind her across the pillows. "It's good. To be here, like this, with you...."

"Mmm." She smiled at him and cuddled closer, letting her eyes drift shut.

He brushed his fingers across her cheek. "Are you conking out on me?"

"No way," she muttered lazily. "That would be rude."

"You *are* conking out on me."

"Haven't been sleeping much," she confessed on a sigh. "Man problems."

"That bad?" he asked in a teasing whisper.

"Bad enough."

He drew her closer, kissed her cheek and stroked her hair in the gentlest, sweetest way.

She sighed again. "Just need to close my eyes... Only a minute..."

She woke suddenly in the dark, absolutely certain that making love with him had been a dream.

He wasn't in the bed with her. She sat up and turned on the bedside lamp. The clock by the lamp said it was after midnight. And there were three condoms waiting in front of the clock, next to the pins he'd taken from her hair.

So, then. It had happened. It was real. "Nate?"

"Right here." He emerged from the darkness of the bathroom, wearing nothing but one of those killer smiles of his.

"Come back here."

"Yes, ma'am."

She admired the view as he approached. When he reached her, she flipped back the covers and he rejoined her in the bed.

With a happy sigh, she pulled the covers over them, rested her head on his broad chest and relished the way his strong arms closed around her. "I thought you had left— or maybe you were never here in the first place, that you were just a dream I had."

"Wrong on both counts." He tipped her chin up, kissed the tip of her nose. "Sleep well?"

"I did, actually." She reached up, stroked the manly stubble on his jaw. "Sorry. Were you bored to death?"

"Hell, no. I went to sleep, too. I needed it. Haven't been sleeping all that much, either. See, there's a certain woman I can't stop thinking about...."

She chuckled. Then she asked if he was hungry. He shook his head, reached over and turned off the light.

They should go back to sleep and she knew it. She had to be at the clinic by nine in the morning.

But she started thinking about what he'd told her earlier, that he'd met Collin and Sutter at the Ace in the Hole and apologized to them. And that made her wonder about all the years that he and Collin were at each other's throats. "Nate...?"

"Go to sleep," he told her.

"In a minute," she said. He rubbed his hand down her arm. It felt wonderful, to be lying there in the dark with him. It felt like something she could so very easily get used to. "I was thinking about you and Collin...."

"What can I tell you? We hated each other for years. Now it's getting better. That's about the size of it."

"I've heard the stories."

He grunted. "Hey, it's Rust Creek Falls. Of course you've heard the stories."

"But they're always vague, the stories. I mean, I don't really understand what went on between you two."

He made a low, ironic sort of sound. "Neither do I, really. He was a wild kid who never did what he was told, and I played by the rules, I guess you could say. We disapproved of each other and we always managed to get on each other's last nerve."

"I would like to hear what really went on with Cindy Sellers."

He tipped up her chin and brushed a quick kiss on her lips. "Why?"

She snuggled against his heart again. "Well, the day you agreed to sell me this house, you wouldn't tell me. I'm still wondering about it, that's all."

"It happened years ago. Cindy moved away shortly after the whole mess went down. She never came back. It doesn't matter now."

"It matters to me, Nate. I want to know everything about you."

He was fooling with her hair, combing his fingers through it. "I'm just not that fascinating."

"Yes, you are. Tell me."

He said nothing for several seconds. She was sure he would never tell her the story. But in the end, he relented. "Cindy and I started going out about seven years ago. She wanted to get married, settle down, have a family. I didn't. I was never getting married again and I told her that. She didn't believe me. She kept waiting for me to see the light and propose. In the two years we were together, whenever she would bring up marriage, I would either tell her it wasn't happening or change the subject. She should have dumped me, but instead, she kept seeing me, pressuring me. I should have stopped seeing her."

"Why didn't you?"

"I liked her, or I did until the end. I'd been back home for about a year when I got together with her. It was three years since Zoe's death, and I was lonely. I was ready for a girlfriend, to be with someone in a steady way. But marriage? Uh-uh. I knew it wasn't working with her, that we wanted different things...."

"But you held on."

"Yeah. Looking back, I think she just got madder and madder at me. Finally, one night, she went looking for Collin at the Ace in the Hole. She told Collin that she and I were through."

"How do you know that?"

"A lot of people saw her at the Ace that night. A lot of people heard her say that it was over with her and me."

"So, you'd broken up with her?"

"No. In fact, the night before she went after Collin, we were together out at the ranch. She spent the night. In the morning when she left, she kissed me goodbye, and we agreed that I would take her out to dinner the following Friday night."

"I want to call her a really bad name about now."

"Yeah, well, she wasn't that way at first. Like I said, I just think she got so mad at me for not being the man she wanted me to be. By the end, she only wanted to hurt me."

"Did she succeed?"

"I remember being furious that she had made a damn fool of me. And somewhere underneath the blind rage, yeah, she did hurt me. Because I cared about her. I couldn't be who she wanted me to be and I didn't have sense enough to just break it off. And Collin was still a wild one back then, not one to turn down a good-looking, eager woman."

"So Collin spent the night with Cindy, and when it got back to you, you blamed him."

"Hey. He's a Traub and I'm a Crawford, so blaming

him was always the easiest thing for me to do. Back then, he was the wildest, most troublemaking of all the Traubs, and he and I had gotten into it over and over throughout our lives. I was mad because my girlfriend had climbed in bed with another man. Who better to blame than the other man—especially since that man was Collin Traub? I found him at the Ace and I punched him in the face. He couldn't let that stand, so he punched me back. We ended up pretty much beating the crap out of each other."

"Didn't he tell you that Cindy had told *him* that you two were through?"

"That would have involved discussion. There was no discussion. I went in swinging, and Collin swung back. It was only later I found out that he'd thought Cindy and me were over because Cindy had told him so."

"Who won the fight?"

He gave a low chuckle. "Crawfords will tell you I won. Ask a Traub, he'll swear that Collin wiped up the floor with me."

"Well, whoever won, neither you nor Collin comes off looking like a hero in that story."

"Because we're not heroes. We're just men doing what men do, solving problems with our fists."

"You wouldn't behave that way now."

"I hope not. I like to think I've grown up a little."

She lifted up enough to meet his eyes through the darkness. "You're a good man, Nate."

He shook his head slowly on the white pillow. "Not so sure about that, not so sure about anything anymore, really. Which is pretty damn funny because I used to be certain that I knew everything." He pulled her back down to him again, guiding her head to rest against his shoulder. "Go to sleep."

It sounded like a pretty good idea to her. She closed her eyes.

When she opened them again, daylight was peeking through the blinds.

And someone was ringing the doorbell.

"Huh?" She reached for the clock. "Forgot to set the alarm…"

Beside her Nate came groggily awake. "Doorbell…" He looked wonderful, all rumpled and sexy, with his hair sticking up on one side and a sleep crease bisecting his beard-stubbled cheek.

She tossed back the covers. "I'll get it."

He grabbed her arm. "Close the bedroom door. I'll wait here until you can get rid of whoever it is."

She gave a low, scoffing laugh and pulled her arm free. "Oh, come on."

"Seriously." His lips were a thin line, his expression set. "It could be anyone, including someone with a big mouth, who'll be spreading our business all over town."

The doorbell rang again.

She swung her feet over the edge of the bed and grabbed her robe from the bedside chair. "Nate. Get real." She stuck her arms in the sleeves and swiftly tied the belt. "I'm not sneaking around to be with you. We spent the night together and I don't care who knows it." She headed for the door.

"Spoken like a girl from the big city. Just close the bedroom door," he called after her. "Please."

She did close the bedroom door because he didn't have a stitch on—*not* because she cared who knew that he was in her bed. And then she went straight to the front door and pulled it wide.

Nate's mother was waiting on the other side.

Chapter Nine

Laura Crawford let out a sigh of obvious relief. "Callie. I'm so glad you're home. Sorry to wake you."

Callie reached up to guide a tangled lock of hair behind her ear. "No problem. Uh…come on in."

"Oh, no. Really. I don't want to bother you.…"

"You're not." She stepped back. "I'll get the coffee going."

Laura shook her head and stayed on the porch side of the threshold. "It's just that I've been trying to reach Nathan. He's not picking up either of his phones, so I came on over hoping to catch him at home and, well, he's not there. So I was wondering if you knew where he…" Laura let the sentence die unfinished. She blinked. Callie followed the direction of her gaze to Nate's hat hanging on the peg by the door. "Oh!" she said. "Well." And then she smiled. A big, happy smile. After which, she leaned close and whispered, "He's going to be furious with me for showing up here."

"Come in," Callie tried again, hoping she wasn't blushing like some teenaged virgin caught necking out at Lover's Lane in a '50s romantic comedy.

Laura said, still whispering gleefully, "I didn't realize things were moving so fast." And then, a little louder, "I need to talk to him about what I've heard, that's all."

"Uh, what you've heard?"

"That he had a meeting with Collin and Sutter Traub last night." Now she was scowling. "Can that really be true? And— Never mind, never mind." Laura reached out and patted Callie's arm. "Just tell him to call me, that I need to talk to him."

"Sure. But if you come in, you can tell him your—"

Laura put up a hand. "No. Bad idea. Tell him to call me." She turned for the steps that led down to the front walk.

"But, I—"

Laura kept going, calling over her shoulder, "Have a lovely morning, hon."

Callie just stood there, feeling more than a little foolish, her arms wrapped around herself, watching as Nate's mom got into her shiny red quad cab and drove away.

"Close the door," Nate said from behind her.

It seemed like a reasonable suggestion, so she shut it and turned around to find him standing in the doorway to her bedroom, wearing only his jeans and looking like every girl's fantasy of a hot cowboy lover. She coughed to clear her suddenly tight throat. "Ahem. That was your mother."

"I know. I heard."

"Somehow, she's already learned that you met with Collin last night."

He leaned in the doorway, big arms crossed over that

fine, broad golden-skinned chest. "Of course she already knows."

"She…saw your hat." Callie flicked out a hand in the direction of the hat in question.

"Great. Now we can be certain that our private business will be all over town within twenty-four hours. Was she grinning ear to ear about it?"

"About you and me, yeah. About your meeting with the Traubs, not so much. She wants you to call her."

"I'll bet she does."

"You know, you always seem kind of annoyed with your mother."

He still lounged in the doorway, watching her. "Come here."

"She's a very sweet woman, really."

"I grew up with her. I know exactly how sweet she is. Come here." He said it softly but roughly, too. And there was no mistaking the sexy gleam in his eyes.

Callie felt a hot shiver run up the backs of her bare calves and a sluice of heat low in her belly. "I don't have time to fool around. I have to go to work." She adjusted the front of her robe and gave him a slow smile. "However, *after* work is another story altogether.…"

He reached out his hand to her. "Come on over here to me.…"

"Oh, all right." She went to him and when she got there, she couldn't resist going on tiptoe and lifting her mouth.

Nate took what she offered in a lazy kiss that started out smoldering and quickly burned hot. When he lifted his head, she had a hard time not grabbing him and pulling him down to her again. "What time do you have to be at the clinic?"

"Nine."

"You have eggs?"

She nodded. "There's even bacon. And bread for toast. I'll fix us some breakfast. If I hurry, there's time." She turned from the warm circle of his arms.

But he caught her and pulled her back. "I'll do it. You go ahead and get ready."

She sighed and leaned into him again, burying her nose against his chest and breathing in the wonderful scent of him. "A hot cowboy lover who makes breakfast? Is this a dream?"

He took her by the shoulders and turned her toward the bathroom. "Go. Now. Otherwise, I'm going to get you out of this robe and get to work showing you all the reasons you need to call in sick."

Callie took a quick shower and put on her scrubs. When she joined Nate in the kitchen, he had the table set and the food ready. The bacon was crisp, the scrambled eggs light and fluffy. She thanked him for the meal.

He warned, "Expect advice. A boatload of it."

She sipped her coffee. "What kind of advice?"

"Advice about how you need to watch out with me, that I'm not a good bet for a long-term relationship."

Callie laughed. "I've heard that exact advice from *you* already."

"Be ready to hear it again from just about everyone in town—except my mother, of course. She'll tell you the opposite. That I'm just the man for you and we should get married right away and you should make me promise never, ever to leave Rust Creek Falls."

She put down her fork. "Nate."

"What?"

"Stop being glum. Put on your happy face."

"I have a happy face?"

"Seriously. We're in this now, right? You and me, together. We're a thing."

He scowled, thinking about it. And then he said, "Hell, yeah."

That made her smile. "Good, then. Let's enjoy every minute and not borrow trouble."

He broke a piece of bacon in half and stared down at the two halves as if he didn't know what to do with them. "You're right. You're absolutely right." He looked up at her and commanded, "Dinner. Tonight. My place."

"You're cooking?"

"Well, you'll be working all day. Seems like the least I can do is pamper you a little when you get home."

"I do like the way you think. Most of the time, anyway."

Gruffly, he demanded, "Is that a yes on dinner?"

"Absolutely. I'll be there. I get off at five."

When Callie left for the clinic, Nate went back to his house. He'd barely gotten in the door before the phone started ringing.

He knew who it would be and he was right. "Hello, Mom." Just for the heck of it, he checked his cell, which he'd left on silent page. She had called him on it, too. "What's up?"

She answered stiffly, "I would like to speak with you."

"Fine. Speak."

"Face-to-face, Nathan. In private."

Might as well get it over with. "Where?"

"I'll come there," she said. "Ten minutes."

Nine and a half minutes later, she was knocking on his door. He ushered her in, led her to the kitchen and made her a cup of café mocha.

She took the coffee, sipped and then shook her head at him. "I don't know where to start, Nathan."

"Then, don't," he suggested hopefully and sipped from the mug he'd filled for himself.

She failed to take his advice. "I'm happy for you and Callie."

"Great."

"Come to Sunday dinner. Bring Callie. Please."

"I'll invite her."

"Wonderful. As for your visit with the Traub brothers…"

He realized he didn't want to hear her running down the Traubs. "Look. Don't start, okay?"

"You don't even know what I'm going to say."

"Yeah, but I'll bet I can guess."

She blew out a sharp, annoyed little breath and went right on. "I didn't get any details. All I heard was that you met with them and you all ended up shaking hands."

He figured she might as well hear it from him than wait around for the rumor mill to provide all kinds of outlandish stories about what had gone down at the Ace last night. "I apologized to Sutter and Collin for playing dirty during the mayor's race."

She huffed a little. "I wouldn't say you played dirty."

"Well, I would. I apologized, the Traubs accepted and they asked me to invest in a little project they've got going."

"What kind of project?"

He really didn't feel like talking about the resort idea with her. She would only try and warn him off it. "It's an investment they offered me, that's all."

"But what kind of investment?"

"It's in the very early stages and I don't want to go into it right now."

"It's only that I don't want you to throw your money away."

"Let it go, Mom."

Surprisingly, she did. "All right." She gave a heavy sigh.

"Enough said about the Traubs' mysterious investment opportunity."

"Wonderful."

"And, well, I know that to you, I may seem set in my ways. But even your father and I understand that things change. And we do have a daughter who's married a Traub."

He couldn't help razzing her a little. "You noticed?"

"Nathan, there is no need for you to be sarcastic with me." She said it in her best injured-mother voice. "Yes, I *have* noticed who my daughter married. And Nina and Dallas seem to be very happy together. They've made a lovely family, with his boys and baby Noelle. I want us all to get along."

"Well, good. So do I."

"And I want *you* to be happy. I truly do. I know how much you loved Zoe and I am sorry you lost her and the child. So very sorry..."

He stared across the table at her, vaguely stunned. It had been years since she'd said Zoe's name or referred to her in any way. "What are you up to here, Mom?" She gazed steadily back at him, looking sad and...older. The lines around her mouth and at the corners of her eyes seemed suddenly deeper somehow. "You never talk about Zoe. Why start now?"

She drank from her mug, set it down with care. "Because we have to start somewhere, don't we, to try and make a change, make things right?"

"It's too late for you to make things right with Zoe." He said it softly, even gently. But he meant the words to wound her all the same.

And she knew it. A film of tears made her eyes shine. But she was tough, always had been. She blinked the tears away and squared her shoulders. "I should have been kinder to her. I know it. She was a lovely person. And still, I judged her as not right for you—and not because she waited tables for a living, as I know you've always thought. But because she was from out of town and reluctant to move to Rust Creek Falls."

He couldn't let that go. "She was reluctant because you weren't welcoming to her."

His mother pressed her lips together and seemed to be taking slow, careful breaths. "All right," she said at last. "Yes. I behaved distantly to her when I should have opened my arms. My behavior made her feel unwelcome here. But think back. She loved her mama in North Dakota. She wanted to live there, near Anna. Deep down, you know that." He ached to argue just for the sake of disagreeing with her, but he didn't. She was right, after all. His mother's behavior aside, Zoe *had* wanted to live in Bismarck. "I wanted you to find a nice local girl who would ground you here, keep you at home with us. But you found Zoe. And instead of being happy that you had someone to love who loved you in return, I was bitter because you never came home. I blamed *her*. I was wrong."

Was this really happening? Laura Crawford sitting across from him, drinking a café mocha and admitting she'd been wrong?

Never in his life had he expected to have this conversation with her, for her to come right out and admit that she should have behaved differently. He didn't know quite what to make of it. It didn't feel all that good, not really, to hear Zoe's name from his mother's mouth after so many years of silence, of her acting as though his wife had never existed. There was a raw feeling within him, as if someone had taken a cheese grater to his heart.

Finally, he said flatly, "Yeah. You were wrong. And what brings this on?"

She sipped at her café mocha and answered thoughtfully, "I don't know exactly. Maybe I'm old enough to start being a little bit wiser. Or maybe it's this thing with the Traubs. First Nina and Dallas. Now you, going to Collin and making peace. Something that can never change is changing. That gets a person thinking. It truly does. Or maybe it's Callie."

He didn't understand—and he wasn't sure he wanted to. But then he heard himself asking, "Why Callie?"

"*You* and Callie."

"Still not following."

"Oh, come on—the way you looked at each other in the store last week, on the day of the storm?"

"Yeah, so…?"

"You'll never know how happy that look made me."

"You're happy because I finally have strong feelings for a woman who loves Rust Creek Falls?"

She didn't smile, exactly, but somehow she did look less sad. "Believe it or not, the simple fact that you have strong feelings for Callie matters more to me than that she might keep you here in town. All these years…" She stared into the middle distance, a faraway sort of look. "A decade since your Zoe passed away, and there's never been any woman who could reach you. I'd slowly come to accept that Zoe was it for you, that no other woman ever would touch you the way that she did, that I had blown my chance to cherish her for showing you what real love from a good woman can be. And then I saw you look at Callie in that special, deep way, and I realized that anything is possible, Nathan. I saw that you are finally moving on from a terrible heartbreak."

Again, he wanted to take issue with that, just on principal somehow. But what would that prove? That he knew how to be a douche to his mom? He was thirty-three years old, for pity's sake. Grown up enough to sit there and listen while she had her say.

She spoke again, leaning toward him, intent and sincere, "I see things differently now. I see that even the most hidebound of us really can change—if we want it bad enough, if we're willing to do what we have to do to make up for the things that we've done wrong." She fell silent and watched him expectantly.

He knew it was his turn to say something profound. Too bad he had nothing.

She gave him a funny, quirky little smile then and waved a hand at him. "It's okay." She pushed back her chair and carried her empty mug around the peninsula of counter to the sink. "You don't have to say anything. I just came to apologize for what I didn't do for Zoe. And I came to tell you that I am proud of you. And if you want to invest your money in some Traub brothers' project, well, I can't say I'll keep my mouth shut, but I will respect your choice and support you in every way I can." She came back around the jut of counter to stand a few feet from the table and suggested, wincing, "I know this is a lot to ask, but could I maybe have a hug before I go?"

He went to her and put his arms around her. She sighed and hugged him back.

Then she clapped her hands on his shoulders and met his eyes. "You're a good man, Nathan."

He remembered Callie last night, telling him the same thing, and he almost laughed. "Let's say I'm working on it."

"It wasn't your fault that Zoe and the baby died. It was just the way it happened, that you got trapped at the ranch that day. It was tragic and wrong. But not in any way your fault."

He gave her a crooked smile. "I could have made other choices, that's all. Better choices…"

The sad look came back into her eyes again. "Oh, honey. Couldn't we all?"

At a little after ten that morning, Callie was in her office cubicle writing a couple of prescriptions and continuing-care instructions for a patient she'd just seen when her phone chimed.

It was a text from Paige: Lunch? My house. 1:00? Paige knew her schedule. Emmet took lunch early, at eleven-thirty. She went at one.

Callie bit her lower lip and tried not to feel apprehensive that Paige might be gearing up for more dire warnings about Nate. But then she shook it off. She and Paige were friends, and friends were supposed to tell you what they really thought—even if what they really thought was that they didn't much care for your boyfriend.

She texted back: Gr8. I'll b there.

Emmet was back by quarter of one. "Go on, go ahead," he said when she told him she wanted to walk over to Paige's for lunch.

Paige invited Callie in with a hug and a smile and led her to the kitchen, where Paige served pasta salad, warm rolls and raspberry-leaf iced tea. Callie's apprehensions faded a little as they ate. They chatted about everyday things—like how much Paige, who taught at the elementary school, enjoyed teaching summer school.

"I miss it this year," she said. With the baby coming, she'd decided to take the summer off. "The kids are so much fun."

They discussed Brighter Horizons. Paige thought the town's mystery benefactor was probably some rich out-oftowner who'd read Lissa's blog and gotten swept up in the story of the little town coming back against all odds from the flood of the century. "I know Lissa thinks whoever it is has to be local, but I don't agree, necessarily. It could just be some rich old guy with a generous spirit, someone who wants to help."

Callie was more of Lissa Roarke's opinion, that it was someone local.

While they talked, she kept thinking about what Nate had said that morning, that in no time everyone in town would know that the two of them were together. And the more she thought about that, the more she wanted to be the one to tell Paige that Nate had spent the night at her house. Even if your friend didn't like your boyfriend, she shouldn't be getting hot news about your love life from somebody else.

So when Paige brought out the fruit tarts for dessert, Callie said, "There's something I've been wanting to tell you...."

Paige didn't miss a beat. "Is this about Nate?"

"It is, yes." And Callie went ahead and told her that Nate had slept at her house last night, that she didn't really know where it was going, but it was serious. "I care for him, Paige. I truly do. And tonight he's cooking me dinner at his house."

Paige ate a glazed strawberry. "I appreciate your telling me."

"I wanted you to hear it from me first."

Paige nodded. "Thanks. And I really can't say I'm surprised."

Callie peered at her more closely. "I thought you were going to be upset. But you don't seem all that bothered, really."

Paige ate a slice of kiwi fruit. "Did he tell you that he

apologized to Sutter and Collin?" At Callie's nod, she went on, "He's never been my favorite person, but that took guts, to find Sutter at the ranch and say sorry, and then, when Sutter challenged him to say the same to Collin, to meet them at the Ace, bold as brass, right in front of everybody, and offer his apologies all over again. I do admire a man with guts, even when his name happens to be Nathan Crawford. And now he's admitted what a horse's ass he was, well, it wouldn't be right to hold the past against him, would it?"

Callie scooped up a bite of flaky crust, sweet custard and summer berries. "So…you're okay with this, with me and Nate?"

Paige arched a brow at her. "Would you break up with him if I wasn't?"

Callie didn't even stop to think about it. "Sorry. Not a chance." She popped the sweet treat into her mouth.

"I didn't think so."

"I really, really like him, Paige."

"What about how you were swearing off men?"

"You're absolutely right. I was. But the man just…gets to me. There's something so sweet and steadfast in him. And he can be so funny and perceptive. Plus, well, he's just plain hot. What can I say? I'm crazy about him."

"I know, I know. It's written all over your face whenever you talk about him or even when someone just mentions his name."

"I'm that obvious, huh?"

"Well, at least to me, you are. And it's kind of humorous, actually…."

"Terrific. I'm so lovesick, it's funny."

"Come on now." Paige reached across and patted her arm. "That's not what I meant."

"Right."

"No, really. What's humorous is that last year about this time, I was warning Willa Christensen off of Collin, predicting dire consequences if she didn't stay away from him, reminding her that he'd always been a wild one and she didn't need that kind of trouble in her life. Willa wouldn't listen to me. And as it turned out, she had it right. Here they are, happily married, and wild man Collin is the mayor of this town. Life is full of surprises, don't you think?"

Callie agreed that it was. And she couldn't help imagining what it might be like, if she and Nate ended up a couple in a permanent way. The hopeless romantic within her just loved that idea.

But her more realistic, modern-woman self wasn't so sure. Nate was…special to her. Important. And she worried that she'd already let him become *too* important.

Deep inside she feared that his heart would always and forever belong to the woman he'd lost ten years ago.

She got back to the clinic at two, right on time.

There were three patients in the waiting room. One of them was hers, eight-year-old Teddy Trimmer, who'd fallen out of his tree house three weeks ago and ended up with a simple fracture of his left wrist. He was there with his mom, Georgia, to get his removable splint off for good.

Callie gave the boy and his mom a smile, and Teddy held up his splinted wrist and called, "All better, Nurse Callie."

She laughed. "Excellent, Teddy. This could be the big day."

And then Brandy, behind the check-in desk, said, "Callie. At last." She got up from her computer, came around to Callie's side, took her by the arm and pulled her halfway down the hall and into a storage closet, where she shut the door and flicked on the light.

"Brandy, what in the…"

"It's Emmet."

"Is he all right?"

Brandy rolled her eyes. "He's getting so eccentric."

"Hey. Come on. It's part of his charm."

"He took the mail into his office forty-five minutes ago. He said he'd be just a minute, but he's still in there and he's got patients waiting. I can't just stall them forever, you know."

"Did you buzz him?"

"I did. Twice. The first time, he picked up, growled 'Just a minute' at me and then disconnected the line. The second time he didn't even answer."

"Did you knock?"

"I tried that next. He said I should leave him alone, that he just needed a minute—and, Callie, he didn't sound right. Kind of choked up, you know? That was fifteen minutes ago. I'm starting to wonder if somebody died or something."

Well, that was alarming. "Somebody like…?"

"Oh, how would I know? One of his Vietnam war buddies? It's just a guess."

"You want me to try?"

Brandy sighed heavily and smoothed a few loose tendrils of hair back up into the strawberry-blond knot on the top of her head. "Well, I'm all out of new approaches, and that's the truth."

"I'll take care of it. You go on back to the desk."

Emmet's office was the one at the end of the hall. Callie went down there and gave the door a gentle tap.

Nothing.

Quelling her rising apprehension, she tapped again.

"In a *minute,* Brandy," came the weary-sounding reply from within.

"Emmet, it's me…" She had no clue what to say next, so she just let the words trail away.

"Callie?" He sounded more alert.

"Yes. I'm here."

"Come in here, will you?"

Ridiculously anxious as to what she was going to find on the other side of the door, Callie turned the knob. She pushed the door inward, and there was Emmet, looking perfectly fine, sitting at his desk, a sheet of paper in one hand and what looked like a check in the other.

He waved the sheet of paper at her. "Shut the door. Sit down."

She slid into one of the two guest chairs and asked gingerly, "Are you all right?"

"Yeah. I'm fine. I'm better than fine. I'm so fine, I've been sitting here for forty-five minutes asking myself if this is really happening."

"Um, something is happening?"

He handed her the paper. "Take a look at that."

It was a letter. And as soon as she read the letterhead she knew. She blinked and glanced up at him, dazed. "Brighter Horizons. Emmet. It's from Brighter Horizons!"

Emmet's angular face broke into a wide grin. "You've heard of Brighter Horizons?"

She went back to the letter again and started reading. "Everybody in town has heard of them…." And then she gasped. "Omigod. *Three hundred thousand?*"

By way of an answer, he passed her the check.

She gaped at it. "Will you look at all those zeroes?" And

then she glanced up at him again and couldn't stop herself from letting out a loud, "Wahoo!"

At which he fisted both hands and brought his elbows sharply down to his sides. "Booyah!"

And then they both started laughing like a couple of crazy people, shouting out "Wahoo!" and "Booyah!" and giving each other a series of high fives across the desk.

The door swung inward. It was Brandy, scowling. "Have you two lost it completely? Are you out of your minds?"

They both turned to stare at her and then looked back at each other, after which Emmet put on his most severe expression and said, "Brandy, you will be getting that raise you're always bugging me for."

"Right." She made a snorting sound. "Heard that one before." And then she accused, "Your patients are beyond tired of hearing me promise that you'll be right with them."

"Brandy." Still straight-faced, Emmet gestured at the other guest chair. "Come in. Sit down. We have something to show you...."

The rest of that afternoon went by in a happy haze of good feelings. Brandy carried the check to the bank and when she got back, she never stopped smiling.

The three of them took a meeting after the last patient of the day had been sent on his way. Each of them kept a long list of priority purchases, including equipment and other improvements to the clinic, improvements that they'd all three constantly doubted they would ever be able to afford. They could afford them now. It was agreed that the priority lists would be taken care of.

And then they would start on their optional lists.

Callie walked on air all the way home. She couldn't

wait to tell Nate that Brighter Horizons had come through for the clinic.

But he was cooking for her and she hoped that maybe she'd end up spending the night at his place. She wanted to freshen up a little before knocking on his door.

She went to her house first and called him.

"You're late," he grumbled.

"Sorry. Really. It's been quite a day. I want to hop in the shower, and then I'll be right over."

"Want company?"

"Don't tempt me. We'll never have dinner."

"Dinner can wait."

"Just let me get a shower."

"I think I missed you...." His voice was velvety soft.

A lovely, warm shiver went through her and she teased, "What? You're not sure?"

"I'm sure enough. Hurry."

"Don't worry, I will. I promise. I will."

Twenty minutes later, she was running up his front steps. The door swung open before she reached it, and he was there, in jeans and a soft blue Western shirt, the sleeves rolled to expose his muscular forearms. His feet were bare. They were beautiful, strong, tanned feet.

Her heart did a quick little stutter inside her chest. "Hey," she said. It came out all breathless and dreamy.

He reached out, grabbed her hand, pulled her inside and shoved the door shut. "Kiss me."

"Absolutely."

His mouth swooped down and covered hers.

It was a great kiss, a kiss that made her forget everything, even the giant check that had arrived at the clinic, even that she was holding the bottle of wine she'd brought as her contribution to dinner. She almost dropped the wine.

But he must have felt it slipping. He caught it. "Whoa," he said against her lips. He put the wine on the entry table.

And then he pulled her close again. She went eagerly, lifting her arms to twine them around his neck, kissing him back with fervor, laughing in happy excitement as he lifted her off the floor and she wrapped her legs around him, hooking her sandaled feet at the base of his spine.

Oh, she could feel him, right there at the womanly heart of her, feel the ridge of his arousal beneath the fly of his jeans. She pressed herself closer, wrapped herself tighter, kissed him even more deeply than before.

He carried her that way, with her all over him like a hot coat of paint, their mouths fused together, up the wide staircase, through a sitting area and into his bedroom.

The room was big and luxurious, with a triple-coffered ceiling, beautiful dark furniture and a turned-back bed about half the size of Kansas. He set her down beside the bed, and she blinked and looked around. "This is beautiful, Nate."

He made a low sound in his throat and got to work undressing her. After a few dazed seconds of gaping at the gorgeous room, she helped. Laughing, pausing to share quick, hungry kisses, they undressed each other. He was quicker. She barely got his shirt off, and there she was, in only her panties and little red sandals.

She kicked off the sandals, took down the panties and tossed them away. And then she grabbed his arm and pulled him to her again and kissed him while she undid his belt, whipped it off and then ripped his fly wide.

He didn't wait around for her to do the rest but just shoved down his jeans and stepped out of them. Yanking open the bedside drawer, he produced a condom, which he had out of the wrapper and rolled down over himself so fast it made her head spin.

"Callie. At last…" And he put his hand on her, splaying his fingers on her naked belly, making her groan at the wonderful heat of his touch. He moved lower, fingers seeking, through the short, dark curls at the top of her thighs and then lower still. She groaned again as those warm fingers found her. She lifted her body to him, needful of him, very wet and so ready.

He clasped her waist again. "Callie…"

"Oh, Nate…" She twined her arms and her legs around him once more as he lifted her high.

A hungry moan escaped her as he brought her carefully down onto him, filling her in the most complete and satisfying way. And then they were reeling, turning in circles, endlessly kissing, as he carried her to the other side of the room. By the door to the sitting room, he braced her gently, using the wall for extra support.

After that, it all flew away, everything but him and the pulse of their pleasure. She was free and soaring, rocking with him. And his hands were all over her, stroking, caressing. He bent his head and captured her breast and she cried out and let her head fall back against the wall.

Oh, it was so good, like nothing she'd ever known before.

Nothing careful or wary in it, no sense of otherness, not a hint of self-consciousness. They were in this together, and it was exactly, overwhelmingly right.

It went on for a glorious, fulfilling eternity. Until she hit the peak, crying out as her body contracted around him. He drank that cry right into himself as the finish took him, too.

In the end, they sagged together against the wall, his forehead to hers, both of them breathing hard and heavy as they came back to themselves. He stroked her hair, guiding it out of her eyes, tucking it behind her ear. She buried her face against his throat, breathed in the musky, hot scent of him, couldn't resist sticking out her tongue to lick the sweat off his golden skin.

He kissed her, a tender, so-sweet caress of his lips across her cheek.

And then he was gathering her even closer. She tightened her legs and arms around him as he carried her back across the room to the wide bed. He lowered her onto it with such tender care, coming down with her, gently shifting her until her head rested on the pillows. She curled into him. Content in a way she couldn't remember being before, she closed her eyes and listened as his heartbeat slowed.

After a time, he kissed her temple. "You asleep?"

"Mmf."

"Is that a yes?"

She smiled to herself. "I'm awake."

He lifted her chin and kissed the tip of her nose. "Be right back."

"No, no, please don't go…." She pretended to cling.

But of course, he only rolled away and off the bed. She lifted her head enough to watch him walk away. He did look so fine from behind—as good as he looked from the front.

And then he disappeared through the door into the master bathroom. When he came back, he gathered her nice and cozy against him again.

"Hungry?" He kissed the word into her tangled hair.

"Soon…" She braced up on an elbow, her head on her hand. "But first I have news."

His eyes were very soft, green as new grass. "Good news, I hope."

"Oh, yes. Lots of it, too. Some rather nice news. And also some exciting, fabulous news." She beamed at him.

He caught a thick lock of her hair and wrapped it around his hand the way he liked to do. "I'm waiting."

She pretended to think it over. "I think I'll tell you the rather nice news first. I had lunch with Paige today. She knows that you apologized to Sutter and Collin, and she's pretty much decided you're not so bad, after all."

"I'm happy to hear that," he said sincerely.

"I thought you would be—and now for the fabulous, unbelievably wonderful news."

"Hit me with it."

"You were right." She traced a heart onto his chest. "I should have had faith."

Now he was frowning, unwinding her hair from around his fingers. "Faith about...?"

And then she couldn't tease him any longer. "Brighter Horizons has given the clinic three hundred thousand dollars," she announced with a laugh of pure glee.

"Wow," he said. And then he grinned. "Congratulations."

She flopped back against the pillows. "Every time I think about it, I just want to dance around the room."

"Be my guest."

She giggled at the coffered ceiling. "Yeah. A naked-lady dance. That would be something."

He canted up to bend over her. "Sounds pretty good to me—especially if you're the one dancing."

"Oh, Nate." She hooked her arm around his neck, pulled him down and gave him a big, smacking kiss. When he lifted up so he could meet her eyes again, she told him, "You should've seen Emmet and me today, high-fiving each other, laughing like a couple of moonstruck fools.

Even Brandy, who's always annoyed about something, couldn't stop smiling once we told her the news. That money is needed, Nate. It's going to make a huge difference in the quality of the care we're able to provide."

"Good," he said—and only that. He said it firmly and seriously, his gaze determined. "Good."

Serious. Determined. Why should that seem strange to her?

As she asked herself that question, a weird, prickly shiver went through her. Time spun to a stop in a real, honest-to-goodness déjà vu moment, the kind that people never believed in until it happened to them.

The night of the storm, she thought.

The night of the storm, when she'd told him for the first time how much the clinic needed funds. He'd looked at her kind of strangely then, too, hadn't he? As though he was mulling over what she'd told him, coming to some kind of decision about it.

And right now, the way he'd said *Good*—approvingly, with satisfaction. As though he'd been involved somehow with the clinic getting all that money. As though this moment, this conversation, was a natural conclusion to that other one the night Faith had Tansy.

She was staring at him too sharply.

And he noticed. Suddenly, he was all smiles, faking lightheartedness for all he was worth. "It's terrific, Callie. I can hardly believe it. This is really great news."

She only kept staring at him, convinced beyond any reasonable doubt by then, absolutely positive that the money had come from him—and not knowing exactly why she was so sure.

A certain look, a tone of voice. Was that any kind of proof, really?

Maybe not.

But still. She *knew*.

"What?" he demanded, openly uneasy now.

And she couldn't think of anything else to do but just go ahead and ask him, just lay it right out there and see what he said.

"Callie, what's going on?"

And she did it. She asked him straight-out. "It's you, isn't it, Nate? *You* are Brighter Horizons."

Chapter Ten

Nate stared down into her beautiful, flushed face. She was waiting, looking at him so hopefully, *willing* him to admit it.

How in the hell had she put it together, read him so easily? Nobody else had. Everyone was talking about Brighter Horizons, trying to figure out who could be behind the trust. Not a soul in town had guessed it was him—not his parents or his brothers or the ranchers he'd known all his life, not one of the town council members he'd worked side by side with for years.

And he *had* been careful with her, hadn't he?

But apparently, not careful enough.

He didn't want her to know. Didn't want anyone to know. That was the point, for him to do what needed doing just for the sake of the doing alone. He needed to fix this situation and fix it fast.

So he opened his mouth to give her a bald-faced but sincere-sounding lie.

And before he could get a word out, she reached up, cradled his face between her cool, soft hands and said, "Don't. Please, Nate. Don't lie to me. Ever."

He thought of Zoe then. Zoe, who was nothing like Callie, at least not in looks or in her personality. Zoe, with her red hair and pale skin that couldn't take the sun. Zoe, who was shy and a little insecure.

The truth had always been Zoe's bottom line. *Just don't tell me any lies, Nathan Crawford,* she used to say. *Stick to the truth and I'm yours forever.*

And he had. He'd always told the truth to her.

He realized he wanted that with Callie now. He wanted honesty between them.

Nate lowered his head to her, kissed that sweet, soft mouth of hers. And then he breathed the truth against her lips. "Yeah. All right. Brighter Horizons is a trust I had set up. The money in the trust is mine."

She hitched in a tiny gasp. "I knew it. I just...knew it."

He kissed her again. "I don't want anyone to know. But you figured it out and I don't want to lie to you. Will you keep my secret for me?"

"Of course," she said without hesitation, her eyes huge and serious. "And...thank you, Nate. I think this whole town thanks you, even if no one but me knows that it's actually you we're so grateful to." She combed her fingers through the hair at his temple, and a chuckle escaped her. "You look embarrassed."

"I guess I am. A little." He rubbed his nose against hers, breathed in the sweet, tempting scent of her hair. "Come on. I promised to feed you. Let's get going on that."

They pulled on their clothes. Still a little stunned at what he'd revealed to her, Callie followed him down to the kitchen, detouring in the front hall to grab the bottle of wine he'd left on the table there.

He fired up the grill in back. The meal was the kind men usually cook: steak, baked potatoes and corn on the cob. She volunteered to cut up the salad.

"You grill a mean steak," she told him after the first bite of tender, juicy T-bone.

"All Crawford men know their way around a good steak." He plopped a big spoonful of sour cream onto his potato. "It's a matter of family pride."

He offered a beautiful Boston cream pie for dessert and confessed that his housekeeper, who came in twice a week to keep things tidy, had baked it at his request. Callie couldn't resist having a generous slice. It was as good as it looked.

She helped him clear off and load the dishwasher, and then they took second glasses of wine out onto the deck, where night was slowly falling. He had a wooden bench out there with a carved back and a nice, thick cushion, a long, low table in front of it.

"Sit with me." He pulled her down onto the cushion beside him and wrapped his arm around her shoulders. "Put your feet up."

She hoisted her feet up beside his on the low table and watched the shadows deepen, the stars appearing.

He told her that Laura had come by that morning. She wasn't surprised. Laura Crawford was a determined sort of person, just like her oldest son. "She wanted the details of my meeting with the Traubs—and also to gloat about you and me getting together." Callie leaned her head on his shoulder. "And then she brought up Zoe…"

Callie popped up straight again. "Wait a minute. I thought you said she never talked about your wife."

"She hasn't. Not for years. But I guess making amends

is catching. She told me she was sorry, that she should have made more of an effort to get close to Zoe, to get to know her, to make her feel welcome in the family."

"Did you…accept her apology?"

"Yeah. I did." He seemed easy about it, relaxed.

"Well." She clicked her wineglass against his. "Good for you. Good for *both* of you."

"I had a feeling you'd see it that way."

A minute or two passed. It was quiet. She heard a car go by out on the street, and a dog barked a block or two away.

She sipped her wine and broke the silence hesitantly. "About Brighter Horizons…"

He made a low sound, which she hoped was meant to be encouraging. And he still had his arm around her; he hadn't pulled away or tensed up.

So she went for it. "People want to show their gratitude."

"What are you getting at?" He narrowed his eyes at her.

"Hey." She gave him a nudge in the side. "It's okay. I said I won't tell anyone, and I won't. But have you thought that it would be better for the people you're helping if they knew who to thank?"

He grunted. "Better how? I've known most of them all my life and they are proud people. If some faceless, do-gooding foundation gives them a break, they'll take it and say a prayer of thanks. If it's me giving it to them, they owe me, no matter how hard I try to tell them that they don't. Obligation wears on a man. I don't need that from my neighbors. I'm in a position where I can give where the money's needed and let it go at that."

"But—"

He squeezed her shoulder. "You won't change my mind. Might as well stop trying."

She realized she believed him. "All right. You don't want anyone to know. I'll let that one go."

"There's more?"

"Well, I do have more questions."

"Why am I not surprised?" At least he said it in a good-natured tone. And then he leaned in closer and nuzzled her ear, catching her earlobe between his teeth, toying with it a little, making her breath tangle in her throat, sending a thrill zipping through her.

"You're distracting me."

"I like distracting you...." He whispered in the ear he'd been teasing, "What else?"

She hitched in a slow breath and pressed on. "I just... I mean, I kind of figured you must be doing okay, but I had no idea you were rich enough to donate hundreds of thousands to needy causes."

He withdrew from her then, just a little. He still had his arm around her, but he'd turned his head and now he stared out at the darkening sky. "It's a long story...."

She should probably leave it alone. But she didn't. She clasped his hand, where it rested on her shoulder. "I've got all night."

He was quiet. She let go of his hand and wondered if she'd pushed him too far. He'd clearly made up his mind about how he wanted to give his money away and he didn't seem eager to talk much about it. But then he said, "I won four hundred eighty million in the North Dakota Lottery, but I took a lump-sum payout, so I ended up with about half that."

A laugh burst out of her. "Oh, come on. You're kidding me. Back in January, you mean?"

"Uh-huh. That same day I picked you up with your gas can outside Kalispell."

"No...."

"Yeah. I bought the winning Powerball ticket at a Dickinson, North Dakota truck stop about twelve hours after you put the gas in your SUV and drove away."

She turned beneath his arm so she was facing him. Setting her wineglass on the table, she kicked off her sandals and brought her legs up to the side. "So you collected your winnings anonymously?"

"That's right. I hired a lawyer. He set up Brighter Horizons to collect the money."

She stared at him and shook her head. "Amazing."

He set his glass beside hers. "Callie, I'm no man's fool."

"I don't... What does that mean?"

"I've read about what happens to people who win the lottery, the way they kind of go crazy, the way they become the center of a media circus with everybody after them for a piece of what they've got. A lot of them get completely messed up and messed over. They end up practically throwing their winnings away."

"Well, but you..." She stopped herself.

He caught her chin. His eyes were dark, deep as oceans. "Go ahead. You can say it."

"You seem to be doing that, giving a lot of your money away."

"Believe me, what I've given away so far has hardly made a dent in what I've got." He let go of her chin and trailed the back of a finger along the side of her throat, slowly, with great care, as though he couldn't get enough of touching her. She understood the feeling. She couldn't get enough of *being* touched by *him*. "I plan to give a lot more away, as time goes on. And giving it away through the trust is not the same thing as having everyone know I've got money to burn. This way, I'm not being pressured by anybody. I can sit back and see where help is needed and give where and when *I* want to give."

"I can see how that would be wise," she had to admit.

"I've had some rough breaks in my life. And I've also lost track for a while of what really matters. I didn't want to screw up again. I didn't want all the crazy stuff that comes with winning the lottery to happen to me, you know?" At her nod, he continued, "So when I won, I did a little research and figured out what to do—hire a lawyer who could set up a trust for me and keep my name out of it. I got lucky because North Dakota is one of the six states where winners are allowed to be anonymous. Brighter Horizons claimed the money, so my name isn't even on confidential record with the state of North Dakota."

"I can't believe you could be so coolheaded about it all."

"I'm a coolheaded kind of guy."

She leaned close to him, close enough she could feel his warm breath across her cheek. "Not with me, you're not."

He didn't even bother to try and deny it. "I know. It kind of scares me, how I am with you, if you want to know the truth."

"Don't be scared. I'm not." That wasn't completely true, so she qualified, "At least, not right at the moment, anyway."

He whispered, "Stay the night."

She kissed him. "I thought you'd never ask."

They sat out there on the deck until the sky was awash in stars and the half-moon glowed bright above, like a silver lamp lighting their way.

Later in his darkened bedroom, after making slow, delicious love again, they whispered together, coming to certain agreements: not to spend *every* night together, to take this lovely thing between them more slowly, to proceed with care.

And then in the morning, he made her breakfast again before he sent her off to work. That night, they stayed at her house. And the next night, at his.

Friday night, Faith and Owen Harper had them over for barbecue. It was fun. They ate out in the Harper's backyard. The men drank beer and tended Owen's smoker barbecue. The women talked about Tansy and how Faith was getting along with all the stress of having a new baby. They also discussed the famous Montana psychic, Winona Cobbs. Lissa Roarke had invited the Cobbs woman to town to give a lecture at the new community center next month. The story went that the psychic, who lived down in Whitehorn, Montana, had contacted Lissa at the urgings of her psychic guides. Winona even had her own syndicated newspaper column, *Wisdom by Winona*.

When they sat down to dinner, they all joked about what psychic messages Winona Cobbs might be planning to deliver. And then Owen brought up the town's mysterious benefactor. He'd run into Emmet at the Ace a couple of days ago and heard that the clinic had received a big check from Brighter Horizons. Callie said how thrilled they were to have the extra funding and was careful not to look in Nate's direction lest she give him away.

They left Faith and Owen's at a little past ten and went to Callie's house. Later, after making love twice, they discussed again how they were going to give each other some space. They didn't need to rush this thing between them. Nate still hadn't decided whether or not he was leaving town. And Callie didn't think she was ready for anything permanent with a man, anyway. They were going to take it slow.

And then the next morning, he made them breakfast as usual, and they spent the day out at the Shooting Star Ranch. Jesse picked out a sweet-natured, patient mare for Callie to ride. Nate chose his favorite gray gelding. They rode for hours, just Callie and Nate, stopping for a picnic way out at the edge of the property in a field of wildflowers beneath the skimpy shadows of some box-elder trees. While the horses munched the summer grass nearby, Nate and Callie canoodled like a couple of teenagers. Later, as they rode back to town, they decided they needed to get busy on the whole giving-each-other-some-space thing.

So when they arrived at home, he went to his house and she went to hers. After all, they were going to be together again the next day for Sunday dinner at his mom's house. They were certainly due a night apart.

Callie made herself a light meal and then tried not to wonder what Nate might be doing. She hadn't called either of her best girlfriends back in Chicago in a while, so she picked up the phone. One of the two, Janie Potter, was at home. They talked for half an hour. Janie asked Callie's advice on some problems she was having at work and Callie tried not to talk too much about Nate.

But Janie wasn't fooled. "You're gone on this cowboy, huh? Good for you."

"Well, I'm trying not to be *too* gone, you know?"

"Why? You like him. He likes you. Enjoy yourselves."

"He might not even be staying in town."

"So? All the more reason to spend every minute you can with him."

"He was married before. His wife died. He hasn't been serious about anyone in the ten years since he lost her."

"Which proves the guy is truehearted, a keeper."

"You think?"

"Callie. Come on. Life is too short. If you like the guy, *be* with him."

They talked a little longer and when they said goodbye, Callie couldn't stop thinking about what Janie had said.

Who knew how long she and Nate might have together? And why *should* they waste a single moment?

Before she could talk herself out of it, she was out the

front door, down the walk and on her way up the steps to Nate's house. She couldn't see any lights on inside, but she rang the bell, anyway.

And then she tried not to be too disappointed when he didn't answer. Evidently, he'd gone out.

Which was great. Wonderful. The guy deserved a little time to himself, for crying out loud. She was not going to be disappointed about it. She was not going to wonder what Nate might be doing now....

In Rust Creek Falls, if you wanted a little Saturday-night fun, the Ace was the place.

Nate stood at the bar, facing out, nursing a beer, not having any fun at all. Mostly, he was just trying not to think about Callie, not to wish for her there beside him—or better yet—for the two of them to be at home together. Maybe sitting out on the deck, watching the stars come out, or in her cozy kitchen, raiding the fridge.

Or in bed.

In bed with Callie. His bed or hers, he couldn't think of any better place to be.

But the space thing was important. He supposed. She deserved a little time to herself now and then. So he was giving it to her, trying to be a sensitive and understanding kind of guy.

He gave the crowded room a slow scan, nodding whenever he made eye contact with someone he knew. A pretty, black-haired girl down at the end of the bar shot him a big smile. He tipped his hat in her direction to be polite, then looked away. Leaning his elbows on the bar, he stared into the middle distance and wondered what Callie was doing about now.

"Hey, cowboy," said a soft voice at his elbow.

He looked over. Sure enough, the black-haired girl. She

put her hand on his arm and he glanced down at it and back into her big baby blues.

"Whoa," she said. "Taken, huh?"

Taken? Was he? "Sorry." He left it at that.

She shrugged and tried the guy on her other side.

He finished his beer, turned around to put his money on the bar and was just about to get the hell out of there when Collin Traub appeared on one side of him and Sutter on the other. The hairs on the back of his neck stood up.

But then he remembered that he had made peace with them, more or less. Which made it unlikely that they'd surrounded him in order to start a fight.

"Hey, boys." He tipped his hat at them.

"We were just talking about you," said Sutter.

"Should I be worried?"

Collin laughed. "Maybe."

"I don't know if I like the sound of that."

Sutter clapped him on the back. "Let's see if our favorite booth is available—three longnecks, Larry," he added over his shoulder to the bartender.

Nate wasn't sure why he followed them into the back room. It didn't seem like a very good idea, but he was trying to be cordial with them. What good did it do for a guy to humble himself apologizing and then act like a jerk the next time he ran into the men he had wronged?

Wouldn't you know, even with the Ace full of customers, that booth stood empty.

As before, Nate took one side and the Traub brothers the other. A waitress appeared and plunked down three beers. They tapped bottles and drank.

Sutter said, "Heard you been seeing Callie Kennedy."

"I am, yes."

"Everyone likes Callie," said Collin, as if that was news. Then he warned, "You treat her right." Which was kind of ironic if you thought about it, coming from a man who'd spent his first twenty-five years or so breaking every heart in sight.

"I'll do that," Nate replied, after reminding himself that he was trying to be a better man and being a better man meant making an effort not to take offense at the insulting things other men might say.

"Willa's over at our place with Paige," Sutter explained. "They're working on some summer-school project or other. Paige isn't teaching summer school this year, with the baby coming so soon and all, but she loves to help out when she can."

"They told us to go get a beer," Collin added. "They don't like us in their hair when they're doing crafty stuff."

Nate wasn't following. "Uh, crafty?"

Sutter clarified, "You know, craft projects. Things with colored paper and glue and glitter and rickrack."

"Ah," replied Nate, as if it all made sense to him now, though it really didn't.

Collin said, "So, we came to get a beer and we were talking about the resort project—and here you are, the main guy."

"Er, the main guy for…?"

"The resort project," Sutter said, as though it was completely self-evident.

It didn't seem self-evident to Nate. "Ahem. I'm not the main guy. I said I would be happy to put some money in, but—"

"Well, see, Nate, this is the deal," Collin cut in. "We need someone to spearhead this thing, get it off the ground, you know? And who better than you? I mean, you know people. You got the education and the background and the connections to get something like this moving."

"Oh, come on. I don't know anyone you don't know.

And I've never been in the hospitality industry. I told you I know nothing about building or running a resort."

Sutter shrugged. "You can learn."

"We'll get you hooked up with an expert, Grant Clifton," added Collin. "Grant is the genius behind the Thunder Canyon Resort. He can fill you in on anything you need to know."

"But I may not stay in town and—"

Sutter didn't let him finish. "It shouldn't take that long. We're thinking we start out kind of modest, some kind of really nice vacation lodge but on some prime, scenic acreage with the potential for a ski run and great riding trails, with a river or a creek running through it, for rafting and fishing. Then you can build onto the lodge later, add condos, whatever. Eventually it could be a year-round destination. The thing is to get the right property and get the whole thing moving, get the first stage done this year."

"This year?" Nate narrowed his eyes at the other two. "Wait. This is a joke, right? You're yanking my chain."

Collin frowned. "The hell we are." His eyes got that look, the one he always got prior to throwing the first punch. "You think it's funny, that we want to get this project moving?"

For the second time that night, Nate felt certain a brawl was in the offing. And he didn't want that. He wanted peace with the Traubs. He wished he'd never come to the Ace that night. And he *shouldn't* have come, *wouldn't* have come. If not for the damn space issue, he would be home in Callie's arms.

He put up both hands and got to work backpedaling. "I didn't say I thought it was funny. I just think it's impossible and I thought you were joking with me."

"Oh." Collin thought that over. When he spoke again,

his tone had turned mild. "Well, no. Not joking." Then he added with enthusiasm, "And *anything* is possible."

"I'm not arguing with you, I'm only—"

"Yeah," Sutter cut in. "You're arguing with us."

Nate insisted, "But it would be impossible to get this... this lodge opened by Christmas."

"Nothing's impossible," Collin decreed. "You just need the right attitude. And yeah, okay. It's kind of shooting for the moon, but why not?"

"That's right," put in Sutter. "Why not aim for the stars? And right now, you're not running the ranch anymore. It's great that you help out at the family store, but your folks and Nina do most of the work there. You're not in town government. You got your investments to live off of and plenty of time on your hands. It's perfect. You're in a position to take this project on and give it your all."

"But I don't want to take this project on."

"I think you do," Collin piped right up.

"I don't."

"Nate." Collin shook his head. "Come on now. Think about it. Rust Creek Falls needs this. You and me, we've had our differences, but we both love our town. We both want the best for the folks who live here. You spearhead this project. Even if you end up leaving, you know you want to leave your town better and stronger than you found it. This resort project is a way for you to do just that."

Nate gaped at the man he'd hated for so much of his life. "How do you do that?"

"Do what?"

"Tell me all the reasons I want to build a resort when I've told you repeatedly that I don't."

Sutter elbowed Collin in the ribs and proudly announced, "He's a born politician."

Nate had to hand it to him. "He is, indeed."

Collin beamed. "So, then. Say you'll do it."

No way was he saying that. But he did want to be on good terms with them—and that meant a flat-out no right now wouldn't fly. He decided his best option was to stall them until he could figure out a way to let them down easy. "I need some time to think this over."

Collin winced. "Not a great idea, being as how time's the thing we're short on."

"I still have to think about it."

"For how long?" Sutter asked grudgingly.

Maybe he could find someone to step in and get the project off the ground. And he was willing to put in some serious cash. He had to find a way to back out of actually running things—but do it gracefully so he could preserve the goodwill he'd humbled himself to achieve. "Until the end of the month. On August first, I'll tell you exactly what I'm willing to do."

"That's three weeks!" Collin blustered. "We don't *have* three weeks."

"Sorry. Best I can do."

Sutter frowned. "You don't look very sorry."

"Oh, come on. Remember, anything is possible. What's three extra weeks when you're shooting for the stars?"

Collin grunted. "Now you're yankin' *our* chain. But, hey. All right. Three weeks, and then you tell us yes and get to work."

"I don't think that's exactly what I said."

Sutter chuckled. "Yeah, but see, the thing you don't re-alize yet is that you *are* going to do this."

"No, I didn't say that I would."

Collin grinned. Slowly. "Last Monday, we got you to agree to invest. Today, you're considering spearheading the project. We are moving in the right direction here. Be-cause we keep a positive attitude."

* * *

About ten minutes later, the Traubs got up to go. Nate walked out with them. They shook hands in the parking lot. And Nate got in his quad cab and headed for home.

As he pulled into his driveway, he just happened to notice that the porch light was on at Callie's. He didn't see any other lights on, though, and it was full dark by then.

Maybe she was back in the kitchen. Or in the master bathroom, also in the back of the house, next to the kitchen. She might be having a bath.

Now, there was an image to torture a man. Callie in the bathtub, enjoying her space, her hair all pinned up on her head, but bits of it tumbling loose to curl along her flushed, wet cheeks. She'd have fat candles burning, making her smooth skin glow. And bubbles, wouldn't she? Little bath bubbles clinging and dripping between her breasts, down her thigh and along the perfect curve of her calf when she raised her leg out of the water to give it a nice going-over with one of those loofah things women liked to use.

He parked the quad cab and pointed the door opener over his shoulder to bring the garage door rumbling down. And then he just sat there, staring blankly through the windshield, wondering if Callie was even home.

Probably not. She could be anywhere. She had a lot of friends. Maybe she'd gone into Kalispell to catch a movie.

Not that it was any of his damn business where she'd got off to. He had no chains on her. They were giving each other space tonight, and the woman had a right to enjoy her space any damn way she chose.

And why was he sitting here in the garage staring at the wall?

He seriously needed to get a grip.

Muttering bad words under his breath, he got out of the pickup and went inside. And then, when he got there, he somehow couldn't stop himself from going right on through the laundry room into the kitchen and out the back door.

No lights on in her kitchen. There might be a light on in the bathroom, but it was on the other side of the kitchen and he couldn't really tell.

So maybe she was in there, with the bubbles and the loofah.

Or maybe not.

And either way, it was none of his business.

So, then, why was he turning, yanking open the back door, striding fast through the kitchen and the central hall? Because he was an idiot, that's why.

An idiot who just kept going, out the front door, down the steps, over to her house and right up to her front door. An idiot who rang the doorbell and then waited, hoping against hope that she might be there, not really believing that she was.

Nothing happened. She wasn't there. He needed to turn around and get back to his house, where he belonged.

But then he only lifted his hand again and punched the doorbell a second time.

Nothing.

She wasn't there and he was hopeless. He needed to leave it alone. He turned for the steps again.

And right then, the door swung inward.

Chapter Eleven

"Nate." She said it softly, with a glowing, pleased smile.

He took in the short, silky robe and the bare feet and the hair piled up just the way he'd pictured it, her skin all flushed and moist. "Tell me to go," he commanded in a growl. "Tell me to get lost and give you your space, like I promised I would."

She just went on smiling, shaking her head—and then stepping back and gesturing him inside. He couldn't clear that threshold fast enough. She shut the door. She smelled of flowers and oranges and all manner of sweet, wonderful things. And steamy, too.

He fisted his hands at his sides in order not to reach for her. "I don't know what's wrong with me."

She went on tiptoe and kissed him—a sweet, quick brush of a kiss. He had to fist his hands harder because he really, really wanted to haul her tight against him.

"It's okay." She smoothed the collar of his shirt. "I

missed you, too. I went to your house but you weren't there."

"I went for a beer at the Ace. I was trying to stop thinking about how I wanted to be with you. Sutter and Collin cornered me. Now they've decided I should not only invest in their crazy resort project, I should run it."

She laughed then. And then, with a soft sigh, she rested her head against his shoulder. "What did you tell them?"

He dared to wrap his arms around her, slowly. With care. It felt so good to hold her. "I put them off, said I'd have to think about it."

She tipped her head back and looked up at him, dark eyes bright as stars. "You don't want to do it?"

"What do I know about building a resort? And they want it done by Christmas. It's completely insane."

"You might enjoy it. It would be a challenge for you."

He groaned. "I might enjoy piloting a spaceship. Or performing open-heart surgery. That doesn't mean I'm an astronaut or a surgeon."

"It's not the same. You wouldn't be building the thing yourself. You could get advice from experts, hire an architect and a builder. And I know you've got the vision and the brains to make it happen."

He kissed the tip of her nose. "You're worse than the Traubs. I can't afford to be pinned down with something like that."

Those bright eyes dimmed just a little. "Oh. Right. Because you need to be free to leave town any day now...."

He thought about that, about leaving her, and doubted he could do it. But something within him still couldn't quite admit that. "I'm a jerk, huh? And you're mad at me now."

She gave him the sweetest, saddest little smile. "Why should I beat you up? You're doing such a fine job of it all on your own."

He pulled her closer, breathed her in and whispered, "Since Monday..."

"What about it?"

"Monday was our first night together."

"Right." She gave a little nod.

He confessed, "Five days of you and me. And already I can't see myself ever leaving you."

She tucked her head beneath his chin, fitting herself against him as though she was born to be there. "Hold that thought." And then she reached around behind her and captured his hand. "Come on. Let's go to bed."

He pressed his lips into the fragrant silk of her hair. "I get to stay?"

"Of course."

"I really like the way you say that." It came out gruff and ragged, freighted with emotions he'd never thought to feel again.

She turned, unwrapping herself from his arms but keeping a firm hold of his hand. "This way...."

The door to her bedroom was right there, off the entry. He followed her in.

She led him to the bed, which was turned back to reveal soft sheets printed with flowers. "Sit down." He did. She knelt and pulled off his boots and his socks. "Stand up again." He rose. And she unbuttoned and unzipped and took the rest of his clothes away. "There." She stood back to admire her handiwork. Her eyes were dark velvet. "Oh, Nate..."

He just wanted her naked. Naked in his arms. "Take off the robe." He said it much too roughly.

But she didn't argue or even seem to mind that his tone wasn't as gentle as it should have been. She simply untied the belt, slipped it off and stuck it into the pocket. Then she peeled back the sides of the robe and eased it down her shoulders. It floated to the floor.

And there she was, all womanly curves, velvet skin, with that long, softly curling silky hair he loved to wrap around his hand.

"Callie…" It felt so good it hurt, just to say her name.

"Yes, Nate?"

"Come here."

It was only one step and she took it. He pulled her close and then he guided her down to the bed.

The rest was all he wanted and more than he'd ever hoped for. Her hair, her scent, her skin surrounded him. She made all the lonely years fade to nothing. She was all the answers to the questions a man didn't even have the sense to ask.

And later, when she turned off the light and he tucked her in spoon-style, her back to his front, when he wrapped his arm around her to hold her close to his body through the night, he thought that here, with her, was where he wanted to be.

For now.

And forever.

But he didn't say so. Forever was a mighty big word and a man had to choose just the right time to say it.

The next night was dinner at his parents' house. His brothers and sisters were all there, even Nina, with Dallas and baby Noelle and the boys.

His mom served her famous fried chicken and mashed potatoes, beans with bacon, and apple pie for dessert. She and his dad beamed at each other from either end of the long family table, to have their whole family together for a Sunday-night meal.

Callie fit right in, as Nate had known she would. She

chatted with Nina and Natalie and spent a lot of time holding baby Noelle. His mom got her alone in the kitchen for
a few minutes.

Later, at his house, Nate asked her what his mom had
said.

"Just that she thinks we look good together and she
hopes I'll come to Sunday dinner again."

"Will you?" He couldn't stop himself from asking.

She put her hand on his chest, right over his heart. "Anytime you ask me to."

"She doesn't make you crazy?"

"Your mother? No way."

The days took on a satisfying rhythm. Weekday mornings, Nate cooked breakfast and saw her off to work. They
might sleep at his house or hers—but they always slept
together.

They let the whole "space" issue take care of itself. She
went out on a Tuesday evening with her newcomer girlfriends. And the following Saturday afternoon, she went
to a baby shower for Paige.

He had his own independent routines. He helped out
at the store, had weekly meetings with Saul in Kalispell,
trying to decide which business investments to put money
in. And when his brothers needed him, he pitched in at the
Shooting Star. He and Callie might be apart all day and all
evening. But from bedtime on, it was always the two of
them. And she seemed to like it that way as much as he did.

They didn't speak of the future. But he thought about
it a lot, thought about how well they got on together, how
he never wanted what they had together to end.

He thought about the things he'd never planned to think
about again: wedding rings and the two of them standing

up before a preacher. About which house they would live in if they made it official.

About the good years ahead of them, building a life.

About children.

After what had happened to Zoe and the baby, thinking about children scared the crap out of him. He'd never planned to get married again. He'd told himself he couldn't do that after what had happened. He would never marry, never have a kid. His wife and son had died. End of story.

Except that now there was Callie. And she was so very much alive. And he was thinking on forever, thinking of the ways to give her everything she wanted.

And if a baby was what she wanted, well, maybe he could even do that. For her sake. Maybe...

On the last Saturday in July, the Traub family was planning a big barbecue out at the Traub ranch, the Triple T. On the Tuesday before the barbecue, Nina asked him to come to it. Then on Wednesday, Paige invited Callie. And then on Thursday, he got a call from Collin of all people.

"Grant Clifton's coming up from Thunder Canyon for the barbecue on Saturday," Collin said. "You'll have all your questions answered."

Grant Clifton. The name was vaguely familiar. Nate asked, "All my questions about...?"

Collin laughed. "You don't remember? Grant Clifton runs the Thunder Canyon Resort."

He remembered then. Unfortunately. "Ah."

"August first is right around the corner." Collin sounded way too pleased about that. "See you Saturday."

Nate hung up and felt guilty, which thoroughly pissed him off. He'd never wanted anything to do with the resort project. Yet somehow the Traub brothers had messed with his mind until he'd started to feel responsible for it. How in hell had they managed that?

He drove over to Kalispell for a quick meeting with Saul. Saul thought the resort was a fine idea—or could be, if Nate got the right team together. Nate was in a good position to get into something like that, Saul said, because he had access to plenty of capital. He wouldn't go under if it took a while for the project to pay off—and hospitality businesses were notorious for taking a long time to turn a profit. Nate drove back to Rust Creek Falls no closer to knowing what to do about the resort project than he'd ever been and muttering bad things about the Traub brothers under his breath.

Saturday, he and Callie headed for the Triple T at two in the afternoon. The barbecue was set up in a pretty spot not far from the barns and the houses owned by various members of the family. They'd put up several canopies for shade and five long picnic tables to accommodate the crowd. There were kids running everywhere, grills and smokers going, beer and soft drinks in coolers and plenty of folding chairs, so you could sit down and visit whenever the mood struck.

Nate got a beer and stuck close to Callie. She wore tight jeans and a little red T-shirt, those red boots and her red hat. What man wouldn't want to stand at her side?

But then Paige and Willa, Collin's wife, grabbed her and took her away with them to do whatever women did at gatherings like this one. He went looking for Dallas and Nina, thinking he'd visit with them for a while, kid around with Dallas's three boys and spend a little quality time with baby Noelle.

He'd just spotted them under one of the canopies when Collin appeared at his side. "Nate. There you are."

"Nice day for a barbecue." That was Sutter. On his other side.

"Come on," said Collin. "We'll introduce you to Grant."

Nate surrendered to the inevitable. The brothers took him over to a shady spot under a maple tree where a tall, blue-eyed man in his late thirties stood with a pretty green-eyed blonde.

Collin made the introductions. "Nate Crawford, Stephanie and Grant Clifton."

Nate shook hands with Grant and told Stephanie how pleased he was to meet her. Sutter went off and came back with folding chairs, so they all sat in a ring under the tree. There was chitchat about life in Thunder Canyon, about how much Grant was enjoying his first visit to Rust Creek Falls.

Eventually, Collin guided the conversation around to Grant's work at the Thunder Canyon Resort. Grant talked easily, comfortably. About everything from startup costs and property acquisition, to staff hiring and training, marketing and advertising, operations, growth projections and ongoing management. Nate found the conversation fascinating and had to remind himself more than once that he was supposed to be coming up with a way to get *out* of this crazy project—not allow himself to be drawn in deeper and deeper.

When Collin mentioned that they wanted to get the resort up and running by the holidays, Grant did a double take that had Nate biting his lip to keep from laughing. "Now, there's a real challenge for you," Clifton said at last. "Best of luck, boys."

"No law says we can't try," Sutter put in.

Clifton agreed that there was nothing wrong with setting a challenging goal. He promised to make himself available for future consultation as the project moved forward.

About then, Bob Traub, Collin and Sutter's dad, rang the bell to get everyone to start moving toward the tables.

Collin said, "Let's eat." He took over, herding them toward a table under a canopy where Willa, Paige and Callie were already seated.

Callie looked up and grinned at him as he took the chair beside her—and right then, at that exact moment, as her shining eyes locked with his, it happened.

Everything changed. Right then, as he started to sit down beside her under that canopy at the Traub family barbecue, Nate Crawford knew the whole truth at last.

He knew it from the crown of his hat to the toes of his tooled dress boots, in his stubborn head, as well as his yearning heart. There were no more maybes. No more hesitations. No more need to keep thinking things over.

The simple, perfect, undeniable truth was that he loved her. He loved her and he wanted a life with her.

And he was a jackass, and a fool one at that, to keep holding on to the idea that he might leave town. He was never leaving Rust Creek Falls. He wasn't going anywhere that she didn't want to be.

A breeze lifted the long waves of her hair beneath that red hat. She tipped her head sideways and gave him a look both tender and questioning.

He opened his mouth to say it, right then and there, in front of God and the Traubs and everyone.

But before he got the words out, Paige Traub let out a cry and shot to her feet. "Something's…" She let out another shocked, guttural sound. Her body curved over her giant belly. Her face was so red it looked purple, eyes bulging, the veins in her neck standing out in sharp relief. She clutched for Sutter, who had jumped to his feet beside her. "Sutter, oh, no…." Kicking her chair away, she staggered back, groaning some more, her hand, fingers splayed, supporting the heavy weight of her belly. Fluid thick with green streaks ran down between her legs below the hem of the denim maternity dress she wore.

Sutter barely managed to catch her as she crumpled toward the ground.

Chapter Twelve

Sutter scooped Paige up and headed for the nearest house.

"Callie!" Paige cried. "I need Callie…."

"I'm here," Callie promised. She gave Nate's hand a squeeze and followed.

The house was Dallas and Nina's place. Nate watched as Nina rose from the table several yards away. She gave Noelle to Dallas and raced for the house, too, probably to see if there was anything she could do to help.

Nate stayed with the others. Nobody ate. They all just sat there, waiting, praying, whispering quietly to each other. Even the children were subdued.

Nate didn't talk to anyone. He just waited. Collin said something to him at one point, something meant to reassure—Nate knew that by the gentle tone of Collin's voice. Nate turned to him and stared at him blankly. Had Collin heard about Zoe and how he'd lost her? Nate had no idea. And he certainly wasn't about to discuss it now. He couldn't even make his mouth form words.

He only kept seeing Paige, crumpling to the ground, clutching her big belly, that green-streaked water running down her legs. He only kept remembering Zoe. His lost Zoe. And the little boy they named Logan, who never drew a single breath.

Meconium. That was the green stuff, they told Nate later. Logan had experienced fetal distress. He'd aspirated meconium, breathed it in, gasping for air that wasn't there, trying to be born and not making it.

Never making it…

Nate closed his eyes. As if that could help him blot out the memories, blot out his failure all those years ago. Blot out his wrong choices, that had led to the worst conceivable outcome.

Blot out the horrible possibility that what had happened to Zoe and Logan might be happening in Nina's house to Paige and her baby, too.

He didn't know how long he sat there. It couldn't have been all that long before he heard the siren. The ambulance came speeding down the long road from the highway, kicking up a high trail of dust in its wake. It stopped in front of Nina's house and the EMTs went in with a stretcher.

They emerged a few minutes later, carrying Paige, who had Sutter on one side and Callie on the other, Nina trailing behind. Even from way over at the table where he sat, Nate could see the way Paige clung to Sutter, could hear her cry out that she wanted her nurse practitioner and her husband with her in the ambulance.

They put her in the back. Sutter spoke to Callie briefly. She nodded, patted his arm. And then he went around and got in with the driver.

Callie and Nina turned and came toward the silent people clustered at the tables. Nate stood up then, without even realizing he was doing it. One second, he was sitting there staring, and the next, he was on his feet. Callie came to him. She wrapped her arms around him.

He looked down numbly at her bare head. She must have left the red hat in the house.

And then she looked up at him. Her eyes were so dark, full of worry. "Come on. I need you to take me to the hospital."

Some of them, including Nina, stayed behind to look after the children. But everyone else formed a caravan and headed for the hospital in Kalispell.

The short drive seemed to take forever. Callie didn't say much. That was fine with him. He didn't know what to say, anyway. Everything seemed way too clear to him now.

Clear in the most final kind of way.

At the hospital, there were so many of them, they overran the waiting room. There weren't enough chairs for all of them, so they stood around, silent as they'd been back at the ranch. Waiting for word.

Callie stayed with Nate. They stood near a wall with a framed picture of a mother holding a laughing, healthy baby. Nate looked at that picture once.

And never again.

Some Daltons showed up—one of Paige's sisters and her mom and dad, Mary and Ben.

Eventually, Sutter came out looking a decade older than he had just an hour before. Everyone stood to attention.

Sutter went to Paige's mom and whispered something. Mary Dalton nodded. Then he looked toward where Callie and Nate stood by the wall. "Callie," he said. "She's asking for you. They said it's okay if you come."

So Callie went with him.

When the two of them had disappeared down the long hallway and through the double doors at the end, Paige's mom told them all that the baby and Paige were hanging in there and there would be a cesarean.

Hanging in there, Nate thought. What did that *mean,* really? It was one of those things people said when it would be too big of a lie to say everything was all right.

They waited some more.

After a while, Nate went and got some awful coffee from a vending machine and drank it—not because he wanted it, but because it was something to do to help pass the time that seemed to crawl by at the speed of a dying snail.

Finally, a woman in green scrubs with a surgery mask hanging around her neck came out of the double doors. She asked for Mary and Ben Dalton. When they stood up, she said she was Dr. Lovell. She said the surgery had been a success and that the baby and Paige were going to be all right.

She led Paige's parents away to see their daughter and have a look at their new grandson.

After that, everyone started talking excitedly, shaking hands and clapping each other on the back. They hugged each other; they cried happy tears.

Nate sank slowly onto a chair. Through the numbness that seemed to enclose him, he was vaguely aware of a feeling of relief.

They made it, he thought. *Paige and the baby will be all right.*

He was glad for them. So glad. Glad for Sutter and all the Traubs. And the Daltons, as well.

Collin, grinning widely, said something to him and clapped a hand on his shoulder. He looked up and replied, nodding, forcing a smile, hardly knowing what words he said.

Now that the danger was passed, people started leaving. Nate stayed in the chair, waiting for Callie, who would need him to take her home.

Eventually, she emerged from the long hallway. She stopped and spoke to the people who were left, telling Collin and Willa that Paige was a trouper, that the baby, little Carter Benjamin, was breathing on his own and doing well.

Nate stood when she finally came to him. He thought that she was so very fine, beautiful inside and out. Everything he could have wanted.

She took his hand. "Let's go home."

He got up and they got out of there.

She didn't say much on the way back to town. That was fine with him. He didn't know what to say, anyway. He kept remembering that moment at the table before everything went wrong, that moment when he knew that his heart was hers and there was no going back.

That moment seemed a million years ago now. He couldn't find that moment again, couldn't be the man who knew the way to make a life with her.

He didn't love her any less.

He only knew that he couldn't.

Just couldn't.

And that was all.

Something was very wrong with Nate. Callie knew it in her bones.

She understood that what had happened to Paige had affected him deeply, and she understood why. Because he'd told her. In detail. The night that Faith Harper had given birth to little Tansy.

What she didn't know was what to do about it, how to reach him—or even when she ought to try. Sometimes the wisest thing in a situation like this was to leave it alone for a while.

She decided to do that. To give Nate a chance to work through his reaction to the events of the day for himself.

They were halfway home when it started raining, fat drops splattering against the windshield, the wind rising, lightning forking twice across the sky, followed by two long, deep rolls of thunder.

When they got to South Pine Street, she half expected him to say he wanted some time alone. But he surprised her and went to her house with her. The rain drummed on the windows as they threw together some sandwiches, watched TV for a little while, sitting on her sofa, not saying a word. She took his hand twice. Both times he accepted her touch and let his hand rest in hers. But then, within a few minutes, he gently withdrew.

At a little after ten, his cell rang. He got it out of his pocket and checked the display. "It's my mom. She'll want to know about Paige. Would you...deal with her?"

So Callie took the phone and told Laura what had happened. At the end, Laura asked, "Nate?"

"He's right here." She tried a smile for him. But he only jumped up from the sofa and backed away, shaking his head at her. So she told Laura he was busy and would give her a call later.

Laura said, "Is he okay?"

Callie hardly knew how to answer that. "He's... Well, it's been a rough day."

"Take care of him, honey," his mother said softly.

"I will. I promise." She said goodbye.

Nate stood in front of the dark fireplace and stared at her. She watched him, not knowing what to say, until he demanded, "What?"

And she couldn't just go on pretending that nothing was wrong. "Your mother asked if you were all right."

"So?"

"You heard what I told her. We both know it was an evasion. You are not all right."

He waved a hand. "Look. Don't get on me."

"Nate, I'm not getting on you. I just think it would be better, you know, if you talked about it. If you told me what's eating at you."

He put up both hands then, as if she held a gun to him. "Look."

She waited for him to say something more. He stared at her through haunted eyes, slowly lowering his hands until they hung at his sides.

Finally, he spoke again. "Callie." Her name seemed dredged up from somewhere way down deep inside of him. "I...I've really screwed up and I'm so damn sorry. I can't do this, you know? I can't go on and do this anymore."

She gaped at him, her throat clutching, her stomach sinking. "I don't... What do you mean, Nate? What are you telling me?"

He raised his arms again, raked both hands back through his hair. "I thought that I...that we could..." Again he let his hands drop. And this time he drew his broad shoulders back and faced her squarely. "I have to go. I have to let *you* go. This isn't right. You are so fine, so good. So true. You deserve everything, all the best from a good, solid man. I'm not the one for you. You saw what happened to Paige today."

Slowly, she rose. "Nate. Come on. Paige came through okay. The baby is going to be all right. This isn't ten years ago. What happened to Zoe *does* happen. But not very often if there's medical help available." She went to him.

He watched her, warily. "Fine. Right. I know that. But I can't... What if it *did* happen to you? What if we had a baby and it happened to you?"

"It's not going to happen to me." She reached up, brushed her hand along his beard-rough cheek.

He caught her wrist and carefully put it away from him. "You don't know that. You can never know that. Not for sure. You just can't."

She didn't know what else to do, how to get through to him, so she just went ahead and told him what she'd been holding back while she waited for him to admit to her that he loved this town and he loved her, that all his talk about moving away was just that: talk and nothing more. "I love you, Nate. I love you with all my heart."

He winced as if she'd struck him. "Don't love me. Don't."

"Too late. I love you. That's how it is." She let out a sad little laugh. "I used to be afraid that Zoe would always stand between us. But I'm not afraid of that anymore. I know that you loved her, and I'm glad that you did. I know she would want, above all, for you to be happy. And you *can* be happy. I promise you can, if you'll only allow yourself to be."

"Don't."

"I know what's in your heart, Nate. I know that you love me, too." She took his hand, laid it above her breast. "Here. I know it here."

Something flared in those shadowed eyes. For a moment, she dared to hope he would grab her close and tight, that he would confess that she was absolutely right, he loved her, too.

And then he did reach for her. She let out a cry of pure joy as his arms closed hard around her. She felt his lips against her throat, heard the rough groan he couldn't suppress. She knew that it would be all right.

Until he muttered, harsh and low, "I'm sorry, Callie. So

damn sorry for what a complete jerk I am, for the way I'm letting you down. But it's over."

She shoved back from him and gripped his shoulders, gave him a shake to bring him back to his senses. "No. No, that's not true."

"It is. And I have to go." He lifted his hands, took hold of hers and, gently, tenderly, pushed her away.

"Go?" She stared at him as he circled around her and headed for the front door. "Go where?"

He took his hat off the peg. "Hell if I know." Then he opened the door and stepped out into the storm.

Nate was wet to the skin by the time he mounted his front porch steps.

He didn't care. He just knew it was time.

Time to go. As he'd gone from Zoe and Logan's funeral ten years back—driving and driving until he had to stop. Getting away, staying on the move, from one state to another. Trying to forget. Trying to put his love and his hope behind him, trying to outrun a loss so deep it hollowed him out right down to the core of him.

He let himself in the house and went straight up the stairs to his bedroom. He got his big suitcase from the closet and piled some clothes in it. Then he moved on to the bathroom, where he grabbed his shaving gear and stuck it into the zippered leather case he kept under the sink. That went in the suitcase, too. He zipped the damn thing closed, grabbed it by the handle and went out of the bedroom, down the stairs, to the kitchen and out into the garage through the laundry room. He tossed the suitcase into the back of the quad cab and climbed in behind the wheel.

No, he had no clue where he was going. He only knew it was time—past time—to leave. To get away from home, from Callie, from everything and everyone who mattered to him.

He backed out of the driveway, sent the garage door rumbling down, turned the wipers on high and got out of there.

It was a hell of a rainstorm, almost as bad as the one the night Faith Harper had her baby. Lightning fired up the sky and thunder boomed. The wipers could hardly keep up with the sheer volume of water pouring down.

He was careful. He watched the road and kept his speed under control—not so much because he gave a damn what might happen to him, but because he didn't want to endanger anyone else who might be out in the storm.

Almost to Kalispell, he saw a flash of movement at the side of the road.

A deer. It kept coming, bolting across the highway, directly in front of him. He swerved to miss it—and must have hit a slick spot. The truck started spinning like those whirlybird firecrackers on the Fourth of July. Nate worked the wheel, trying to give it play and steer into the slide as he spun across the center line all the way over to the opposite shoulder of the road.

A big tree loomed in the windshield. There was no steering free of that. He squinted at the sudden wash of hard brightness, the reflection of his headlights on the tree trunk right before impact. A tire exploded. Metal screamed and screeched.

And then nothing.

When he came to himself again, he had a face full of air bag. It hurt, as though someone had whacked him in the mouth with a dead fish. For a moment, he just sat there, listening to the sighs of twisted metal and the wheezing of the wrecked engine.

Then he pushed the air bag aside, unhooked his seat belt and tried the door.

Wonder of wonders, it opened with only a loud creaking sound of complaint.

He got out. And then he bent at the knees and took a moment to wait for his breath to come even, his heart to stop trying to beat its way out of his chest.

The rain was still coming down, not as hard as before but damn hard enough. He'd lost his hat. It was probably in the backseat with his suitcase somewhere. Water ran down his forehead and into his mouth.

When he finally stood straight, he saw pretty much what he'd expected to see. The good news? The deer had gotten away. His pickup? Totaled. The front of it was wrapped nice and cozy around the tree, one headlight still beaming, its light canted crazily toward the sky.

It took him a minute longer to register where he was.

The rain came down, and a shiver worked its way up the back of his neck, a shiver that had nothing at all to do with cold. Beyond the tree that had eaten his pickup, he saw the fence with the For Sale sign on it. Beyond the fence, that thicket of new-growth ponderosa pines. And farther out, in the distance, on a high point looming into the dark sky: *Bledsoe's Folly*.

Nate had crashed his truck in the exact same spot where he'd picked up Callie on the fifteenth of January.

Callie.

He knew then. He saw it all. She'd come into his life and changed everything.

What in hell was he thinking, to leave her? He could never leave her. She was everything to him.

The rain ran down the sides of his neck and under his collar. It plastered his hair to his head, and he had to be careful with every breath not to suck it up his nose. But he hardly noticed all that.

The fog of fear and panic had lifted somehow, leaving him seeing it all so clearly now—what to do, how it would work out.

He stared at the dark shape of Bledsoe's Folly and thought about all those beautiful acres surrounding it, about the mountains farther out where there would surely be just the right spot to put up a ski run. And there was more than one pretty little creek on that property, lots of access to national forest and plenty of horse trails.

The house itself? He could see it now—not as it was, but as it would be. They would put a talented architect to work on it, and it would become the main lodge of the resort. The plumbing and electric was already in place. With a little bit of luck, it might even be possible to have a grand opening sometime during the holidays, just as Collin and Sutter had insisted would happen....

Headlights cut the night, coming from home. He stood there, with the rain running down his face, as the silver-gray SUV pulled in next to the smoking ruin of his truck.

His heart seemed to fill up his whole chest when Callie got out. She'd had the sense to put on a rain slicker. She came and stood at his side, the yellow hood of the slicker hiding her face from him.

Finally, she turned and looked at him. God, there was no woman on earth like her. He could see she was torn between laughing and crying.

"There was a deer," he offered lamely. "It got away."

She stared at him for a moment more, then faced the pickup again. "Did you call for a tow truck?"

"The wreck's well off the road. It can wait till morning."

"You should maybe call Sheriff Christensen, at least, to let him know what happened."

"I'll do that. Yeah." But he didn't reach for his phone.

Silence from her. The rain poured down. All the things he needed to say to her were tumbling around in his head.

And then she asked, "Need a ride home?"

It was more than he could take. "Callie…" He grabbed her hand and hauled her close.

She let out a cry, and her slicker made silly squeaky sounds as she wrapped her arms around him. "You're soaking wet," she scolded.

"I'm a damn hopeless fool." He pushed the hood away from her neck so that he could bury his nose there and breathe in the scent of her. "I love you. Callie. I love you more than I know how to say."

"Yeah," she said on a soft, little sob. "I know that."

"I completely freaked out."

"Know that, too."

"But damned if I could ever really leave you. There is no way. You are everything I thought was gone, and more. You are the hope I hardly dared to have. And I want us to get married and somehow, I want to find a way to be the husband you need. The, um…" He had to swallow hard before he could say it. "The father of your children."

"Nate." She stroked his streaming hair, cradled his wet cheek. "Oh, Nate, you think *you* got scared? You scared *me.* I heard you drive away. And I stood at my front window and didn't know what to do. Finally, I just got in my car and came after you."

"I'm sorry. So sorry…"

She caught his face between both hands. "I think you maybe need to talk to someone, you know? Work out this fear you can't seem to shake."

He let out a disbelieving snort. "A shrink. You want me to see a shrink?"

"Yeah. Yeah, I do. Someone to help you work this thing through, someone to make it so you can finally, truly move on."

He didn't even argue. Because it was what she needed from him. And because, well, he knew she was right. "I will. Yes. I'll get a little counseling."

She sniffed and palmed water off her streaming brow. "All right, then. Wonderful."

"Callie..." He couldn't get enough of just holding her, of looking at her dripping face. "Callie. If I work it out, if I get past this crap, will you maybe marry me?"

"Of course I'll marry you," she said without a second's hesitation. "And there are no 'ifs' about it. I love you, Nate Crawford. You're the guy for me."

He kissed her then, standing there in the rain by the wreck of his pickup, a kiss that was his promise to move on from the past, his vow to be with her now and forever, for as long as they both drew breath.

Then they got in her SUV. He was about to call Gage Christensen when a highway patrolman pulled up. The patrolman turned in an accident report and agreed that morning would be soon enough to have the wreck towed away.

On the way home, Nate told Callie about his idea for Bledsoe's Folly, how he couldn't wait to tell Collin and Sutter all about it. She laughed and said it was going to be fabulous.

And up ahead, the sky was clearing. He could see the stars. Tomorrow would be a beautiful day.

* * * * *

Her eyes twinkled. "Are you flirting with me?"

"If you have to ask I must not be doing it right."

She laughed some more. "I'm glad not everything about you has changed. You were always a great guy in my book."

Her gaze lifted up to meet his. The tender look in her eyes touched something deep inside him—a part of him that he'd thought was long dead. In that moment he felt more alive than he had in months.

Without thinking he reached out and caressed her cheek. "Thank you."

She leaned into his touch, short-circuiting the logical side of his brain. The only coherent thought in his head was to pull her close and kiss her. And this time he wouldn't be kissing her rosy cheek. This time he planned to find out if those cherry-red lips were as sweet and passionate as they were in his daydreams.

THE RETURN
OF THE REBEL

BY
JENNIFER FAYE

Published in Great Britain 2014
by Mills & Boon, an imprint of Harlequin (UK) Limited,
Eton House, 18-24 Paradise Road, Richmond, Surrey, TW9 1SR

© 2014 Jennifer F. Stroka

ISBN: 978-0-263-91299-9

23-0714

Harlequin (UK) Limited's policy is to use papers that are natural, renewable and recyclable products and made from wood grown in sustainable forests. The logging and manufacturing processes conform to the legal environmental regulations of the country of origin.

Printed and bound in Spain
by Blackprint CPI, Barcelona

In another life **Jennifer Faye** was a statistician. She still has a love for numbers, formulas and spreadsheets, but when she was presented with the opportunity to follow her lifelong passion and spend her days writing and pursuing her dream of becoming a Mills & Boon® author, she couldn't pass it up. These days, when she's not writing, Jennifer enjoys reading, fine needlework, quilting, tweeting and cheering on the Pittsburgh Penguins. She lives in Pennsylvania with her amazingly patient husband, two remarkably talented daughters and their two very spoiled fur babies, otherwise known as cats—but *shh*…don't tell them they're not human!

Jennifer loves to hear from readers—you can contact her via her website: www.jenniferfaye.com.

In honor of my grandmother...

An amazing woman who had the patience to teach a very eager and curious little kid how to work a needle and thread. In the process she taught me that with perseverance you can achieve your dreams, whether they be big or small.

CHAPTER ONE

"You won't regret giving me this opportunity."

And hopefully neither will I.

Cleo Sinclair kept the worrisome thought to herself as she held her cheery smile in place. With the meeting at last over, she sailed out of the office of the vice president of player development, barely remembering to pull the door closed behind her. Away from Mr. Burns's cool demeanor and skeptical stare, she rotated her shoulders, easing the tension.

At the end of the hall, the elevator chimed and the door opened, allowing an employee to exit. Cleo stepped up her pace and slipped into the open car. Her pink manicured nail pressed the button for the main floor. Once the doors swished shut, the air whooshed out of her lungs and she leaned against the wall for support.

Step one was done. She had the job, albeit on a trial basis. Now on to step number two.

She had to prove to the ever-doubting Mr. Burns that she was up to his challenge. She could and would bring in wealthy clientele eager to gamble at one of Las Vegas's most luxurious establishments, the Glamour Hotel and Casino.

A glance at her image in the polished doors had her adjusting her cheery yellow dress, which dipped a little lower than she'd like. When she'd worked in the accounting department, her attire hadn't been so important. But now working the front-end of the casino, everything about her appearance mattered. She smoothed her hands over the skirt. It wasn't the fanciest outfit she'd ever stitched. In fact, she'd worried that she'd made a mistake by choosing to wear it, but with each compliment from her fellow employees, her nervousness had eased... That was, until her meeting.

She halted her rambling thoughts and inhaled a deep breath.

It was too late to second-guess herself. The train had left the station. The ship had sailed. Oh heck, it didn't matter what phrase she used. Her plan was in motion. And she would succeed.

After all, she'd just put her entire future on the line. There was no going back. No changing her mind. If this arrangement didn't work, she couldn't stay in Vegas nor would she be able to return home to Wyoming.

The elevator doors silently slid open, revealing lush carpeting leading to the casino area. The soft lighting added to the ambiance while the blinking lights on the slot machines lured guests to try their luck at winning a fortune. Without windows or clocks, minutes stretched into hours. In fact, she had found herself losing track of time on the numerous occasions she'd spent on the floor training for this promotion.

A cheer echoed through the room and she glanced around to see an excited crowd at the craps table. The palpable energy charged the room. Someone must be on a roll of luck. She hoped this would be her lucky day, too.

As of yet, her whale, the big client, hadn't checked in. The VP himself would be greeting the guest and then he'd phone her when her presence was required. Her boss had gone over the guest's preferences, including his favorite game—blackjack. Her job was to keep the whale happy by comping his meals and getting him tickets to whatever shows he preferred. But the utmost important thing was to maintain this guest's privacy, above and beyond their normal discretion. Even she didn't know his name yet.

With her family's ranch deep in debt, this was her only chance to chip in and prove to them that she was still a Sinclair. And she was doing what any Sinclair would do—taking a necessary calculated risk and making sure it paid off.

She wanted to be close by, so she headed for the China Cup, a little coffee shop just on the other side of the reception area. Her mouth watered in anticipation of her first sip of a mocha java latte. Her steps came faster and when her blue suede heels hit the marble floor by the front doors, they made a rapid staccato sound.

A line of guests waiting to check in trailed past the sculpted fountain, blocking her passage. She paused, finding the line almost reached the entrance. They must be here for the car convention that opened today. It was the biggest event along the strip. The hotel had sold out months in advance. This would be an ideal time for her to fish for new clients—if only Mr. Burns didn't have her on such a short leash, insisting she cater to this one whale only.

"Hey, buddy," grouched a man near the front of the line, "how about moving aside?"

"Yeah," chorused a screechy female voice. "The rest of us have reservations."

Shouts and complaints rippled through the lushly decorated lobby.

Cleo glanced at the front desk to find one employee on duty. What in the world? There were supposed to be three people helping with check-in, but the only person standing there was Lynn, their newest hire. The girl was so green

that she made the grass on the eighteen-hole golf course
look dull and grayish. Why would they leave her alone at
the front desk, today of all days?

"There has to be a mistake." Rising frustration laced
the voice of the man standing at the counter.

But it was more than the angry tone that drew Cleo's
attention. A note of recognition chimed in the far recesses
of her mind. She craned her neck for a better look. Only
the back of his short brown hair and his blue-and-white-
striped collared shirt were visible. She knew that voice,
but from where?

She glanced around, hoping to find someone qualified
to assist the now flustered desk clerk. When Cleo didn't
see any hotel employees moving in to help, she stepped
forward. The least she could do was maintain crowd control until someone showed up to help with registration.

"Check again." The man's posture was rigid. "It's under
Joe Smith."

"I am, sir." Lynn studied the computer monitor. "I can't
locate your name in our system."

"Call your supervisor."

"I—I can't. She's just left. She's ill."

"Then call her boss. Surely there's someone around here
who knows what's going on."

While Lynn frantically stabbed at the phone pad trying
to reach someone to straighten out things, Cleo stepped
up behind the disgruntled man. He didn't notice her as he
leaned both elbows on the counter, peering at the computer monitor. Her gaze slid over his broad shoulders to
his tapered waist, where his jeans accentuated his finer
assets. Realizing what she was doing, she jerked her attention upward.

"Excuse me, sir. Can I help?"

When the man straightened, he was much taller than

she'd anticipated. As he turned to her, she found herself straightening her spine and lifting her chin. His assessing glance sent a shiver of awareness down her arms. She shook off the sensation. Obviously she'd been concentrating on the problems with her family and her job a little too much. It had been years since a man had such an effect on her. Not since...

Jax Monroe!

His cool blue-gray gaze met and held hers. The chatter of excited voices and the jingle of the slot machines faded into the background. Her breath caught as she waited for a sign of recognition. But none came. No smile. No hug. Nothing. What was up with that?

She smiled at him. "Hey, Jax. Still making trouble, I see."

He made a point of checking out the ID badge pinned to her chest. Was it just her imagination or was he taking longer than necessary to verify her name?

"Jax, it hasn't been that many years. You've got to recognize me."

Sure she'd changed some, but so had he. His long brown hair had been cut off. Her fingers itched to brush over the supershort strands. And his face was now pale instead of the tanned complexion she recalled—back when they spent most of their time outdoors.

But not everything about him had changed. If you knew to look for it, there was still a little scar that threaded along his jaw. She clearly remembered the day he'd gotten it. They'd been fishing at the creek. He'd been goofing off when he'd slipped and fallen on rocks. He'd clambered back upright and laughed at himself until she'd pointed out he was bleeding.

They'd practically grown up together...even if he was five years her senior. Hope Springs, Wyoming, was a very small town and it was great seeing someone from home.

It'd been so long since she'd been there. And her last visit had been such a nightmare—

Her throat tightened. Could that be the answer? It might explain why he was acting as if he didn't know her. Even though he'd left Hope Springs years ago, it was possible he kept in contact with someone from there. Her stomach churned. Did he know about what she'd done?

"Jax, stop acting like you could forget the girl who used to follow you to our favorite watering hole."

"I think you must have me mistaken for someone else." He turned his back to her and waited while the clerk spoke in hushed tones on the phone.

Mistaken? Not a chance. She'd know those baby blues anywhere. They could still make her heart flutter with just a glance.

Even with the passage of time and some outward changes, it was impossible he'd forget her. She'd had a teenage crush on him of megaproportions. To say she thought the sun rose and set around him was putting it mildly. She'd have done anything for him. She *had* done anything for him, including lying. So whatever he had going on with this alias of his, she refused to lie for him again. Not here. Not when she could lose her job and so much more.

"Stop acting like you don't recognize me. We need to talk—"

He glanced over his shoulder at her. His eyes darkened and his voice lowered. "No, we don't."

"Your name is Jax Monroe. You're from Hope Springs, Wyoming—"

"Stop." He turned fully around. "You aren't going to let this drop, are you?"

She crossed her arms and shook her head. When his eyes flared, she realized she'd made the wrong move. Her arms pushed up on her chest, which was now peeking out from the diving neckline. She wanted to change positions but stubborn pride held her in place. Let him look. Maybe now he'd realize what he'd missed out on when he'd brushed off her inexperienced kiss and skipped town without a backward glance.

Jax Monroe couldn't help but stare at Cleo—all grown-up and filled out in the right places. Long wavy honey-gold locks just begged for him to run his fingers through them to see if they were as soft as they appeared. Wow! If he had known how hot she'd turn out, he might have reconsidered returning to Hope Springs. After all, she'd had a crush on him that was apparent to everyone in their hometown... But then he recalled how young she'd been back then—much too young for him.

And now, as much as her body had grown and changed from the gangly teenager he'd once known, there were other parts of her that were annoyingly the same. She still spoke her mind at the most inopportune time and without any thought of who might be listening.

What in the world had made him think that flying across the country to hide in plain sight was such a good idea? On second thought, maybe he should have stuck it out in New York until it was time for his courtroom testimony. But he'd already made his choice. And now that he was here, he was looking forward to seeing if Lady Luck was still on his side.

Now if only he could just get Cleo to quiet down before she revealed his identity to everyone in the hotel. Frustration bubbled in his veins as he considered clamping his hand over her pink glossy lips. Then a more tempting thought came to mind of how he might silence her—lip to lip.

One look at the agitation reflected in her eyes and he knew she'd slap him if he dared kiss her. Definitely not a viable option, even if Cleo wasn't his best friend's kid sister. Kurt had been the one guy who'd always accepted him as is—the same guy who'd saved his bacon more than once when he'd acted out after his old man had called him a good-for-nothing mooch. The only thing Kurt had ever asked of him was to keep his hands off his little sis.

Jax smiled as he recalled Cleo with knobby knees, freckles and a long ponytail. Boy had things changed. She was smooth and polished like a piece of fine art.

Cleo's green eyes narrowed. "Am I amusing you?"

"Um, no." He struggled to untangle his muddled thoughts. "I take it by your name tag that you work here."

Lines creased between her fine brows. "What's the matter with you? Have you been drinking?"

"What? Of course not." He'd watched his father live his life out of a scotch bottle and the way his mother tried to please him, with no luck. Jax refused to follow in his father's unhappy footsteps. "I don't drink."

"So why are you calling yourself Joe Smith?"

"Let's talk over there. Out of the way." He pointed to the edge of the counter, away from the incoming guests.

She turned to observe the long line before following him. "I don't know what game you're playing, but I won't let you cause trouble here."

"Lower your voice." Luckily no one appeared to notice them or their conversation. The guests were more interested in the arrival of an additional desk clerk than in what Cleo had to say. "I promise you I'm not here for any nefarious reason."

"Why should I believe you? I covered for you when you 'borrowed' the school mascot and when you pulled those numerous other pranks. I know the trouble you can cause."

"You've got to trust me."

She arched a disbelieving brow. "Says who?"

Little Cleo had certainly gained some spunk. Well, good for her. It was also a relief to know she wasn't still carrying that crazy torch for him. The last thing he needed at this critical juncture of his life was more complications.

Her finger poked his chest. "You're up to something and I want to know what it is." Her tone brooked no room for debate. He wouldn't be wiggling out of this confrontation with some flimsy story. "You can start by explaining your need for an alias."

"Just leave it be."

She shook her head. "I can't look the other way. We aren't kids anymore. This is where I work and I can't let you jeopardize my job." Cleo's voice rose with every word. "But if you turn around and leave now, we can forget we ever saw each other."

He doubted he'd ever be able to wipe her sexy image from his memory. Her polished persona stole his breath away. She may have been a cute kid, but she'd grown up to be a real knockout. And as for leaving here now, he wasn't about to do it. He had as much right to be here as anyone else.

Cleo leveled her shoulders and tapped her foot. He hated to tell her but if she was angling for an intimidating pose, she'd missed her mark. She was more alluring than scary.

"Don't make me call for security."

Heads were turning in their direction. The very last thing he wanted was to become a spectacle for the masses. "You wouldn't do that to an old friend, would you?"

"A few minutes ago you didn't even know me."

He raked his fingers through his hair. Back in New York when he'd started receiving phone calls where the person at the other end wouldn't speak, followed by notes warn-

ing him not to testify, this vacation had sounded like the
perfect plan. What could be better than getting lost in a
crowd while testing his luck at the blackjack table?

Ever since the assets of his investment firm had been
frozen by the government until the trial was completed,
he'd missed the rush of working the stock market—the
flood of adrenaline. He'd hoped Vegas would give him a
similar high—a chance to feel truly alive again instead of
living his life from one medical test to the next.

When his doctor gave him the green light, he'd picked
a spot on the map far from New York and booked a plane
ticket. He'd requested an alias be used while he was at
the Glamour just as a precaution. But he had no idea how
much of that he should tell Cleo. If only she would trust
him…for old times' sake.

"What's going on here?" A short, round man in a business suit approached them. He glanced at Cleo. "Do you
intend to interrogate all of the casino's important guests
in the middle of the lobby?"

Her expression morphed from frustration to one of
shock. Her gaze moved back and forth between the two
men as though waiting for an explanation.

When none came, she said, "But he is—"

"Your client. And you will treat him with respect."
The man turned to Jax and held out his hand. "Hello, Mr.
Smith. I'm Mr. Burns. We spoke on the phone. Let's talk
someplace a little more private." He led them to a hallway
just off the casino's main floor and into an empty office.
"I think there must have been some sort of mix-up. I'll see
about getting you a new casino host."

Jax's gaze moved to Cleo. Beneath the makeup her face
had taken on a sickly pallor. And her eyes held a deer-in-
headlights panic. His initial instinct was to ride to her
rescue. She'd always been the one to offer him a helping

hand all those years ago back in Hope Springs. There was a strange satisfaction in seeing the roles reversed. But that was then, and this was now.

And it only complicated matters that he couldn't keep his eyes off this grown-up version of her. She was no longer too young for him. In fact, the reasons he had to keep her at arm's length became more muddled the longer he was around her. It was best to end things right here. After all, it wasn't as if the man was going to fire her over this.

CHAPTER TWO

THIS COULDN'T BE HAPPENING.

Jax was her whale?

How was she supposed to have anticipated that? The last time she'd seen him, he barely had two coins to rub together. And now he was an important player in Las Vegas. How exactly did that happen?

Cleo's gaze shifted between the men. Neither of them seemed to notice that she was in the room. Did they think they could decide her future without even so much as consulting her? She wasn't about to let that happen.

"No other host is needed." Both men turned. She leveled a determined stare at each man before continuing to make her point. "Mr. Burns, you misunderstood what you overheard. Jax and I are old friends."

Her boss turned a questioning gaze to Jax. "Is this true?"

Cleo begged Jax with her eyes to back her up. After all, he owed her.

As the quietness stretched on, Cleo shifted her weight from one foot to the other. What was Jax thinking? His silence was even worse than any words he could say. She had to do something, anything, to keep from being canned for arguing with a MVP. Jax? A whale? The world could certainly be a strange place at times.

Cleo turned to face her disapproving boss. "We both come from the same small town in Wyoming."

Mr. Burns crossed his arms. "And do you always treat people from your hometown with such hostility?"

"I wasn't—"

Her boss's bushy brows arched. "I know what I heard."

"But you misunderstood—"

"Enough." Mr. Burns's hand sliced through the air. "I will deal with you later. Go wait for me in my office."

She hated being dismissed as if she was a child. She hated the thought of walking away with things unresolved, but she didn't want to make things worse... But then again could they get any worse? It was almost a certainty that when Mr. Burns joined her it would be to dismiss her. Not even a full day in her new position and she was being fired.

As she started for the door, her thoughts turned to her family. Even before learning of her family's financial problems, she'd made plans to transfer to the casino floor. She was bored senseless working in the accounting department. To think she left the family ranch because the work was isolating and she'd ended up taking a position where she spent her days alone in an eight-by-eight cubicle where silence was the status quo.

But then one day out of the blue her brother had called. She'd been so happy to hear from a family member. She hadn't heard a word from them since the funeral.

However, Kurt hadn't phoned with the intent of mending fences. He had news—bad news. The ranch was in arrears on its mortgage. And considering her Ivy League tuition was in large part the reason the ranch had been mortgaged in the first place, he thought she might want to help save their heritage.

The news totally blindsided her. Never once in her life had she imagined that the family had money problems.

And to know that she was about to be condemned for yet another Sinclair tragedy was not something she could let happen. She could not change the past, but going forward, she hoped to bridge the gap with her family.

Her fingers gripped the cold metallic door handle. One thought rose above the others: Sinclairs do not give up. No matter what.

Her grandfather had taught her that the first time she'd gotten thrown from a horse. If you wanted to succeed, you had to get back in the saddle and ride. That's what Sinclairs did—roughed things out.

She leveled her shoulders, released the door handle and turned. "Mr. Burns, you're right." His eyes lit up as though he was shocked by her bold confession. But before he could utter a word she rushed on. "Jax and I were having a disagreement. However, at the time I had no idea he was your special guest. I merely thought he was—"

"Here to check up on her for her big brother." Jax stepped between them to gain Mr. Burns's full attention.

At last, Jax found his voice, but why now? What convinced him to finally come to her aid?

The answers would have to wait. His motives paled in comparison to her losing her job and letting her family down…again. At the moment, she didn't have much choice but to go along with his fabricated story.

"That's right," she chimed in, trying to sound as genuine as possible. "And I didn't want Jax reporting back to my family about what I've been up to since moving away."

Surprisingly Mr. Burns's lips lifted at the corners as amusement danced in his dark eyes. "Let me guess, your family doesn't know that you've been working in a casino and they wouldn't approve of it."

This time she didn't have to lie. "That pretty much sums it up. They are old-fashioned in their beliefs."

Mr. Burns's eyes narrowed. "Then unless you're planning to find another job, I suggest you treat all of Glamour's guests with a pleasant demeanor."

She forced a smile on her face. "Of course. It was just a mix-up."

Mr. Burns turned to Jax. "The question still remains… Would you like me to assign you another host?"

He rubbed the dark scruff on his jaw. "No. Cleo and I will be fine. And we have some catching up to do."

Mr. Burns's gaze shifted between them as though making up his mind. "If that is your wish, Cleo will remain as your host. I have you set up in our most exclusive residence." He handed Jax the key card. "The bungalow should provide you with the privacy you're seeking. Cleo can show you the way. Do you need anything else?"

"Not at this time. I'm sure if something comes up Cleo will be able to take care of it."

Mr. Burns nodded. "But remember, I'm just a phone call away."

"Thank you." Jax extended his hand to the man.

After they shook hands, Mr. Burns moved past her, pausing long enough to say softly, "One more slipup and you're done."

A cold chill ran down her spine. The man had it in for her ever since the episode that occurred shortly after she'd started working in the accounting department. She'd pointed out some irregularities in his expense account, which were subsequently rectified.

Still, rumors were circulating that the only reason Mr. Burns had agreed to the promotion was because it was an all-or-nothing proposition. Either she was successful at endearing the high rollers to gamble at the Glamour Hotel and Casino or she was out on the street. And without a good reference, no other business on the strip would touch her.

"Don't worry. I'll make sure Jax is well cared for." She pasted on a smile, hoping it would suffice.

"I would expect nothing less."

The irritating note of superiority in Mr. Burns's voice grated on her razor-thin nerves. If the man hadn't been so eager to please Jax, she would be out on the curb right now. The fact she felt indebted to Jax ate at her.

With the door firmly shut, Cleo turned to Jax. Her mouth moved but the words wouldn't come. At last, she ground out, "Thank you."

His brows rose in surprise. "You're welcome. But the part I don't understand is why your brother didn't mention that you are working here in Vegas—"

"You've been talking to Kurt?" The thought left her unsettled.

Jax nodded. "We've kept in touch since I left Hope Springs."

Why was this the first she'd heard of it? Kurt was five years her senior, but she'd been closest to him out of all four of her brothers. When she'd needed someone to talk to, he was the one she'd turned to. So how had she missed hearing about Jax?

She tilted her chin and met his gaze. "You know, it's funny he's never mentioned you since you skipped town."

"Maybe he thought it was for the best."

"Why would he think that?"

Jax gave her a do-you-really-need-to-ask-that-question look. "As I recall, his kid sister had a massive crush on me—the kid from the wrong side of the tracks. I'm guessing he wouldn't want you having anything further to do with me."

Heat flamed in her chest and licked at her cheeks. "That was a long time ago. You can't fault me for my lack of judgment. I was just a kid. I've grown up since then."

"Trust me, I've noticed."

The implication of his words only multiplied her discomfort. Why was she letting him get her worked up? Back then she'd been a teenager with raging hormones and a complete lack of sense. And the fact that her family disapproved of Jax had only made him all the more attractive. What girl didn't go through a stage of falling for a sexy bad boy?

But even now with this mature version of Jax, his sexiness had only escalated. And his dreamy smile still had the power to penetrate her defenses and turn her insides to mush.

"We aren't here to talk about the past." She cleared her throat and schooled her facial features into what she hoped was a serious expression. "Why don't I show you to your bungalow?"

"Listen, I don't want to get you in any more trouble with your boss, but this arrangement obviously isn't going to work. So I don't care how you want to explain it to him, but you can't be my casino host. Better yet, don't say anything to him and you'll officially be my host but from a distance. A long distance."

"What?" Her chest tightened. "I—I can't do that. You're one of the casino's most valuable players. Upper management would find out immediately and accuse me of neglecting my duties."

"I don't need a babysitter." His brows gathered. "I just want a quiet vacation."

"And you'll have one while I take care of you...er, manage your needs." She pressed her lips together, knowing that with each attempt to dig out of this uncomfortable hole, she was only making it deeper for herself.

A deep chuckle rumbled from his chest. "Cleo, you still have a way of making me smile."

She glanced up, noticing how his face lit up when he smiled, easing his worry lines. Maybe his new life of luxury wasn't all chocolate and roses. From the obvious size of his bank account, she couldn't imagine what problems might be plaguing him. For a second, she considered asking but resisted. It wasn't any of her business.

"Does that mean I can go ahead and do my job?"

"Still as persistent as ever." Jax shook his head. "All right. Maybe we can try it on a trial basis. But that's no guarantee it'll work."

It was so much better than a no and it would give her time to soften him up. Hope bloomed in her chest. She would make this work…one way or the other.

Before she could say anything else to amuse him and embarrass herself, she turned to exit the office. "I'll show you around. I'm sure you're anxious to get to the tables."

"Actually there's no rush."

Cleo glanced back. "Really? Because if you're concerned about unpacking, don't be. I can have the staff do that for you."

"Are you that eager for me to start losing my money?"

Her gaze narrowed at his snide comment. "I get paid based on how much you wager, win or lose. So if you'll follow me, I'll give you a quick tour of the casino on the way to your lodging."

"That won't be necessary. I'd just like to get there quickly and discreetly."

If he wasn't up to something, why was he acting so strange? And did this have anything to do with his newfound wealth? The questions buzzed through her mind.

He was no longer Jax Monroe, Hope Spring's rebel. The truth was she never believed that he was a bad boy, more likely misunderstood and living up to people's low expectations of him. Back in the day he'd been so sexy with his long hair and holey jeans. Every girl in town had her eye on him—including her.

Cleo couldn't wait to tell her mother about this amazing transformation. Suddenly her excitement dipped. The gaping hole in her heart throbbed. Sometimes when she got excited, she'd forget that her mother was no longer speaking to her.

"Was there something else?"

Cleo glanced up at him, unable to recall their discussion. "What?"

"You were about to show me to my room." Jax's penetrating gaze met hers, making her turn away before she said or did something stupid.

"Follow me." She started toward the players' area.

"Is there a back way to my room?"

She nodded and turned around, guiding him down a long nondescript maintenance hallway. Jax may be tall, handsome and mysterious, but she had to remember that he was her client—a stranger to her now.

She didn't even know if she should trust him, but a little voice in the back of her mind said that he was still the same good guy down deep where it counted. He was also the guy her family didn't approve of—at least not for her. It niggled her that he was good enough for her older brother to pal around with, but when it came to her, she'd been forbidden to hang out with him—not that it had stopped her.

The silence between them stretched on. She didn't do well with awkward moments. "We're having a vintage car show in our convention center, if you'd like to look around—"

"Maybe later."

So much for conversation. She didn't recall Jax being this quiet when he was a kid. In fact, there were times he hadn't known when to shut up. She couldn't believe she was missing that smart-mouthed kid—the same kid who would go out of his way to put a smile on her face. What in the world had changed him so drastically?

She stopped and pushed open a heavy steel door. The glare of the Nevada sun nearly blinded her. She blinked and her eyes soon adjusted. As she moved along the secluded footpath, the sound of laughter, the cacophony of voices and the splash of water filled the air.

Jax grabbed her arm, giving her pause. "I thought we were taking the back way to my room."

An army of goose bumps raced over her skin. She pulled away from his touch and ignored the fluttery feeling in her chest.

She lifted her chin to face him. "We are. Your bungalow is in a secluded area just beyond the pool. Don't worry, there's a path over here on the side that we can use."

As they passed the pool she found herself glancing over at the crowd of young people on summer break, enjoying themselves. Her family were ranchers—and ranchers didn't take holidays. Or so her parents told her every time she asked them if they could go on a trip like her friends did.

It was always expected that when she wasn't in class, she would be at home helping out. It's what her brothers did. No one ever seemed to understand she was different. Was it so wrong to want to hang out with her friends? Or take vacations?

It was always presumed she'd become a rancher's wife—just like her mother and grandmother. After all, she was a Sinclair and ranching was in their blood. Except somehow the love of ranching had skipped over her.

"This sure is different from Hope Springs," Jax said, as though he, too, were thinking about the old days.

"Is that good or bad?"

"Neither. Just an observation."

The desert air was dry and hot as it rushed past them. Even though the private walkway was ensconced with palms trees, large rocks and various types of greenery, she gazed longingly at the glimpses of the enormous pool that had a wall of granite with a beautiful waterfall on one side. A dip in the cool water was so tempting. But employees were forbidden to indulge. She wondered if that rule could be suspended if someone like Jax invited her for a swim. After all, her priority was to keep her clients happy.

"What has you smiling?"

She was smiling? She hadn't realized that her thoughts had transferred to her face. She'd have to be careful in the future. The last thing she needed was Jax getting any ideas about her meandering thoughts.

"I was just imagining how nice it'd be to take a dip in the pool."

"It is hot out."

"It's always hot in Vegas."

"So how is it that the only Sinclair girl ended up in Las Vegas? I'd have thought you'd be back in Hope Springs with a cowboy by your side and a baby in each arm."

Cleo stopped short on the narrow path. He almost ran into her. "Not you, too. You sound like my parents."

"Calm down. I can see I struck a chord. I just thought that with your close-knit family that you'd never want to leave."

"Well, you're wrong. Besides, you did the exact same thing. I don't see you rushing back." She eyed him accusingly.

"That's different—"

"How?"

"You know I couldn't stay there." His posture grew rigid. "After my mother died, my father only got meaner. I wouldn't wish that life on anyone."

The pieces of the past started to drop into place. "That's why you were always out and about. You were trying to avoid your father."

Jax nodded. "It was easier than having to deal with him."

"But why did you have to play into the negativity by being at the center of all of the trouble in Hope Springs? How was anyone supposed to give you the benefit of the doubt when you never gave them a chance to trust you?"

His blue eyes stared straight at her. "Why didn't you write me off like the rest of them?"

"Because I saw there was more to you than you were willing to let on." She wasn't going to say that she'd had a bad case of puppy love. Thankfully they arrived at his bungalow, putting an end to this awkward conversation. "This is where you'll be staying."

She swiped her master key card and pushed open the door. When she stepped back to let him pass, he shook his head and waved at her to go ahead. "Ladies first."

She smiled. "Thank you."

So the bad boy had transformed into a gentleman. She definitely approved of this change. But that didn't mean she'd let her guard down around him. In her experience, people only showed you the side of them that they wanted you to see.

She'd been so foolish in the past, always looking for the good in people. She'd been too trusting—too understanding. And what had that Pollyanna attitude gotten her? A broken heart and being disowned by her very own mother.

In the end, people always let you down.

"This is nice," Jax said, drawing her back to the here and now.

"Yes, it is. It's our most private and exclusive residence on the grounds."

This was actually the first time Cleo had been inside

the bungalow. Only the most valued players were invited to stay here. And it was hard to believe Jax was now one of the elite. A man like that would not need or want for much.

But that still left her wondering, what was up with him using an alias? And his request for privacy was so different from the Jax she knew back in Hope Springs. In those days, he seemed to open his mouth just to annoy someone who was hassling him. Now he put thought into what he said and, more important, what he didn't say.

So what twist of fate had put him in her path? And why did it have to be him who held her future in the palm of his hand? Her stomach dipped. How did she get him to agree to keep her on as his host—permanently?

CHAPTER THREE

JAX KEPT HIS eyes on the room and not on Cleo. Did she have any idea how irresistible she looked? How in the world did she think that they were supposed to spend time together with her wearing a dress that accentuated her curves? But then again she'd look good in anything, including a paper bag.

"Do you like what you see?" Cleo glanced at him from the entryway.

Oh, he definitely liked the view. Way more than he should. He cleared his throat. "Yes… Yes, I do."

Forcing his attention back to his surroundings, he observed the oversize leather couches. They looked inviting. He could easily envision settling in and watching a baseball game on the big-screen television. In fact, the idea sounded like something he'd enjoy indulging in right now.

Not so long ago, he used to work nonstop. But then he'd gotten sick and everything had changed. He had yet to regain his stamina after his medical treatments. It frustrated him to have to slow down, but until this court case was resolved there really wasn't any work he could do. This was his first vacation. He was curious to see if it was as great as people let on. Or if he ended up as bored as he imagined.

"If there's anything you're missing, just let me know and I'll take care of it for you."

He was positive the one thing he wanted, she would not supply. Not that he should or would act on the desire to taste her sweet lips. Cleo was the very last person he'd have a fling with. She deserved so much more—more than he could offer anyone.

"Would you like me to get you anything? Extra towels? Some food?"

"I don't think so. You can go." He didn't miss the frown at his dismissive tone and total lack of manners. His weariness was messing with his mind. "Thank you for showing me here, but I'll be fine on my own."

He turned his back to her and eyed up the couch. After a little television and some shut-eye, he'd be good as new—he wished. But with each day that passed, he was feeling a bit more like his old self.

Cleo firmed her shoulders. "I'd like to finish our talk about me staying on as your casino host. Perhaps we can come up with some sort of compromise."

He was intrigued. "What sort of compromise?"

She shifted her weight from one blue suede stiletto to the other, deciding just how much information she had to impart. Considering that not only her job but also the possibility of mending fences with her family was riding on her bringing in a large influx of cash, she had no choice but to be totally honest.

"I'd better start at the beginning." She worried her bottom lip as she sorted out in her mind a good starting point. "The thing is I sort of went over Mr. Burns's head to get this position and now he's out to get me."

Jax's eyes lit up as a smile tugged at his lips. "What do you mean sort of went over his head? You either did or didn't do it."

She hated how he put her on the spot. "Fine. I went over his head. But I wouldn't have had to if he hadn't kept passing me over every time there was an opening. And I'd already impressed his boss with a special project I'd previously worked on."

"Some things don't change." Jax laughed, remembering how he'd envied the way her father catered to her. He'd never known anything close to that amount of love. His own father had been too caught up in his own needs to worry about his son. The sobering thought killed off his laughter. "Why should I care about this mess you've gotten yourself in? I'm not the one who decided to buck the chain of command."

"So beneath that designer jacket and short haircut, you're still the tough, 'don't care' Jax, aren't you?"

"You don't know a thing about me." The fact that she didn't think he'd changed stung more than he'd expected.

"Then why don't you tell me how you ended up in this exclusive bungalow?"

He let out a frustrated sigh as exhaustion coursed through his body. "This is exactly why I need another host. I shouldn't have to explain myself. A stranger wouldn't butt into my life."

A pained look crossed her face, making him regret his heated words.

"You're right. You don't owe me any explanations. I just need you to forget everything that happened up until this point and give me another chance to be the best casino host you've ever had." She twisted her hands together. "But there's one more thing you should know."

His patience was wearing thin and he was so tired. "What is it?"

"This job isn't just for me." Her voice was so low, he almost missed what she'd said.

"What are you talking about?" Then a thought struck him. His gaze sought out her left hand, finding her ring finger bare. But that didn't mean she wasn't a single mother. "Who's relying on you?"

She wrapped her long honey-gold hair around her finger in a similar manner to the way she used to twist her father and brothers around her pinkie. But they were a long way from Hope Springs and he wasn't so easily swayed. If only he could get past his fascination with this grown-up version of Cleo. It was just a lot to take in at once.

"It's the ranch—the Bar S." Her worried gaze met his. "It's in a serious bind."

The worry in her eyes ate at him. "Kurt never mentioned anything about problems with the ranch when we've talked."

"I'm sure it's a matter of Sinclair pride. That's what got us into this trouble in the first place. It seems my father had been juggling money to cover his bases for quite a while without telling anyone that the Sinclair fortune had dwindled to nothing."

The knowledge that the high-and-mighty Sinclairs had come down off their lofty spot in the community didn't give Jax the satisfaction he once thought it would. Maybe it was the distressed look on Cleo's face that drove home the reality of what she was telling him. People were about to lose their way of life—their home.

"But I don't understand. What does any of that have to do with you being my casino host?"

"I need money to send home to put toward the mortgage. It's in arrears."

The Bar S was mortgaged to the hilt? He'd always looked at that ranch in awe and dreamed of one day having a spread just like it. Why hadn't Kurt mentioned any of this to him?

Later he would have to call Kurt and see if there was something he could do to help. Just as quickly, he realized he couldn't do that without mentioning Cleo. This would take a lot more thought before he acted. And right now, he needed to straighten things out with Cleo.

In his exhausted state, his brain just wasn't making all of the necessary connections. "So you want to be a casino host to make money for the family?"

She nodded. "The position pays a lot more than being an accountant."

He leaned back on the banister at the bottom of the steps. "Oh, yes. You mentioned making a percentage of what I wager."

She cocked her head to the side and stared at him intently. "Are you okay?"

"Of course. Why?"

"It's just… Oh, never mind."

This wasn't good. The last thing he needed was for her to figure out that something truly was wrong with him. It was difficult for him to maintain a normal existence while waiting for his test results without having to deal with the pitying looks or the sympathy.

"Jax, you have to do this. You owe me."

This sparked his attention. He always made it a policy to pay his debts. The thought of owing Cleo didn't sit well with him. At all. "I do? Since when?"

"Remember when I saw you on the day you left town? You asked me not to tell anyone what you were up to and I kept that secret for you."

Getting away from Hope Springs had turned his life around. If his father had his way, Jax never would have made anything of himself. Only his father hadn't lived long enough to learn how he'd graduated from college at the top of his class and had made a killing in the stock market. Not that it mattered. All of that, including Cleo, was in his past. And he wasn't going to get caught up in looking back—he didn't when his biopsy came back positive and he refused to look back now.

Oblivious to his inner struggle, Cleo continued, "I knew what you were running from and I wanted to help. If your father had known where you went, he'd have tracked you down and dragged you back. He'd have made your life miserable."

"You knew where I went? How?"

"I didn't know for sure. But I had a pretty good guess. You didn't talk about your family much, but when you did, you mentioned your mother's sister in Virginia. I figured that's where you went."

He nodded. "It is. I spent the summer with her before I went on to college."

"Your mother would have been so proud of you."

He grew uncomfortable with all of this digging around in his past. His mother had been sick off and on most of his life until her frail body finally gave in and she passed away when he was a teenager. No one ever spoke of her because very few people knew her since she was usually housebound from one ailment or another. The doctors would have him believe that she had a weak body, but he never believed that was what did her in. He was convinced her spirit had been broken by his father, who bullied everyone and ruled the house with an iron fist.

"I'm sorry." Cleo stepped closer to him. "I shouldn't have brought it up."

"It's okay. It's nice having someone else around who remembers her. You were always kind to her and she liked you."

"I liked her, too."

He remembered how Cleo would stop by the house with school fund-raisers. She never rushed off. She'd sit down with his mother at the kitchen table and chat. At the time he hadn't liked Cleo wedging her way into his life, but now looking back he realized she'd recognized a loneliness in his mom and had tried her best to fill it.

"Your mother was a really nice lady. And she made the most delicious chocolate chip cookies."

Before he could say more, his phone buzzed. Adrenaline pumped through his veins. At last, he'd know his test results. He glanced over at Cleo. "I'll be right back."

He moved to the kitchen, seeking privacy. No one knew about his brush with death, and he intended to keep it that way. He didn't want people looking at him as if he was less of a man.

He went to answer the phone but the other party had already disconnected. Jax rushed to check the caller ID but it was blocked, leaving him no clue as to who was trying to contact him. If it was important, they'd call back.

He returned to the front room, where Cleo was studying what was bound to be an expensive painting. He could never tell a Rembrandt from a Picasso. He just knew what he liked.

Jax stuffed his hands into his pockets. His fingers brushed over the smooth metal of the old pocket watch that he kept with him as a good-luck charm. More times than he could count it had brought him peace of mind. Only today its magic hadn't worked.

Today it reminded him of the past and the fact that Cleo's grandfather had given him the watch. Jax's gut was telling him that her grandfather would want him to help Cleo, no matter how hard it would be for him.

Cleo could feel Jax's presence before she heard him. She turned and noticed the dark shadows beneath his eyes. She didn't know what the man had been up to lately, probably too much. He certainly needed some rest.

"I'll get out of your way. But before I go, I'd like to confirm our arrangement."

Jax's brows rose. "I didn't realize we'd come to any agreement."

"Seriously, you're going to make me plead with you?"

He looked as though he were weighing his options. "You really want to put up with me for the next few weeks?"

Was he talking about catering to his every whim and desire? Her mind filled with the vision of him pulling her close and pressing his lips to hers. Okay, so maybe she hadn't totally outgrown her childhood crush. But fantasies were one thing. Acting on them was quite a different subject.

She'd learned her lesson about love. Men were to be treated with caution. She may date now and then, but she never let those relationships get serious. By dating the same guy less than a handful of times, she never let herself get close enough to risk her heart.

With Jax, it'd be a temporary arrangement—no chance for either of them to get the wrong idea about their relationship. "If you agree, I'll do a good job for you."

He glanced down at his phone as though expecting it to ring again. "In exchange, you'll keep my identity a secret. As far as everyone is concerned I'm Mr. Smith."

"I will make your privacy my top priority. But what's up with all of the secrecy?"

"Let's just say I'm on a much-needed vacation and I don't want anyone to disturb it."

"If you're supposed to be here for some R and R, you might consider turning off your phone. There's nothing so important that it can't wait. Why don't you let me reserve you a blackjack table for later today?"

Jax smiled and shook his head. "With your determination, I think you'll do quite well in your new position."

She straightened her shoulders. "I plan to."

He moved toward the couch and picked up the television remote. It was almost as if he'd forgotten she was in the room.

"Mr. Smith." When he didn't respond, she added, "Jax, if you're going to go by a fake name, you should at least answer to it."

He looked over at her. "I'm sorry. I didn't hear you."

"I'll make sure your line of credit is established and your table is ready. I'll be back as soon as everything is in place."

"There's no need to rush. I'll be fine."

"The fridge is stocked. Help yourself." She started for the door. Curiosity was eating at her. Something was troubling him and she was starting to worry about him. "Jax, just tell me one thing, are you in trouble with the authorities?"

"Why would you ask that?" He expelled a weary sigh. "You're still puzzled by the alias. Did you ever just want to get away? Want to be someone else for a little bit?"

Sure she had, especially after growing up in a small town where everyone knew everybody else's business. She used to daydream about the day she'd get to leave. The funny thing was the farther she got from her hometown, the more she missed it. Not the ranching part but the people.

And now that her father was gone and the ranch was in trouble, she felt as though she should be there to help out. But she wasn't wanted. The backs of her eyes stung as she recalled how her mother had told her to leave at her father's funeral, accusing her of being responsible for his death.

Jax stepped closer. "Cleo, what is it?"

She blinked back the unshed tears. "Nothing."

"You sure don't look like it's nothing."

"Well, you would be wrong. So we'll keep each other's

secrets. Yours from the rest of the world and mine from my brother. Deal?"

He frowned but nodded.

She slipped out the door. It was only then that she could breathe easy. Jax was here for more than just a vacation. Of that she was certain. He had a problem and if she had to guess, it was what had him looking so run-down. It must be something big and troublesome. But what could it be?

And why was she letting herself get drawn in when she had enough of her own problems?

CHAPTER FOUR

WHAT HAD MADE him think a trip to Las Vegas was a good idea?

Jax grabbed a bottle of water from the fully stocked fridge. In the past two days, Cleo seemed to be everywhere he turned. It was almost as if she had him under surveillance. He paused, considering the possibility. Then realizing he'd watched too many spy movies after his treatments, he dismissed the idea. Even that would be too much for her.

The stress of waiting for his latest test results combined with a restless night had his imagination on overdrive. He really did need this vacation more than he'd originally thought.

The afternoon sun filtered through the sheers on the windows, casting a golden glow over the room. The couch beckoned to him. If he just sat down here for a minute, he'd be fine. Putting his feet up on the coffee table, he leaned his head back against the smooth leather upholstery and closed his eyes. This felt so good…

"Jax."

He turned down a dark alley. Rapid footsteps sounded behind him. A gunshot pierced the night. He flinched. His legs moved faster.

He glanced around. The alleyway was empty. His heart pounded harder. No place to hide. No place to rest.

His muscles ached. His lungs burned. Still, he couldn't stop. He had to keep going.

"Jax."

The female voice was growing closer. Where were they? He couldn't see them. He had to keep moving, keep one step ahead of the man in black.

A brick wall reared up in front of him. He stumbled. Fell. Before he could get to his feet a hand clutched his shoulder.

He jumped.

"Jax, you're safe."

One second he was in the alleyway and the next he was staring into the most amazing forest-green eyes. He blinked, trying to make sense of what was real and what was a dream. He jerked himself away from her touch and sat upright.

Cleo knelt down in front of him with concern etched across her face. "You were having a nightmare. Are you okay?"

"Um, yeah." He ran a hand over his forehead. "It's a bit warm in here."

She grabbed the cold water bottle from the coffee table and handed it to him. "Have a drink. I'll adjust the thermostat." She moved across the room and adjusted the touch pad on the wall. "Sorry I'm late. I had to pick my cat up from the vet."

"No problem. I wasn't in any rush." He raked his fingers through his hair.

The nightmares had started when he'd been diagnosed with cancer. With both of his parents dead at an early age, he didn't hold out much hope for himself. He'd lost count of how many nights he'd woken up with his heart racing and drenched in sweat, but back then the dream had been a blur. As time went by he remembered more of the details. Thankfully he didn't have them every night, only those times when his illness was weighing heavily on his mind.

"Are you sure you're okay?" She sent him a questioning stare. "I could call a doctor."

"What? Why would you do that?"

It was impossible for her to know about his medical condition. There were no loose ends for her to pull. No stones for her to turn. He got to his feet, stretched and headed to the minibar for a fresh bottle of water. He unscrewed the cap and took a long drink.

"If you're sick—"

"Why do you keep insisting I'm sick?"

"Because you're pale and perspiring. And obviously exhausted if you didn't hear me knocking on the door."

"It's just jet lag."

"Jet lag? Three days after the fact? I don't think so."

She had a point, but he kept quiet. Let her think what she wanted. He wasn't about to tell her that he'd just finished up a round of chemo and was now awaiting test results to see if he was in the clear or if the dreaded disease was still lurking within him.

"Maybe you should sit back down and take it easy." She fluffed a throw pillow before returning it to the couch.

He'd been taking care of himself since he was a kid. He didn't need her mollycoddling him like...like his mother used to do when he was sick. And this illness was not something that you shared casually over coffee. He could barely admit to himself the changes that had taken place in his life over the past year.

Now he just needed to be treated as if he was normal. And maybe then he'd start to feel normal, too.

She turned a sympathetic gaze his way. "I can get you some aspirin."

"Stop fussing over me." The hurt expression on her face had him regretting his outburst. She was only trying to be nice. "Thank you, but I'm fine."

Her brow arched as she pressed her hands to her hips. "If you're so fine, prove it. Let's head over to the casino and see if you can win back some of that money you lost yesterday."

Actually that sounded like the best suggestion he'd heard in a while. Because there was no way he was going to fall asleep again anytime in the near future. "Lead the way."

Surprise lit up her eyes, but for once she didn't argue. She turned on her stilettos and headed straight for the door. His gaze drifted to her derriere, nicely displayed in a red skirt that showed off her curves. He had no idea where she bought her clothes, but it was as if they were tailored just for her.

His throat grew dry and he gulped down the rest of the water. She'd certainly grown up to be a knockout. He couldn't believe Kurt let her out of his sight. If she was his little sister, he'd definitely keep her under wraps—away from men like himself.

Then again he wasn't anyone that her brother should be worried about. He was far from being classified as a ladies' man these days. That was one of the reasons he'd decided to come to Vegas—to distance himself from the stark reality of his diagnosis. Here he could be Mr. Smith—Mr. No Worries.

He rushed to catch up with her on the footpath. For just a bit longer he could hang on to the illusion that he was the man he'd always been—a man with a promising future. Now that future was littered with uncertainties.

"Have you lived in New York long?"

"Ever since I finished college." He glanced her way. "Did you move here after you graduated?"

Sadness filled her eyes and she nodded. "My family wanted me to return home. They'd even made arrangements for me to work for Mr. Wetzel in town, processing taxes."

"I take it that wasn't what you had in mind for your future."

She shook her head. "I thought I knew everything when I finished college. At last, I was free to make my own choices—to forge my own direction wherever it led me."

"It looks like you did well with those choices."

Her shoulders drooped. "Looks can be deceiving."

He concurred wholeheartedly. Things were never quite what they seemed from the outside. He was just sorry that Cleo had to learn that lesson the hard way.

"Hang in there. I'm sure life has some amazing things in store for you."

"We'll see."

The fact that she felt comfortable enough to open up to him warmed a spot in his chest. But he couldn't let himself read too much into it. She was probably lonely being so far from her family. And it wouldn't do either of them any good if he tried to fill that empty spot. It'd only make it that much harder to walk away.

"You know, I can be on my own today. I don't want to take up all of your time. I'm sure by now you have other guests to look after."

"Actually you're my one and only guest. Mr. Burns has me on a very short leash." Her cherry-red lips lifted and her eyes sparkled. "So name your pleasure and I'll make sure it's provided."

The sweet lilt of her voice and the sight of her tempting lips sent his mind spiraling back in time. He clearly remembered the one and only kiss they'd shared. He hadn't even seen it coming and it was over before he could react. The strange thing was that after all of these years, he had never forgotten that innocent moment.

He'd been kissed countless times since then and by experienced women who knew how to turn a kiss into an adventure. So why had the memory of those other kisses faded while hers stood the test of time?

Every detail of that moment stood out in his mind. He recalled how the morning sun peeked over Cleo's shoulder. The golden rays made her hair glisten, giving it the illusion of a halo. Her cheeks were rosy with color and her eyes sparkled like fresh-cut emeralds.

He'd been so mesmerized by the stunning image that he hadn't expected her to lift up on her tiptoes. Her gaze met and held his as she leaned forward. Her puckered lips pressed to his mouth. In the next heartbeat, she pulled away. And then, as if horrified, her eyes grew round. She'd pressed a hand to her mouth and run off.

The buzz of his phone drew him back to the present. At last, it had to be his doctor with the confounded test results. He glanced at Cleo. There was no way he was having this conversation in front of her.

He never wanted her to know that he had…Hodgkin's lymphoma.

He swallowed hard, still not comfortable with the "C" word.

He held up a finger to Cleo. "You can go ahead. I've got to get this."

He took a step back toward the bungalow. In fact, he took numerous steps before he pressed the phone to his ear. "Hello?"

Nothing but silence greeted him. Not again.

"Hello? Who's there?"

Frustration bubbled through his veins. Was it possible the anonymous phone calls were starting again just like in New York? But how had they gotten this number? He'd just had it changed.

He checked the caller ID. It was blocked. But then he noticed the reception bars were down to just one. The knot of tension in his gut eased. Perhaps the calls hadn't started again. Perhaps it was just a case of spotty reception.

His gaze moved to Cleo. She was standing next to a large palm tree. In the background was a glimpse of the waterfall at the edge of the pool. Her striking beauty drew him in. A year or two ago, he'd have tossed caution to the wind and lived in the moment.

But the here and now was all he had these days. He couldn't forget that. And he noticed the more time they spent together, the more he had to remind himself that he was in no position to offer her anything. His life was a continual question mark. And that was no way for anyone to live.

Her gaze caught his and held it. He found himself smiling back. Maybe he was thinking about this all wrong. Would it be a crime to let down his defenses just a little and enjoy Cleo's company?

It had been so long since he'd let someone in, even if it was just to kick back and chat over a meal. He longed for a little companionship. But he'd have to be careful around Cleo. She had a way of sneaking past his defenses. And he couldn't afford to let her get too close. They'd both end up hurt.

These thoughts made him all the more determined to check out early. Once he spent a little more time at the tables and made it look good for her, he was leaving Vegas.

He didn't know where he'd go, but that didn't matter. Still, it'd sure be nice to take a few happy memories of Cleo's smile with him.

Cleo stood next to a palm tree, wishing Jax would hurry up.

It was a hot day even by Vegas standards. Perspiration trickled down her cleavage. If this was going to take a while, she'd wait for him inside.

She glanced over at him and noticed how his brows were drawn into a dark line. And his eyes were narrowed as though he were upset. Something was definitely wrong. Should she go to him?

She stepped forward. Then stopped. It wasn't her place to interfere. As long as she saw to his needs while he was here at the Glamour, her job was done. Maybe once he got a few winning hands, it'd cheer him up.

Yet when he joined her, she couldn't help but ask, "Is everything all right?"

He smiled but the expression didn't reach his eyes. "Things couldn't be better. I'm on vacation and being escorted by the most beautiful woman in Las Vegas."

Without warning, he held up his phone and snapped her picture.

"What'd you do that for?"

He shrugged. "Why not? This way I have a reminder of my trip."

"You already had one from the other day."

His smile warmed her insides. "I could never have too many pictures of you."

His compliment caused a fluttering sensation in her stomach and silenced any further objections. Instead she returned his smile and when he offered her his arm, she gladly accepted. In a peaceable silence, he escorted her into the casino.

Inside, colorful lights twinkled while the murmur of voices filled the room. A group cheered at the roulette table. There were plenty of things going on in here to distract both of them. While Jax played blackjack, Cleo checked in with the pit boss to see if there were any new high rollers she could introduce herself to.

After all, Jax wouldn't be here forever. When he was gone and she'd proven herself, she'd need other clients. She may only be on a trial period right now, but she didn't intend for it to stay that way for long. And for her to be successful, she needed to plan ahead.

Sadly today there weren't any new leads for her. So after making the rounds on the casino floor, she gravitated back to Jax's table.

"And how are we doing?" She flashed him her practiced smile.

He didn't smile back. "Seems Lady Luck is on holiday."

"I predict things will turn around."

He cocked a dark brow at her as though gauging her sincerity before playing another hand. And losing again. Cleo's anxiety rose. If he didn't start to win soon, he'd quit. Or worse, take his business to another casino on the strip. Vegas was full of choices.

She wondered if that held true for her, too. At first, being a casino host seemed like an exciting challenge, but even though she was new to the job, she was finding that it didn't give her a sense of fulfillment, either. Now the only reason she wanted this job was to help her family get the ranch out of arrears. Once that was achieved, she knew she'd be moving on to something else. Because one thing she knew for certain, being employed in a casino didn't make her any happier than working on her family's ranch.

The most fun she'd had since arriving in this town was buying a secondhand sewing machine and returning to a hobby she enjoyed immensely—creating fashions. Her family may think her passion was a waste of time, but it'd saved her a bundle of money by allowing her to dress in style for a fraction of the price.

After the last losing hand, Jax turned to her. "That's it! I'm done. And don't say a word. No platitude or hokey prediction is going to fix this. I just hope you don't ever try to make a living off being a fortune-teller," he teased. "Because you're lousy at it."

"I—I'm sorry."

"I know how you can make it up to me."

"How's that?" She'd do it as long as it wasn't too over-the-top.

"Have an early dinner with me."

He was asking her to dinner? Excitement bubbled up inside her. She just as quickly tamped it down. He was her client. She had to stay focused.

"Thank you. But I don't date clients."

This brought an unexpected smile to Jax's face. "That's good because I'm not interested in a date. I just thought if you're going to follow me around, you might as well eat, too. But if you're not hungry that's fine."

"Oh." Her stomach growled. Heat filled her cheeks. Strike that. She was a lot hungry. "I'll join you if you tell me how you ended up going from ragtag jeans to designer ones."

His brows lifted. "You really find it so surprising that a person can turn their life around?"

"From what I've witnessed, people say they're going to change, but they're usually lying."

Jax stopped walking and turned to her. "Since when

did Hope Springs's very own Pollyanna become such a pessimist?"

She glared at him. "I was not Pollyanna."

"Oh, yes, you were. There was hardly a time you weren't smiling, and you seemed to think it was your job to make everyone else in town smile, too."

She hated that he still thought of her as some foolish kid with unrealistic expectations. "I grew up and found out that life isn't like in the movies. It doesn't come with rainbows and happily-ever-afters."

She started to walk again, not caring now if he followed her or not. Of course she'd always been smiling when he was nearby, it was how he made her feel. He surely didn't think she was that happy around everyone. But then again maybe it was best she didn't squelch his misconception. It was for the best that he didn't know those smiles had been just for him.

"Hey, slow down." He grabbed for her arm but she pulled away and kept on moving. "I didn't mean to upset you. I just miss seeing you smile and laugh. You're always so serious these days."

"I smile." She lifted her chin and pasted on a smile.

"I meant a real one. Not one of those practiced smiles you use for guests."

Cleo paused at the restaurant entrance, waiting for the hostess to seat them. She didn't know why she still let him ruffle her feathers. She really needed to loosen up.

The hostess seated them in the corner where there was dim lighting and a candle burning in the middle of the table. She inwardly groaned at the romantic setting. She glanced around, finding the restaurant empty, except for one gentleman across the room.

Jax leaned back against the cushioned bench as though the atmosphere didn't faze him. "So tell me about him?"

"About who?"

"The guy who made you stop believing in happily-ever-afters."

Her initial instinct was to tell him to look in the mirror. He'd been the first guy to break her heart. But she didn't dare admit it to him. He'd think she was being ridiculous. After all, she'd just been a silly kid.

But to this day she could still remember how crushed she'd been when she'd acted on impulse. She'd stood up on her tiptoes and kissed him. He hadn't kissed her back. He hadn't said a word. Not even a smile. In fact, all he did was stare at her. She'd been mortified.

The next time she saw him, he'd been leaving her grandfather's house. She'd run to catch up to him. She didn't know what she'd been expecting him to say, but it sure wasn't goodbye. Nor had she anticipated him leaning forward, kissing her cheek and saying, "See you, kid."

She'd been so devastated by him leaving town that she hadn't eaten her dinner and had hidden in her room all night. Luckily being the only girl afforded her the luxury of having her own room, where no one could see the tears she cried.

Jax took a drink of ice water and studied her over the rim. "Aw, see, I was right. It was a man who turned you into such a jaded person."

Cleo was not about to confess her long-ago teenage crush on him nor mention her college boyfriend, who got her to trust him—to believe they might have a chance at a future—before he two-timed her with her roommate. Some things were better not discussed.

"Let's just say I grew up and learned that people always let you down." She had to remind herself of that hard-learned lesson when Jax was around. With him it was too easy to fall into old patterns and let down her guard.

Throughout the meal they compared notes about college life and who had it worse. When Jax claimed he lived a semester with not much more than a can of tuna for his supper, he won hands down.

Since he'd started asking questions, it was time he answered a few. "Now, tell me more about your life in New York. You've said very little about what you do there."

"What can I say, I like to be a man of mystery."

Now that she couldn't argue with. He'd been a mystery for as long as she'd known him. He'd give just so much of himself before a solid wall would come up and block everyone out. She always thought that it had something to do with the way his father mistreated him. She inwardly cringed remembering how that man would call Jax rude names in the middle of town.

"Well, I hate to tell you this, but you aren't as mysterious as you seem."

"Really?" Jax propped his elbows on the table and leaned forward. "And what is it you think you've uncovered about me?"

"I know you work in New York City for some investment firm."

"So far you're right. I run a hedge fund on Wall Street."

"That sounds very impressive." She couldn't hold back a big smile. "I'm so happy for you. I just wish your mother was still around to see what you've done with your life."

"I think she would have approved."

"I know she would have. She was always proud of you." Cleo's thoughts filled with memories of the people of Hope Springs. "Do you ever think about going home?"

"This from the girl who moved to Connecticut for college and then graduated and moved to Vegas. I don't see you rushing back to Wyoming."

She shrugged. "I'm not cut out to be a rancher, even

if I am a Sinclair. I just wish I could have convinced my family."

"Ah, so you're off in search of yourself."

After all of these years it was as if he could still read her thoughts. Before she could tell him more, shouting came from behind her followed by the sound of shattering glass.

CHAPTER FIVE

WHY NOW?

For the first time in forever, Jax had been enjoying himself. Instead of worrying about his test results or the upcoming trial, he'd taken time to enjoy a good meal and an easy conversation. Cleo was perfect, from her sparkling smile to the way the candlelight made her blond curls shimmer. This was the closest he could ever envision himself getting with a woman and he hated that the moment had come to an abrupt end.

Stifling a groan of frustration, he turned his head. A man stumbled to his feet while berating a young waitress as she set a cup on the table. The woman's face was splotched with color while all around her on the floor were shards of broken glass.

"I'll get security," Cleo said, scrambling to her feet.

Jax wasn't about to stand by and watch the scene unfold. He strode across the empty dining room, hoping to reason with the man. "Is there a problem here?"

"What's it to you?" The man slurred his words.

"It looked like you might need some help." He'd had his share of experiences with men in this guy's condition and knew they could be unpredictable.

"Yeah, get her to bring me another drink." The man's

bloodshot eyes glared at him and then turn to the young waitress. "I don't want this coffee."

"I'm sorry. I can't serve you any more alcohol," the waitress stammered.

Before the man could move, Jax situated himself between the two of them. He'd seen enough of this thing when he was a kid, when he was too young to do anything about it. Now he wouldn't just stand by and let a man take his frustration out on this woman.

"Why don't you try the coffee?"

"Fine." The man glared at him before grabbing a large brown mug from the table behind him. "If you're so interested in the coffee, you have it."

The next thing Jax knew warm liquid hit him in the face. His hands balled at his sides and a growl started deep in his throat. With every muscle tensed, he stood there soaked as coffee continued to drip from his chin.

"Enjoy." The man staggered away.

Jax took a step in the man's direction then stopped. More than anything he wanted to go after him, but he knew better. Nothing good would come from exacerbating the situation.

He glanced over in time to see Cleo standing at the entrance to the restaurant with two burly security guards. "That's the guy."

While security dealt with the obnoxious man, Jax turned to the waitress. "Are you okay?"

She nodded and handed him a towel. "Thank you. I don't know what I'd have done if you hadn't been here."

He proceeded to dry his face. "Glad I could help."

"I tried to make him understand that I have to follow the rules. I—I wasn't sure what to do. I'm new and no one has ever acted like that before. I should have handled it better." The girl grew flustered and he felt bad for her.

"You did fine. He was just a difficult man. Here, let me give you a hand cleaning up." He knelt down and started placing the big pieces of glass on the tray.

"If there's ever anything I can do for you, just ask for Marylou."

"Thank you." He flashed her a reassuring smile. "I'll keep your offer in mind."

Cleo returned with a mop and bucket. She looked him over. "Are you okay? Did you get burned?"

"I'm fine. Luckily the coffee had time to cool down. I'm just a little wet."

She gave him one last look as though to determine whether he was telling the truth. Then she started mopping the floor. The three of them worked together until the mess was nothing more than a distant memory.

"Well, hero," Cleo said, smiling up at him, "let's get you back to the bungalow and into some dry clothes."

He shook his head. "I'm no hero."

"Yes, you are. Just like all those years ago when you stood between me and Billy Parsons when he insisted I hand over my lunch money. You're still playing the modest hero. That's one of the things that I always—" She clamped her lips together and glanced away.

His black mood started to lift. "That you always what?"

"That I…I always admired about you."

The way she stammered around, he couldn't help wondering if that was what she'd originally intended to say or if there was some other hidden truth that was making her look so uncomfortable. He knew she had a crush on him way back then. And in all honesty, he'd thought she was pretty great, too. But way too young for him.

"Come on. Let's get you out of these." She tugged at his damp, clingy T-shirt. "Then again your new cologne, eau de coffee, might be a big hit with the ladies."

"You think so? How's it working for you?"

Her petite nose curled up. "I don't think it's your scent."

Her soft laughter was the sweetest sound he'd ever heard. And her smile started a funny feeling in his chest. If only he could keep her smiling.

Her eyes twinkled. "Are you flirting with me?"

"If you have to ask, I must not be doing it right."

She laughed some more. "I'm glad not everything about you has changed. You were always a great guy in my book."

Her gaze lifted up to meet his. The tender look in her eyes touched something deep inside him—a part of him that he thought was long dead. In that moment, he felt more alive than he had in months.

Without thinking he reached out and caressed her cheek. "Thank you."

She leaned into his touch, short-circuiting the logical side of his brain. The only coherent thought in his head was to pull her close and kiss her. And this time he wouldn't be kissing her rosy cheek. This time he planned to find out if those cherry-red lips were as sweet and passionate as they were in his daydreams.

His head started to lower when he heard footsteps behind him. He pulled away. Frustration bound up in his gut. He'd been so close—a breath away from satisfying his desires.

His hands clenched at his sides as he worked to compose himself. A little voice in his head assured him that this was for the best, but it didn't stop the wave of disappointment. Only a moment or two more and he'd have had a tantalizing memory to take back to New York.

"What's going on here?" Mr. Burns demanded. "Security said there was some sort of incident."

Cleo stepped forward. "Mr. Smith played hero. Everything is fine now."

Mr. Burns frowned as he surveyed Jax's stained shirt. "I'm sorry about that. Please stop by the men's shop and pick out a replacement. Charge it to my account."

Cleo clasped her hands together. "I can explain—"

"Trust me, you'll get your chance in my office. I have something to take care of first, but I'll be there shortly."

"Yes, sir."

Cleo's worried gaze moved from Mr. Burns to Jax. He wanted to reassure her that everything would be all right. That if he had to he would go over this man's head because he was really starting to dislike her boss and the tone he used when speaking to her.

Not wanting to do anything to make her even more uncomfortable, he decided to wait until she was gone before he had a word with this man. Then he'd set him straight.

Talk about a long, miserable evening.

Not even the magnificent sunset with its brilliant orange-and-pink glow could lift Cleo's spirits. She strode along the path to Jax's bungalow, grateful for its privacy. Her steps picked up speed as she continued contemplating what had just happened.

What made everyone think they knew what was best for her? First her overbearing family. Then her two-timing boyfriend. And now Jax…

She'd been a fool to think Jax was different—that he respected her ability to take care of herself. Even if it was to learn from her mistakes. She could just add him to her ever-growing list of people who'd disappointed her.

Her lips firmed into a line, holding back a string of heated words. She only had herself to blame. When would she learn to be more cautious?

There had only been one other time when she'd been this worked up—the last day she'd argued with her father on the phone. Her stomach churned as the chilling memory surfaced. She recalled how her father had yelled and then the phone had gone dead. Not knowing what had happened to him, she'd practically climbed the walls waiting for him to call her back. Nothing could ever be that bad. And thankfully this day wouldn't end with someone dying.

But before she was done, Jax would get an earful.

She stopped outside the bungalow and took a deep breath, trying to calm her racing heart. Her tightly clenched fist knocked solidly on the door. She waited. No answer. She once again pounded on the solid wood door.

"I'm not leaving until you talk to me," she shouted.

The door yanked open just as she raised her clenched hand.

"I think the entire resort heard you." He glanced both ways. "I'm surprised no one has come running to find out what's wrong."

She lowered her hand and marched past him into the bungalow. "Do you know what I just spent the last hour or so doing?" Without even waiting for Jax to respond, she motored on. "I had to justify exactly why I should continue as a part of the player development team. And Mr. Burns wanted to know if there was something going on between the two of us. Otherwise he just couldn't understand why you'd be so adamant about keeping me on as your host."

Jax closed the door and turned. "And, gee, I thought you came here to thank me."

"Thank you? If it wasn't for you, I wouldn't be in this mess."

"Hey, this isn't my fault. And as I recall, in the beginning I suggested another casino host take over."

The fact he was making perfect sense was not helping

matters. "Still, did you have to threaten my boss? He already dislikes me. Now he outright hates me."

Jax crossed his arms, his biceps bulging. "I didn't exactly threaten him."

She pried her gaze from his muscles and looked into his blue eyes, which were just as disconcerting. "Are you saying you didn't mention something along the lines of if he fired me, you'd take your business elsewhere? As well as that of your friends?"

Jax shrugged. "Someone needed to put that man in his place. He couldn't keep treating you like that."

"But that wasn't your responsibility. I can take care of myself. Stop acting like one of my overprotective brothers." She started pacing through the spacious living area. "I know how to handle men like Mr. Burns."

"Fine. Maybe I did come on a little strong, but that man is annoying. I don't know how you can stand working for him." Jax strode out of the room and quickly returned with some water. "Drink this. It'll cool you off."

She placed her sunglasses and phone on the table in the entranceway and accepted the tall glass. After a long sip, she said, "I know I should be thanking you."

"That's not such a bad idea."

She drew in a deep breath and leveled her shoulders. "I'm sorry. I shouldn't have blown up at you."

"Apology accepted."

"But you don't understand. My entire life my brothers have interfered with everything I do, never letting me stand on my own two feet. And my mother was constantly overriding my decisions. I thought that it was all behind me when I left Wyoming."

"I remember how your brothers policed every guy who looked in your direction. Did you ever have a date in high school?"

She nodded. "Mama finally put her foot down and made them back off on the couple of boys she approved of."

"But not the guys you had your eye on."

She shook her head. "You know how old-fashioned my family can be, and Kurt is no better. He doesn't understand why I had to get away to try different things and find what makes me happy."

"I guess I hadn't thought of it that way." Jax placed his hand over his heart. "I promise in the future to let you fight your own battles."

"Thank you. But you do realize once you check out, Mr. Burns will find a way to get rid of me."

"Are you saying that I have to stay here indefinitely?" Jax smiled, causing her heart flutter.

"Yes. But in order to do that, you'll have to start winning."

He rubbed his jaw. "I suppose you're right. Maybe we should go give it another try. I'm feeling lucky now."

"Are you serious?" There was still a chance of turning things around if Jax continued to test his luck at the tables.

The light from his smile snuck between the cracks in her dark mood and lightened her spirits. She was drawn to him, but she steeled herself against the desire. There was still so much she didn't know about him.

She'd never met anyone who could affect her so deeply. She'd come in here ready to tell him what to do with the job he'd secured for her, but instead she was walking out the door with a smile on her face, anxious to prove Mr. Burns wrong.

In the warm evening, the lights along the pathway gave off a soft glow. Jax was just behind her and she could sense his gaze on her. What was going through his mind?

Was he remembering how he'd almost kissed her in the restaurant? Drat Mr. Burns for ruining the moment. After all, it wasn't as though they were starting something serious. It would have been a simple kiss.

"It's a beautiful evening," Jax said from behind her.

"Yes, it is." But it wasn't the darkening sky or warm breeze that held her interest.

When Jax made another comment, she couldn't quite catch his words. Afraid she missed something important, she stopped short. He bumped into her. His hands reached and wrapped around her waist. She automatically turned in his arms.

Her gaze met his and her heart skipped a beat. "I didn't hear you."

"I said the sunset wasn't nearly as beautiful as you."

He was so close. She could smell his male scent combined with a spicy aftershave. A much better fragrance for him than the coffee.

Her good intentions evaporated as his intense gaze held hers. In his eyes, she detected mounting interest. She reveled in the fact that she could evoke such a reaction in him. She moved a little closer and heard the swift intake of his breath. He might fight it, but he was as attracted to her as she was to him.

Then she did something spontaneous. She lifted up on her tiptoes and pressed her lips to his just the way she had all those years ago. But this time she didn't stop there. She was no longer young and inexperienced. And she fully intended to make an unforgettable point.

Her lips moved against his very still mouth. Surely he couldn't be that surprised. This had started long ago and tonight she wanted to turn her fantasy into reality. So that when they each went their separate ways, she would have this memory to hang on to during those sleepless nights.

Her hands slid up over his solid chest and his muscled shoulders and wrapped around his neck. Her fingertips slid through his hair. With a moan, he tightened his hold on her, drawing her closer. His lips moved beneath hers. And like a timeless dance their mouths opened and their tongues met. Was it possible that this kiss—that Jax himself—was even better than she ever imagined in her dreams?

His kiss became frenzied with need. She met him stroke for stroke. His excitement increased her pleasure. Time slipped away. The only thing that mattered now was the man holding her.

Then as quickly as the kiss had started, it ended. Jax released her and stepped back. His breathing was as rapid as hers but his gaze lowered. He refused to look at her. What was that all about?

"That shouldn't have happened." He raked his fingers through his hair, scattering the short strands.

This was not the reaction she'd expected. She inwardly groaned. Why should this time be any different? He didn't want her. The acknowledgment stung.

"You're right." What had she been thinking? "It was my fault. It won't happen again."

She went to turn away when he reached out to her. "Hey, this has nothing to do with you. You're beautiful. Any man would be crazy to turn you down."

"You're making too much of it."

When would she learn to think before acting? Every time she put herself out there, she'd been rejected, first by her ex and then by her very own mother. People couldn't love her as is. They always wanted her to be more outgoing, more compliant, more something. There was always an area where she fell short in their eyes. She didn't even know what Jax found lacking in her and she wasn't about to stick around to ask.

She sucked down the bruising ache in her chest. It wasn't as though she still carried a torch for him. The kiss had been nothing more than a passing fancy, not something serious.

Swallowing hard, she levelled her shoulders and met his gaze. "I have some stuff to do. You can go ahead without me. I'll call and make sure your blackjack table is ready." It was then that she realized she didn't have her phone. "I must have left my phone back at the bungalow."

Jax turned as though to walk with her.

She held up her hand to stop him. "Just go into the casino. I'll get it."

He looked as though he was going to argue but then thought better of it. "Are you sure?"

"Yes. Go ahead into the casino. You should be all set up at the same table as earlier."

"Cleo, I'm sorry. I didn't mean to hurt you—"

She waved away his platitude. "I'm fine. It was a mistake kissing you all those years ago and it was a mistake tonight."

His mouth opened but she didn't wait around to hear anything he had to say. She strode away, completely mortified by the way she'd thrown herself at him. What in the world had gotten into her? She'd like to blame it on a full moon, but there was none. This mortifying disaster was all her fault.

When she arrived at Jax's bungalow, she realized her pass card was with the phone locked inside. She expelled a sigh. Just what she needed now was to tell him that she had forgotten not only her phone but the hotel pass card, as well. Could she look any more incompetent this evening?

The sound of footsteps had her taking a calming breath. A shadow fell over her. She turned, expecting to find Jax, but instead a tall, muscular man dressed in a dark suit stood before her. The stranger was built like a linebacker and under different circumstances this might have intrigued her, but tonight she didn't want to be bothered.

Her gaze rose to his face. She was caught off guard by his dark, menacing eyes. "I'm sorry but this is a restricted area. Are you a guest of the hotel?"

The man's tanned face creased with an intimidating frown. "I'm looking for someone. A Jax Monroe."

She had no idea who this man was or who had pointed him in this direction, but the first rule about being a casino host was abiding by their client's wishes. And Jax had no wish for anyone to find him here.

"I can't help you. Did you try at the front desk?" She knew that they wouldn't release guest information, but she hoped this man didn't know that and would go away. "Maybe they can give you some information."

"Just tell me where I can find him."

An uneasy feeling inched down her spine. Was this the man Jax was avoiding? If so, she fully understood why Jax wouldn't want anything to do with him. Her mouth grew dry. The guy looked as though he could bench-press a car. And the menacing look in his eyes gave her the creeps.

Something definitely wasn't right here. Her palms grew moist. Standing alone with this man was not a good idea. It was time to get moving.

"I really need to be going. I have people waiting for me." She started walking, but instead of taking the private path back to the casino, she veered toward the pool, hoping there might still be some stragglers hanging out.

"Don't walk away from me. This is important. Just tell me where to find him and there won't be any trouble."

She didn't need to hear any more. She walked faster. The man easily kept pace.

The hairs on the back of her neck lifted. When she reached the pool area, luckily some young people were still milling about. Not that they were paying her any attention. Still, whatever this man meant by his threat, he wouldn't be foolish enough to try something with so many witnesses... Would he?

She got as far as the first line of lounge chairs when his meaty fingers reached out and clamped around her upper arm, halting her progress. She jerked her arm, but his grip was like a vice. Her heart jumped, lodging in her throat.

He pulled her to him. Her back pressed to his chest and he wrapped his hand over her mouth. "I want you to give Jax a message—"

Cleo bit down on the man's finger.

A curse thundered in her ears. He yanked his hand away. Never taking her eyes off him, she backed up. He lunged for her. In the ensuing struggle, her foot got caught in a lounge chair. She lost her balance and fell backward, hitting the concrete.

CHAPTER SIX

"OPEN YOUR EYES."

Jax stared down at Cleo's pale, lifeless form on a stretcher in the back of an ambulance. His chest tightened as he said a silent prayer to the big guy upstairs. She just had to be all right. She had to be.

His thumb stroked the soft skin of her limp hand. He had no idea what had happened. When he'd heard there was a commotion out by the pool and Cleo hadn't returned, he'd gone looking for her. He never expected to find Cleo in a crumpled heap on the ground.

There hadn't been time to stop and ask questions. All he could think about was her opening her beautiful green eyes again. But one thing he knew in that moment was that the girl who'd given him a peck all those years ago still meant the world to him. He reached into his pocket. His fingers traced over the pocket watch—his good-luck charm. He was about to pull it out and press it into her limp hand when he noticed her fingers move.

"Jax? Where am I?"

Cleo's voice was weak but clear. He'd never heard anything so wonderful in his whole life. He longed to pull her into his arms and hold her close.

"You fell, but don't worry, you're going to be fine now." She tried to sit up, but the straps on the gurney held her down. "Not so fast, they still have to check you out. You got quite a bump on your head."

She glanced over, noticing the paramedic reading off her stats to the hospital.

"My leg hurts and I can't move it."

"They immobilized it. Looks like you banged it up pretty good."

She closed her eyes and he worried that she had slipped into unconsciousness, but she quickly opened them again. "I'm sorry to be such a bother."

He held her hand between both of his and gave it a re-assuring squeeze. "You could never be a bother. Right now all you have to do is concentrate on getting better."

He wanted to ask her what happened, but now wasn't the time to get into it. Still, Cleo wasn't a clumsy person. When you lived on a ranch, you learned to be fast on your toes. So what exactly had happened to her?

He was still holding her hand as they backed up to the emergency room entrance. Her fingers were cold as she kept a firm grip on him. When he tried to pull away, she wouldn't let go.

"It's okay. They'll take good care of you." He stared straight into her eyes, noting the worry reflected in them. He lifted her hand and pressed his lips to her delicate skin. "You're safe now. I promise."

"Will...will you stay?"

"You bet. They couldn't drag me out of here if they tried."

"Thank you."

The fact that she wanted him with her, that he was able to provide some sort of comfort, stirred a strange sensa-tion in his chest. It wasn't the protective feeling of a big brother watching over a little sister. No, this was something different—something much deeper. Much more powerful.

The scare had been of a magnitude that he'd never experienced before. He didn't know where the feelings came from or what to do with them—he just knew his place was right here by Cleo's side.

The ambulance doors swung open and they rushed her off. He wanted to go with her—to make sure that nothing happened to her. But as he started to follow Cleo's gurney, a nurse stepped in front of him and pointed the way to the waiting area, promising they would notify him when he could see her.

Frustration knotted his gut. The last time he'd let her out of his sight something bad had happened. But Cleo was safe now. She was in the hospital. Doctors and nurses would be seeing to her needs.

He entered the spacious waiting area lined with rows of black cushioned chairs. He took a deep breath as the reality of his location struck him. It wasn't so long ago he'd been the patient. Even though it had been a different hospital, the memory had him on edge. He didn't want to be here—not at all.

But he'd promised Cleo he'd stay. He wouldn't break his promise to her. It was the least he could do for her. He tried sitting but that lasted all of thirty seconds. He paced the length of the room. Back and forth. He wasn't the only one wearing a concerned expression. The waiting area was filled with young and old people all waiting for word on a loved one.

"Excuse me, Mr. Monroe."

He turned to find a police officer. "Yes."

"I'm here about the incident at the Glamour. Did you see anything?"

The police were involved. This wasn't good. "No, I didn't. I was inside and heard about the commotion by the pool. I went to investigate and that's when I found Cleo. Do you know what happened?"

"I'm still piecing things together. We have a report of a man getting into a scuffle with Ms. Sinclair and your name was mentioned."

"Have you talked with her?"

"Not yet. That's where I'm headed next."

Dread dug at Jax as he wondered if it had anything to do with his mysterious calls. "There's something you should know."

The officer turned his keen, observant eyes on him and listened intently as Jax revealed how he was a key witness in a federal money-laundering case. He also mentioned the strange phone calls that had started in New York.

The officer asked a few more questions, jotted out some notes and gave Jax his contact information. "If you think of anything at all that might be helpful, let me know."

"I will." And he meant it. He wasn't going to take unnecessary chances with the woman he...he...cared about.

Whether he liked it or not, she was definitely getting to him. She was making him feel things that he didn't have any right to feel. The only way to stop this growing attraction was to follow through with his plan to leave Vegas. He eyed up the exit. But he couldn't break his promise to her. He'd wait until he saw her and was certain she was going to be fine.

Almost a half hour later, a nurse stood at the security door that led into the examination area. "Mr. Monroe, you can come back now."

When he came to a stop next to Cleo's bed, he was stunned by what he saw. A white bandage was wrapped around her forehead. Her face was nearly as pale as the sheet. And her injured leg was elevated. He didn't know what he'd been expecting, but it wasn't her looking weak and helpless.

She studied him. "Do I really look that bad?"

He'd obviously let his poker face slip again. Still, the sight of her lying there injured had shaken him more than he'd anticipated. "Sorry. I wasn't expecting to find you all bandaged up."

"Jax, there's something I need to tell you—"

"And how's the patient?" A male voice came from behind him.

Jax turned to find a doctor in a white lab coat standing at the opening in the curtains surrounding the bed. He glanced back at Cleo. "We'll talk later. I'll just wait outside."

"It's okay." She grabbed his hand. "You can stay for this."

The doctor cleared his throat. "Ms. Sinclair has a mild concussion. We're still not certain about the extent of damage to her leg. I'm waiting on the films. However, I want to keep her in the hospital under observation. She was unconscious for a bit and I want to make sure there aren't any complications. But she's insisting that she's going home."

Jax turned to her. "You need to listen to the doctor. He knows what he's talking about."

"I'm not staying." A stubborn glint reflected in her eyes. "I can't sleep in hospitals. Besides, I feel fine now."

"She can go home as long as she isn't alone," the doctor said while looking directly at Jax. "Can you stay with her?"

"I don't need him." The sincerity in her pointed words poked at Jax. "I can take care of myself."

The doctor's brow drew together. "I'm sure you can in most cases, but you've got a serious bump on your head and you need to stay off your leg as much as possible. So either you stay here and let the nurses look after you or you can go home with..."

"Jax. Jax Monroe. And I'll see that she's taken care of."

Cleo worried her bottom lip. And in that hospital gown, she looked like a child again. All he wanted to do was take care of her any way possible…even if it meant getting closer to her instead of beating a trail into the sunset. That would have to wait for another day.

Cleo's worried gaze turned to him. "Are you sure about this?"

"I wouldn't have said it otherwise."

The doctor's gaze swung between the two of them, deciding if he could trust them. "Now that it's settled, I'll go check on things. If you wait in the lobby, we'll call you when she's ready to go."

Jax didn't mind a few minutes to himself to pull his scattered thoughts together. He started for the doorway when Cleo grabbed his hand.

"I need to talk to you. I just remembered something."

"Don't worry. We'll have plenty of time for that later."

"But this is important." Her distressed tone caught his attention.

He wondered if this had something to do with the police poking around. "I'm listening."

"There's a man after you."

"What?"

As though recalling her fingers were still gripping his hand, she let go and made a point of straightening her white sheet. "When I went back to the bungalow a man approached me. He wanted to know how to find you."

"And he attacked you?"

"Not really. When I tried to get away from him, he followed me. He grabbed my arm and put a hand over my mouth. He said he had a message for you."

Alarm arrowed through Jax's chest. "What is it?"

Cleo's gaze lowered. "I don't know. I bit his finger before he could relay the message. He let go of me and the rest is kind of a blur."

His gut was telling him trouble had followed him from New York. And Cleo had ended up paying the price. Guilt beat at his chest.

"Don't worry. He won't bother you anymore."

"How do you know? Who is this man? What does he want?"

Jax held up his hand, halting the flow of questions. "I don't know him, but I promise you won't have to deal with him again. Remember from here on out I'm in charge of your safety. Doctor's orders."

She started to sit up. "Jax, I need to know what's going on."

"Calm down." He placed a hand on her shoulder, pressing her back against the pillow. "When I learn something I'll tell you. Now I have a couple of phone calls to make."

Jax hated the thought that he'd dragged Cleo into his problems. He had no proof that this mystery man was tied into the money-laundering case, but he'd be willing to bet his fortune that he was right. His priority now had to be keeping Cleo safe. And since that hired thug knew her name, her face and where she worked, it wouldn't take long for him to track her down at home, either.

Just then the doctor returned. "We'll have you fixed up in no time."

That was Jax's cue to leave. He turned back to Cleo. "Don't worry. I'll take care of everything."

As he strode away, she called out, "What are you going to do?"

He didn't pause to answer because, at that moment, he didn't have a clue. It was obvious that he needed to get Cleo and himself out of Las Vegas. But how far could he take her with her injuries? If she needed further medical attention, he didn't want to be stuck out in the middle of nowhere. There had to be a compromise. A place where the thug hired to scare him into silence wouldn't think to look for either of them.

Free at last.

Cleo settled back against the leather seat of a large SUV. Even though her hospital stay had only lasted a matter of hours, for her it felt like days. And now Jax was playing the dutiful hero and riding to her rescue. She had no idea where he got this sweet ride, but she appreciated its spaciousness more than she could say.

"Thank you. But you really didn't have to go to such lengths. I could have called a taxi to take me back to my place."

"I don't think so. Remember I'm the one who promised the doctor I'd take care of you."

At the next traffic light, he turned left instead of right.

"You went the wrong way. Wait. How do you know where I live?"

"I don't."

"It's the other direction. I live at 331 Villa Drive, apartment C3. You can just turn left up here and loop around." When he kept going straight, she sat up a little straighter. "Where exactly are you taking me?"

"Do you always ask so many questions?"

She glared at him. "I demand to be taken back to my apartment."

"Not today. We're going someplace where you can rest and not worry about any unwanted guests."

"But I can't." She didn't like the sound of this. "I have a job…er, at least I hope I still have a job."

"Of course you do. You were injured on Glamour grounds while performing your duties. Therefore you're entitled to workers' compensation. Not even Mr. Burns would be foolish enough to let you go and face a lawsuit."

The medication they'd given her at the hospital was making her head woozy. "The doctor said it wouldn't be long until I could get around."

"And until then you need to rest as much as possible. Now just relax. I've got everything under control."

"How am I supposed to do that when you won't even tell me where we're going?"

"We aren't going far. Just north of the city. And I promise you'll like the accommodations."

He was trying to sound upbeat, but she knew he was worried. "You think that guy is going to come back, don't you?"

"He won't bother you where we're going."

She wanted to believe him, but she didn't even know what he was mixed up in. The adrenaline that had been driving her drained away, leaving her feeling wiped out. She was with Jax. Nothing would happen now because the one thing she did know was that she still trusted him. She instinctively knew that he'd protect her.

She leaned her head back, fighting to keep her eyes open. The image of her kitty came to mind. She'd called her neighbor Robyn McCreedy to check in on him. Still, it wasn't the same as being there, especially since he'd just been neutered.

"I can't stay here long. I have to get home."

"Don't worry. I'll get you home soon." Jax glanced over at her. "You can sleep. I'll let you know when we're there."

She really shouldn't trust him so easily, but her eyelids felt so very heavy. If she could just close her eyes for a minute, she'd be all right…

"Cleo, wake up. We're here."

Her eyes snapped open, not recognizing her surroundings. The bandage around her forehead was getting itchy so she rubbed at it, wanting to take it off. But the doctor had warned her to leave it on until the stitches on the back of her head had a chance to heal.

She gazed up at a large gate that was automatically opening for them. "Where are we?"

"Someplace safe."

Jax maneuvered the vehicle between the gates and down a road lined with jaw-dropping mansions. It was dark out, making it difficult to see the details of each impressive estate until they pulled into the driveway of a humongous home. She'd only ever seen something this extraordinary in glossy magazines.

Soft rays from the full moon bathed the white stucco home, giving it a magical glow. And it was two…no, wait, make that three stories high. With the lights on inside, it looked like a gem against the velvety night. Its sweeping length and elegance left her in awe.

"I hope you won't mind staying here."

She blinked, making sure that it was real. "Mind? It's amazing." Then she turned to him. "Is it yours?"

He shook his head. "I don't have any use for a place this big. It belongs to a friend of mine."

"That must be some friend. Is he famous?"

Jax chuckled. "You might say that. Remember the movie from last summer, *Shooting Stars?*"

"You mean the Western romance? I think everyone went to see it, including me. It was a great mix of action and passion."

"My friend will be glad to hear you're such a fan."

"He filmed it?"

"No, George starred in it."

Cleo's mouth gaped as she sat there trying to process

this information. "No way. Are you totally serious? He's drop-dead gorgeous."

Jax smiled and shook his head. "I do believe you're starstruck."

"Did you see the movie?" She fanned herself. "He's so hot. In the film he was the marshal and he was on the hunt for train robbers. He ended up rescuing the heroine from a train accident the robbers had caused. It was so romantic how he cared for her and kept her safe."

Jax cleared his throat. "I'll be sure to tell George when I talk to him. Now, is there any chance you want to go inside?"

"And see the rest of his house? You bet." She reached for the door.

"Wait! I'll help you. We don't need any more accidents tonight." He alighted from the vehicle and circled around to open her door.

"But how did you get George to lend you his house?"

Jax gave a nonchalant shrug. "It's not his primary residence. He spends most of his time in Hollywood."

"I still can't believe he's letting us stay here."

"Let's just say that he owed me a favor and I called it in. George is a really good guy. He was happy to do it."

"Did you tell your friend that we are on the run from some ape?"

"Ape, huh?" Jax smiled. "I'm glad to see your sense of humor hasn't been injured."

She thought back to her run-in with that man and a shiver ran down her spine. "I just refuse to give him power over me by calling him a big, mean, scary dude…even if he was one."

Refusing to dwell on what happened, she turned her attention to the long sweeping steps that led to the front door. And then she glanced down at her leg. This was going to be a challenge, especially when she wasn't used to getting around on one good leg.

But before she could ask Jax for the crutches, he scooped her into his arms. Her body landed against his solid chest. He'd definitely filled out in the years they'd been apart.

"What are you doing?"

"Taking you inside."

Her hand automatically slipped around his neck. "But I can manage—"

"Do you have to argue about everything?"

She pressed her lips shut. If he wanted to carry her up all of those steps, why should she complain? She wasn't feeling exactly steady on her feet. Tomorrow would be plenty early enough for her to prove her independence, even if she had to be aided by those confounded crutches.

Her head rested on his shoulder as he moved up the steps. Beneath the moonlight with the warm breeze swirling around them, it would be so easy to let her guard down. If she closed her eyes and inhaled his masculine scent, she could let herself get swept up in this very romantic scenario. Not that she had any intention of making a fool of herself again. If there was any more kissing, it would be Jax who made the first move.

One night here and then she'd return to her apartment to finish recuperating. Being situated in the middle unit of a young people's complex, tenants were coming and going at all hours of the day and night. She wouldn't have to worry about being alone. They'd be around if she called out for help. Yes, that would work. One night with Jax and then they'd go their separate ways.

Her thoughts turned back to Robyn, who was more than a neighbor—more like the sister Cleo never had. It was nice to have someone in her life now who cared. She'd told Robyn that she'd be home sometime that night. She really should let Robyn know that her plans had changed. She didn't want her to needlessly worry. Cleo reached for her phone but realized she didn't have it.

"Jax, I left my phone back at the bungalow."

"It's for the best."

"What? But I need my phone. How am I supposed to contact people and let them know that I'm okay?"

"They'll just have to wait. Phones have GPS tracking units in them. It's possible that thug could track us down that way. Don't worry. I got a disposable phone for emergencies."

The hairs on the back of her neck lifted. "Jax, how much trouble are you in?"

CHAPTER SEVEN

ALONE AT LAST.

Jax gently lowered Cleo down onto a long white couch in the expansive living room. He regretted having to let her go. There was something so right about having her slight figure curled up next to him. It'd taken every bit of willpower to concentrate on climbing the stairs instead of turning his head and kissing her.

His gaze dipped down to her lips while remembering how sweet they'd tasted. This wasn't right. He should be worried about the man who'd run into Cleo at the hotel, not contemplating repeating their kiss because the one they'd shared earlier had been far too brief. And even worse, it had left him anxious for more of her touch.

He'd never had a woman distract him to this extent. What was so unique about Cleo? Could it be the fact she'd always been forbidden fruit? After all, she was one of Hope Springs's highly respected Sinclair clan whereas his own family had been barely tolerated.

The attraction appeared to be all one-sided as Cleo sat up and looked around the expansive room. "Did you see those posters in the hallway? This really is an honest-to-goodness movie star's house."

"Are you saying you doubted me?"

Her gaze darted around the room. "Look at the mantel. There's an award. Do you think he'd mind if I touched it?"

"I don't see why he would have to know." When she went to stand, Jax placed his hand on her shoulder. "I'll get it for you."

"Can you believe we're here? And look over there." She pointed to the wall to the left. "There's pictures of him with actresses and politicians. Look at that one of him with the president."

Jax chuckled at Cleo's awestruck face. He retrieved the gold figurine, surprised to find it was rather heavy, and handed it to her.

"I just can't believe you're friends with him. Can you get me his autograph?"

"I'm sure that can be arranged. Now sit there and don't move. I'll be back."

"Wait." She looked up. "You promised we'd talk."

"And we will right after I get our stuff. Just enjoy checking out that award."

The events of the day were catching up to him, and he couldn't wait until he got Cleo settled in bed. He inwardly groaned at the thought of her stretched out on some silky sheets. He gave himself a mental shake. That wouldn't and couldn't happen. Being a total gentleman tonight was going to be a feat all of its own.

Jax made a few trips to the car and deposited the final items next to the couch.

Cleo eyed up the stash. "What is all of that?"

"Things you'll need while we're here."

"But both of those bags look full. What did you buy?"

He handed over a shopping bag and she peered inside. Her lips formed an O and he realized too late that he'd given her the pink bag. Still, the color filling her cheeks matched the bag and made him smile.

"Don't worry. I didn't pick out the lingerie. Marylou helped me out."

Cleo's thin brows rose. "Marylou? You mean the woman from the restaurant? The one you rescued from that rude guy?"

He nodded. "She said that if I ever needed anything to ask. I couldn't risk going back into the Glamour and I didn't want to risk going to your place, so she discreetly picked up some of my things from the bungalow and bought you some essentials at the guest shops."

Cleo grimaced and adjusted her leg. "You're making this sound like we're going to be here for more than just tonight."

He glanced at his watch, realizing it was time for her pain medication. "We are. But don't worry. I have plenty of groceries."

She sat up straight. "I can't run off with you. I have responsibilities. People who will be worried about me."

"Listen," he replied as he got to his feet, "I'm not any happier about this than you are. But until the police track down this guy, we're staying put. Now it's time for your pain meds. I'll be right back."

"Jax, you're being ridiculous. I can get these things for myself."

He headed for the kitchen, ignoring her protest. Why did she have to be so stubborn? Couldn't she relax and let him take care of her? Did everything have to be a struggle?

He returned quickly, handing over the glass and the medication, which she took without so much as a comment. He sank down into the armchair across from her and folded his arms behind his head.

"You have to admit staying here won't be so bad." He was trying to convince himself as much as her. He leaned his head back. One by one the muscles in his body relaxed. "Even the furniture is comfortable."

He closed his eyes. This was the most relaxed he'd been in a long time. Was it the house? Or was it the company—Cleo's company—that had him thinking about the here and now instead of the uncertainty of his future?

"I'm still waiting."

Her voice startled him as he started to doze off. He lifted his head to look at her. "Waiting for what?"

"For you to explain why we're here. Who's the ape that's hunting you?"

Jax ran a hand over the evening stubble trailing down his jaw. "I honestly don't know who the man is. But the police are on it now. With the aid of the surveillance cameras at the casino, they'll be able to identify and locate him."

He hoped.

"But you do know why he's here and what he wants." Her eyes grew round. "Jax, what did you do?"

The fact she thought he might be on the wrong side of the law dug deep into his chest and pulled at the old scars on his heart. Years ago, when all of Hope Springs saw a delinquent kid, she'd looked at him as somebody worth befriending. Cleo always made him feel as though he mattered.

But for the first time, the look in her eyes had changed. Was she now looking at him as her mother had done and seeing him as the no-good Monroe kid who could never amount to anything but trouble. Anger and hurt churned in his gut. He thought he was far past these old feelings—yet being here with Cleo had rolled back time.

"I'm not a criminal," he ground out.

Color filled her cheeks. "I—I didn't mean it like that. This whole thing has me on edge."

"I guess once you're considered the bad boy, the reputation sticks." His jaw tightened, holding back old resentments.

"That's not true. You're forgetting all of the people who cared about you. People like Kurt and my grandfather."

"You're right." He sighed. "I shouldn't have gone off on you. It's just been a stressful day."

"And I deserve some answers."

"Yes, you do." Although he was certain his words would not give her the peace of mind she was seeking, he owed her the truth. "I'm a key witness in a federal court case."

"A witness." She leaned forward, resting her elbows on her knees. "I take it this isn't a simple murder case."

He couldn't help but smile at the way she classified murder as a simple case. "No, this isn't about murder. It's actually a white-collar crime."

The worry lines on her face smoothed. "Well, that doesn't sound so bad."

Would it be so wrong to let her cling to the idea that this case was no big deal? Then she wouldn't have to worry. But she also might decide to let down her guard, giving that thug a chance to get near her again. No, she definitely needed to know the whole truth.

"It's a money-laundering scam that involved my business partner. I blew the whistle on him before he could take us both down. I wore a wire and gave the government all the evidence they needed to make their case against him and his shady affiliates."

Cleo's face grew ashen. "That sounds dangerous."

"Let's just say these men aren't the friendliest people to cross."

"That…that man… Does he want to—"

"Scare me off? Yes, he does. But it won't work. I will finish what I started."

"Oh, Jax. What if—"

"There are no what-ifs. I just have a few more weeks until I return to New York for the trial and then this will all be over. Now it's time to call it a night. I don't know about you, but I'm exhausted. It's been a long day."

In truth, not only was he truly tired but he also needed some space. He was still smarting over the fact that Cleo thought he might be a criminal.

Her fine brows gathered. "You can't expect me to stay here with you until the trial."

"We'll have to see how things go. But for now you're staying where I can protect you."

He yawned. Maybe tonight he'd be able to fall asleep without the endless hours of staring into the dark. Or even worse, to drift off only to have that blasted recurring nightmare where he was chased down a dark alley. Stupid dream.

"Come on." He knelt down beside her and held out his arms. "Your chariot awaits."

Cleo's head felt fuzzy. She didn't know if it was the painkillers or the information she'd just learned. Either way, it didn't matter. She was tired of being treated as if she was helpless. And she didn't need Jax making decisions for her.

When Jax reached out to her, she pushed aside his offer. "Thanks, but I can get to the bedroom on my own."

His face creased with frown lines, but he didn't argue. Instead he grabbed her crutches and held them out to her. "Are you sure?"

She nodded and placed the crutches under her arms. A bump on the head hadn't made her forget the way Jax had rejected her earlier that day. The memory still stung. Why should things change just because she got hurt?

They weren't a happy couple. They never would be.

She paused at the bottom of the long line of steps.

Suddenly, sleeping on the couch didn't sound like such a bad idea.

"Sure you haven't changed your mind?" Jax prodded in a persuasive voice.

"I can manage." All she had to do was focus. Soon she'd be upstairs and then she could lie down.

"You don't look so good."

"Thanks. You sure know how to give a girl a compliment."

"That isn't how I meant it and you know it. You're just being difficult."

He was right. But tonight she didn't care. Maybe it was the medicine or hitting her head, but she didn't feel like acting as if everything was all right when it clearly wasn't.

He followed her into a spacious bedroom with a king-size bed done up in peaches and cream. She sat down on the edge, very aware of Jax's presence. He knelt down in front of her to remove her shoe from her good leg. Why did he have to be so nice when she wanted to be angry with him?

"I can do it." She attempted to take over.

He brushed aside her hand. "You don't need to. That's what I'm here for."

His gentle tone smoothed her agitation. "I'm not even sure how I'll sleep tonight. Every time I close my eyes I see that ape man. You have to promise to be careful. He isn't a nice guy. He totally gave me the creeps."

"I'll be careful."

"You promise?"

"I do. I brought us here, didn't I? He won't know where to find us."

She lay back against the bed and closed her eyes, willing away the image of that man. Jax's warm fingers touched the bare skin of her calf, snapping her eyes open. What was he doing? Then she realized he was removing her sock. How could such a mundane task feel so amazing?

Dropping the sock, his fingers continued to work their magic, kneading and pressing on the sole of her foot. One by one her muscles relaxed and she turned to putty in his hands. The most amazing sensations coursed through her body. If he could do this massaging just one foot, she couldn't even imagine what other tricks he had up his sleeve.

"This will help you relax." His voice was soft and soothing.

She hadn't realized that she'd moaned out loud until he said, "I'm glad you're enjoying it."

"What can I say? I'm a sucker for a foot massage."

"Scoot back on the bed."

She did as he said, wondering what he was up to next. He grabbed a couple of pillows and propped up her injured leg. Then he sat down and put her other foot in his lap. The pad of his thumb rubbed up and down over the arch of her foot. She watched him as he used both hands to stretch her foot and then run both thumbs in circular patterns.

"Close your eyes," he said, still working his magic fingers.

She was in the midst of ecstasy and didn't want it to stop so she complied. Tomorrow she would stand her ground— yes, tomorrow. Tonight she would let him feel as though he were taking care of her… Just so long as his fingers kept moving.

Time slipped by and, at last, he stopped. She was lost somewhere between floating on a fluffy cloud and half-asleep. He got up and turned off the light.

"Don't go." She reached out to grab his hand. "Not yet."

"Cleo…"

All she knew was that she was in a happy place and she

didn't want it to end. Her body felt like mush. The darkness made her feel safe from his scrutinizing stare. She felt as though she could say anything to him. And in a sleepy haze she decided to throw caution to the wind.

"Why don't you find me attractive?"

She heard a swift intake of his breath. Then an awkward silence hung there.

The edge of the bed dipped as he sat down. The back of his hand glided over her cheek. "Who says I don't find you attractive?"

"When we kissed earlier, you pulled away. You didn't like it."

His voice was soft. "Did you ever think that I liked it too much?"

"Then kiss me now." He groaned but she wasn't giving up. "I've kissed you twice. You owe me."

Again there was an elongated silence. It had to be the medication because she'd never asked a man to kiss her. And it was so much easier to blame it on the painkillers than to admit how very much she wanted him. She'd never desired a man as she did Jax.

Then without warning he leaned over. His lips were just a breath away from hers. "Cleo, you don't know what you're asking of me."

"Yes, I do. I want you to kiss me. I want to know what it's like to be desired by Jax Monroe. Hope Springs's bad boy. Now a Wall Street tycoon. Kiss me, Jax. Please."

With a moan, his mouth pressed to hers. His kiss was hungry and needy. And her heart swelled. Somewhere in the haze of her mind there was a warning voice, but it was garbled and she didn't feel like heeding to caution. Here in the dark there was just the two of them.

His lips moved hungrily over hers like a starved man. And she met him kiss for kiss. Her fingers worked their way over his muscular shoulders to his neck and then her nails raked through his short hair.

The kiss went on and on and she never wanted it to end. She just floated along in the moment, enjoying having Jax so close. Because come the stark morning sun, she'd come to her senses. A relationship wasn't in the cards for her. But a fleeting moment of ecstasy was too tempting to pass up. Tomorrow would come all too quickly.

As though he could read her thoughts, he pulled back. His breathing was uneven and rapid. But as she reached out to him, he jumped to his feet.

"Cleo, you couldn't be more wrong. I want you more than I've ever wanted anyone. But this, you and me, it can't be."

"Of course it can't be," she spat out. No matter what he said, he didn't find her attractive enough. She blinked back the tears swarming in her eyes.

She'd miscalculated. Instead of the kiss making her feel better, she felt even worse knowing that he still thought that they were a mistake—that she was a mistake. She wanted to get as far away from him as she could, someplace where she could lick her wounds in private.

"I want to go home. Charlie needs me."

She rolled over onto her side, craving the company of her tabby cat. Anytime she was upset, he was right there with a loving rub and a cheerful purr. Her wounded body ached but it was nothing compared to the great big bruise on her heart.

CHAPTER EIGHT

JAX YAWNED AGAIN. At this rate he'd need to brew another pot of coffee before lunch. He'd done nothing but toss and turn for hours last night. He'd finally dozed off sometime after three.

His mind had been crammed full with thoughts of the thug who had hurt Cleo. He'd even checked in with the police to see if the ape, as Cleo called him, had been arrested. So far, nothing. But the good news was they had his image from the resort's tapes and were working on identifying him.

Jax grabbed a spatula for the scrambled eggs. He wasn't used to cooking for anyone, but he didn't mind. What did bother him was having Cleo long for another man after he'd just got done kissing her. He snatched up a plate and placed it with a thunk on the counter.

The fact that she had Charlie in her life was for the best. A man in his position needed to keep clear of romantic entanglements. And even if his latest set of tests came back clear there was no guarantee they'd stay that way.

He drew his thoughts up short. None of it mattered because he had no intention of letting Cleo into his life—into his heart.

After the thug was arrested, Jax's plan was to return to his solitary life. With all of the money he'd made in the stock market, he could retire young. He didn't want to be one of those people who died at their desk. He wanted to get out and experience the world for as long as he had... And just as soon as this court case was over he'd get started.

No longer feeling so tired, he piled the scrambled eggs on the plate next to the buttered toast. When his friend said the housekeeper kept this place stocked, he hadn't been kidding. Jax really need not have bothered stopping at the store last night after he'd picked up the rental vehicle.

He placed the food and the orange juice on a tray, along with a red rose from the bouquet on the dining room table. Then on second thought, he returned the flower back to the vase. There was no reason to muddy the waters any further.

He carried the tray to the bedroom and tapped on the door. "Cleo, are you up?"

Silence greeted him.

He knocked louder. "Cleo, I've got your breakfast."

Still nothing.

Balancing the tray with one hand, he eased open the door and stepped inside. He came to a halt when he saw that the bed was already made up. His gaze flicked to the bathroom door. It was open and no sounds came from within.

Erring on the side of caution, he called out, "Cleo, are you decent?"

Again there was no response. He envisioned her passed out in the tub or worse. He set the tray on the end of the bed and rushed into the bathroom. The room was spacious, just like the rest of the house, but there was no sign of Cleo. He didn't understand. Where could she have gotten to?

The food long forgotten, he searched the other five bedrooms. She wasn't anywhere in the upstairs. He rushed to the sweeping staircase, which faced the wall of glass overlooking the front lawn and the drive. That was when he noticed the SUV was gone.

She'd run out on him!

But why?

Was she that upset about the kiss last night?

Did she feel guilty for cheating on Charlie?

His chest tightened. The doctor said she was supposed to be resting. What if she made her injuries worse? A knot formed in his gut. Or what if that thug caught up with her again?

He had to find her, but where did he start?

Cleo wished she hadn't been so spontaneous. Trying to get about with the aid of crutches was more work than she'd imagined. And now Jax had made her paranoid about the ape man staking out her place. She'd driven around the block three times looking for anyone or anything unusual, but nothing appeared to be out of place.

She pulled to a stop in a handicap parking space in front of her unit. She figured due to her unusual circumstances, she could park there for ten minutes—long enough to grab a few essentials and scoop up Charlie.

She'd just opened the driver's-side door when Robyn came up the walk, pushing a pink polka-dotted stroller. "Hey, girl, where have you been?"

Robyn was a good friend, but she was known for staying on top of the latest gossip in the complex. And this place was always rife with juicy stories. Cleo just hoped she wouldn't make a big deal over her injury.

Cleo reached over to the passenger seat and grabbed the crutches. With the crutches positioned outside the door, she carefully lowered herself to the ground. Her ankle pulsated with pain. It probably didn't help that she didn't take any of those pills the doctor prescribed for her. But she needed to be clearheaded for driving.

Cleo swung the door shut, almost losing her balance. She really did have to get the hang of the crutches since she was going to be on them for a while. "Sorry I didn't call again, but I didn't have my phone."

"I was hoping you were off with some hot guy, but by the looks of you, I guess that's wishful thinking. Unless you had a McSteamy doc taking care of you."

At the mention of a hot guy, her thoughts immediately went to Jax. He was definitely sexy in anyone's book. But she wasn't about to open that can of worms with Robyn, who was far too eager to help her find a "forever" guy. No matter how many times Cleo told her she wasn't interested, Robyn would still introduce her to any hot new tenants.

"Sorry. No hot doctors."

"When you called yesterday, you didn't say anything about it being this serious." Robyn frowned at her injured leg.

"I'm not that bad off." Cleo forced a smile, wanting to ease her friend's worry. "And the doctor said I was fine to go home."

It wasn't exactly a lie. She just left out the part about needing to be supervised for forty-eight hours. Come to think of it that probably meant she shouldn't be driving. But this was important.

"I don't know." Robyn gave her a hesitant stare. "You look about as appealing right now as Stephie's mashed peas. Definitely a bit green around the edges."

"Thanks. You really know how to cheer up a person," Cleo teased.

Robyn wasn't the type to mince words. And right about now, Cleo did feel pretty rotten. She hoped she never saw that ape man ever again. If it wasn't for him, she wouldn't be in this mess. The memory of him had her glancing around.

"You'll be back to normal after you get some rest." Robyn kept pace with her as they headed for their side-by-side apartments.

"You haven't seen any strangers lurking about, have you?"

"No." Robyn raised her brows. "Should I have?"

How much should she say? Probably as little as possible. Robyn had a good heart, but she had a habit of saying too much.

"There was just this creepy guy hitting on me at the casino. You know, the kind who won't take no for an answer."

Robyn's brunette bobbed hair swayed as she nodded. "Sometimes guys can be such jerks. And with you being so pretty, I'm surprised you don't get hit on more often."

"So if you see some tall guy with dark hair lurking about, call the cops."

"But what do I tell them?"

"Hmm…let's see." She stopped and thought for a moment. "I know, tell them that he's trespassing."

"Consider it done."

Luckily she lived on the first floor, saving her the task of going up and down more steps. They stopped at Cleo's door and it was then that she realized she didn't have her purse or her keys. Everything was back at the casino in her locker.

She turned to her friend. "I'm afraid I forgot my key. Would you mind letting me in?"

"Oh, sure. Let me grab the spare one. It's a good thing you gave it to me. I'll be right back."

Cleo hobbled around until she could lean against the wall. She wondered if Jax was awake yet. She'd considered telling him what she was up to, but when she'd gone to his room, the door was open and he was out cold. He was sprawled across the bed on his stomach while wearing nothing more than a pair of boxers.

He'd looked good—real good. She also remembered how he didn't want her—how he'd withdrawn from her. The memory dug at her heart.

Before turning away from his sleeping form, she'd noticed how the sheet had been pulled loose and kicked about. The pillows had been tossed off the bed as though he'd had a rough night. At least she had the satisfaction of knowing that he hadn't had a good sleep, either.

In no time, Robyn returned with the key in one hand and a baby monitor in the other. "If you lost your key during your accident, I can call the manager and have them change the lock. Of course, you know they're going to charge you for it. Like we don't already pay enough in rent."

"Thanks. But I know where it is. I just didn't have time to grab my things before they took me to the hospital." She wasn't about to add that she'd blacked out.

"Okay. But if you need anything, just phone me. By the way, Charlie wouldn't eat last night. I don't know if he's not feeling well or if he just missed you."

"I was worried about that. After his surgery, I want to keep a close eye on him. He didn't react well to the anesthesia." Cleo made her way over to the couch, where Charlie was curled up. He eyed her up but didn't make any movement. "Hey, buddy, it's okay. I'm here." She ran a hand down over his striped fur before scratching beneath his ear. Finally a faint purr started. "I'm sorry I wasn't here last night."

Instead of taking him with her, she was actually thinking of just staying home. According to Robyn there hadn't been any strangers lurking about. Apparently ape man had other people to push around.

The sound of the baby stirring came across the monitor. "I better go check on her," Robyn said, stepping out onto the walkway. "If you need anything else just let me know."

With her neighbor gone, Cleo turned to Charlie. "You do know that I'm going to be in trouble when Jax finds out I'm here with you."

Charlie blinked and licked his paw.

"I see you aren't the least bit worried. That makes one of us." She ruffled the fur on his head before locking the front door.

It was nice that Marylou had picked her out some new clothes, but they weren't really her taste and right now, she needed soft, stretchy shorts to get over her cast. And a comfy T-shirt. She may enjoy dressing up on most occasions, but this was different. Her body ached in places she didn't even think had been injured. Some loose-fitting clothes were definitely in order for today.

She hobbled toward the bedroom with Charlie leading the way. His tail hung low and he wasn't chatty like normal. The poor fellow. She felt really bad for him having surgery. At this point, she could kind of relate to not feeling so chipper. She'd have to remember to grab a bag of his favorite treats to take with them.

When her gaze landed on her bed, she thought that it never looked so inviting. So soft and snug. Maybe if she just lay down for a moment, she'd get her wind back. And she could give Charlie some much-needed attention as his love meter seemed to be low.

When Charlie eyed the bed hesitantly as though he wasn't so sure he could jump that high after his surgery, she scooped him up and deposited him in the middle of the bed. She could tell he was going to get as much babying out of this recovery as possible. And she didn't mind it a bit. She smiled as he circled once, then twice and finally sank down on the blue comforter.

After struggling to get changed into some comfy clothes, she lay down next to him, anxious to discard the crutches, which were as much a hindrance as a help. Her hand smoothed down over Charlie's back and his purr machine kicked into full gear.

"Sorry I wasn't here to take care of you last night. Some meanie sent me to the hospital."

Charlie yawned and then she yawned.

"I don't think he'll be back. Maybe we can both stay home."

She adjusted her pillow and closed her eyes for just a moment. After all, this guy was after Jax, not her. And Jax would be a lot safer if he didn't have to worry about caring for an injured woman. Especially after he made it perfectly clear that he wanted nothing to do with her. He felt an obligation toward her—nothing more.

Staying home was sounding ever-so-tempting. And with Robyn watching her back, she didn't have to worry.

"We'll be fine. Right, Charlie?"

CHAPTER NINE

JAX KNOCKED ON the apartment door.

When there was no sound, he thought of trying the doorknob. But considering he might have mixed up Cleo's unit number, he wasn't going to risk it.

He rapped his knuckles again. Louder this time.

An adjacent door swung open and a young woman with straight brown hair, no makeup and stains on her blue shirt stuck her head out. She eyed him up suspiciously.

Maybe she'd know Cleo's whereabouts. He stepped toward her when she held up a cell phone. "Don't come any closer or I'll call the police."

"Hey, I don't want any trouble. I'm just here to see Cleo. This is her apartment, isn't it?"

"Don't play innocent with me. Cleo told me you'd be showing up and causing trouble. She's not interested in you. Time to move on, buddy."

Cleo told her neighbor about him? And what exactly had she been saying? It sure sounded bad.

Turning away from her kiss had been one of the hardest things he'd ever done. And if given another chance, he didn't know if he was strong enough to resist her.

Just then the door to Cleo's apartment opened. "Jax, how'd you get here?"

For the first time since he found her missing, he

breathed easy. His initial instinct was to pull her into his arms, but one glimpse of the wounded look in her eyes had him frozen in place. It was for the best, even if it didn't feel like it at the moment.

Giving in to his desires was what kept getting them into trouble. First they kissed and she took off only to run into ape man. And then there was last night's kiss, where she got upset and left without a word. This time he wasn't giving her another reason to walk away.

"Do you want me to get the police?" The young woman looked far too eager to place the call.

Jax rolled his eyes. "Please tell her that I'm not here to hurt you."

Cleo smiled as though she was enjoying this. He didn't find it the least bit amusing. He hadn't thought about anything besides her safety on the ride here. A tension headache spanned his forehead. He didn't know what he'd have done if she hadn't been here.

"It's okay, Robyn." Cleo smiled at her neighbor. "Jax is an old friend of mine. He's been looking after me since my accident."

The woman's whole demeanor changed and a smile pulled at her lips. "No wonder you didn't come home last night. I wouldn't have, either."

Cleo sighed. "Robyn, it's not what you're thinking."

"Then you must be blind, girl. Otherwise how could you pass him up?" Robyn flashed Jax a bright smile before backing into her apartment and closing the door.

Color flooded Cleo's cheeks, giving them a rosy glow. "I'm sorry about her. Robyn means well but is a bit misguided at times."

He nodded, understanding why Cleo wasn't eager to hook up with him the way her neighbor thought she should be. And that reason was named Charlie. Jax's jaw tightened. He at least wanted to get a look at this guy.

Cleo adjusted her crutches. "How did you get here?"

"I didn't have much choice. I took a taxi."

"Oh. Sorry. I was only borrowing the SUV. I would have brought it back."

From the looks of her in a rumpled T-shirt and mussed-up hair, he'd just awoken her from a nap. "I take it you weren't in any hurry to come back." He pressed his hands to his waist and frowned at Cleo. "Mind telling me what's so urgent that you had to go and run off without saying anything to me?"

"Charlie needed me. And…and you were sleeping. I didn't want to bother you since I figured you'd try to stop me."

"You're right. I would have." Jax's body tensed. "This Charlie, is he that important to you?"

She nodded. Just then there was a meow and Jax looked down to find a tabby cat rubbing against Cleo's ankles before stepping outside.

"Charlie, come back."

That was Charlie? Her cat? The knot in his gut eased. Then in spite of himself, he laughed. He'd been jealous over a cat.

"Don't just stand there laughing," she said. "Grab him."

Charlie appeared to be enjoying himself, exploring the great outdoors. When Jax set off in pursuit, the cat picked up speed.

"Here kitty, kitty."

"His name is Charlie."

Of course it was. He felt like such an idiot for getting bent out of shape over a cat. Not that he had any right to be jealous of anyone. On second thought, it would have been better if Charlie had turned out to be her boyfriend.

He could put her safety in another man's hands and walk away. At least he wanted to believe he could have turned his back and forgotten her.

The cat stopped to investigate a potted plant and Jax made his move, wrapping his hands around the cat's rib cage.

"Be careful," Cleo called out. "Support his back feet."

Jax adjusted his hold and the cat seemed to relax. That was good because he didn't know one thing about felines. His family didn't have cats or dogs. Not even goldfish. His father thought that they were a waste of money. That was what he'd loved about the Sinclair's ranch. They had lots of animals, from cats to steers. He'd always dreamed of living on a spread like theirs. So when the senior Sinclair took him under his wing and showed him how to work on a ranch, he was thrilled. He'd done something he enjoyed while making some pocket money.

"What are you smiling about?" Cleo eyed him. "Did Charlie find your ticklish spot?"

"Not hardly." He wasn't ticklish.

Cleo sighed. "Well, bring him inside and be gentle. He just had surgery."

Jax stared down at the furball. It didn't look as if anything was wrong with him. But Jax would take Cleo's word for it and as carefully as possible placed the cat on the couch.

"Enough about the cat. What I want to know is why you took off. Don't you realize that the thug who hurt you is still out there?"

"I was careful."

"I talked to the police on my way here." He waited to see if the reminder of their situation would gain her attention.

She didn't raise her head to look at him. Instead she

fussed over the cat. "What did they say? Has he been arrested?"

"No. And he was spotted in this area last night, but he eluded the police in the darkness."

She glanced up. The light in her eyes dimmed. "Oh. I didn't think—"

"Exactly. Now let's get you out of here."

He strode over and reached for the door.

"Wait. I'm not ready. I want to grab a few things. And you'll need to load the litter box in the car while I put Charlie in his carrier."

"I don't think so. I'm not hauling some howling cat around in the car."

Cleo frowned at him. "Charlie doesn't howl. He's not a dog."

"Howl. Meow. It's all the same." He wasn't a cat person.

"And don't forget to scoop the litter before loading it."

"No way. I'm not hauling around a litter box and a cat."

A few minutes later, Cleo settled on the passenger seat of the SUV. "Did you remember to grab extra kitty litter?"

"Yes." Jax's grumpy tone made her smile. "I don't know how something so small can require so much stuff."

He'd grow to like Charlie. She was sure of it because beneath all of that gruff, Jax had a big heart, even if he refused to acknowledge it.

"It's okay, Charlie. He's not normally this grouchy. He just woke up on the wrong side of the bed."

"I did not," Jax grumbled from the hatch as he stowed away her crutches.

In no time at all, they were on the road. She noticed how Jax kept checking the mirrors. She supposed she hadn't made the wisest choice this morning. Her gaze moved back to Charlie—but he needed her.

She glanced at Jax as he focused on traffic. "How long are you planning to keep us hidden away?"

Jax's fingers tightened on the wheel. "As long as it takes to make sure you're safe."

"I'm not your responsibility. I moved to Las Vegas to get away from my family and their overbearing expectations and overprotectiveness. Now you're trying to do the same thing."

"Well, if you don't like staying with me, I can get you an airline ticket. I'm sure your mother would enjoy the visit—"

"No!"

Jax glanced her way. She pressed her lips together, feeling stupid for reacting so strongly. If she wasn't careful Jax would start asking questions—questions she didn't want to answer. Once he knew what she'd done—the irreparable damage she was responsible for—it'd only confirm his decision that she was not worthy of his attention. She couldn't bear to have him look at her the way her mother had done.

"I can't go back there. Hope Springs is in my past."

"And does that include your family?"

She shrugged. A mix of feelings churned in her stomach, making her nauseous.

"What's going on, Cleo? Your family used to mean everything to you. Now you'll do anything to send them money, but you balk at the mention of visiting them."

His voice was soft and soothing, inviting her confidence. Still, she worried about what he'd think of her once he knew.

"Cleo, I'm concerned about you. Something serious is going on. And if you won't give me the answers then I'll have to go to Kurt for the truth—"

"No!" Her fingers twisted together. "Don't do that. I— I'll tell you."

He had her between a rock and a hard place and she hated it. Dredging up these painful memories would be torture. And for the first time to speak them out loud would just make what happened so fresh in her mind.

While living in Las Vegas, she'd been able to pretend that things were okay. To colleagues, she'd act as though she had a loving family missing her back in Wyoming. She was able to bluff her way through most days, but not today.

Maybe it would do her some good. Getting it off her chest might help. For so long now she'd been choking down the anger and hurt. She drew in a deep breath to steady her nerves.

"Things haven't been the same since my father died."

Jax cleared his throat. "Your brother mentioned that there'd been some drama at your father's funeral, but he didn't go into details and I didn't push. I figured he'd tell me if he wanted me to know."

"It was all about me." The weight of guilt settled on her chest. "The funeral was…was my fault…"

"What?" Jax pulled off the side of the deserted roadway and put the vehicle in Park. "Cleo, you aren't making any sense."

His face started to blur behind a wall of unshed tears. She blinked repeatedly. "It's my fault that my father died."

"How? Weren't you living here in Las Vegas at the time?"

"I'd just moved here." She inhaled a steadying breath. "I was on the phone with him and we were arguing. I didn't know at the time that he was in the pickup, transporting a mare he'd bought in hopes of luring me home. I might not like working around the ranch, but I still have a big soft spot for horses and he knew it."

Jax didn't say anything. He just reached out and squeezed her hand, allowing her to proceed at her own

pace. This was something she'd never shared with anyone...ever.

Somehow it seemed fitting that she turned to Jax. He
wasn't as close to the situation as her family and yet he
wasn't so distant, either.

Cleo inhaled a steadying breath. "He kept telling me
to come home. He was always going on about how much
my mother missed me, but I didn't want to hear it. I was
so stubborn. So determined that everything had to be my
way. I was finally away from that suppressive atmosphere
and making decisions for myself. I didn't want to go back
and marry one of the locals. It might be the right life for
some people...but not me."

The backs of her eyes smarted as a tear spilled onto
her cheek. She dashed it away. This wasn't the time to
fall apart. She needed to get through this. After all, Jax
deserved to know what sort of woman he was putting his
neck on the line to protect.

"No one can blame you—"

"But they do. And they should. If only I hadn't fought
with him...he wouldn't have died."

"You don't know that." He placed a finger beneath her
chin and lifted her face to meet his gaze. "And you can't
live your life according to someone else's wishes. At some
point you have to stand your ground."

She shook her head. "Sometimes the price is just too
steep."

He gave her hand a squeeze. She drew strength from
his touch.

"I—I told him—" her throat grew thick as she pushed
through "—that there wasn't anything that he could say
or do to get me to come home."

Another tear splashed onto her cheek. She sniffled and

ran the back of her hand over her cheeks. Why had she been so stubborn? So determined that she was right?

She pulled her hand from Jax's, no longer feeling worthy of his understanding. And he'd have no choice but to agree once she told him the price of her independence.

Her voice cracked with emotion. "Those were the last words I spoke to him."

She stared straight ahead at the desert, not wanting to see the look of disgust in Jax's eyes. She wouldn't be able to finish if she looked at him.

"The line... It went dead. I thought he'd hung up on me. I thought... Oh, it doesn't matter." She sniffled, trying to maintain a bit of composure. "I found out later...that he'd blown through a stop sign. He...he was broadsided."

Jax leaned forward, squeezing her shoulder. "It was an accident. It could have happened to anyone."

"But it didn't." She turned to Jax. "If I hadn't been arguing with him, he wouldn't have been distracted. He always obeyed stop signs. This is all on me."

"How do you know that he wasn't tired? Or he hadn't been distracted by something falling off the dashboard or the seat. Maybe he reached over to pick it up."

She shook her head, taking a second to collect herself. "I know what happened because there was an investigation. The police determined he was talking to me at the time of the accident."

"I'm sorry, Cleo. But this isn't your fault."

"My mother would disagree. She totally flipped out on me. She ordered me out of the funeral home. She said as far as she was concerned, she...she had no daughter."

"She didn't mean it—"

By now the tears were running unleashed. "Yes, she did. I was banished from Hope Springs. I tried to call a couple of times after that, but she hung up."

"She was in shock and mourning the loss of your father. I'm sure she didn't mean it."

"Even my brothers have changed. They speak to me, but it's not the same. Nothing is the same. Everyone blames me and they're right. This is my punishment."

Jax placed a finger beneath her chin and turned her head until she was facing him. "None of them had any right to lay this at your feet. You didn't know he was on the phone while driving. Not to speak ill of the dead, but the decision to talk on the phone while driving is all on him. And second, he didn't have a right to demand you come home."

Had she heard Jax correctly? Wait. This wasn't the way she thought this conversation would go.

"You don't blame me?"

"Of course not. And if your mother had been thinking clearly, she wouldn't have blamed you, either. It was an accident. And no one person was to blame. It was a culmination of events."

She wanted to believe him—wanted to shed the weight of guilt that had kept her isolated in Las Vegas through the lonely holidays, missing how her brothers would gather around the tree on Christmas Eve passing out gifts. And later how they'd argue over who got to carve the turkey.

Cleo blinked repeatedly. She might not have wanted to be a rancher, but that didn't mean she wanted to walk away from her family. She just wanted them to respect that she was grown-up now and fully capable of making her own choices on where she lived and how she lived her life. In her worst nightmare, she never dreamed she'd be labeled a black sheep and banished from her home.

"Remember when you were a kid, you always had your head in the clouds." Jax looked her in the eye. "You dreamed about those fancy fashion shows and how you wanted to travel to Milan and Paris. I never saw anyone who liked clothes as much as you."

She lifted her head to look him in the eye. "You remember that?"

"Those days that you'd sit and talk about places you'd learned about in one of your magazines taught me something important. You made me realize I could dream bigger than Hope Springs."

"I thought you were bored stiff listening to me."

"Not at all. You were like a breath of fresh air after hearing my father rant on and on about all of the injustices in this world." Jax leaned toward her. "You don't know how much I enjoyed our talks down by the creek."

"You mean when you were supposed to be fishing. And I was supposed to be quiet so as not to scare off the fish." They shared a smile.

"But you were so much more interesting." He leaned closer. "I had a hard time keeping my attention on my fishing pole. I'm lucky a big fish didn't swim off with it because you were all I could think about."

He'd noticed her? How had she missed the signs?

His fingers stroked her cheek. "But you were far too young and most definitely off-limits back then."

"And now?" Where had that question come from?

"And now I can do this..."

His hand slipped down to cup her neck. Could he feel the way he made her pulse jump? Did he know in that moment she couldn't think of anything but him?

With mere inches between them, she wondered if he'd put her out of her misery and kiss her. Her gaze moved from his tempting lips to his eyes. They were dark with a definite glint of interest in them.

Her heart pounded so loud that it was the only sound

she could hear. Logic fled her. Instead she mentally willed him closer. Her eyelids slid shut as her anticipation grew.

And then he was there. His lips tentatively pressed to hers.

Butterflies fluttered in her stomach. This was like an out-of-body experience where her body did what it desired and she sat back luxuriating in the most exquisite sensations. She didn't think it was possible but with each kiss, they got better. She wasn't sure how he could improve on perfection, but somehow he did.

She leaned into his kiss, meeting his hunger with her own. Her head spun and she didn't want this moment to end. She reached out to him, wanting to pull him closer, but the darn seat belts did their jobs and restrained them, as did the cat carrier in her lap.

Charlie meowed his protest at being jostled around. They pulled apart. But Jax's gaze held hers and she wanted to know what he was thinking—what he was feeling. But a louder protest from the cat carrier drew her attention.

She squeezed her fingers past the metal bars, trying to soothe Charlie. "It's okay, boy. I didn't mean to bounce you around."

Jax shifted the SUV into gear. "You know if it wasn't for you and your dreams, I never would have dared to imagine another life for myself. I'd have most likely given up on school and ended up just as disillusioned about life as my father. It's hard to tell where I'd be now."

She smiled through her tears. "You probably wouldn't be sitting on the side of the road with a crying woman who's holding a cat on her lap."

"Probably not. But right now, I can't think of anyplace I'd rather be."

Jax eased back onto the roadway and they headed north

to their five-star getaway. Her stomach quivered as she wondered where they went from here. Was this all some sort of sympathy? Or was there a deeper meaning to that kiss?

CHAPTER TEN

TREAD CAREFULLY.

After a week of sharing the mansion, Jax found himself susceptible to Cleo's enchanting spell. He'd found her fascinating as a kid, and as a woman, she was near irresistible. But no matter how sweet and enticing she may be, he couldn't keep finding excuses to touch her—to kiss her. The best thing he could do was find a way to reunite her with her family.

But first, he had something he had to do. He was tired of waiting for the doctor's office to call. He could only figure they'd lost his new number and that was why they hadn't called with his test results.

He glanced around for Cleo. Not finding any signs of her, he grabbed the cell phone from the kitchen counter and dialed the familiar number. After two rings, it switched to a prerecorded message announcing the doctor was out of the office for the next week.

Jax cursed under his breath and resisted the urge to throw the phone across the room. Of all the times for the doctor to have a personal life, why did it have to be now?

The distinct sound of Cleo's crutches echoed down the hall. He cleared the number and placed the phone back on the counter. He'd just turned around when she entered the room.

She stopped in front of him with a frown marring her beautiful face. "Have you seen Charlie?"

"I wasn't exactly looking for him. Why?"

"I don't know. He's just usually wherever I am, and I haven't seen him since first thing this morning."

"In a house this size it wouldn't be hard for him to find a hiding spot."

A frown settled on her face. "I know, but I just worry."

She fussed over that cat like a mother caring for a young child. The image of her holding a baby in her arms came to mind. That was yet another reason why they shouldn't be playing house.

Jax shifted his weight from one foot to the other. "I'll... um, go look around for him. Why don't you sit down? You know what the doctor said about resting."

"How could I forget? You remind me every day." She started toward the family room before calling over her shoulder, "While you're upstairs would you mind grabbing the blue tote bag from my bedroom?"

"Your wish is my command."

He took the steps two at a time. His gaze scanned the hallway for any sign of the feline. How in the world was he going to find a little cat in this big house? He'd probably found a nice dark corner to take a catnap.

But first Jax needed to get the bag for Cleo. He worried that she was overdoing it and he didn't want her to reinjure herself. He told himself that it was no more care than he'd give to a coworker or neighbor... But then again he wouldn't be kissing them. And with each passing day it was getting harder to keep Cleo at arm's length.

Not only was he painfully attracted to her, but her passion for life made him want to set out on a new adventure. He found himself daydreaming about having a full life— no longer spending his days chained to a desk and computer. His thoughts trailed back to Hope Springs with its wide-open spaces and its endless possibilities. But most of all, he envisioned Cleo by his side.

However, for that to happen, he'd have to sentence her to an eventual life of caring for an ill man with a tenuous future—only to wind up a young widow. Cold fingers of apprehension gripped his throat, cutting off his breath. He refused to do that to Cleo. He banished the unsettling thoughts to the back of his mind. No matter how tempting a life with her might seem, he couldn't put her in that horrendous situation.

With the blue bag in hand, he returned to the family room, where Cleo had turned on the big-screen TV. A fashion design competition was on. "I take it you still enjoy clothes."

She nodded while rummaging through the oversize bag and pulling out a sketch pad and a pack of pencils.

"Some things don't change."

"Did you find Charlie?" She glanced at him expectantly.

He'd forgotten about the furball. Where in the world did he even begin to look for the cat?

As though reading his mind, Cleo said, "You'll have to get down on all fours. He likes to nap in cozy, dark spots."

Jax expelled a sigh. He might as well start in here. "Here kitty, kitty."

He crawled around on the floor looking under every piece of furniture in the room. There was no cat to be found.

Jax sat up on his knees next to Cleo. "He isn't in here." His gaze moved to the sketch pad in her hands. "What are you doing?"

She jerked the pad against her chest. "Why?"

"I'm curious."

"You'll just laugh."

"Why would I laugh? Obviously you're drawing something that's important to you. I'm just curious what it is."

Her shoulders drooped and the lines in her face eased. "It's just that when I was growing up my brothers would always poke fun at my drawings. I guess I didn't realize, until now, how touchy I've become."

"Can I see? I promise to be on my best behavior."

Her mouth pulled to the side as she thought it over before she nodded. When she turned the pad around, he sat up straighter, truly interested. There was the outline of a woman with no face, but the details were in the soft pink dress with a long skirt and a halter-style top.

"That's impressive." He meant it. "Instead of going to college to become an accountant, you should have considered pursuing art."

"You really think it's that good."

He nodded. "If I had to draw it, there'd be a stick figure on the page. It wouldn't be that good of one, either. And as for the clothes, um…do rectangles and squares count?"

"I don't think so. They'd be awfully uncomfortable."

The rays from Cleo's smile filled his chest with warmth. Until that moment he hadn't realized how empty his life had been, even before the cancer. Sure, he had his work, and his amazing success at such a young age was very rewarding. But when he returned to his apartment in the evenings, it was dark and empty. There wasn't so much as a fish or a Charlie waiting for him.

He didn't know how he'd ever go back to that solitary life after sharing this place with Cleo…and her furball. The cat really wasn't so bad after all. In fact, he rather liked the little guy, which was probably a good thing since the cat had taken to snuggling up on his chest when he was sleeping. He'd surprisingly grown used to Charlie's nightly visits.

Jax knew he was setting himself up for a fall because this arrangement was not permanent—no matter how much he might like it to be otherwise. But he had resolved not to fight it. There was no harm in enjoying Cleo's company—as long as he kept his hands to himself.

"So what do you do with your drawings?"

"Actually they are sketches of clothes I plan to make." Her eyes never left his, as though she was anxious to gauge his reaction. "Aren't you going to say anything?"

"I don't know what to say except...wow! You're a lady of many talents."

"You're really impressed?"

"Of course I am. Did you make what you're wearing now?"

His gaze moved to the pink-and-white tiny T-shirt and gray sweat shorts. It didn't matter what she wore, she always looked beautiful.

Cleo shook her head. "I only make dress clothes like the ones you saw me in at the Glamour Hotel."

"Have you been doing this for long?"

She nodded. "My grandmother taught me how to sew at an early age. She was a very patient woman. More so than I could ever hope to be."

He glanced through her sketchbook. Each drawing was more impressive than the last. "Have you sent these out to professionals?"

Color infused her cheeks. "I couldn't do that."

He caught the uncertainty in her eyes. "I'm no expert, but I think you should follow your dream. If you want I can make some calls."

"No!" She grabbed the sketch pad from him. "I already

know my clothes aren't good enough. I've been told they're too frivolous. It'd be a waste of time."

Anger warmed his veins. "And who told you that?"

"My parents. They said that if I insisted on going to college that I must take up a skill that was practical and would eventually provide me with a substantial income when I finished."

He wanted to argue with her and those misconceptions that her parents drilled into her head. They had stolen her dreams. And now he was determined to find a way to give them back to her.

Jax sat down on the carpet and leaned an elbow on the couch near Cleo's pink-painted toes. "Boy, your parents were more set in their ways than I ever imagined."

"Now you're seeing why I moved across the country for college and why I was arguing with my father…"

Not wanting her to return to that dark, quiet place where she locked him out, he said, "So this sketch, is it an outfit for yourself?"

Her gaze snapped back from that faraway look. "Um… no. It's actually for Robyn. She's always going on about my clothes and how pretty they are, which is so sweet. Anyway she wanted me to make an outfit for her. It's nice to have someone appreciate my efforts."

If Cleo ever hoped to make peace with her mother, she had to lighten up on her. Maybe he could try to help bridge that gap. He hated the thought of Cleo with no family. He wouldn't wish a solitary existence on anyone, especially when he knew as sure as he was sitting there that deep down where it counted, her mother loved her.

"Cleo, did you ever think that maybe your parents saw your fashion magazines and your high-class creations as a rejection of the life they chose to lead? Or maybe they were afraid that if they encouraged you to follow your dreams that you'd up and leave Hope Springs—leave them."

A light shone in her eyes. "But I never looked down on them or the ranch. It's my...was my home."

"But every time you complained about having to ride the fence line or feed the herd, maybe they took it as a strike against their lifestyle. I'm not saying it was right what they said or how they made you feel, but maybe they thought if you lost interest in fashion that you would realize the ranch was the right place for you."

Cleo's fine brows arched. "You really think that's what it was about?"

Jax raked his fingers through his hair. "I don't have all of the answers. I just know that a mother's love runs deep. You've both made mistakes. How long has it been since you tried to talk to her?"

"Almost two years. The last time I called was a month after the funeral. She told me never to call again." Cleo's eyes shimmered and she blinked repeatedly.

"Try to forget what she said in a moment of grief and follow your heart. When you talk to her be honest about who you are and what you want in life. Maybe she'll surprise you. What do you have to lose?"

Cleo shook her head. "I—I can't do that. I can't have her say those hurtful things again. I'm fine with the way things are now."

"Then you're lying to me and yourself. This distance isn't making you happy. You may have all of the independence in the world, but it'll never replace the love of your family. And don't doubt that they love you just as much as you love them." He got to his feet. "Now I have a cat to track down."

He didn't want to push Cleo too far too fast, but before they went their separate ways, he hoped she'd work up the

courage to call home. The sooner, the better. Otherwise
he wasn't sure if he could just walk away from her and
leave her alone.

A few days later, Cleo was still thinking over Jax's words.
The fact that he'd come to her mother's defense she found
confusing. Why was he pushing this? There had never
been any love between him and her mother. In fact, as a
kid, Jax used to revel in egging her mother on by doing
things to irritate her. So why was he suddenly coming to
her mother's aid?

It didn't make any sense. But more than that, Cleo didn't
feel worthy to be part of the Sinclair clan any longer. Not
when her actions contributed to her father's death—the
man who gave her the dream of an Ivy League school even
though he'd had to put the family's heritage at risk to do
it. And how did she repay him? By her last words to him
being ones of anger.

Cleo gave herself a mental jerk. She wasn't going down
that painful road again. She'd thought she'd tucked all of
these memories into a locked box in the back of her mind.
Now the memories had broken the padlock and were spill-
ing out faster than she could push the lid closed.

What she needed to do was quit thinking. She'd done
enough of that all afternoon and right about now, the most
delightful aroma was coming from the kitchen.

Tired of sketching, she closed the pad and placed it on
the glass coffee table alongside her colored pencils. She
grabbed the crutches that she was now more adept at using
and made her way to the kitchen.

From the hallway, she could hear Jax talking but she
couldn't make out what he was saying until she got closer.
"Don't look so down. Us guys have to stick together. I'm
sure that surgery wasn't easy."

Surgery? Oh, having Charlie neutered. She smiled as she listened to Jax sympathizing with the cat. He continued to talk as if Charlie understood every word he said.

"Here. Maybe this will cheer you up."

Cleo turned the corner in time to find Jax doling out some treats before turning his attention back to the stove.

"So you and Charlie are buddies now?"

Jax jerked around from where he'd been stirring a steaming pot. With the spoon still in his hand, the tomato sauce dripped all over the black-and-white floor tiles. The sheepish look reminded her of the expression her brothers would get when caught stealing one of her mother's cookies fresh from the oven.

"You heard that?"

"I did." She worked her way over to the island and pulled out a stool. "I told you Charlie would grow on you."

Jax turned away and busied himself cleaning up the mess. "There. All cleaned up." He tossed the paper towels in the trash and washed his hands. "I hope you like pasta."

"Smells delicious to me. What is it?"

"My version of Sicilian pasta." He broke up some capellini and dunked it in a pot of boiling water. "It'll be ready shortly if you want to go back to the family room. I can bring it in there."

"I'm bored with my own company. Mind if I stay and watch?"

He cocked a smile. "Is that your way of saying that I'm interesting? Or am I just the best of the worst?"

She laughed. "Hmm...I'm not going to answer on the grounds that it might incriminate me."

"I see how you are," he said teasingly as he moved to the fridge.

She wouldn't have missed this for anything in the world. As he bent over to retrieve some salad makings, she couldn't help but take in the way his faded jeans accentuated his backside. There wasn't an ounce of flab on the guy. Between his good looks and wealth, why was he still single?

"So do you do this often?"

He turned around with a head of iceberg lettuce in one hand and a large tomato in the other. "No. I rarely cook."

Then an unhappy thought came to mind. "Is that because there's a woman around to do the cooking for you?"

His gaze caught hers. "And what would you say if I told you that she cooks, cleans and folds my underwear, too?"

The thought that he'd be involved with someone hadn't even crossed her mind. An uneasy feeling stirred within her. She didn't know why she'd just assumed he was available. He was sexy and rich. He could have his choice of women.

"Before you go jumping to the wrong conclusion," Jax said, "you should know that she's my cleaning lady. She's old enough to be my mother and she's happily married."

Cleo breathed easier. "That's good because I'm never going to be the other woman. Especially when I know firsthand how much it hurts everyone involved." Then realizing she'd said too much, heat licked at her cheeks.

She glanced up, catching the slack-jawed look on Jax's face.

"I would never want you to be the other woman. If you were mine, there wouldn't be anyone else in my life but you. You'd be all I'd need."

Her gaze met his. Her heart thump-thumped in her chest. She'd only ever dreamed of someone speaking such endearing words to her.

The kitchen timer buzzed. In a blink the fairy-tale moment ended.

Jax moved around the counter. "I have to take care of

the pasta, but don't go anywhere. We aren't through with this conversation."

She watched as he drained the pasta, dribbled some olive oil on it, gave it a toss and put the lid on the pan. She thought of sneaking off while he stirred the sauce, but she was certain that he'd track her down. She might as well get this over with. Her stomach growled its agreement. Her only road to dinner was a detour through her past.

After turning down the heat and giving the sauce one final stir, Jax joined her at the counter. He settled down on the stool and faced her. "Now, what is this about you being hurt by another woman?"

"It's not worth getting into the details. Let's just say the moral of the story is I let myself fall for the wrong guy. And now I know better. So let's have dinner and forget all of this."

"Not so fast. I want to know the parts you're skipping over."

She exhaled an exasperated sigh. She hated to think about how naive she'd been. She'd never be that trusting again because putting your heart on the line was just asking to be hurt—even from those that you'd least expect.

"It was my last year in college and I'd fallen hard for this guy from my public speaking class. He was charming and charismatic. Let's just say he aced the class without breaking a sweat."

"And you fell for his charms, not knowing that he had a darker side?"

She nodded. "He was perfect. Good-looking. Talkative. Funny. Or so I thought at the time."

"What kind of things did he like to talk about?"

She shrugged. "His classes. His future plans. Football. Nothing specific."

"Did he ever care about what was important to you?"

"Not really." She stopped, not realizing until that moment that most of their conversations had revolved around him. "When I had news, he'd quickly change the subject back to him. I guess I should have seen the warning signs earlier."

"It's not your fault. You tried. He obviously didn't. So what made you see him as the jerk that he is?"

"We'd been dating for a little more than six months when I didn't feel well and came back to my dorm room early from a class to find him in bed with my roommate."

Jax clenched his hands. "If I'd been around, he wouldn't have gotten away with that."

She took comfort in hearing the protective tones in Jax's voice. "Well, I'm glad you weren't there."

Jax's brows rose in a question.

"He wasn't worth you getting into trouble. Besides, I've lived and learned, even if it was the hard way. The important part is I won't be making those same mistakes again."

"But you have to know that all men aren't like him." Jax's voice grew deep. "If you were mine, I'd never look at another woman as long as I lived."

Her gaze met his. Her heart once again went thump-thump. "Seriously? You'd really only have eyes for me?"

"You're the most beautiful woman in the world." His thumb stroked her cheek, followed her jawline and rubbed over her bottom lip. His gaze never left hers.

His touch sent her insides quivering with excitement. She was drawn to him like a butterfly to a field of poppies. Not waiting for him to make the first move, she pressed her lips to his thumb. His eyes lit up with excitement. She was enjoying this new side of herself and she didn't want this moment to end.

The tip of her tongue darted out, stroking the length of his finger. She immediately heard the swift intake of his breath. He wanted her. And she wanted him. There were no strings. No promises. Just the intrigue of finding out where this moment might lead.

Jax pulled away. "I have to get the sauce… It's getting too hot. It's bubbling over. I don't want it to…uh, burn."

He moved away and Cleo smiled to herself knowing that she'd gotten to him. This thing between them, whatever it was, was not over. Not by a long shot.

Jax kept his attention focused on the food. "You know there are good guys in this world."

"I know. You're one of them."

He shook his head. "I don't mean me. I'm not right for you. But there's someone better waiting to find you."

"I doubt it." The smiled faded from her face. "Besides, the people that you're supposed to be able to trust the most are the first ones to let you down when you really need them."

"We're not talking about jerk face anymore, are we?"

She shook her head and lowered her gaze to the floor. She couldn't help but think of her family. They were the ones she always thought she could count on—no matter what.

"I honestly think you should call you mother."

He was really pushing for a mother-daughter reunion. Buy why? Was he that anxious to get rid of her and he just couldn't bring himself to say it?

Dread filled her heart. She'd been down this road before. Her instinct was to leave and not look back. She could return to the casino and he could fly back to New York. But as much as she wanted that to happen, some ape man out there was looking for them. For now, they were stuck here together.

CHAPTER ELEVEN

BY THE END of the week, Cleo had promised she'd call her mother if he'd just quit pestering her.

Now the moment of truth had arrived. She stared at the disposable cell phone the same way she would a rattler—one false move and she'd be in a world of regret. Whatever made her think calling home was a good idea? Oh, yes, Jax. He seemed to be full of all sorts of advice these days.

And the part she hated most was knowing he was right. She missed her family. After fighting to follow her own path in life and to be able to make her own choices, she still didn't feel complete. There was a gap in her life—her mother and brothers.

Jax's voice echoed in her mind. *Deep down she still loves you. What do you have to lose?*

Inhaling a steadying breath, Cleo picked up the phone. She didn't know if she was strong enough to do as Jax suggested, but she could do the next best thing. She dialed an old, familiar number. Her stomach quivered like a dried leaf on a blustery fall day. What if—

"Hello?"

She knew the deep timbre of the male voice. "Kurt, it's Cleo."

"Cleo?" Her oldest brother said her name as if he was

talking to a ghost. "What are you doing calling? Is something wrong?"

It was not exactly the greeting she'd been hoping for. This was nothing like the cheerful calls she'd used to make from college. But then again that was another lifetime. Things had changed irrevocably since then.

"I—I— How are things there?"

"Not so good. I've been putting off telling Mom about the mess with the bank, but I need to do it soon."

"You know Mom has no head for business. That's why Dad left you in charge. If you tell her, she'll just worry." And have one more thing to hold against Cleo.

"And if we don't come up with some money soon, there won't be a business for any of us to worry about."

Cleo worried the inside of her lip, wondering if she should mention her promotion. After her accident and now with her missing work, she didn't know if she'd still have a job when she returned. Although Jax seemed certain that her job was protected. Maybe he was right.

"I got a big promotion at work." Then in her excitement, she forgot that she hadn't told her family about her job at the casino.

"That's nice, sis. But we need more than a bump in your paycheck to cover the arrears on this loan." He sighed. "I should tell you that I've had to sell off some of the stock, including Buttercup."

Cleo gasped. She loved and missed the even-tempered mare. The backs of her eyes started to burn. It was the last gift her father had given her—no, it wasn't. There was the horse her father had bought for her as a bribe to move home. But the horse had died in the same accident that snuffed out her father's life. With that sobering thought in mind, she knew she had no right to complain about her brother's actions.

"I'm sorry, Cleo. I've had to drastically reduce the over-head."

She swiped at her eyes and sniffled. "I—I understand."

Maybe Jax was right. Maybe now was the time to be up front with her family about her choices. It was time to quit sneaking around and pretending to be the person they wanted her to be instead of showing them the real Cleo.

Taking a calming breath, she gripped the phone tightly. "Kurt, this promotion is a lot more than a bump in my check. I'm now working as a casino host."

"What?" There was a pause as though he were letting the news sink in. "You mean you wear slinky outfits and flirt with men to get them to gamble more?"

"No. I wear really nice clothes. In fact, I design and make my own clothes."

She considered mentioning that Jax was one of her clients so her brother wouldn't worry so much, but under the circumstances, she realized that it was best to keep Jax and this mess with ape man to herself. It would be safest for everyone—especially Jax. And she didn't want to jeopardize Jax's friendship with her brother, if Kurt decided to act all protective of his little sister.

Without giving her brother an opportunity to hassle her about her career choice, she hurried on. "I'll forward you some money as soon as I get paid." And now for the real reason she'd called. "How are Joe, Stephen and Cassidy?"

"They're fine. Cleo, what is it you really want to know?"

Kurt always knew when she was hedging around something. "And how's Mom doing?"

"You know, same as always. Busy with this and that. But the arthritis in her fingers is getting worse. If you're really curious to know how she's doing, you should call her."

Her chest tightened at the thought of being rejected by

her mother again. She didn't know if she could open herself up to the potential for that kind of pain.

"I—I don't think that's a good idea. I tried calling her after the funeral. She told me not to call back and hung up."

"I'm sorry, sis." He expelled a weary sigh. "Mom wasn't herself after Dad died. She was angry with everyone for a long time. Most of all I think she was angry with Dad for leaving her. She's been lost without him."

"I remember how in love they were after so many years. I always dreamed of having a marriage like theirs."

"You can still have that, if you want it."

"Listen to who's talking. You're older than me and you have yet to settle down and start a family."

"I have a lot of responsibilities. I don't have time for that stuff."

Another pang of guilt assaulted her. If she hadn't been arguing with her father that day, he wouldn't have died. Her mother wouldn't have melted down. And her brother wouldn't be devoting his every waking hour to keeping the ranch afloat. Kurt might be happily married by now with a baby on the way.

"I should go." She didn't know what else to say. There were no words to repair the damage that had been done.

"Cleo, call Mom. Enough time has passed. I think she'd want to hear from you."

After promising to think it over, Cleo disconnected the call. She still wasn't sure about calling her mother. After all, her mother was right. The tragedy of her father's death was her fault—no matter what Jax said. Why should her mother forgive her? If the roles were reversed, she didn't honestly know how she'd deal with such a profound loss.

The phone buzzed, startling her. She glanced at the screen, but didn't recognize the number.

"Jax! Jax! Phone."

She didn't know where he'd been but he entered the family room at a dead run, grabbed the phone and punched the talk button. "Yes." A pause. "Yes, it is."

He strolled out of the room.

That was strange. She thought that it was dangerous to let people have their phone number because of the GPS tracking system. So who did Jax trust enough with their location? The police? And why was his face creased with worry lines?

Jax's entire body tensed as he waited for the doctor to come on the line. He paced back and forth on the veranda. The afternoon sun was hot, but his need for privacy trumped being comfortable. He didn't normally pray, but in this instance if he had any points with God, he could use some help now.

"Jax, this is Dr. Collins. How are you doing?"

Did he mean besides the stress of knowing that his clients were up in arms because the funds in his investment accounts had been seized as evidence until this trial was over? Apart from the fact some thug attacked the woman that he…that he considered a close friend? Or aside from the fact that he was secluded in a ritzy home with a woman who could make him want her with just a look?

"I'm doing good," he lied.

"That's what I like to hear from my patients. But something tells me even if you weren't feeling like your old self yet, you wouldn't say anything. Don't push yourself too hard, too fast. And if you won't listen to me, at least listen to your body. It'll tell you what it needs."

Enough of this, he needed to know where he stood. "Doc, what did the tests reveal?"

"Nothing. That is to say there's nothing wrong with you. At this point, you are fit and healthy."

"Really?" His legs felt like jelly. He sank down on a chair. "You're absolutely positive?"

"I am. You can relax now. There's no reason you can't continue with a normal, healthy life."

Immediately Cleo's face came to mind. "But the cancer, it can come back, can't it?"

There was a distinct pause. "I won't lie to you. It can. For the next couple of years we'll keep a close eye on you. If anything develops, we'll catch it early. But I would think positive."

"Thanks, Doc."

They talked a few more minutes and Jax promised to schedule a follow-up appointment in six months. By the time he got off the phone, he was so relieved, he pumped his fists and yelled, "Yes!" like a pro football player after scoring the winning touchdown in the final seconds of the game.

This was the game of his life. After months of tests and treatments, the endless wonder and worry, he could at last relax. For the moment, he was healthy.

He let himself back in the house, eager to seek out Cleo. She was curled up again with her pencils and sketch pad. She glanced up when he entered the room.

"Is everything okay?"

"Um, yes." Had she heard him cheering? He doubted it. The house was far too big for voices to carry that far. "I actually got some good news."

"You did? That's great." She smiled and patted the spot on the couch next to her. "Come sit down. You can tell me your good news, and I need your opinion on something."

For the first time since he had found the lump under his arm, he had energy and felt as if he could run a marathon. Okay, maybe not a marathon but at least around the block.

The invitation to sit next to the most gorgeous woman

in the world was just too tempting to resist. However, he forced himself to leave a comfortable distance between them.

Charlie lifted his head from where he was sleeping on the opposite side of Cleo, eyed him up and then promptly went back to sleep. He was going to miss Charlie. Every time he opened the fridge and grabbed for the bag of lunch meat, the cat knew it and made a beeline for the kitchen so he could have some, too.

Needing a moment or two to sort out what to say to her, Jax said, "First, tell me how the conversation with your mother went."

"It didn't."

He turned to look directly at her. "What do you mean, it didn't?"

"I didn't call her."

"But I thought that's why you borrowed the phone."

She went on to tell him how she called her brother instead. Jax's body tensed as he wondered if this thing between Cleo and himself could ruin a lifetime friendship with Kurt. He hated the thought of losing yet another person from his life.

"Did you mention anything about us?" He braced himself for the answer.

"No, I didn't." Cleo's eyes filled with compassion. "I didn't feel it was my place. I know how protective Kurt can be, and I know he made you promise to stay away from me."

"You do?"

She smiled at him. "Let's just say that a little sister can have big ears when the need arises. I figure if there's ever anything to tell him about us, you'll find a way to tell him. After all, it isn't like I'm a teenager any longer."

"Maybe you're right." He desperately wanted to believe

her. But he knew he was jumping too far ahead. It wasn't as if they had a future. "And right now Kurt has enough on his mind."

Two V-shaped lines formed between her brows. "Do you think I'll get paid much for the time I was your casino host? You know, before ape man ruined things?"

"You don't have anything to worry about. I wagered a sizable fortune while I was at the Glamour. And lost quite a bit. All in all you should get a generous paycheck."

"Oh, good!" Color immediately rushed to her cheeks and she glanced away. "Sorry. I didn't mean I was excited about your loss...just that I'd have some money to send home to Kurt. He sounded defeated on the phone."

"I understand." Jax wanted to ease the worry on her face, but he still wasn't sure how to go about it without overstepping. "I'd like to help."

"You would?"

"Yes. I've been doing some thinking about this even before I heard that the Bar S was in trouble."

"We could definitely use the help." She looked up at him with a hopeful gleam. "What did you have in mind?"

He wasn't so sure how Cleo would feel about his idea. In fact, he was hesitant to bring it up. Maybe he should just go directly to Kurt with it. But then again if he couldn't get it past Cleo, he'd never get her brother to agree.

"I want to buy your grandfather's ranch."

Cleo sat back. Her eyes opened wide. "But why?"

"I'm tired of New York. I accomplished what I went there to do."

"Make yourself into a business success?"

He nodded. "Now I want to try something different."

"But I would have thought you'd be settled in New York. Won't you miss it?"

He shrugged. "Some. Certainly the coffee shop down

the street from my apartment building. They have the best bagels. But I need something more."

"What did you have in mind?"

"I thought of returning to Hope Springs. I miss the wide-open space."

"You mean to move there permanently?"

"It's one possibility. I was planning to explore the idea when the strange phone calls started. I didn't want to travel to Hope Springs and have trouble follow me there. That would just reinforce some folks' opinions that I'm still bad news."

"No one would say that."

He eyed her, knowing she was lying just to make him feel better. "Your mother might disagree."

She reached out and squeezed his arm, sending a sensation zinging through his veins and settling in his chest. He stared deep into her eyes, wanting to pull her into his arms. Since he'd talked to the doctor, he felt as though he had a new lease on life.

But before he could move, Cleo's smile morphed into a frown.

"What is it?" He'd fix it if he could. Right about now, he'd do anything for her.

"I'm just worried about my job at the casino. I can't lose it."

At least he could reassure her. "You don't have to worry. Your job will be there waiting for you as soon as you're ready."

"I don't know. I didn't complete the one task Mr. Burns gave me."

"What was that?"

"Keeping you happy."

"Oh, trust me. You've made me very happy."

"Really?"

He nodded and her eyes twinkled with mischief.

She leaned forward and in a breathy voice said, "Maybe I could make you happier."

In an instant, her lips pressed to his. His heart slammed into his ribs. Now wasn't the time for overthinking things. It was a time for decisive action. His hands slipped around her waist, pulling her closer. Every nerve ending sprang to life. He hadn't felt this free, this alive, in forever.

Cleo smelled like a field of wildflowers. He didn't know if it was her perfume or shampoo, but there was something about her that had an intoxicating effect on him.

Who'd ever think that the girl who gave him that inexperienced peck all those years ago would grow up to give such passionate kisses? Her lips moved over his in a fervent hunger. And when she moaned, it was his undoing. In that moment, it didn't matter what she'd ask of him, he'd be helpless to deny her.

Her fingers trailed up his neck. Her nails scraped against his scalp. It was the most stimulating sensation. He couldn't believe the girl whose ponytails he used to pull and who would flash him a smile lined with braces was now this red-hot siren in his arms setting his whole body on fire.

She pulled back just far enough to murmur, "Let's move this to the bedroom, where my cast won't be in the way."

It was as if she'd dumped a bucket of icy cold mountain water over his head. He…he couldn't do that, no matter how much he wanted her. He turned his head away, trying to get a grip.

"We can't." He couldn't look her in the face.

She placed her fingers under his chin and attempted to turn his head, but he resisted. He felt like a wild animal that had been caught in a trap. There was no getting away.

No pretending that he was the same Jax that he'd been all those years ago.

"You can kiss me, but you can't even look at me now." Irritation threaded through her voice. "What's the matter? Don't my kisses stack up to the other women you've known?"

He swung around and looked at her point-blank. "They aren't even in the same ballpark. Yours are so much sweeter. You're amazing."

"Then I don't understand. What's the problem? Why do you keep pulling me close only to shove me away?"

For the lack of anything better, he fell back on a cliché. "It's not you, it's me."

Cleo rolled her eyes. "You've got to do better than that. I want to know the truth."

"Can't we just forget this happened?"

"No, we can't. I want you. And you obviously want me. You owe me the truth. What's holding you back?"

There was no way out of this. He supposed he did owe her the truth, but somehow that didn't make it any easier to say.

CHAPTER TWELVE

JAX COULDN'T BELIEVE he was about to bare his soul to Cleo.

His gut knotted as he pictured her withdrawing from him—of her looking at him differently. He didn't want to make this confession. But what choice did he have? She needed to realize here and now that they could never be more than friends.

He lifted his head to meet her questioning gaze. "I'm not the same man you used to know."

She squeezed his hand. "And I'm not a kid anymore. But I think you figured that out."

He pulled away, needing to think straight. "This isn't easy for me to say."

She reached out and gripped his thigh. "You've listened and understood my problems. Trust me to understand yours."

Realizing he needed more distance between them if he was ever going to say this, he got to his feet. If she kept touching him, he'd never get these words out.

He strode over to the wall of windows and wished he could just keep walking off into the desert—where no one knew him and no one cared about his story. He honestly never planned to have this conversation with anyone. Yet somehow when he wasn't looking, Cleo had snuck past his defenses. She'd gotten closer to him than anyone ever had in his life. And now he had to give them both a strong dose of reality.

He leveled his shoulders and turned. "I have cancer."

She fell back against the couch as though his words had physically knocked the breath out of her. "Are…are you dying?"

He shook his head. "I have Hodgkin's lymphoma. Luckily I found the lump early on. And I've since been through the treatments."

"Are you cured?"

He shook his head. "But I just found out that I'm in remission."

The fright in her eyes eased to a look of concern. He wished she would say something. Do something. Even if it was to walk away. At least then he'd know where they stood.

As the silence stretched on, his patience snapped. "Cleo, did you hear me? I have cancer."

"I heard you. I'm just wondering, with both of your parents gone, did you go through this all by yourself?"

He didn't see why any of that mattered now. "Yes, I did."

"You know if you'd called me or even Kurt, we'd have been there for you."

Her words stirred a spot in his chest. The thought that she'd even offer to stand by him through such a tough time said so much about her sweet nature. Cleo may have grown up and changed on the outside, but inside, where it counted, she was still the caring and thoughtful person he'd known all those years ago.

He drew his thoughts up short. He was letting himself get distracted. He had to be sure she understood what he was trying to tell her—that he couldn't be with her the way she wanted. That this thing between them had gone as far as he could let it go.

"I'm so sorry you felt you had to go through that all alone."

"Cleo, you aren't understanding what I'm trying to tell you."

"Yes, I am. You told me that you were very sick and you had no one there to stand by your side. But now you don't have to face the future alone. You have me. I'll be there to hold your hand. Or read you silly stories from magazines. Whatever you need."

She wanted to be there for him? Really be there. Not just with words but with action, too. His gaze blurred and he blinked rapidly. No one since his mother had ever put his needs first. He glanced away and rubbed at his eyes. Someday Cleo would make some man amazingly happy. He envied that person.

Jax cleared the lump in his throat. "You won't need to do that. My treatments are done for now. But that's no guarantee there won't be a recurrence."

There. He'd said it all. She knew now she'd be wasting her time on him. He turned his back, unable to watch her walk away.

He waited. Listening. Longing for this agonizing moment to be over. Just like when he was a kid and got caught stealing a locket for his dying mother. She always wanted one to hold pictures of the two men in her life, but his father told her it was a waste of money. Some people had looked at Jax with pity and a certain amount of resignation. Others had turned their backs on him. He hadn't cared. It was the only thing he'd been able to do for her on her deathbed and it had been worth every cruel look. Why should he think that now would be any different?

But in the next moment, he remembered how Cleo paid for the necklace. He'd been so embarrassed, he'd run off. Afterward she'd never mentioned it. And it had taken him time, but eventually he'd paid her back every single penny he owed her.

The next thing he knew Cleo's arms wrapped around him—hugging him. Her cheek pressed to his back. And he could feel the dampness through his T-shirt of what must surely be her tears. Just like all those years ago, she was there for him.

He carefully turned, trying not to knock her off-balance and reinjure her leg. He wrapped his arms around her, taking comfort in her warmth. He braced himself as she hesitantly raised her gaze until she met his.

In her eyes he found understanding. How could he have ever doubted her?

He held her to his chest and lowered his cheek to the top of her head. He stayed there in her embrace, absorbing the peace that came with her acceptance of what had happened to him. He didn't know until that moment just how much he needed her to understand—to make him feel normal.

"Thank you," he whispered into her hair.

She squeezed him tighter.

He breathed in her strength and let it settle his nerves. He didn't know that it was possible to feel even better than when he got the test results from the doctor. But right now, he felt as though he could take on the world...and win.

Jax eased back from Cleo just far enough to look into her eyes. He needed to hear it with his own ears. "You're really not put off by my cancer?"

"I think you are the most wonderful man both inside and out. No disease can change that." She followed her words with a kiss that left no doubt about what she had in mind.

Believing in her words, he gave in to his long-withheld desires. He scooped her up into his arms and carried her upstairs, leaving Charlie to finish his catnap alone.

* * *

Cleo woke up and ran her hand over an empty bed.

Her eyes sprang open. The golden rays of the setting sun mocked the fact that she was alone.

"Jax?" She glanced toward the bathroom, finding it dark and empty.

Old insecurities plagued her. Her stomach roiled. What had she done opening herself up to him? When would she ever learn?

She threw on her clothes and worked her way down-stairs, unsure what reaction she'd receive. Did he regret their time together? Did he consider what they'd shared a mistake?

It was better to get this over right away than to let it drag out, no matter how much it hurt. It was as her grand-father told her as a kid. The bandage hurt less when it came off fast.

She found Jax in the kitchen—a room in which he'd spent a lot of time creating such amazing meals. Not that she had any appetite right now.

He turned to her. "Hey, sleepyhead. I wasn't sure when you were going to wake up." He put down the dish towel in his hands as his brows gathered. "What's the matter?"

"I woke up and you were gone."

He approached her. "Is that all that's bothering you? I mean, if I did something wrong—"

"No. You were amazing." Her stomach shivered as she continued to open herself up to him. "It's just that when I woke up and found you gone, I thought… Well, I didn't know what I thought."

He wrapped his arms around her waist. "I didn't mean to worry you. I couldn't sleep so I thought I'd make you something to eat."

"Really?"

"Honest. I thought you needed some rest. Otherwise I would have stayed and done more of this…"

He nuzzled her neck. Shivers cascaded down her arms as his lips moved over the sensitive part of her neck. Maybe she was crazy for letting down her guard with him, but she wanted so badly to believe that he was different from the others in her life.

She lifted his chin until her lips could claim his. She'd never ever tire of his kisses. She finally understood the age-old adage that the best things in life are worth fighting for. She'd known for years that Jax was special, but it wasn't until now that she knew exactly how special.

He pulled back and looked at her. "You know if you keep this up, I'm going to burn dinner."

"Would that be so bad?" she teased.

"Aren't you turning into a little temptress."

He moved to the stove and her gaze followed him, drinking in his good looks. There was just something so sexy about having a man cook for her. She noticed his off-white T-shirt and the way it clung to his muscular shoulders and broad chest. She smiled when she spied a few drops of his culinary creation dribbled down the front of his shirt. Still, he was the hottest cook she'd ever laid eyes on.

He paused from adding some spices to the pot on the stove. "See something that you like?"

"Most definitely." And she wasn't talking about the food.

She wanted to share her happiness with someone—she thought of her mother. She'd been so eager for Cleo to fall in love with someone from Hope Springs and now her wish would come true. Cleo reached out for the phone resting on the counter. Then paused. She clenched her fist and pulled back.

Her hand returned to her side. Even if she and her mother were speaking again, she'd never approve of this match. Not that this was anything permanent, maybe it never would be. She and Jax still had so much to figure out.

"What are you thinking about?" Jax stood next to the stove with a spoon in his hand.

"What?" It took her a moment to process what he'd said. "Oh, nothing important."

"It sure looked like it was important. One second you're smiling like the Cheshire cat and the next you're frowning. What gives?"

"Is that soup?" She inhaled the gentle tomato aroma and forced her thoughts away from her mother. "I smell bacon, don't I?"

"You're changing the subject. If this is about us making love, I want to know."

She shook her head, anxious to assure him that his lovemaking had rocked her world. "You definitely don't have a thing to worry about in that department."

"I don't?" He put down the spoon and approached her. "Are you sure?"

She pulled on his arms, lowering his face to her level. She kissed him thoroughly just to be sure not to leave any lingering doubts in his mind.

She pulled back and flashed him a big smile. "Now do you believe me?"

He smiled back and nodded. "Now I better get back to the stove before the tortellini soup burns."

"It smells delicious."

He gave the pot a stir before adding the pasta. "So have you thought any more about calling your mother?"

Well, that question had certainly come out of left field. What had he been doing, reading her thoughts? She sure hoped not.

"Um…some. But I don't know."

"I do." He sent her a reassuring look. "Time has passed since the funeral. I'm sure that she's thinking much clearer now. This is your mother. You need to give her a chance. The phone's on the counter."

"I don't know. Maybe I'll call tomorrow."

"There isn't always a tomorrow. I can tell you that I would do anything to hear my mother's voice again."

Her gaze strayed to the phone. Was he right? Should she seize the moment?

A movement out of the corner of her eye caught her attention. She jerked around to glance out the French doors leading to the veranda. The sun was setting, sending splashes of purples and pinks streaking across the sky. The breeze over the desert rushed past the palm trees, rustling the fronds. But she didn't see anything out of place.

Figuring it was probably just a bird or something, she turned back to Jax. "I promise, I will call her."

"Soon?"

"Yes, soon."

"How about tomorrow?"

"You aren't going to give up until you have an exact time, are you?"

"Maybe just the hour. It doesn't have to include the very second," he teased.

"Fine, tomorrow after lunch, I'll call. But I don't want to ruin tonight. It's a new beginning for us."

"Cleo, about that. We need to talk this over. We have to be realistic about things between us. Your life is in Las Vegas and mine is in New York—" His head snapped around to the French doors.

She knew where he was going with the conversation and she didn't like it. It was inevitable that sooner or later he'd want out of this relationship. "Jax, I think we should—"

"Shh…"

She followed his gaze to the doors. "Did you see something?"

His hands balled up and his arms tensed. "More like someone."

A shiver raced over her skin. "Do you think it's ape man?"

"I don't know. But I'm not waiting around to find out. Call the police. I'm going to investigate."

"But you can't. It's not safe."

"Close the blinds. Turn off the lights. And stay inside."

The thought of losing someone else she loved had her bottom lip quivering. She grabbed for the phone and panicked. She stared at the electronic device, willing her jumbled thoughts to settle. Her finger trembled as she punched out 911. Her heart echoed in her ears. Taking deep breaths, she forced herself to calm down long enough to answer all of the operator's questions.

Nausea rolled through her stomach, one wave after the other. She grabbed for the crutches, fumbling and knocking one to the ground. She cursed under her breath. With jerky movements, she struggled to reach it.

Should she hide? Yes, that was a good idea. Her head swung around the kitchen, looking for a hiding spot. She moved to the living room, but it was an open floor plan. But in the entranceway was a coat closet. She'd just opened the door when she heard the distant wail of a siren. Thank God they were close by.

Minutes later, Jax returned and she was never so glad to see someone as she was him. He rushed over and held her in his strong arms.

"Everything's okay now," he murmured.

After a reassuring hug, she pulled back. "Was it ape man?"

Jax nodded. "I was able to give the police a description and they're tracking him down. Hopefully this will be over soon."

"I'm not holding my breath. That guy seems to slip away at every turn."

"Everyone's luck runs out eventually. He's bound to make a mistake and they'll be waiting for him."

Her gaze met his. "I was so worried about you. You shouldn't have gone after him."

Jax shot her a reassuring smile that lit up his eyes. "You're talking to a man who fought cancer and won the first round. Chasing down a thug is nothing compared to that."

She hugged him close, knowing they still had to talk but this wasn't the time. Right now, she just wanted to appreciate what they had at this moment. The future would be here soon enough.

CHAPTER THIRTEEN

The time had come to keep her promise.

The following day, Cleo sat down in the family room. The cell phone sat atop the sketch pad. She reached out but then pulled back. She was making too big a deal of this. If Jax was brave enough to chase after ape man, surely she could find the courage to call her mother. After all, what was the worst that could happen?

Her mother could simply hang up. Tell her that she didn't love her. Tell her that—

Cleo halted her rambling thoughts. If she was going to fill her mind with doom and gloom, she might as well experience the reality. It couldn't be as horrible as she was imagining. Right?

After all, Jax and Kurt both thought that it was for the best. They wouldn't intentionally set her up to get hurt. But she worried that they based their opinions on wishful thinking. Drawing in a deep breath, she dialed the number. Her hands grew damp and her fingers were ice-cold. Maybe her mother wouldn't be home. Maybe she'd be out visiting—

"Hello?" The warm, easy strains of her mother's voice sounded the same as ever.

Suddenly the words Cleo had planned to say balled up in the back of her throat.

"Hello, is anyone there?"

Drawing together her scattered thoughts, Cleo swallowed hard. "Mom, it's Cleo."

She waited for the phone to be slammed down, but there was no click. In fact, there were no sounds at all. Had the connection dropped?

"Mom, are you there?"

"I'm here." Her mother's voice took on a weary tone. "I've been praying that I hadn't run you off for good. You don't know how many times I've wanted to call you."

Cleo's chest swelled with hope. Did this mean that they could bury the past and move forward? She wanted to ask but didn't want to jump ahead. Slow and steady wins the race, her grandfather used to say.

After a deep breath, Cleo asked, "Why didn't you call?"

A noticeable pause ensued.

"Because I...I wasn't sure you'd want to talk to me after what happened. I knew you were right. I'd overstepped in your life too many times. I had to give you this chance to decide if you still wanted to return to this family that isn't always perfect."

"I do," Cleo choked out past the ginormous lump lodged in her throat. "I miss you."

There was a big sigh on the other end of the phone as if her mother had been holding her breath. "You don't know how grateful I am to hear those words. I'm so ashamed of how I've treated you...of how I talked to you."

"It's okay, Mom. I understand. I deserved your anger."

"No, you didn't. Don't ever believe that. I've had a lot of time to think this over. I realize now that when you lived here, I tried to make all of your choices for you. I'm the reason you went so far away to school."

Cleo couldn't deny the truth of her mother's words. "There were other reasons for choosing the college that

I did. Like their amazing reputation. And the fact I got a partial scholarship."

"I know you're trying to make me feel better, but you don't have to. I understand what happened."

"The main thing is I miss my family and I've realized how important you all are to me."

Her mother's voice grew soft as though she was crying. "The day you were arguing with your father, it was because you didn't want to come home because I would be here." Her mother's sob ripped through the scar on Cleo's heart. "I'm the reason the family was torn apart. It was me! Not you."

"Mom, that's not true. It was me, too. I needed a chance to find out what makes me happy."

Her mother sniffled. "And did you? Find out what makes you happy?"

"I'm working on it."

"Cleo, I know that I don't have any right to ask this but could you forgive me for the way I treated you at the funeral and afterward? I can't even believe the things that came out of my mouth. I'm so ashamed that I spoke to one of my children in that manner. I'm a terrible mother."

"No, you're not. Everyone makes mistakes. Especially me. This whole nightmare is of my making. If I hadn't been so stubborn when Dad called—so certain I knew everything—"

"The accident was not your fault. And I'm so sorry that I said it was. I don't know if I'll ever forgive myself for turning my pain and anguish on you like I did." Her voice cracked and Cleo knew that her mother was crying, which brought tears to her own eyes. "I don't have any excuses except that I was out of my mind with grief. I had to be to speak to you like that."

"Mom, I love you. And I understand. A friend of mine explained it to me."

"Tell your friend that I'm deeply indebted to them."

That touched upon another sensitive subject—Jax. Maybe it would be best to wait—to put it off until things were more stable between them. But if this was to be a new beginning for them, she wanted to get things out in the open. There was no way that she could go back to pretending to be the complacent daughter.

"Mom, the friend who talked me into calling you, it was... It was Jax."

"No. Not him."

The palpable disapproval in her mother's voice caused dread to churn in Cleo's stomach. She recognized her mother's tone and whatever followed was never good news.

"Mom, he's changed—"

"Cleo, are you trying to tell me that you're involved with that man?"

Anger warmed her blood. Jax deserved a lot more respect than being call "that man." She may not have stood up for him back in Hope Springs, but she wasn't about to let him down now.

"His name is Jax. And...and yes, we're involved."

"But, Cleo, you could do so much better for yourself. The Riley boy is just down the lane. He's still single and he's taking over his father's ranch—"

"Mom, I thought you just got done saying that you regretted trying to make my decisions for me. Listen to me. I'm interested in Jax. I've been crazy about him since I was a kid."

"I know." Her mother groaned. "The whole world knew."

A smile pulled at Cleo's face, easing some of the tension. "I wasn't very good at hiding my feelings, was I?"

"Not at all. But why you had to choose him over the other boys in Hope Springs is beyond me."

Cleo accepted that her mother would never approve of her choices. There was nothing she could do to change her mother's attitude, but Cleo promised that she'd stay true to herself. Going forward, her choices would be made based on what was best for herself and not just to please someone else.

"But I don't understand," her mother continued, pulling Cleo from her thoughts. "When Jax left Hope Springs all those years ago, no one knew where he went. How did you find him?"

Obviously Kurt excelled at keeping secrets. It seemed she wasn't the only one not to know of his ongoing friendship with Jax. Instead of being upset with her brother, she was grateful to him for being such a good friend to Jax.

"It was fate, Mom. He walked into my life one day and we've been playing catch-up ever since."

Her mother let out an unimpressed "hmprf" sound.

"Mom, he's changed—"

"People don't change that much. Look where he came from. The nut doesn't fall far from the tree."

"You're wrong about Jax. He's nothing like his father. He takes after his mother. He's kind and thoughtful. I wish you'd give him a chance."

"To watch him break your heart? I don't think so."

"He won't do that."

Her mother rushed the conversation on to other subjects and since they hadn't talked in close to two years, a lot had happened in and around Hope Springs. In the end, Cleo grew quiet and listened. She wasn't going to convince her mother that Jax was a good guy and the knowledge ate at her.

Was it possible to reconcile with her mother when she was so outspoken in her objection to Jax?

"How did the conversation go?"

Cleo jerked around to see Jax entering the room. "Where did you come from?"

"I was out talking with the security guys. Now that we know that the thug is in the area, I've hired extra protection. I want him caught and I want this over."

"But will it ever be over? If you stop him, won't someone else fill his place?"

"It isn't likely. Remember the court case isn't far off now. Soon I'll be stepping on a plane to testify. Once that's done there won't be a reason for them to try to intimidate me or anyone I care about."

She looked him in the eyes. "You really believe that?"

"I do."

She relaxed. "Then let's hope he's caught soon."

"And now back to my question. How did the conversation with your mother go?"

"Not like I'd hoped." Cleo slouched against the couch and crossed her arms.

"You didn't expect miracles, did you?"

"She said that she'd made a mistake by trying to make my decisions for me. And then she turned around and tried to do the exact same thing. It was like she hadn't really heard me."

Jax pulled up a barstool next to her. "How exactly did she do this?"

"You don't want to know." And she didn't want to hurt him by repeating her mother's unkind words.

The frustration churned inside Cleo. If only she didn't have this cast, she'd go for a walk. But then again she couldn't do that, either, because crazy ape man was out there somewhere. Her body tensed.

Jax placed a reassuring hand on her leg. "Something tells me that you mentioned my name to her and that it didn't go over so well—"

"No, it didn't. Then she tried hooking me up with the guy down the road who's taking over his father's ranch. And she thinks that you can't change. She's the one who hasn't changed."

"Slow down. Take a breath." He reached for her hand and held it. "I think she's trying, but she's still your mom. And she'll always want what's best for her little girl."

"But that's just it. I'm an adult now. And she has to start trusting me to know what I want—right or wrong. I've got to learn these things for myself."

"Maybe it's best if you avoid talking about me. I won't come between you and your family."

"Speaking of which, Mom might tell Kurt about us. I didn't even think to tell her to keep it to herself."

"Don't worry about it." But by the frown lines framing Jax's face, he was worried. "I told you that I'm not going to come between you and your family and I meant it."

"Why?" She wasn't going to let him off the hook until he answered her. "This thing between us is special. It's worth fighting for."

He raked his fingers through his hair. "It isn't that easy. There's still so much we don't know about each other."

"I'm willing to learn."

"And what if you don't like everything you learn?"

"Why are you making this so difficult?" She crossed her arms and stared at him. "Are you trying to tell me you're having second thoughts about us?"

"I just want you to slow down. Don't rush things, Cleo. There's a lot to take into consideration."

"I'm not rushing. But obviously we see things differently."

"Maybe. I don't know." His face was creased with frown lines. "I came in here to tell you that I have to go to the police station. They might have a lead. I'll be back later."

This wasn't the end. It was just the beginning. With time Jax would come to terms with that. She wasn't about to let him walk out of her life again.

Cleo felt like a canary in a gilded cage. Only the saying didn't quite fit. Though she loved to sing, her voice was best not heard.

She was tired of being confined, even if it was in this luxurious mansion. She would do anything to get out. Today's follow-up appointment with the doctor sounded like a vacation. She couldn't wait to kick back and feel the sun on her face while the breeze rustled through the open car window.

During the past few days, Jax had withdrawn from her. He was hiding behind a wall of indifference and acting as though they were nothing more than friends. When he said he didn't want to rush into anything, he hadn't been kidding. So how did she get through to him? How did she convince him to take a chance on them?

Not even her drawings could hold her attention—they had no flash or flair. They were flat and boring. She tossed the pad aside. It didn't help that she had no fabric to work with or sewing machine to stitch together her ideas. She missed bringing her art to life. And as luxurious as this house was, it didn't come with the one place she liked to unwind and lose herself—her sewing room.

The simple truth was she missed her life, even as mundane as it was compared to living here like royalty.

The buzzer on the dryer went off. She glanced down at Charlie, who was curled up on her lap. His eyes opened but his head didn't move. She ran her hand over his silky smooth coat. With Jax holed up in the office at the back of the house, working on the computer, she'd decided to do some laundry.

"You've got to move, kitty." She picked up Charlie and placed him on the couch cushion. "I might as well make myself useful since I don't seem to be inspired to draw at the moment."

With the laundry room on the second floor, she headed up the steps. In no time, she had a load of Jax's clothes folded and placed neatly in a basket. The next task was figuring how to get the clothes to the bedroom. She couldn't imagine juggling a full basket while using her crutches, so she got creative. She shoved the basket along the floor with her foot. Granted it wasn't exactly the fastest approach but it did the trick.

She opened the dresser drawer to put away Jax's T-shirts when she noticed the glint of a gold chain. She'd never seen Jax wear jewelry beyond a watch, not even as a teenager. She lifted a couple of T-shirts and froze.

She blinked, but the pocket watch was still there.

What in the world?

Her fingers trembled as she picked it up. She moved to the bed and dropped down on it. When her grandfather had suddenly died, no one could figure out what had happened to the watch—her grandfather's pride and joy.

What did it mean that Jax had it?

She clutched the watch as the past unfolded itself in her mind. Like an old projector, the scenes of yesteryear started to come into focus. Her thoughts swept back to the last time she was with Jax in Hope Springs.

She'd been walking home from her best friend's house after doing homework. She saw Jax hightailing it from her grandfather's house. She'd rushed to catch up to him, wanting to show off her new outfit. It was the latest rage at the mall and she'd even put on some of her friend's makeup, hoping to convince him that she was not just a little kid anymore… After all, she was going to be fourteen the following week. Looking back now, she realized how foolish she'd been. But at the time, no one could tell her that an eighteen-year-old was too old for her.

So she'd stopped on the road and waited for him to catch up, but he just kept walking. No greeting. No teasing her. No nothing. She'd rushed to keep up to his long-legged pace.

When he noticed that she was going to follow him wherever he went, he stopped and looked at her. "Hey, kid, can you keep a secret?"

She'd nodded, reveling in the fact that he was going to take her into his confidence. She'd thought that it meant something special—that she was special. She hadn't been expecting the next part.

"Okay. But first pinkie swear you won't tell anyone, not even Kurt."

Once she'd given her heartfelt pledge to keep his secret, he surprised her.

"I'm leaving Hope Springs."

"When are you coming back?"

"I'm not. That's the point."

She remembered how she'd struggled to hold back the tears and failed miserably. Maybe that was why he'd broken down and kissed her…right on the cheek.

And that was the last time anyone from Hope Springs had laid eyes on him…except for her brother. She stared at the pocket watch, wondering what it meant that Jax possessed it. She knew that he did errands for her grandfather, but was there more to their relationship than mucking stalls and fixing fence lines?

She had to be sure to phrase her questions just so. She

didn't know want transpired between Jax and her grand-father so she didn't want to accuse him of anything. But then again, she needed to know the truth.

"Cleo, we've got to leave for the doctor's or we'll be late," Jax called up the steps.

She hastily put the watch back where she'd found it. They'd have plenty of time to discuss this later. Right now, she needed the doctor to assure Jax that he didn't have to watch over her any longer—that she was perfectly fine to take care of herself.

She didn't need him.

The bold lie settled front and center in her thoughts, weighing her down. The truth was she wanted him in her life so much it scared her.

When had Jax come to mean so much to her? Her thoughts rolled back in time, unable to nail down a spe-cific moment when things had dramatically changed be-tween them. Her feelings for him had grown and changed gradually as they spent day after day together.

And this was nothing like the schoolgirl crush she'd had on him all those years ago in Hope Springs. These feelings went far deeper and had a sharp edge when she thought of Jax leaving—and he would soon. He'd said more than once that his life wasn't here in Las Vegas.

This appointment was the beginning of the end for them. Her shoulders drooped. Once they got the all clear from the doctor, it'd be one less reason for Jax to stick around. And from the sounds of it the police were closing in on ape man. In no time at all, Jax would be on a plane for New York. And their time together would be nothing but another memory.

CHAPTER FOURTEEN

JAX GLANCED OVER at Cleo, noticing that she'd had something on her mind during their trip into the city.

"Is everything okay?" he asked.

She smiled, but it didn't quite reach her eyes. "You heard the doctor. I'm healing up nicely."

"This isn't about the doctor's visit. Something has been bothering you since we left the house. I thought you'd be happy getting out of there for a while."

"I am." Her tone was flat.

She was lying, but why? He sure didn't understand women. Give them what they want and they are still unhappy. Maybe she was hungry. He could whip them up an early dinner and perhaps that would lighten her spirits. She always liked his cooking.

He eased the SUV onto the highway. "What sounds good for dinner?"

"Didn't you hear the doctor? I can take care of myself. You don't have to keep hovering and doing things for me."

"But why should you have to cook when I'm around and I don't mind?"

"But that's the thing, you aren't always going to be around. As you keep reminding me, your life is in New York. Not here."

He glanced in her direction, noticing her crossed arms

and the frown on her face. She'd been in an unusual mood ever since he told her that it was time to leave for her appointment. He sure wished he knew what had triggered it.

But before he could probe further, he spotted a much larger problem. A big black pickup truck was quickly gaining ground on them. Jax picked up speed as he kept glancing in the mirror at the vehicle's reinforced front bumper and the exhaust pipes trailing up each side of the cab.

The truck had been tailing them since they'd pulled out of the parking lot at the doctor's office. He did not have a good feeling about this. Not at all.

"Maybe now is the time to talk," Cleo said tentatively. "I found something earlier—"

"Can this wait?" His gaze strayed to the rearview mirror. The pickup was closing in fast.

"I think it's waited long enough."

"Hold on!"

He swerved over into the fast lane and accelerated. The pickup did the same. Definitely not a good sign.

"What are you doing?" Cleo screeched. "Have you lost your mind?"

"I think we're being followed. Our exit is just ahead."

He didn't bother with his turn signal. Instead he waited until the last moment then swerved over through the slow lane and onto the exit ramp. Horns blared. Jax kept going.

The pickup followed.

He just had to keep Cleo safe. He'd do anything for her. And in this particular moment, he didn't have time to contemplate exactly how deep that feeling went.

"Grab the phone from my pocket and call Detective Jones."

Any other time he might have gotten a cheap thrill out of Cleo fishing around in his pants pocket, but his attention was on more important matters. He had no idea what the thug behind him had in mind and he didn't want to find out.

Cleo quickly found the saved number on the phone and spoke with the detective. She disconnected the call. "He said to head for the house. He already has units in the area."

"Good."

A loud thump and they lunged forward, restrained by the safety belts. The SUV shuddered. The pickup had hit them from behind and Jax wasn't giving the creep a chance to do it again. Jax tramped on the accelerator. The SUV rapidly gained speed, putting distance between them. He sure hoped Detective Jones was right about the nearby units.

Cleo reached out and squeezed his leg. In that moment he acknowledged something that he'd been fighting for so long—he loved her. And he would do anything to keep her safe and happy.

More determined than ever to get them to safety, he turned right toward their gated community. And that was when he spotted the nail strips on the road and was able to cut the wheel and avoid them. Fortunately the truck behind them didn't have the luxury of time and hit the strips, blowing out the tires.

Jax slowed to a stop and threw the SUV in Park. He glanced out the side window in time to see the police arrest the thug.

Cleo took off her seat belt and shimmied over next to him to peer out the side window. "Is it really over?"

"Let's hope so."

Instead of throwing her arms around him and kissing him, she settled back in her seat. "It's about time."

What a strange reaction. Ever since they left for the doctor's office it was as if a wall had gone up between them. And he didn't like it. Not one little bit. But until he knew what the problem was, he couldn't fix it.

Jax entered the house smiling. It had certainly been a day for good news. First Cleo's doctor's appointment and now the police had made an arrest. At last, their problems were truly over.

"Cleo." He glanced around the living room. No sign of her.

He moved to the family room. She wasn't there, either, but he noticed her sketch pad on the coffee table and Charlie curled up on the couch. Something told him that she hadn't been gone long, because where Cleo was, Charlie wasn't far behind.

Next he checked the kitchen. It was empty, too.

"Cleo!"

When she didn't answer, he started to worry. Maybe she'd fallen. She'd been getting around with ease, but she did have a habit of pushing her limits. He took the steps two at a time.

"Cleo, where are you?"

He scanned her bedroom. Then he glanced in his room. She was sitting on the bed with her back to him.

"Hey, didn't you hear me calling you?"

She shrugged but didn't say a word.

He stepped farther into the room. "Are you okay?"

She shook her head this time. He sure wished she'd speak, it would make this so much easier. At least then he'd know what was wrong. He started around the bed and stopped in front of her. She was gazing down at something in her hands. It took him a second to recognize the familiar object in her hand.

"Cleo, listen. I can explain this."

"I always wondered what happened to this watch. It

was one of my grandfather's most treasured possessions. I just never would have guessed that he'd given it to you."

Jax sat down on the bed next to her. "Your grandfather was a very special man. I've never known anyone with a bigger heart."

She smiled. "I'm so glad you got to know that part of him."

"He took me under his wing and showed me that a man could make his own happiness. He showed me how to work hard for my money. And he taught me respect. In all of the ways that count, your grandfather was more a father to me than my biological one."

"I'm glad he was able to be there for you, especially after your mom passed on. He liked you, too. But that doesn't explain why he gave you this." She dangled the pocket watch.

Jax reached for it, but she jerked it out of his reach. He sighed. "It isn't what you're thinking."

"Really? And now you're a mind reader—"

"Obviously you think I came to have it by some underhanded way. But I didn't." He knelt down in front of her. "You've got to believe me. I wouldn't have done anything to hurt your grandfather. If it wasn't for him, I wouldn't be here today. I'd probably still be in Hope Springs, following in my father's unhappy steps."

Her brow crinkled as her lips pursed together in thought. "For him to give you this, it had to be for some really important reason because this is a family heirloom. Did you know that it belonged to my great-grandfather? It was supposed to be passed down to my father. And then to my oldest brother, Kurt. So you'll see why I'm confused about how you ended up with it."

"Your grandfather gave it to me the day I left Hope

Springs." Jax got to his feet and started to pace. "He told me to sell it when I got to where I was going."

She shook her head. "But why this? And what do you know about the money missing from his bank accounts?"

"I don't know anything about his bank accounts, but..." Jax wasn't so sure how she would take this and he hated the thought of letting her down. "He took care of my college tuition as well as my room and board. I didn't know how he arranged it and he wouldn't say. But when you were dirt-poor like I was and someone drops you a rope to pull you out of poverty, you act first and think later. Can you understand that?"

She continued to look at him. He could see the wheels in her mind spinning. But he hoped he was getting through to her. Finally she nodded. But he didn't give her a chance to say anything, he kept going. He had to make sure she believed he wouldn't hurt her family in any way. In secret, he'd always dreamed about what it would be like to be a Sinclair—to be a part of a loving, close-knit family.

"By the time my brain caught up with everything, your grandfather had passed on and all I could do was make the most of the generous gift he'd given me."

"And that explains the withdrawals from his bank accounts that no one could account for."

"I'm sorry." He felt really bad for upsetting the family. "I never meant to take away your inheritance. I was young and I hadn't thought through his generous offer. All I could envision was an escape from an unhappy life."

"Don't be." Her words shocked him. "If anyone should understand about rushing off to chase your dreams without thinking about what it took to get you there—it's me."

"Does this mean you believe me about the money and the pocket watch?" He held his breath waiting for her confirmation.

"You know, it's almost like my grandfather knew something all those years ago that we didn't have a clue about. It's like he knew someday we'd find our way together." She held up the watch. "And this is like his blessing for us."

She was being a bit dramatic, but he had to admit that he liked the idea. "You really think your grandfather would approve of you being in my arms?"

She nodded and smiled up at him.

Jax stood and drew her up into his embrace. He never ever wanted to let her go. She fit so perfectly against him. It was as though she'd been made just for him.

She pulled back and looked into his eyes. "What did you come in here to tell me?"

"That's right. I have good news." He paused, thinking about kissing her now and saving the talking for later. "But it can wait."

He leaned forward, but she pressed a hand to his chest. "It can't wait. I need to know what's happening."

Jax tightened his hold on her, not wanting the moment to end, but realized he might as well get this out of the way. "Okay. Apparently ape man wasn't a hired thug. He's actually the brother of my former partner. He was a one-man team out to protect the goose that laid his golden egg. Now that he's been arrested, we don't have to worry."

"Are you certain?"

"Positive. He confessed."

Cleo threw her arms around Jax and hugged him tight. But instead of following it up with the kiss he'd been anticipating, she pulled back and gave him a serious look.

"What does this mean?"

He brushed a strand of hair from her cheek. "As tempting as it is to stay, we can't go on living here forever. Eventually my friend will want his house back."

"I suppose you're right. Even if it's the fanciest house I've ever been in. Do we have to leave now?"

Jax shook his head. There was absolutely no other place he wanted to be. "I think we can stay another night."

"Good." She snuggled closer to him. "I'm just so glad you're safe."

"How glad?" He smiled and glanced at her very kissable lips.

In the next moment, her mouth pressed to his. She was bold and persuasive, leaving no doubt of what she had on her mind. And he liked it. He liked it a whole lot.

He met her move for move, needing to feel their closeness once more. As she opened up to him, she tasted of chocolate. It had never tasted so good. A moan grew deep in his throat.

Things were about to change for them. They could move forward—think about the future. And the past could fall away behind them. They could make their own memories starting with today.

Because with Cleo, he was alive. She cared about him as no one else ever had. The knowledge sealed the hole in his heart—the empty spot where the love of a family was supposed to be. Cleo was all of the family he'd ever need.

CHAPTER FIFTEEN

"JAX, YOU MISSED my street."

He glanced in the rearview mirror as the street sign faded into the distance. He'd been distracted by the way her hand rested on his leg. "Sorry. I'll turn around."

"No need. You can just circle the block." There was a slight pause. "It's great to be going home. Don't get me wrong. Staying in a movie star's mansion was an experience I'll never forget. It sure is a long way from Hope Springs, Wyoming."

"Is that good or bad?"

"Part of me misses Hope Springs, but another part doesn't want to be stuck in that small town for the rest of my life. There are so many places to see and things to do."

"You know, your fashion designs could be the key to having the best of both worlds."

"You think so?" He nodded and she continued, "But I haven't even shown anyone my drawings."

This was his moment to confess what he'd been up to while she'd been drawing. He just hoped she approved. If not, this might very well be the last time she talked to him and that thought knotted his gut.

"Actually I've been told by an expert that you have amazing talent and a bright future, if you pursue it."

"What? But how?" There was a pause as though she was trying to make sense of things. "Jax, what did you do?"

He pulled into a parking spot, put the SUV in Park and turned off the engine. He rubbed his head, suddenly in doubt of his actions, which was so unlike him. He was a man of decision—split-second decisions. That was how he'd been able to amass a fortune.

But when it came to Cleo, he felt constantly off-kilter. But surely she'd be happy about this, right? No point in delaying the inevitable.

"I sent some of your sketches to a friend of a friend. And I included a picture of you in that yellow outfit you had on at the casino."

"You didn't?" She looked at him as though she was waiting for him to say he was joking.

"Cleo, I'm serious. I sent your stuff to an industry professional. He is interested in meeting with you."

"Why didn't you ask me first?"

"I thought about it, but I didn't know how it'd work out. I mean, I'm no judge of fashion. I just know what I like—"

"So if this expert didn't like what they saw, you didn't want to hurt me."

He nodded, relieved that she understood his motive. "Exactly. I have his name and number written down." Jax reached into his pocket and withdrew the slip of paper. "He's expecting your call."

"I should be upset with you for going behind my back, but I'm grateful. Thank you. You're the first person since my grandmother to believe I could make my dreams come true without just settling for what is expected of me."

He reached out for her hand and took it in his own. "You can do whatever you set your mind to. And I'm going to enjoy watching you succeed."

She leaned over and hugged him. His heart pounded

beneath her cheek. What had he ever done to be lucky enough to have someone so special in his life?

Cleo lifted her head and looked at him. "But next time you have a brilliant idea, talk to me first. Agreed?"

He expelled a pent-up breath. "Agreed."

"Now let's get inside. Charlie is anxious to get out of this carrier."

Jax dashed out the door and strode around the front of the vehicle to assist her. "Would you mind taking Charlie while I grab my crutches? We can come back out later for the rest of our stuff. Not that there's a lot of it."

He did as she asked and escorted her up the walk. Cleo smiled and greeted the other people coming and going. This place was crawling with young people, from college students to young mothers with strollers. He could imagine Cleo fitting in well here.

"I've never had a houseguest before." Cleo sent him a hesitant glance. "You'll be my first. I wish I'd known you were staying. I'd have cleaned up some."

Staying? Here? With her? Like an honest-to-goodness couple? The reality of the situation was setting in and all of the uncertainties in the back of his mind came rushing forth—from the potential for his cancer to return to her mother's dislike of him. Jax shoved the doubts away. After all, this was what he wanted—Cleo in his life.

"I'm sure you don't have to worry." He sent her a reassuring smile even though he was feeling anything but assured. "Remember I was already here and the place looked great."

Before they could say much else, Robyn exited her apartment. She was pushing a pink baby stroller in their direction.

"Oh, look! Robyn has her daughter all dressed up in an outfit I made her." Cleo picked up her pace on the crutches

"Welcome home." The young woman's face lit up with a broad smile. "Stephie is wide-awake and anxious for Auntie Cleo to visit with her."

Cleo stopped and leaned over the stroller. "Hey, cutie, aren't you adorable."

Jax had never seen Cleo with a baby. Her whole demeanor changed. She almost glowed as she oohed and ahhed over the child. What was it about babies that could affect women of all ages so deeply?

Jax stood back as the women went on and on about the baby. He tried his best to act as if nothing was bothering him, but inside their words were shattering the dreams he'd had about his future—a future with Cleo. With each laugh and smile, his hopes were splintering into shards that cut deep.

What made him think Cleo would fit into his predetermined world?

She was still so young and full of possibilities. His life choices had been drastically narrowed when he'd received his cancer diagnosis. Having a family of his own was not an option for him.

Aside from the question of the lifesaving treatments causing fertility issues, he wouldn't subject his child to the uncertainty of his cancer making a recurrence. He knew the agony of being a child and losing a parent. He didn't want to pass on that unhappy legacy.

Cleo had him thinking about all sorts of things he'd never thought about before. Like moving to Las Vegas instead of Hope Springs. He'd let himself get caught up in the moment. First the doctor called with the news that his test results were good and then he'd given in to his desires. It'd been like the fall of dominoes—one thing leading to another. And now Cleo was expecting him to make her happy and as much as he wanted to do just that, he couldn't.

The truth of the matter was he lived a life of uncertainty. It was bad enough that he had to live every day with a big question mark over his head. It wasn't fair to ask Cleo to give up her chance to be a mother to live with a man who could become sick again.

The best thing he could do for Cleo was walk away. Forget his dreams of making a future with her. He'd never felt so awful about a decision as he did now. How was he supposed to walk away from the woman whose smile could light up his whole world? He couldn't even imagine his life without her in it. But it wasn't as if he had a choice. He had to do what was best for her.

And that wasn't him.

He carried her belongings into the apartment and Cleo followed him. When she closed the front door, the walls seemed to close in on him. He didn't belong here. He didn't belong with her.

She proceeded to give him the grand tour of her two-bedroom apartment. "And this is my sewing room. Don't mind the mess. I've been working on an order for Robyn. Her older sister is pregnant and she wanted me to make some clothes and stitch up a comforter like I'd done for Stephie."

His gaze took in the array of baby blue, yellow and green fabrics. The knife of guilt stabbed at him for even considering asking Cleo to spend her life with him. And when she held up little bib overalls and her face scrunched up into a huge smile as if she was imagining her own baby someday in the outfit, he couldn't breathe.

He needed to leave. He needed space. Someplace where the pain wasn't so severe. Where there weren't reminders of everything he'd never have.

"I've got to go." He started for the door.

"Leave? Where are you going? I thought you'd stay here until your flight to New York."

"I—I can't."

"What's wrong? You've been acting strange ever since we got here."

He wanted to walk away without her hating him. The thought of her looking at him with loathing in her eyes made his stomach roil. There had to be a way to part on good terms. After all, soon he'd return to New York.

Maybe that was the answer. He could remind her that they led separate lives miles from each other. In no time, she'd get on with her life. She'd forget him. With her beauty, she could have any guy she set her heart on.

"I'm just tired." He could feel her staring at him, trying to guess if he was telling the whole truth or not. "I thought I'd go back to the casino and make sure things are squared away there."

"The casino?" A frown pulled at her face. "Are you tired of me?"

The sadness in her eyes cracked his resolve. "Of course not. I just… We can't pretend that my life is here. I belong in New York. I have the court case coming up. I can't back out now. Too much is at stake."

Her eyes shimmered. "This thing that happened between us. Are you saying it was all a lie?"

He shook his head. "It was a beautiful dream. One I will always treasure."

"Then why?" Her voice cracked with emotion. "Why are you doing this?"

"Because it isn't fair to you." The truth came tumbling out. "I can't tie you down to a life with a cancer patient."

"But you're cured. You said your tests were clear."

"But if it spread once there's no reason to think that it

might not recur. And I can't put you through that. Living with this uncertainty is horrible."

"But we can lean on each other. We can get through it together."

She had an answer for everything. But he had something she couldn't fix.

"And I can't give you children."

"I don't want kids." She said it way too fast—like a needy child desperate to say anything to get what they wanted without thinking of the ramification of their words.

"Your lips say one thing but your body says something else. I watched you just moments ago with that baby. I never saw that peaceful look on your face before. You were in your element. You practically glowed."

"But…but—"

"There's no but for this. I've tried to do this as nice as I could but you won't let go. Cleo, your mother was right. I'm not the man for you. I take what I want and I wanted you."

"Because you love me."

He stilled himself, holding back the rush of emotions. He'd never lied to her, ever—until now. But it was necessary. It was for her own good. But when he searched for the words to deny his love for her, his voice failed him.

She stepped up to him and stabbed him in the chest. "You can't deny it because it's true. We've shared so much. We're building something. We…we're falling in love."

"This is all my fault. I'm selfish and an uncaring jerk."

"That's not true."

"Yes, it is, or I wouldn't be putting you through this."

In that particular moment, he hated himself for hurting her. He wasn't deserving of her love.

He dipped his head and planted a quick kiss to her cheek. "Have a good life. You deserve the best."

He turned and started walking. He had to get away before she wore through the last of his resistance. She had no idea how hard it was to act as if he didn't care about her when his heart thumped out her name with every beat.

It was only after he was headed down the sidewalk to the SUV that he realized they'd done this scene once before…long ago when he left Hope Springs. Back then he was walking away from one of his dearest friends. This time he was walking away from the woman who held his heart in her hands.

CHAPTER SIXTEEN

Unable to sleep since Jax walked out the door, Cleo found herself spending all of her time in her sewing room. It was where she lost herself when the world turned dark and gray. And thanks to her sketch pad, she had plenty of creations to keep her hands busy. But her mind kept stumbling back to Jax.

She wanted to yell at him and tell him that he didn't know what she was thinking, but the truth was he had been pretty accurate. She'd blurted out that she didn't want kids in desperation to keep him from leaving.

It pained her to admit it, but she was doing exactly what she promised herself she wouldn't do. She was making a monumental decision based on what Jax wanted—not what she wanted. And that was a recipe for disaster.

Jax had been right to turn down her plea. She didn't know how she felt about kids. In all honesty, she hadn't given the subject much thought. At this point in her life, she still had lots of time to start a family—if she chose to.

She found herself in Robyn's living room to drop off the baby items Robyn had ordered for her sister's upcoming baby shower and yet somehow Cleo had ended up staying for a chat. While she waited for her friend to return with the coffee, she pulled her grandfather's pocket watch from her pocket. Her thumb rubbed over the engraved design.

She'd found the watch in her duffel bag she'd brought back from the mansion. She knew for certain she hadn't placed it in there because she'd given it back to Jax. Obviously her grandfather had loved Jax and wanted him to have the watch. The fact that Jax still had it and hadn't sold it as her grandfather had given him liberty to do was a tribute to Jax's feelings for him.

No man who was selfish and uncaring would carry around a memento and then hand it over to her because he saw how much it meant to her. Only a man with a heart of gold would be that thoughtful and generous.

"What's that in your hand?" Robyn asked as she placed a cup of steaming coffee in front of her.

"It belongs to Jax. He forgot it."

"He'll be missing it. You should catch up to him before he heads to the airport."

"Maybe." But she still had something to get straight in her mind before she faced Jax. "How did you know if you wanted kids?"

"That's easy. I always enjoyed them. And Mike comes from a big family. So we agreed to have at least two babies. Why?"

She could feel her friend's intent stare while Cleo concentrated on stirring the sweetener into her coffee. "The strange thing is I've never really thought about kids... until now."

"Are you pregnant?"

Cleo's head jerked up so she could gauge the look on her friend's face. She was serious. Cleo inwardly groaned. Maybe agreeing to stay and talk wasn't the best choice. She already had enough problems on her mind.

"No. I'm not pregnant. And don't even think of wishing it on me. You've got the mommy genes. The jury is still out for me."

Robyn held up her hands all innocentlike. "Sorry, I jumped to the wrong conclusion."

"Stephie's adorable, but I'm not ready for that kind of commitment. Is that bad? I mean, I'm only twenty-five. If I don't want kids now, do you think I'll never want them?"

Robyn shrugged and sat back in her chair. "I pretty much knew what I wanted early in life, but everyone is different. Do you have to know now? Does this have something to do with Mr. Tall, Dark and Dreamy?"

"He has reason to think he can't have kids and he doesn't think it's fair to tie me down. He thinks that eventually I'll want them."

"He could be right."

"Or he could be wrong." Cleo sent her friend a pointed stare.

She didn't want Robyn siding with Jax. She wanted her friend to say his logic was flawed. Because deep inside, her gut was screaming that they belonged together...no matter how her mother felt. And she certainly wasn't going to let the worry of cancer dictate her future. Life didn't come with guarantees. If only she could convince Jax of that.

Robyn shrugged and sipped at her coffee. "You said he couldn't have children. You know that's different than him not wanting children. Does he want children?"

"I—I don't know. We never really discussed it."

"If it's a matter of him not being able to father a baby, you must realize that in this day and age you have so many options to choose from."

"You're right." Hope bloomed in her chest. "I wish I'd thought of that before."

Cleo honestly didn't know if he was interested in having children or not. She'd been so caught off guard by his abrupt turnaround regarding their relationship that her mind hadn't been able to string two thoughts together much less ask intelligent questions. But Robyn had brought up a valid point and Cleo wasn't about to let him off the hook until he gave her an honest answer.

She refused to stand by and let him make a unilateral decision about their relationship. He needed to hear her thoughts on the matter. And there was no time to waste. If she had to follow him all the way to New York, she'd do it. This was too important to let the moment slip by. If there was even the slightest possibility they could make this relationship work, she wanted that chance—they deserved it. And she wouldn't be dissuaded by a truckload of what-ifs.

"I've got to go. I have a pocket watch to return." With the aid of her crutches, she stood. "Thanks for the coffee."

"I wish I could see this." Robyn let out an exaggerated sigh. "I miss all of the good parts. Just promise me you'll fill me in on the details later."

"Maybe."

While Robyn sputtered and spurted over her noncommittal answer, Cleo rushed out the door. There were some things that didn't need to be shared even with her closest friend. She just hoped there would be some special memories created today.

With a quick change into a red-and-white-flowered sundress, she felt more feminine and confident. Nothing like a beautiful outfit to bolster one's nerves. She tramped the gas as she zipped across town to the Glamour Hotel and Casino. She just hoped she was in time. She knew that Jax had booked his flight for home today, but she had no idea when it would depart. If she had to, she'd track him down at the airport and buy a plane ticket if that's what it took. They weren't finished talking. Not by a long shot.

She hustled up to his bungalow. Ignoring the Do Not Disturb sign, she knocked. When he didn't answer right away, she pounded harder on the door.

The door swung open. "What's all the racket about?"

Jax stood in the doorway. His hair was rumpled. His torso was bare, revealing his rock-solid abs. And his khaki shorts were wrinkled and hung low as if he hadn't been eating. She didn't have to ask. She could see he wasn't any happier with this separation than she was.

She drew her gaze back to his unshaven face. "You've had your say, now I'm going to have mine."

"Don't, Cleo. Everything has been said." He started to shut the door in her face.

She moved quickly, angling her crutch in the way. "What gives you the right to speak for me? And to make up my mind for me?"

She pushed him aside and entered the bungalow, which looked as if it hadn't been visited by housekeeping in days. Clothes were strewn about. Pillows and blankets littered the couch. And through all of the mess, she didn't see any signs of food. This whole mess was so unlike the clean-up-after-himself Jax who she'd been living with for the past month.

She turned to him, finding that he'd closed the door, giving them some privacy. "I've had time to think things over and you're wrong."

His brows drew together into a dark line. "I'm not wrong. You just want to believe the impossible."

"What's impossible? Us being together?" When he nodded, she rushed on, "I disagree."

He sighed and rubbed the back of his neck. "Cleo, you're just making this harder on both of us."

"Good. It should be hard to walk away from someone you care about, especially when you're doing it for all of the wrong reasons."

"I'm doing what is best for you."

"But see, I don't want you deciding what's best for me.

I already went through that back in Hope Springs. It was why I left. And now you're trying to do the same thing. It's time people listen to me and respect my feelings."

"I've always respected you and your feelings."

At last, she felt as though she was making some progress. "Then it's time you stop talking and listen to what I have to say."

"Can I at least put on a shirt?"

She nodded. But that was all she was going to wait around for. This needed to be said before she burst. Because she wasn't going anywhere until he heard her out about everything. Including the part she'd been too afraid to come straight out and say before now—she loved him.

Jax needed a moment to gather his thoughts.

In reality, he needed to back away before he pulled Cleo into his arms and kissed her into silence. Secretly he'd been wishing she'd show up, but logic told him that this talk would not end happily—for either of them. Why couldn't she have just left things alone?

He walked over to the couch and grabbed his discarded T-shirt. He'd spent the past couple of days doing nothing but trying to forget the fun and the laughter when he was around Cleo. She was his sunshine and without her, life was like a blustery gray day. But he couldn't be greedy. Her happiness was more important to him. He'd forgotten that for a moment, but he wouldn't forget it again. He just had to make her understand that she was setting her sights on the wrong man…no matter how touched he was that she chose him.

Taking a deep breath in and slowly blowing it out, he turned. "Okay, I'm listening. But I don't have long. I have some packing to do before I head to the airport."

Cleo's gaze slowly surveyed the room before cocking an eyebrow at him.

"Like I said, I have things to do before heading to the airport." He wasn't about to admit to her that he'd been so miserable since he walked away from her that he hadn't wanted to be disturbed by anyone, including housekeeping.

"Then you won't want to forget to pack this." She withdrew the pocket watch from her purse and placed it in his hand, wrapping his fingers around it.

"I can't take this. It belonged to your grandfather."

"And he wanted you to have it. He wouldn't have gone out of his way to help you if you hadn't come to mean a great deal to him. His son was busy with his own family. And my grandmother was gone. I was too young then to understand how lonely he must have been. So you filled in that gaping hole and I'm sure he took great pleasure in being able to help you."

Jax's throat tightened as his hand lowered. He couldn't believe how Cleo was able to be so positive when it would be so easy for her to hate him for taking what would have been her inheritance money and the pocket watch.

He wasn't going to continue to argue about it. "I'll keep it until you or Kurt have children of your own and then you can have it for them."

"Speaking of children, since when do you get to dictate whether I'll have any or not?"

He inwardly groaned. She had a stubborn glint in her eyes. She wasn't going to leave until he convinced her that walking away was the best option. Why did Cleo always have to do things the hard way?

"I saw you the other day with that baby. It was obvious that you're a natural mother. And don't even try to tell me again that you don't want children just because you know that I can't give you any."

She pressed her hands to her hips. "You're right, that was wrong of me."

At last, he was getting through to her. He wanted to be happy for her that she was seeing reason and was no longer willing to throw her life away on him, but it only made him sadder.

She tilted her chin. "The thing is I don't know if I want to have children. As of today, I don't. But tomorrow, who knows. When my biological clock starts to tick, I might totally change my mind."

"Then you accept that we can't be together."

"The thing is I've heard you say that you can't have children, but you've never said whether you want them or not."

"What does that matter?"

She smiled as though she knew something he didn't. "I had to be reminded that being a parent isn't a matter of DNA. And there are so many options open to people wanting to give love to a child, from adoption to foster parenting. And if we want a baby, there are sperm banks."

He was surprised by how much thought she'd put into this after her emotional response the other night. This time he was persuaded to believe she'd really thought this over. She deserved an honest answer.

"Until I spent time with you, I hadn't given kids any thought. My childhood wasn't the happiest so I wasn't inclined to be a family man, but being around you has me rethinking my stance."

"So then kids are a possibility for you, too." She smiled up at him as if she'd bested him.

"You're forgetting one big thing. The cancer. My life is lived one test result to the next."

"Then maybe you should broaden your horizons and quit living test to test. No one says you have to."

"But you don't understand, it could come back."

"And it might not. It's kinda like looking at a glass of water. You can either view it as a glass half-full or half-empty. I choose to look at it as half-full."

He raked his fingers through his hair. "It isn't fair to put a wife and child through the uncertainty."

"So you're saying that my father shouldn't have married my mother and that my brothers and I were a big mistake."

"Of course not. That's not the same thing."

"Why isn't it? My father died young. My younger brothers were still in school. We all still needed him." She stepped up to Jax and looked him in the eyes. "Life doesn't come with guarantees."

"But—"

She pressed her fingers to his lips. "I'd rather live a month or a year with you in my life than fifty years alone. You've been in my heart since I was a teenager."

He took her hand in his. "But your mother..."

"Will have to get used to the idea that you and I belong together."

"And you're absolutely certain that you want me, flaws and all."

Her eyes lit up and she nodded vigorously. "I'm absolutely certain. But I do have one question."

His chest tightened. He wasn't sure he was ready for any more proclamations. His mind was still trying to process everything she'd said. "What is it?"

"I love you. And I need to know if you feel the same for me."

Now this part was easy.

He'd been so busy trying to hide his feelings from both of them that he just now realized he'd never spoken the words of his heart.

He wrapped one arm around her waist and pulled her close. With his other hand, he brushed back her hair and looked into her mesmerizing green eyes—eyes he could see his whole future in.

"I can't honestly tell you when I first started to fall in love with you. There are too many moments to choose from. But I've been having a heck of a time trying to figure out how to go on without you."

"And now you won't have to."

"You're certain this is what you want—that I am what you want?"

"Most definitely."

He lifted her into his arms and pressed his lips to hers. He couldn't imagine how he'd ever gotten lucky enough to have this ray of sunshine in his life, but he planned to do everything he could so she never ever regretted her decision.

EPILOGUE

One year later...

JAX WAS CERTAIN he'd never tire of staring at his beautiful wife. He was so glad that she hadn't given up on him and had made him see things her way—the way they should be. Together.

Cleo sent him a hesitant look. "Are you sure about this?"

He nodded and smiled, hoping to ease her worries. Over the past year they'd learned to rely on each other during moments of uncertainty. And in return, she'd gotten him to appreciate each day and to stop fretting about tomorrow. Whatever came their way, they'd face together.

"Don't worry. Everything will be fine." He pulled on a blue T-shirt. "Your mother loves you and she'll want whatever will make you the happiest. After all, Kurt finally came around to the idea of us as a couple."

She smiled at him, filling his chest with a warm, familiar sensation. "I can't believe you convinced him to be your best man."

"You do know I had to swear on my life to keep you happy, don't you?"

She leaned over to him, her lips almost touching his. The breath in his throat hitched. It didn't matter how many times she kissed him, it would never lose its excitement.

Her mouth pressed to his and he pulled her close, but all too soon she was backing away.

"Now, was making that promise to my brother such a hardship?"

"Um…not when you put it that way." He grinned at her. "Now why don't you come back over here?"

"I have to get ready." Cleo struggled to fasten her necklace. "I just don't understand why we have to tell my mother about our plans. Can't we just tell her we're going on vacation?"

"Because we're all working on building a strong, open relationship." He stepped up and helped her with the clasp. "After all, she loves you enough to give me a chance, right?"

With a shrug, Cleo said, "I guess."

"Then you need to give her a chance and be honest with her."

Cleo rushed into the walk-in closet of their newly built house in Hope Springs. She returned with a pair of blue stilettos.

He eyed them up suspiciously. Obviously his wife was far more nervous about this talk with her mother than he'd originally thought. "Um, are you sure you want to wear those to the Jubilee?"

She frowned at him before rushing back into the closet. He smiled to himself. Life with Cleo was never boring.

After he'd testified in the money-laundering case, he was hailed as a star by both the press and her family. He'd finished up his work in New York City and returned to Cleo in Las Vegas just as he promised. But after a while they agreed that Vegas didn't feel like home to either of them. So Cleo tendered her resignation at the Glamour and they bought her grandfather's ranch from the family, and in the process, they'd put the Sinclair ranch back on solid financial ground.

Cleo slipped on a pair of colorful cowboy boots. "I just don't think Mom's going to be happy with our decision. She's been hinting about grandkids since you and I said 'I do' on Valentine's Day."

"And she's just going to have to understand that my wife has dreams to fulfill. By the way, I have our tickets to New York in my jacket pocket. We take off tonight after the festivities."

"You mean after we tell my mother that we're going to put off adoption and launch a fashion line instead."

"Exactly."

Just then Charlie strolled into the room and rubbed over Jax's legs. "Hey, boy, where have you been all morning?"

Charlie meowed in response and Jax couldn't resist kneeling down to scratch behind the cat's ear. "And don't worry. While we're gone, you're going to the ranch house to visit with your other feline friends."

"Mom really has become quite the cat lady." Cleo ran her fingers over her hair, trying to improve on perfection. At least that's how she looked in his book.

"It's good for her. Now she has furbabies to fuss over instead of you and your brothers."

"If only it was that easy. I still don't think she's going to take the news well."

Jax approached his wife and wrapped his arms around her waist, pulling her close. "I insist you quit worrying. Where's that fiery woman who told me what was up when I was foolish enough to try to walk away from the best thing that ever happened to me?"

"She's still here." Cleo smiled up at him before planting a stirring kiss on his lips. "And look how wonderful that has turned out."

"And if you keep kissing me like that we are going to be quite late for the Jubilee."

"You shouldn't tease me," she taunted.

"Who's teasing?" He tumbled her onto the bed.

She gazed up at him with happiness reflected in her eyes. "I love you, Mr. Monroe."

"And I will always love you."

* * * * *

A sneaky peek at next month...

Cherish™

EXPERIENCE THE ULTIMATE RUSH OF FALLING IN LOVE

My wish list for next month's titles...

In stores from 18th July 2014:

☐ The Rebel and the Heiress — Michelle Douglas

& A Cowboy's Heart — Rebecca Winters

☐ Not Just a Convenient Marriage — Lucy Gordon

& The Billionaire's Nanny — Melissa McClone

In stores from 1st August 2014:

☐ A Wife for One Year — Brenda Harlen

& From Maverick to Daddy — Teresa Southwick

☐ A Groom Worth Waiting For — Sophie Pembroke

& Crown Prince, Pregnant Bride — Kate Hardy

Available at WHSmith, Tesco, Asda, Eason, Amazon and Apple

Just can't wait?

Join our *EXCLUSIVE* eBook club

FROM JUST £1.99 A MONTH!

Never miss a book again with our hassle-free eBook subscription.

★ Pick how many titles you want from each series with our flexible subscription

★ Your titles are delivered to your device on the first of every month

★ Zero risk, zero obligation!

There really is nothing standing in the way of you and your favourite books!

**Start your eBook subscription today at
www.millsandboon.co.uk/subscribe**

The World of Mills & Boon

There's a Mills & Boon® series that's perfect for you. There are ten different series to choose from and new titles every month, so whether you're looking for glamorous seduction, Regency rakes, homespun heroes or sizzling erotica, we'll give you plenty of inspiration for your next read.

By Request

Relive the romance with the best of the best
12 stories every month

Cherish™

Experience the ultimate rush of falling in love.
12 new stories every month

INTRIGUE...

A seductive combination of danger and desire...
7 new stories every month

Desire™

Passionate and dramatic love stories
6 new stories every month

nocturne™

An exhilarating underworld of dark desires
3 new stories every month

For exclusive member offers go to
millsandboon.co.uk/subscribe

WORLD_ M&Ba